Country Girls:
Carl Weber Presents

Country Girls:
Carl Weber Presents

Blake Karrington

www.urbanbooks.net

Urban Books, LLC
97 N 18th Street
Wyandanch, NY 11798

Country Girls: Carl Weber Presents Copyright © 2015
Blake Karrington

ISBN 13: 978-1-62286-939-8
ISBN 10: 1-62286-939-7

First Trade Paperback Printing June 2015
Printed in the United States of America

10 9 8 7 6 5 4 3 2 1

Distributed by Kensington Publishing Corp.
Submit Orders to:
Customer Service
400 Hahn Road
Westminster, MD 21157-4627
Phone: 1-800-733-3000
Fax: 1-800-659-2436

Book 1

Chapter 1

Prada waited patiently on Oaklawn Road for Niya to pull up. She'd been attentively watching the traffic that was going in and out of the trap house a block away. She was very familiar with the house, considering it belonged to Mayo, a nigga she'd been involved with for about two weeks now. Within that short period of time, she had gained intel on damn near his whole drug operation. *Damn, I got that pussy that would make a nigga give up his whole paper route,* Prada thought.

The lights from a car pulling up and parking right behind her caught her attention. Niya stepped out of the all-black 1995 Impala. She tucked the P80 9 mm Ruger in her front pocket as she headed for Prada's car. She scanned the area thoroughly before she jumped into the passenger's seat.

"Damn, bitch, what took you so long?" Prada joked as she kept her eyes glued to the binoculars.

"Mommy business," Niya shot back. "I didn't even have time to shower," she joked.

"You nasty." Prada chuckled. "Look, in like twenty minutes, homeboy is gonna pull up and park the car. As soon as he goes into the house, just get in the car and pull off," Prada explained, passing her a set of keys.

"How much you think is in there?" Niya asked, taking a piece of gum out of her pocket and placing it in her mouth, as if what she was about to do meant nothing to her. In fact, it honestly didn't. Niya had made up her mind a long time ago that once she decided to take something, it belonged to her and was there for the taking whenever she was ready.

"I'm not sure, but I know Mayo is about to re-up in the next couple of days, and this is his main trap house," Prada told her.

The all-white BMW 760 pulled up and parked a few doors away from the trap house, just as Prada had said. The driver took a minute to get out of the car, but when he did, it was obvious why. He was having a short conversation with the passenger of the vehicle, an unknown female.

"Aaahhh, shit! He got somebody else in the car!" Prada said. She wasn't expecting anybody to be with him.

The female in the car didn't pose a threat, but Prada wasn't taking any chances with her. She couldn't risk her making a scene when Niya jumped in the car. If Mayo's worker even thought something was going on, he would surely come out of the house shooting.

"Let's get out of here," Prada said, starting her car.

"What? Bitch, you must be crazy," Niya said with a serious look on her face. "We here now."

Niya pulled the P80 Ruger out and cocked a bullet into the chamber. For her, it was too late in the game to be turning back. She got out of the car, tucked the gun into her pocket, and fixed her clothes. She waited until the driver of the BMW got out of the car before she made her move.

"When I get up to the passenger's door, pull my car right up next to his," Niya said, tossing Prada the keys to the Impala through the windows.

Niya proceeded to the car just as the worker entered the house. Prada thought Niya had lost her mind as she watched her walk down the street. She quickly snapped out of her trance and headed for Niya's car.

Tap, tap, tap! A knock at the window caught the young woman's attention. She looked up and saw Niya standing there with a pleasant smile on her face. She appeared to be no danger at all to the young girl. As soon as she rolled the window down, Niya's whole demeanor changed.

"It ain't worth your life, baby girl, so just do what I say," Niya said, sticking the gun into the window and pointing it right at the girl's chest.

Just then, Prada pulled the Impala right next to the car. The young girl was so shook that she didn't know what to do. The only thing that she could do was comply, and that she did. Niya quickly escorted her out of the BMW, but not before giving her a quick pat-down.

"Go. Meet me at the spot," she told Prada, tapping the driver's side door. Niya jumped in the passenger's seat of the white sedan. She placed the gun on her lap and waited for the owner to return.

"Where da fuck did she go?" Chad mumbled to himself, looking over at the clock.

He was sure he'd fucked Niya good enough to put her to sleep, but it was he who actually nodded off. If it weren't for one of the kids waking up and coming into the room, Chad would probably still be asleep. He reached for his phone and dialed her cell, but it went straight to voicemail.

"Eleven at night," he mumbled as he walked over to the bedroom window.

He looked down and could see that her Range Rover was still in the driveway. That made him even more curious. He tried her number again, but it went straight to voicemail for the second time.

"Ya mommy gonna make me kill her," Chad joked with Jahmil as he picked him up and walked back over to the bed.

***

Dro swung the book bag over his shoulder as he exited the house and went straight for the trunk. He looked up and down the block before popping the trunk open and tossing the bag inside. He didn't even notice the change of occupants in his passenger's seat. He jumped in shock when the barrel of Niya's gun was jammed into his side. It was at that point that he looked over and realized that it wasn't Lexus.

"Play hero and I'll rearrange everything inside of you," Niya threatened, getting Dro's full attention. "Now pull off nice and easy," she directed, only wanting to get from in front of the trap house.

"You can't be serious, shawty," Dro said in a nonchalant manner. "You really th—"

Niya shoved the gun farther in his gut, making him swallow the rest of his words. Not only did he swallow his words, but he put the car in drive and pulled off, just as she said. They didn't go far, though. Once around the corner, Niya made him pull over and park. After searching his waist for any guns, Niya made him get out of the car with his hands raised over his head. Inside the trunk were three book bags and another large duffle bag. She quickly scanned the three book bags and saw that there was money inside.

"You know who shit you fuckin' wit', shawty?" Dro asked, as if he was surprised that anybody would mess with Mayo's money.

"To be honest with you, I really don't give a fuck," Niya told Dro before slamming the trunk. She walked over and kicked Dro in the back of the knees, causing him to buckle.

"You might wanna kill yaself while you're at it, shawty," Dro said, staring Niya in her face as she got into the driver's seat. "Kill yaself! Kill yaself," he yelled, watching Niya pull off.

***

Faces and names were always changing in the drug game. For now, the south side of Charlotte was in the possession of a young nigga named Dallaz. Ever since he could remember, he wanted to get money like the old heads. Throughout his teenage years, he watched as the OGs caused havoc in the hood.

"Damn, what's up, cuzo?" Ralph said, walking up to the corner. "I see you out here on the late night."

"Yeah, li'l nigga. I'm out here making sure dis money right. You know don't shit come to a sleeper but a dream, ya dig," Dallaz said, passing Ralph the blunt of haze.

The whole time he stood there talking to Ralph, Dallaz kept his eyes on the traffic of crackheads walking up and down the street. Dallaz had the block running like an assembly line, and he made sure that this was a cop-and-roll spot. This wasn't a hangout or a smoke place; it was a business, and he ran it with an iron fist. This had made him one of Mayo's top lieutenants.

Niya crept into the house as quietly as she could. She looked up at the clock on the wall in the living room and noticed it was one thirty-five in the morning.

"Shit," she mumbled to herself, knowing beyond a shadow of a doubt that Chad was upstairs waiting for her.

She headed for the basement, hoping that she could put the large duffle bag in her little stash spot. She moved as fast as she could, but the sound of Chad calling her name from upstairs made her change course. The guns in the bag made more noise than she'd expected.

"Oh, shit, Chad!" she yelled, scared to death when she made it to the top of the stairs and saw he was standing right there. "You scared da shit out of me, boy."

"Where da fuck was you at?" Chad asked with an attitude, curiously looking down into the basement.

"Prada had troubles with her man tonight. I didn't even notice the time, boo," she answered, thinking fast on her feet. "We went and got some drinks at the b—"

"Well, why da fuck didn't you answer ya phone?" he snapped, interrupting her before she could get the lie out. "And don't you gotta go the fuck to work in the morning?"

Niya pulled her cell phone from her pocket and passed it to Chad. She had put it on vibrate, then made Prada call it back to back so that the battery would die. It worked, because Chad couldn't even get the phone on.

"Don't worry, boo. I'll be up in time to get back to work," she told Chad, grabbing the dead phone from his hand.

Niya hated lying to Chad. It weighed heavy on her heart because she loved him so much. They never kept secrets from each other, but the second life Niya was living couldn't be exposed to the love of her life. No matter how she put it, Chad would never understand, and if he told her to stop, nine times out of ten, she would. That was something that Niya was trying to avoid.

"Are the kids asleep?" she asked, trying to change the mood in the room.

Chad just turned around and walked up the stairs, not really feeling like talking. Niya could tell that he was upset, but it was a tough pill she had to swallow for right now. As she walked up the stairs behind him, she felt the bulge in her back pocket. She reached back and her fingers touched the P80 Ruger, stopping her in the middle of her stride. The gun was a vicious reminder of the kind of double life she was leading.

The entire room was deathly quiet; you could hear a mouse piss on cotton. Mayo sat on top of the piano in his living room, while JR, Made, and Spice sat on the large sectional. Dro, the man at the head, sat in a little fold-up chair in the middle of the room. Not only did he feel totally embarrassed, but he also felt scared because he really didn't know what Mayo was going to do to him.

"So, my nigga, run dis shit down one more time about what happened," Mayo said, jumping down off the piano.

Dro did as he was told and broke down detail by detail what had happened to him the night before. JR and Made laughed at him as he explained how he let a female catch him slippin'. He even chuckled at how dumb it sounded. Mayo was probably the only nigga in the room who wasn't smiling. Whoever it was who robbed Dro had robbed him, and 140K lost left no room for laughter in Mayo's heart.

"Ahh, you think it's funny, right? You think it's a joke you let a bitch rob you, my nigga?" Mayo evilly chuckled as he walked over to Dro. "You got a hundred forty K right now to pay me back, nigga?" he asked, pulling a large .357 Magnum from his waist.

"Nah, May, it wasn't even like that, homie," Dro answered, now looking at Mayo with fear in his eyes.

Mayo walked around behind Dro, took a step back, and pointed the gun at the back of his head. Dro could feel the hairs on the back of his neck stand up. The sound of the hammer being cocked back confirmed what was about to happen. Dro just closed his eyes. Everybody in the room tensed up, but before Mayo could pull the trigger, the front door opened and Prada walked in. Everyone in the room turned to see who it was, even Dro.

Prada entered in time to witness a murder. Mayo never took his eyes off Prada as he pulled the trigger. The loud blast from the large revolver made everyone jump. The bullet tore through Dro's skull and planted itself in the center of his brain, killing him instantly. His body slumped over and fell to the floor. Prada stood there in shock, not knowing what to do. This was the first time she'd ever experienced something like this, and she wasn't sure if Mayo was going to do the same thing to her. She quickly got it together and came to the conclusion that she had to play the situation like an old mob housewife.

She walked over to Mayo, looked down at Dro's body, then back up at him. "Have this shit cleaned up before dinner," she said, motioning with her finger as if it didn't faze her. "Chicken or steak?" she asked Mayo before kissing him on the cheek and walking off toward the kitchen.

Mayo just smiled as he responded, "Chicken. You know a nigga trying to chill on that red meat." He watched Prada walk off, thinking that he had finally copped a winner. Mayo knew he needed a strong bitch on his team, one who understood what he was into and didn't have a problem playing her position.

Niya had the kids up and ready for daycare before Chad cracked his eyes open. It seemed like his dick woke up before him, because he was rock hard. The smell of bacon and eggs flooded the whole house, and after washing his face and brushing his teeth, Chad headed downstairs to the war zone. The twins sat in their highchairs making a complete mess out of their breakfast, while Niya juggled between talking on the phone, watching the news on the kitchen television, and preparing Chad's plate. It was chaos, but the regular morning ritual for the Stafford family.

"Good morning to you too," Niya said, hanging up the phone and bringing Chad's plate to the table.

"Good morning, shawty," he responded then turned his attention to the twins.

"Oh, I'm shawty this morning, huh?" It was obvious that he was still upset about last night. "So how long are you going to be mad at me, Chad? I said that I was sorry," Niya whined.

"I'ma be mad until I get over the fact that you walked in this house at one-thirty in the morn—"

"I told you I was with Prada," she said, cutting him off.

"Yeah, that's what you say," Chad responded as he wiped the food from baby Khoula's face.

"So what's that supposed to mean, Chad? Are you insinuating something? I mean, it's obvious you don't believe me, so why don't you say what's really on ya mind?"

Chad didn't say another word. He didn't feel like arguing this morning, and he knew that if he really said what was on his mind, it would get ugly. He did what any man in his right mind would do: he simply got up from the table and took his food upstairs.

Prada sat in the bathroom on the edge of the tub with her face buried in her hands. She still couldn't believe she had witnessed Mayo killing somebody. The tears poured down her face; and it wasn't because she was afraid, but because she felt somewhat responsible for Dro's death. She never thought in a million years that Mayo would take it that far.

"Prada! Prada!" Mayo yelled out as he walked into the bedroom. The voice alone startled her, causing Prada to jump up and grab a washrag for her face. She quickly splashed some water on her face just as he opened the bathroom door.

"You all right in here, ma?" Mayo asked with a curious look on his face.

"Yeah, I'm good, baby. I was just washing up. Did you take care of that downstairs yet?" she asked, referring to Dro's dead body.

"It's being taken care of as we speak. I wanted to talk to you about that too."

"You don't have to explain," Prada said, cutting him off. "You did what you had to do, I'm sure."

"Naw, ma. That's something you didn't have to witness. It's just that when it comes to my money, I have zero tolerance for incompetence," Mayo tried to explain.

Prada wasn't trying to hear any of that. It went in one ear and out the other. Her mind was made up the moment she saw Dro's body slumped over. This short relationship was over, and there wasn't anything Mayo could do to make things right. Prada was already prepared to have the conversation with Niya and let her know she was done spying on Mayo.

Chapter 2

Gwen dropped the last nine ounces of powder into the Pyrex pot that was sitting on the stove. She was a chef when it came to cooking crack, and there weren't too many people in North Carolina who could mess with her. That was one of the reasons JR loved her so much. That and the fact that she was sexy as hell.

"Pass me the ice," Gwen told JR as she continued to whip the baking soda in with the cocaine.

JR brought the ice over to the sink and then slid up behind Gwen. He wrapped his arms around her waist. A soft kiss to the back of her neck gave her the chills.

"You better stop before I fuck this money up," she joked, scraping the thick liquid from around the edges of the pot.

With her skills, it was impossible for her to mess up the product. Hell, she learned how to cook coke from the best: her son's father. It had been a while since she and Chad had actually been together, but many good jewels that she had learned from him stuck with her. Making crack was one of them.

"It's me and you this weekend?" JR asked Gwen, grabbing her and pressing her fat ass up against his dick.

"I don't know. I got to see if Zion's dad can take him. You know that's gonna be a slim chance," she answered as she took the pot of cocaine off the stove and placed it into the sink.

Gwen and JR had been together for about a year, and ever since the day Chad found out Gwen was in love with another man, their relationship had gone south. It was as if they had become enemies. They couldn't get along for anything, not even for the sake of little Zion, their only child together.

"Well, look, if he don't want to take his son, then maybe we can bring him along with us," JR suggested. "It can be like a family outing," he said, planting yet another kiss to the back of her neck.

Gwen dumped the ice and some cold water into the pot of crack and then turned around to face JR. She had to admit to herself that she had love for him; it just wasn't the crazy love she once had for Chad. However, JR had come into her life when she needed somebody the most. Outside of being one of the most vicious niggas to come out of Charlotte, he was also kind and sweet when it came down to Gwen. He was everything a woman looked for in a man: a rough shell, but soft inside. There was no doubt that she really cared about him, but at the same time, Gwen wasn't stupid enough to play the family card with JR.

Chad was a hop, skip, and a jump away, and even though Chad had given up the street life and had a new family of his own, she knew that he was an extremely proud man. If the word got back from the streets that some other man was out there playing father to his child, it would not sit well with him. Gwen was well aware of Chad's temper and had witnessed more than her share of his wrath on those he perceived to be his enemies. *No,* Gwen thought, *sometimes it's best not to wake a sleeping giant.* If she and JR were going out this weekend, it would be without Zion.

***

"Niya is gonna kill us if we can't get this building," Diamond said, looking around the empty warehouse. Her phone began to ring. She excused herself from her friend, Tiffany, and the Realtor who was showing them around.

"Hey, girl, what's up wit' the buildings? How do it look?" Niya asked as she jumped into her car.

"Girl, this place is big as shit. It's more than enough space, plus it got a second level to it."

Niya smiled at the description Diamond was giving her about the place. It had always been her dream to own her own club, and for the past few months, she'd been working toward that goal. That was just one of the reasons why she started taking money from big-time drug dealers around North Carolina. Niya was more than determined. This was the come-up she and Chad needed in their lives. Both of them had taken on jobs just to make ends meet, and currently that was all they were doing. Also, she had the girls of her crew to think about. How long would they be able to continue doing this?

"No, this is the only way out, and I have to make it happen," Niya had uttered to herself.

"So what do the numbers look like?" Niya asked, looking back at the house before pulling out of the driveway.

Diamond was quiet on the phone for a minute before she spoke. "They want one point five million for this building, Niya, and they are not taking anything less than that," Diamond explained. "Where the hell are you going to get one point five million from, Niya?" she asked with doubt in her tone.

"Don't worry about it, D. We're gonna get it," Niya assured her. "If I got to rob every nigga in North Carolina, it's gonna get done fo' sho," Niya said.

"Big sis, we also got another problem," Diamond said, letting out a sigh of frustration. "The Realtor said that he can only hold this building for another thirty days. If we can't come up with the money by then, he's gonna sell the building."

"Damn," Niya mumbled to herself. Thirty days wasn't enough time for Niya to come up with that type of money, and she knew it. Given the couple of jobs she and Prada had lined up, it was possible she could come up with a half million. At times like this, she wished that Chad was still in the game, because $1.5 million would have been paid by the end of the day.

"Diamond, I need more time. I can get the money; I just need more time," she pled. "Just see what you can do," she told Diamond before hanging up the phone.

Gwen watched as the traffic light changed from green to yellow, but at her rate of speed, she wasn't going to be able to stop the car. The only thing she could to do was go through the red light. Everything seemed okay, until she saw lights flashing behind her.

"Fuck," she mumbled to herself, thinking about what was in the car.

Today was Gwen's day to deliver all the drugs to the multiple trap houses that JR had in the hood. She had enough crack in the trunk to trigger a federal indictment, not to mention the 9 mm she had tucked away under her seat. Gwen's anxiety was at an all-time high as she pulled the car over.

After about a minute or two, the officer got out of the police cruiser and approached Gwen's car. His partner walked up to the passenger's side. Slowly and calmly, Gwen reached for her sun visor to grab her license and registration.

"Did I do something wrong, officer?" Gwen asked with an innocent look on her face.

"You ran a red light, ma'am. Can I see your license and registration, with proof of insurance?" the officer said while taking a good look around the inside of Gwen's car.

She complied, giving the officer all of her info. The second cop was making Gwen extremely nervous. He stayed behind while his partner went back to the cruiser to run the paperwork. He asked question after question, mainly pertaining to where Gwen was coming from and where she was going. The whole time he was questioning her, he was looking around the car in a suspicious manner. Gwen just kept her cool. She had been schooled by Chad and knew that a routine traffic stop alone was not probable cause to search the car. For now, she was in the clear . . . unless the K-9 unit showed up.

Chapter 3

"What's good wit' you, homie?" JR said, giving Mayo daps as they walked through the door. They had been friends since grade school, and there wasn't too much they didn't know about each other

"I needed to holler at you about the bull Dro told me before I checked him out," Mayo said as both men took a seat on the couch.

JR could feel that Mayo was on to something, and he knew that Mayo wasn't going to forget about his money. He couldn't let it go, and he was determined to get down to the bottom of who took 140K from him. "Dro told me that when the chick was robbing him, he noticed a tattoo on her wrist. It said *MHB* inside some crazy little sign," Mayo explained.

JR's brain went into overdrive. There was only one person he knew of who had a similar tattoo. It was the last person he thought would have had something to do with the robbery, but a clear vision of the tattoo *MHB* was on Gwen's right ankle. He remembered Gwen telling him a little bit about the tattoo when they first started dating, but he couldn't remember what it stood for.

"You sure the nigga said it was on her wrist?" JR asked.

"Yeah, and he said she had another tat on her arm, but he couldn't make it out."

Prada crept out of the bedroom and down the hall to the top of the steps. She could hear Mayo and JR talking about the situation with the robbery, and she wanted to see just how much Mayo knew. She had missed a lot of the conversation but heard all she needed to hear from Mayo.

"Yo, homie, if it's the last thing I do, I'ma find dis bitch who took my money, and I'ma blow her fuckin' head off," Mayo declared with determination in his eyes.

Prada almost choked on her own spit when she heard that. She feared that Mayo might know more than she thought he did. She slowly backed up from the top of the steps and went back into the bedroom.

"Damn, homie, I'ma put my ears to the streets, ASAP," JR said, giving Mayo daps before getting up from the couch.

As he was leaving the house, the only thing he could think about was Gwen and if she knew anything about the robbery. One thing he did know for sure was that Mayo was going to find out who did it. He recalled the time when he and Mayo were in middle school and a high school kid by the name of Art beat Mayo up and took his lunch money for about a month straight. When Mayo got old enough and started playin' around with guns, he sought Art out, robbed him, beat him up, and then shot him in his face. JR could remember Mayo's words the day after he killed Art: "It wasn't about the fact that he beat me up. I killed him 'cause he took my lunch money!" JR knew that Mayo's determination was going to make him victorious in finding the culprit behind the robbery.

Chad knew the storm was coming; he could feel it in the air. As he opened his front door to leave for work, Gwen was pulling up. She was worse than a storm; she was his baby mama/ex-wifey. Before he met Niya, Gwen was his everything, and the relationship they had was the kind that dreams were made of. They were like the modern-day Bonnie and Clyde. During that time, Chad ran Charlotte in the drug game, but a single bullet to the side of his head put him in early retirement. He knew that he was lucky to survive it, and after beating a federal case, Chad recognized the blessing God had shown him and decided to give up the life and go square.

He got a job with the City of Charlotte, and had been laying concrete for the last two years. He loved Gwen, but he knew she wasn't the type for a regular Joe blow. Gwen wanted the glamorous life and everything that came with it. Gwen had more aggression and drive than most men did.

After Gwen left, Chad made a life decision and chose Niya, the calmer of the two, to build a future with. He knew that having a relationship with Niya would cause a lifelong vendetta with Gwen. She and Niya had been close at one time. They both grew up in Clanton Park and were classmates through elementary, middle, and high school. Chad knew that he couldn't end up with some soft broad, because Gwen would constantly run over her, until she had run her away. He knew that although Niya was calm, she was at heart a very dangerous woman when provoked.

Niya was light-skinned with long hair, and she had to constantly prove herself growing up in the hood. Some girl's boyfriend was always liking her, and this would keep her in a fight. Her hand game was crazy. One time, a girl pulled down on her. Niya grabbed the gun and began beating the girl mercilessly, until one of the other girls drew another pistol and fired a shot to get Niya to stop. Well, she obviously didn't know who she was dealing with, because Niya walked up to her, grabbed her gun as well, and fired a bullet into the young woman's leg.

She stood over her and asked, "You happy now? You got what you wanted. I stopped whooping her ass, and all it cost you was a leg!" From that day forward, everyone in Southside knew that Niya was a sleeping giant no one wanted to wake.

"What seems to be ya problem, Chad?" Gwen began yelling before she even got out of the car. "You haven't seen ya fuckin' son in a month," she continued, slamming the car door behind her.

"Come on, Gwen, wit' da bullshit. I told you I been busy," he shot back.

"Too busy to see ya own fuckin' son?"

"Look, man, you know a nigga out here working, and I got to take all the overtime I can get. You can bring him over here next weekend," he said, flagging her off and heading for his car.

"You sad, Chad. Ya son need you—"

"I'm sad? I'm the one out here breaking my fucking back with this concrete. You cleaning up real good wit' the amount of money you get for child support, and I'm sad?" Chad said, cutting her off. "I'm sure you got JP . . . JT . . . J whatever doin' a good job playin' daddy," he said as he got into his car. Chad really didn't mean the last statement, but he knew that he was getting underneath Gwen's skin, which was exactly what he wanted to do.

He isn't the only one who can play this game, Gwen thought. "Oh, I'm glad you okay with that, because JR wanted to take him on a father-son trip this weeke—" She didn't even have time to get the words out of her mouth before Chad was out of the car and standing in her face with his hand on her chin.

"Gwen, don't you ever play with me like that. You tell that nigga to take his own fucking son, you hear me?" Chad uttered through clenched teeth. He shook Gwen's head up and down for her. Chad gave her a light tap on her cheek and got back into his car and pulled away.

***

Diamond pulled up to the Realtor's office, hoping to catch Mike before he left for the day. She needed to get the extension so that Niya could have enough time to come up with the money to buy the building. When she got to the front door, it was locked, but the lights were on. She looked down at her watch and saw that it was a little after five.

Just as she was about to turn around and leave, she caught a glimpse of someone moving around in the back. It was Mike leaving his office and going across the hall into the copy room. Diamond knocked on the glass to catch his attention.

"Hey, Diamond, I was just about to leave," Mike said, opening the door. "What can I do for you?"

"I know it's kinda late, but I really need to talk to you about the building," she pleaded with a sad, puppy dog face.

Mike stepped to the side and let her into the office. For a second, he couldn't take his eyes off her. Diamond had a way of letting her body speak for her. Standing at five feet six inches, weighing 155 pounds with 34B breasts, a curvy waist, flat stomach, and a nice, petite ass, Diamond was the reason white men lusted over black women the way they did. Mike was no exception. Diamond's light brown skin complemented her long, curly black hair that stopped at her shoulders. Today, it was pulled back into a ponytail, bringing out the beauty of her face.

"I really need ya help," Diamond said, setting her large brown leather printed Gucci bag on his desk. "I really need additional time to buy the building. I know that I can have the money in a couple of months."

"I'm sorry, Diamond. I have someone looking at the building in a couple of days. I won't be able to hold it if he's ready to buy it," Mike explained.

"Come on, Mike," she whined, walking around to his side of the desk and taking a seat on the edge of it in front of him. Her sweetly scented body drove Mike into freak mode. He damn near started to drool, looking at the way her thighs were kissing each other in those jeans. Diamond noticed the attention he was giving her body and decided to entice him some more.

"Sixty days is all I need," Diamond said in a seductive manner, lifting one of her legs up and planting her Zegna heels on his armrest.

Mike got up from his chair, and at first Diamond thought she had messed up. Then, he put his hand on her thigh. He stood between her legs, looking down at her with lustful eyes. "How far are you willing to go?" he said in his most seductive yet playful tone.

Diamond knew right then that she was going to have to take one for the team. She reached for Mike's belt and unfastened his buckle while getting off the desk and taking a seat in his chair. Mike's dick was rock hard before his pants hit the floor, and before he knew it, Diamond was taking his white flesh into her mouth. The warmth of her mouth caused him to lean against his desk. His eyes rolled to the back of his head as Diamond completely devoured his dick. He could feel the head of his manhood tapping the back of her moistened throat, and the sounds of spit splashing around in her mouth heightened the sensitivity of his dick.

Mike couldn't help but to grab the back of her head as she continued to suck. He could feel the tingling sensation in the pit of his stomach, and he knew he was about to nut. He quickly grabbed a handful of her hair and pulled Diamond off his dick. It sounded like a suction cup releasing its pressure when she let his dick go. He pulled her up to him and kissed her.

In the heat of the moment, Diamond returned his kiss, stuffing her tongue in his mouth. With one hand, Mike reached down and unfastened Diamond's jeans. His other hand spun her around and bent her over onto the desk. Within seconds, Mike was pushing his meat inside of Diamond's pink box. She spread her legs apart and loosened up her walls so that she could take all of him inside of her. Mike slammed his meat deeper into her. Her loud moans resounded throughout the empty office as Mike continued pounding and pounding away.

Niya sat on her bed, counting all of the money that she had in her stash. The bed was full of fifties, twenties, tens, and single dollar bills. She could tell that the money she'd been taking was drug money just by how dirty the bills looked. So far, and including the recent take for 140K that she and Prada split, she had a little more than 300K. The whole time she was counting the money, she thought about the club she wanted to own. "One point five million," she mumbled to herself, shaking her head.

Niya was still within reach of being able to set up a mortgage for the property, but she really wanted to buy it straight out, with no strings attached. Niya was so caught up with counting the money that she didn't hear Chad pull up, nor did she hear him come into the house.

Chad tried to be quiet, thinking that everyone was taking a nap. He knew that Niya was there because her truck was still outside. As he crept up the stairs, he could hear some noises coming from his room. It was a familiar sound to him, and as he got closer to his bedroom, he knew that it was money being counted.

The door was cracked open just enough for Chad to see Niya sitting on the bed with a handful of money. He started to just bust through the door and demand an explanation, but he decided against it. He calmly backed up and headed downstairs.

Where da fuck did she get all that money? he thought, pacing back and forth in the kitchen. One thing Chad learned from being in the streets was that things are rarely what they seem. So, before he allowed himself to confront Niya while he was upset, he would just let it be for now. One thing was for sure, and two things for certain: this wasn't going to be the end of it.

"Yo, what's wrong wit' you?" Mayo asked Prada, who was lying in bed with her back to him. He had felt that something wasn't right ever since he killed Dro in front of her, and he was really unsure how he was going to deal with the situation.

"I'm good, May," she responded. "I'm just a little tired."

"Yeah, what, you pregnant or something?" he asked, sliding up behind her and placing his arm around her waist.

That comment was enough to get her attention. She turned around and gave him a curious look. *I hope this nigga ain't tryin'a get me pregnant,* she thought. She had to admit that the sex was good, and there were a couple of instances where she felt him cum inside of her, but there was no way she should or would be feeling symptoms of pregnancy. They had only known each other for about a month and started having sex three weeks ago. After a week of safe sex, she let him go inside of her raw. All of this information played back in her head for a split second.

"Boy, don't be tryin'a jinx me. I'm not tryin'a have no babies right now," Prada joked. "Don't make me have to put a rubber on you," she said, smiling.

"Ah, shawty, dis daddy pussy now," he shot back, climbing on top of her. "You got my nose wide open." He chuckled, leaning in to kiss her soft lips.

He hadn't lied when he said that he was open. Prada had done some things to him that women only do with their husbands; not to mention the fact that she was probably the toughest redbone in Charlotte. She was pretty as all outdoors. Her natural eye color was a golden brown, and she really didn't have to smile in order to reveal her dimples. Her hair reached to the center of her back, and her five foot seven, 170-pound frame was stacked in all the right places. Thirty-eight D breasts, thick thighs, fat ass, and a smile that could make heaven open up the gates.

It wasn't hard for Mayo to fall for someone like Prada, and if Prada wasn't focused the way that she was, she probably would have fallen for him as well. He was everything she liked physically: tall, dark, and handsome. He even had the nerve to have a full head of naturally curly hair. It wasn't too many niggas in Charlotte with curly hair. Prada just had the ability to control her emotions and not get attached. Prada's only mission in life right now was to gain the last two digits to Mayo's safe, take everything in it, then move on to the next nigga. That was what she did. She was an MHB girl and would be that until the death of her.

Chapter 4

Prada pulled into the strip mall where she was supposed to meet up with Niya for their Tuesday ritual at a small eatery. The white Range Rover sitting in front of the store confirmed that Prada was late again, but with what she had to tell Niya, being late would be the last thing they talked about.

"Girl, dis nigga is crazy as shit," Prada began as she pushed the plate of food Niya had ordered to the side like it wasn't even there. "He killed that boy right in front of me," she whispered with her hands cupped around her mouth.

"What? Bitch, you better get the hell out of there," Niya told her with a concerned look on her face. "Dat nigga might kill you next."

"Shit, I'm one digit away from having the combo to his safe. And when I say safe, it look like a walk-in closet," Prada said, snapping her neck back and forth.

Niya had to chuckle at Prada and the way she was trying to look so ghetto. Through everything she had seen Mayo do, she was still in it to win it. Niya admired that part about her. "You MHB," Niya said, smiling and shaking her head.

"Oh, shit, that reminds me: the nigga we robbed told him he saw a MHB tattoo on ya wrist. Mayo was making all kinds of threats about how he was goin' to get to the bottom of it," Prada added.

The Money Hungry Bitches consisted of Diamond, Tiffany, Tiki, Lisa, who had died in a car accident, and lastly Niya's best friend turned archenemy, Gwen. Prada was a new MHB, but she hadn't gotten her tattoo yet. She was waiting for the right time to get it, and now definitely wasn't the time.

Niya was in deep thought, thinking about the first day that she had met Prada, and how far she had come from being that timid, helpless little girl. They were both sitting in the lobby of the abortion clinic. Niya had gotten pregnant by her high school sweetheart when she was fifteen years old. She knew there was no way she was going to be able to tell her saved and sanctified grandmother, whom she lived with, that she was having sex and was pregnant. She knew that her grandmother would ship her off quickly before she let Niya embarrass her to the whole neighborhood and church congregation. So, Niya did the only thing she could think of, and that was to steal the $400 from the money her grandmother kept in her sock drawer and handle her business.

She convinced her boyfriend at the time to give her a ride to the appointment, since he was seventeen and old enough to drive. While in the waiting room, she could hear Prada on the phone, crying and arguing with someone about coming to pick her up, especially since they hadn't given her any money to help. Niya stepped in, and ever since that day, Prada had been at her side.

"So now what?" Prada asked, looking over at the stress in her best friend's eyes. Whatever Niya wanted to do, Prada was down with it. That's just the kind of love and loyalty she had for MHB. She also knew the love Niya had for her, and that whatever she decided was in the best interest of all.

"Hurry up and get that last digit to that safe," Niya instructed before digging her fork into her lunch. She hated the fact that she had to put her girl back in harm's way; however, she also knew that if she didn't make this club dream a reality soon, they would never be able to stop with this lifestyle. Therefore, it was better to take this chance now, for a safer future.

Gwen was sitting at the kitchen table weighing and bagging up ounces and half ounces of crack when JR came through the door. Although JR was pretty much the supplier, Gwen was the engine of the car. Gwen moved most of the coke JR bought. She knew pretty much every drug dealer in Charlotte, along with all the hot spots for heavy crackhead traffic. That was all courtesy of Chad, who had her in the passenger's seat the whole time he flooded the streets back in his day.

"Yo, I need to talk to you about something," JR said sincerely as he came into the kitchen and took a seat at the table with her.

From the way he sounded, Gwen thought someone had died. He was only like this when it was something serious. "What's up, babe?" she said, turning off the scale.

"I need you to tell me everything you know about MHB," he said with a serious look in his eyes.

That caught Gwen by surprise. She couldn't understand why he would suddenly be asking about MHB, considering the fact that Gwen hardly ever talked about the tattoo on her ankle.

"Why? What's going on, JR?" Gwen asked with a curious look on her face.

JR began to explain the whole situation with Mayo and the money. He told her about Dro's story of being robbed, and how Dro told Mayo about the tattoo he had seen on the female who robbed him, and how Mayo really just wanted to get his money back. JR wasn't speaking in a harsh manner, but rather in a concerned tone, something Gwen picked up on the moment he sat down.

"So what do you wanna know, JR?" Gwen probed, trying to see where he was going with his line of questions.

"I wanna know everything. I wanna know everybody who's a part of MHB—where they from, where they live, how many of y'all there is, and most importantly, which chick got *MHB* tattooed on her right wrist," he said, scooting his chair closer to Gwen.

Even though Gwen didn't mess with the people in MHB, that didn't change the fact that she was still a Money Hungry Bitch herself. The rules and regulations still applied in Gwen's life, and it didn't matter what the situation was; she could never cross her MHB family. It was more about who she was, and less about what had transpired. So she responded as if she was at the last meeting.

"Look, I don't know what you plan on doing, but I haven't been a part of MHB for years, boo. Even if I did have info on them, I couldn't possibly get involved."

Gwen wasn't dumb at all. She knew that Mayo was going to kill whoever took his money, just as fast as he killed the person they took the money from. She couldn't have an MHB member's blood on her hands. No matter how much she hated Niya, she wasn't about to tell JR that she was the only member who had *MHB* tattooed on her right wrist.

JR could see that Gwen wasn't gonna budge. She was going to stand firm in her loyalty to her crew by any means necessary. The look she had was the same kind of look he would have if someone were to inquire about Mayo. JR was genuinely concerned about her, because he knew how far Mayo was willing to go about his money. Anybody from MHB was liable to get shot, and that included Gwen, if she wasn't careful.

***

Prada walked into the house to find Mayo already in his safe, putting the money in and taking cocaine out. She was mad because she wasn't there to catch the last two numbers. All she could do was wait until he went back in it again, and when he did, she was going to be ready.

Chad had decided to spend some time with his son, instead of waiting for the weekend. He had been feeling guilty about the lack of time he'd been giving him, due to the rift he had with Gwen. There wasn't a question whether he loved his son, because he did. Zion was his firstborn, the result of a planned pregnancy with the woman he was in love with at the time. Zion wasn't an accident or someone Chad had to learn how to love. His feelings for his boy came naturally.

When Gwen pulled up to the house, Chad was already sitting outside waiting for them. It was rare that Gwen actually came to the house, and that was due to the constant tension between her and Niya. They couldn't stand each other, and Chad was the core of the problem.

"Daddy! Daddy!" Zion yelled, getting out of the car and running up to him.

The love he displayed for his father was so emotional that even Gwen had to smile. No amount of time away from each other could break their bond, and in some ways, Gwen respected that.

"Get out the car. I wanna holla at you for a minute," Chad told Gwen, catching her off-guard.

"I don't have time. I got somewhere to—" she tried to plead, only to pair of deaf ears.

"Get out the car, G," he said again, cutting her off.

He hadn't called her by the name G since they were together, and that by itself compelled Gwen to get out of the car.

Even though she had on something as simple as a pair of thigh-high shorts, a tank top, and some Alexander McQueen sandals, she still looked good. Chad's dick got hard at the thought of sliding between her thick thighs. He could just picture himself biting each thigh right before planting his face into her pussy.

"Yo, listen. This beef between me and you gotta stop. Let me be the first to apologize for everything that got us to this point," Chad began.

"Chad, you don't have to—"

"Chill out, shawty. Let me talk," he said, stopping her. "I'm not the same person I used to be. I changed a lot over the past couple of years, and I've come to realize what's important in life," he continued.

Just listening to him, Gwen could see the change in his attitude. He sounded like someone who was responsible and knew what he wanted out of life. He sounded like a person who had a heart and a conscience, and not like the thugged-out nigga she fell in love with. He sounded like a man, a real man.

"I just want you to know that I'm gonna do better. I'ma do all I can to be a better father," he said with all the humility in the world.

Gwen was stuck for a moment as she listened to him. She couldn't help but to think about how things would have been if they had never parted ways. In some odd way, she wished that she could have grown with him into being the kind of person he was today, but four years ago, Gwen wasn't ready to leave the life of a hustler's wife.

Before Gwen could even get a chance to respond, the white Range Rover pulled into the driveway right behind her car, blocking her in.

Niya jumped out of the truck, and it was obvious that she had an attitude, because she didn't even speak to Gwen. Chad gave her a stern look as if to say, "Don't start," as she walked up and kissed him. Gwen just smiled, finding it funny that Niya thought the kiss made her jealous.

"Well, look, I'm tryin' to leave. Can you move ya truck so I can go?" Gwen asked, breaking the awkward silence. "You know what? I do need to have a word or two with you," Gwen said, looking at Niya.

They both looked at Chad as if to dismiss him, so the women could talk. He was reluctant, knowing how ugly this conversation could get, but he chose to leave them alone anyway. He wasn't going far, though.

"I'll be over here," he said, pointing to Zion, who was sitting on the front steps.

The ladies were silent until Chad was out of hearing range. Niya didn't know what to expect, but she was ready for any physical confrontation Gwen was plotting.

"So when did MHB start robbing people?" Gwen asked with both an attitude and disappointment.

The question caught Niya off-guard. "What the hell are you talking about?" Niya shot back.

"Cut da shit, Ni. I know about the trap house that got robbed last week," Gwen said, leaning against her car. "They say she had a *MHB* tat on her right wrist," she continued, grabbing Niya's right arm.

"You should mind ya fuckin' business," Niya shot back, snatching her arm away. Niya was a little ashamed about what she was doing. MHB was never about violence when Tiki, an OG wife, started it and then passed it on to Niya and Gwen. It started as an empowerment movement for young women to take control of their lives and be more independent. It was over the course of time that both Gwen and Niya changed the movement. MHB was trans-formed into a handful of young women who competed to see who could bag the most infamous drug dealers in North Carolina. *Money hungry* was just a better phrase to use than *gold diggers*, even though that's all they became, just at a higher level.

"You know, robbery is a new low for you, Ni," Gwen rubbed in, as she reached for her door. "If I was you—"

"Well, you're not me," Niya snapped back. "You do you, and let me do me," she said as she headed for the truck so that she could let Gwen out.

When Niya got into her car, a tap at her window got her attention. It was Gwen.

"What?" Niya said as she rolled down the window.

"You might want to cover that tattoo up before you end up having a hundred niggas runnin' up in ya house," Gwen warned.

That was going to be the only warning Gwen would give her, and that was only due to her being a MHB. After waving to Zion and Chad, who were still sitting on the steps, Gwen jumped in her car and left.

Detective Butler walked into the wooded area just off the highway, where he was greeted by a female detective named Rose. Butler was led to the makeshift gravesite where the forensic unit was photographing Dro's body.

"A single shot to the back of his head. He didn't feel a thing," Detective Rose said, kneeling down next to the corpse.

Detective Butler reached into Dro's pockets, looking for identification. It was there along with some money and car keys. "I guess we can rule out robbery," Butler said, looking at the contents. "Jeffrey Davis," he announced, holding the ID to his eyes.

It was simple murders like this that made Detective Butler want to be a cop. He grew up in Charlotte and knew firsthand how violent the city was. He would do everything in his power to solve this case.

Chapter 5

Club Caviar was jam-packed, and it seemed that everyone from Charlotte was in the building. For MHB, it was ladies' night out, a well-needed break from a long week of work. Diamond, Tiffany, and Niya sat in the VIP booth surrounded by bottles of Patrón and Grey Goose. The oldest member of the crew, Tiki, was making her rounds in the club.

Tiki was the original founder of MHB, back in the day when the He-men crew ran the city. Tiki was married to the leader and figured she would form a crew for the women of the male members. After her husband, Andre, was violently murdered, she decided to turn the group into a positive support group. After years of being in the midst of things, she decided to pass the torch to Gwen and Niya, when most of the He-men crew hung up their jerseys. Now Tiki was more of an adviser than an actual member, but the people in the city still loved her.

"What you thinking about?" Niya yelled over the music to Diamond, who was lost in her thoughts.

She hadn't stopped thinking about Mike the Realtor and what happened in his office a few days ago. Most women would have felt bad and degraded for doing what she did, but Diamond liked the crazy wild office sex. Visions of Mike slamming her over on his desk and pounding her from the back raced through her mind.

"I got the extension," Diamond said with a big smile on her face. "Ninety days!" she yelled.

Niya was ecstatic. All she was hoping for was sixty days, but Diamond managed to get ninety. Niya saw the devious grin Diamond had on her face before she took a sip of her drink, and it made her suspicious.

"How da hell did you get ninety days, girl?" Niya asked, already having a feeling what Diamond was going to say.

It was silent at the table for a second. Tiffany even stopped what she was doing to hear the answer. "I gave him a shot of pussy." Diamond laughed. Everybody at the table laughed at the surprising twist.

"You whore," Tiffany joked.

"Yo' ass sittin' up there wit' a big ol' smile on ya face. Let me find out that white boy got ya ass sprung," Niya chimed in.

"Girl, he fucked me like a porn star," Diamond said, taking another sip of her drink. "I know he got some nigga in him."

They all burst out laughing again. Just as they finished laughing, Prada walked into the VIP section. She was rocking a black sleeveless Dolce & Gabbana pencil dress, and a pair of red-and-black Louis Vuitton peep-toe heels. She could've been on the runway, because all eyes were on her.

Niya admired the way Prada dressed when it was time to get fresh. But even with all that was going on in the club, Niya was still on point and aware of her surroundings. About fifteen steps behind Prada was a familiar face. At first she didn't know who or where she remembered the girl from, but as the female got closer, it was like a light bulb switched on.

"The girl from the car," Niya mumbled to herself as she reached into her pocketbook.

It was hard to get guns inside of Club Caviar, especially for a female, but a trusty pocketknife almost always made it in. Through all the smiling faces, Prada noticed the frown on Niya's face when she walked up. She had to think about it for a second, but quickly remembered who she had brought along. It was almost too late, because Niya was climbing out of the booth, knife in hand, and staring right at her target.

"Whoa! Whoa! Whoa! Sis, it's cool," Prada yelled out, stepping in front of her.

"Oh, shit!" Diamond yelled, seeing the knife in Niya's hand.

"What da fuck is going on here, Prada?" Niya yelled with rage still in her eyes.

"Let me explain. Wait, let me explain!" Prada shouted, putting the young girl behind her.

It took a minute for everyone to cool off, but eventually the dust settled.

Diamond, Tiffany, and Niya all stared at the girl standing behind Prada looking scared to death.

"She's only sixteen years old, Ni," Prada began. "She didn't have nowhere else to go, so I took her in and let her stay at my apartment," Prada explained.

"What was she doin' wit' him?" Niya asked, talking about her being in the car with Dro.

"She was doing the same thing I was doing ten years ago when I was her age," Prada answered with a sad look on her face.

Just saying those words brought tears to Prada's eyes, as a recap of her parentless childhood flashed through her head. The hard look in Niya's eyes also faded away and was replaced with a bit of sorrow. Niya knew the trials and tribulations that Prada had gone through. She herself had experienced firsthand how cold the streets could be for a young girl.

By the age of sixteen, Niya and pretty much everyone at the table had known the struggle. It was grown-ass men like Dro who took advantage of teenage girls with nobody to look out for them. For those reasons, Niya became a little more understanding.

"What's your name?" Niya asked, folding the knife up and putting it back in her bag.

"I'm Alexus," the young girl said, coming from behind Prada.

"Yeah, and Alexus got a birthday coming up in about twenty minutes," Prada announced with a big smile. "I was hoping she could ring in her seventeenth birthday with us."

It got quiet at the table for what seemed like forever. The only thing that could be heard was the club music. Everyone looked at Niya to see what was going to be done, because the decision of whether Alexus stayed or left was totally up to her. MHB was going to back whatever the decision was, and that included Prada. Niya took one good look at Alexus, then nodded her head.

"Happy birthday, sweetie. Come take a seat right here next to me," Niya said, managing to crack a smile.

Gwen pulled up and parked two blocks away from the Food Lion on Beatties Ford Road. She was supposed to meet up with Master for a routine drug transaction. She was glad to finally see his blue Cadillac pull up and park a few cars away from hers. The heavy rain beat down on the windshield as Gwen waited for Master to get out of his car.

"I'm not coming out in that rain," Gwen said, breaking the silence in her car. Master wasn't getting out of his car either. For about two minutes, they both played the waiting game, until Gwen decided to call him. She reached into the center console and grabbed her phone, along with the ten-shot 9 mm Glock. Master picked up on the first ring.

"Yo, what up, shawty?" Master said, inhaling the thick green smoke from his Swisher Sweet.

"You gonna get out of the car, or are you gonna make me wait here all day?" Gwen said, looking out of the driver's side window at all the rain puddles in the street.

"Nah, shawty. I be wit' you in a second. I just got to finish countin' my money," he answered, now exhaling the weed smoke.

Gwen just hung up the phone and tossed it back into the console. It was always some shit wit' Master every time she dealt with him—too much shit for him to only be buying one half of a brick.

Minutes had passed, and the rain wasn't letting up at all. It was to the point where Gwen was about to pull off and catch up wit' Master later. When a green Chevy Tahoe turned onto the street and caught Gwen's attention, chills ran through her whole body. Something wasn't right, and she could feel it.

Master still hadn't gotten out of his car, and the SUV was slowly making its way down the street. She grabbed the Glock that was sitting on her lap and checked to make sure there was a cartridge in the chamber. The moment she started her car and put it in drive, the green truck sped up and came to a screeching halt right beside Gwen's car. The Tahoe blocked her car in so that she couldn't move, and then finally the side door opened.

Gwen's heart was racing. Out of the corner of her eye, she could see Master getting out of his car, but she still had her main view on the truck. Gwen didn't waste another second opening fire on the SUV. Several bullets crashed out of her driver's side window and into the open side door, where a hooded gunman attempted to jump out. As she fired, Gwen climbed over into the passenger's side, opened the door, and fell out onto the pavement.

"Get da bitch! Get her and don't kill her," Master yelled out to the occupants of the Chevy Tahoe.

Hearing that, Gwen sent two fireballs his way, forcing him to take cover behind his car. Suddenly, the driver's side and passenger's side doors of the truck opened. The hooded gunmen came out. One attempted to come around to the passenger's side of Gwen's car, but rapid gunfire stopped him in his tracks. She cupped both of her hands around the gun and squeezed. The bullet tore through his chest; then another one knocked off a nice chunk of his face.

Master, along with the other two shooters, watched as their fellow gunman's body dropped to the ground. They all fired heavily in Gwen's direction from all angles. There were only four shots left in her gun, and the only thing on her mind was reaching the extra clip under the driver's seat.

"Fuck dat bitch, dog. We out," one of the gunmen yelled to Master as he backed up to the truck.

A momentary reprieve from gunfire gave Gwen the opportunity to get up from the ground. She fired two shots in the men's direction before reaching under her seat for the extra clip. As she popped a fresh one into her gun, the green Tahoe pulled off. She came from behind her car, firing several more shots into the back of the SUV. She continued firing, hitting the back of Master's car as he tried to pull off. The multiple bullets shattered his back window, and before he could make it to the end of the street, his car crashed into a couple of parked cars. Gwen just stepped over the dead body, jumped into her car, and reversed down the street.

As the club wound down for the night, the heavy crowd of people began to exit the building. Niya and Prada sat at the booth, pretty much waiting for everyone else to leave before they did. Diamond, on the other hand, had an after party to attend.

"All right, bitches, I'm gone for the night," Diamond announced, grabbing her bag from the VIP. "Call me in the morning," she told the girls as she hurried to leave.

"Wait, wait, wait. Bitch, where you goin', and why are you in a hurry?" Tiffany asked with a curious look on her face.

"None of ya damn business, girl. I'm grown," she shot back with a lustful grin.

Everyone couldn't help but to laugh at Diamond, knowing exactly where she was going. Mike had her nose wide open after the first shot of dick, and now she just couldn't get enough. He couldn't either, because he had come down to the club to pick her up.

"What's wrong wit' you?" Prada asked Niya, who was looking across the room at Tiki and Alexus sitting at the empty bar.

"Nothin'. I just got a lot on my mind right now, girl," she said, taking a sip of her drink. "Do you know that the word on the streets is that MHB is the one who robbed Mayo's stash house?" she asked.

"Who told you that?"

"You know Gwen came by my house earlier, talkin' about she didn't know MHB started robbing people," Niya explained with an attitude.

Niya was more worried about whether Gwen was going to rat her out to Mayo and his boys. That would be a death sentence for Niya if she ever got caught slippin'. "Well, look, I think I got the last two digits to the safe, so if you still wanna make it happen, you got to let me know. I'm starting to feel uncomfortable lyin' up in that house," Prada said.

The truth of the matter was that Prada was really starting to catch feelings for Mayo. It didn't matter how she kept her guard up on him; the more time she spent with him, the more she started to see what kind of man he really was. Despite being able to blow a man's head off without thinking twice about it, Mayo was good to Prada. He took her shopping, gave her money, let her drive one of his cars, and the sex was on 100 percent. It was starting to become pointless to rob him when she was at the point where she could get almost anything from him. The only way she could still go through with it was if it was done immediately.

"Go ahead and put it together," Niya said before getting her things and leaving.

As JR walked into the house, the aroma of weed smacked him in the face. This was very unusual, considering nobody in the house smoked weed. On point, he pulled the gun from his waist and cautiously walked through the house. The smell was coming the strongest from upstairs, so that's where JR went. He went from room to room, clearing every inch of the second floor like he was a member of the SWAT team. He made it to his bedroom door in a matter of seconds.

If dis bitch got a nigga up in here, I'ma kill both of them, JR thought, gripping the gun in his hand a little tighter.

He opened the bathroom door and saw Gwen sitting in a tubful of water with a blunt the size of a cigar in her mouth. A bottle of Patrón was also in arm's reach. JR could tell from her glassy eyes that something had happened. Instinctively, he looked around the bathroom then back into the bedroom, just in case a nigga wanted to pop out.

"What's goin' on, baby girl?" JR asked, walking over and taking a seat on the edge of the tub.

Gwen just sat there. She didn't say a word at first. The events that took place in the last three hours were still registering in her head.

"Gwen, I can't help you if you don't tell me w—"

"They tried to kidnap me today," she slurred. "This bitch muthafucka tried to get at me," she said, taking a puff of the marijuana.

Instead of snapping out like he started to, JR did his best to remain calm. He knew that was the only way he was going to get the answers he wanted. "Who tried to kidnap you, Gwen?" JR asked, placing his gun on top of the sink.

Gwen could hardly keep her head from submerging under water as she splashed around, juggling the blunt and the bottle of tequila. JR calmly removed them from her hands and placed them away from her. He then grabbed a towel, picked up Gwen's naked body from the tub, took her into the bedroom, and laid her down on the bed. She just turned over and began to cry. She really wasn't in the mood to talk about it, and JR could see that. Frustrated and hurt, all he could do was wait until morning when the weed and alcohol wore off. Until that time came, he wasn't going to get a wink of sleep.

Chapter 6

A knock at the door woke Mrs. Walters up from the catnap she was taking on the couch. She hadn't seen her son in a few days, and that was unusual, especially since she had his three-year-old daughter there. When Mrs. Walters got to the door, she feared the worst as she looked up at Detective Butler and Detective Rose.

"Good afternoon, ma'am. I was wondering if you knew someone by the name of Jeffrey Davis," Detective Rose spoke in a sorrowful manner.

Mrs. Walters's knees gave out, and the tears poured from her eyes like a river. Dro was her only son, and the detectives didn't even have to say the words for her to know that he was gone. She couldn't speak; she just dropped to her knees and cupped her face in her hands.

"Mama, what's wrong?" a young lady yelled as she ran from the kitchen. "What happened? What's going on?" the girl asked the detectives while she got down and comforted her mother.

"Myyy baaabyyy," Mrs. Walters cried out.

"I'm sorry, but do you know this man?" Detective Butler asked the young lady, passing her Dro's ID.

"Yeah, that's my brother," she responded, looking at the driver's license. "What happened?"

"I'm sorry, ma'am, but we found his body . . ."

The detective couldn't finish his sentence, as both women cried out. It hurt Detective Rose so much that she had to turn her head. This was the hardest part of her job, telling someone that a loved one had been murdered. Butler felt the same way, but his skin was a little tougher.

Gwen's head was pounding before she could even open her eyes. Everything was fuzzy except for the events that had taken place the night before. She rolled over to see JR sitting in a chair next to the bed, with his gun on his lap, looking right at her. He hadn't had a moment of rest all night. How could he? He'd come home to find his girl pissy drunk, talking about somebody tried to kidnap her.

"Wha . . . what time is it?" Gwen asked, trying to clear her throat.

"It's eleven," JR answered, passing Gwen a cup of water and two pills for the headache he knew she had.

The bruise on the side of her face was throbbing. It must have happened when Gwen climbed out of the passenger's side door and fell to the pavement. JR had to look at that bruise all night, which made him furious.

"Now, Gwen, I want you to tell me everything that happened last night, and I don't want you to leave out a single detail," JR demanded in an aggressive manner. The aggression wasn't toward her, but rather toward the nigga who had tried to take her.

Through the grogginess in her voice, she began to tell JR what happened. The more she talked, the more he couldn't believe what he was hearing.

Master must have lost his fucking mind, he thought as Gwen told the story. He knew Master pretty well, and Master knew him. That was the confusing part about it, because Master knew JR didn't play any games and wouldn't hesitate to put a bullet in a nigga's head for fucking with his girl.

***

"Mike, my man," Mayo spoke as he opened his front door.

"Mayo, it's good to see you," Mike said, shaking Mayo's hand before entering the house.

Besides being probably the biggest drug dealer in Charlotte right now, Mayo had his hands in the real estate game. He bought houses and land all over Charlotte and made a killing reselling or renting out the properties. Before Mike, it was hard for him to sell anything. Mike changed all that and made real estate profitable for Mayo.

"I got some good news for you. I sold the lot on Point Breeze last night. The bank should be transferring the money into your account sometime today," Mike told Mayo.

"See, that's why I fuck wit' you, Mike. I don't have to tell you how to do your job like other people I work with," Mayo said, putting his arm around Mike's shoulder and walking him into the kitchen. "Hey, make Mike a plate," he directed Prada, who was already in the process of cooking.

Mike looked over to see who Mayo was speaking to, and noticed Prada. At first, he couldn't figure out where he knew her from, and then it hit him. He remembered her from the club the other night. She was with Diamond when he went to pick her up. Prada noticed him, too, but didn't say anything. She hoped Mike wouldn't say anything either and cause Mayo to start probing.

The relationship between Mike and Mayo had grown over the months, until it became more than just business. They were somewhat friends. Mike was a white man, but he acted just like a black man. That was one of the reasons Diamond was feeling him the way she was. He had swag, most of which came from being around Mayo.

"We gotta celebrate, Mike. Let's hit the club tonight," Mayo suggested.

"Not tonight, Mayo. I got a date already," he said, thinking about the plans he and Diamond had for the night.

"Well, it's me and you this weekend, Mike, and I'm not taking no for an answer," Mayo joked.

Mike, Mayo, and Prada sat at the table and ate their breakfast, talking and just joking around for the rest of the morning. It was a little awkward at the table for Mike and Prada, and at times, Mayo caught on to it, but he didn't say anything.

Niya got out of the shower and headed downstairs for breakfast. When she got there, there was something other than breakfast waiting at the table. Niya almost had a heart attack when she saw her whole stash sitting on the table. Chad even had the twin Glock .40-cals, a .380, a .45-cal, and the AR-15 sitting next to the stacks of money. Chad stood off to the side, just staring at Niya with a blank look on his face. It was so quiet in the house Niya didn't even notice that the twins weren't home. Chad had made sure he dropped them off at daycare so they wouldn't hear the arguing.

"So you're going through my stuff now, Chad?" Niya said, breaking the silence.

"Goin through ya stuff? Last time I checked, this was my muthafuckin' house," Chad barked back. "What da fuck is you out here doin'?"

"Nothin', Chad!"

"Nothin', Chad? What do you think, I'm a fuckin fool? Where the fuck is you getting all this money from?"

The first thing that came to his mind, just like any other man, was that she was stepping out on him. There was too much money to think otherwise, not to mention the fact that she had guns in the stash too.

"Ni, I'm not gonna keep fuckin' asking you. Who fuckin' money and guns are these?" he said, walking toward her.

He was trying to get into striking range, because he was about two seconds away from smacking the shit out of her. She felt it, too, and moved from one side of the kitchen table to the other. Even though Chad was trying to be a different person, Niya knew that he still had that killer in him and was not to be played with.

"It's mine, Chad. The money and the guns. It's all mine," she said, looking down at the table.

Chad inched his way closer. He knew that she wasn't lying. Not one time did he ever put his hands on Niya during their whole relationship, but today he was on the brink.

"Look how we're livin', Chad," Niya started to explain. "You live paycheck to paycheck, and don't get me wrong, I respect you for that, but you deserve to have . . . Don't we deserve to have more?"

"I live paycheck to paycheck because I have to, Niya," Chad yelled in frustration. "I decided to leave the streets alone for one reason and one reason only, and that was for the sake of you and our kids. Now here you are telling me I ain't shit; that I'm not a provider for my wife and kids. Really, Ni, that's what you saying to me? That my woman has to step up for me?"

Chad wasn't a slouch by a long shot, and his retirement from the streets made it possible for niggas like Mayo to eat. There weren't too many people in the history of Charlotte, North Carolina, who had done it as big as him. It wasn't until he got shot and indicted by the feds that he realized the more important things in life, like family. The feds pretty much took everything he had. He beat the case, but the feds wasn't gonna give him back the money that they knew came from drugs. That's when life started to become less luxurious for him.

"Chad, don't do that," Niya said, starting to feel the effects of what he was saying.

"Don't do what? You think I like dis shit? You think I don't miss the money? I work every fucking day so that I can come home to you every night, but I guess that's not good enough!" he yelled. "Now, where did you get this fuckin' money?" he screamed, smacking the stack of money off the table.

He moved closer, but when he did, Niya did something she would later regret. It may have been out of fear, or just a spur-of-the-moment type of situation, but she looked down at the .40-caliber that was still on the table and flinched as if she was about to grab it. She snatched her hand back, but the damage was done.

Chad had seen her reaction. He just looked at her. The anger in him drifted away, but it was replaced by sadness. Niya could see the hurt written all over his face and the moisture it brought to his eyes.

"Oh, yeah, you was—"

"No, boo, I'm sorry," Niya pleaded, trying to walk up to him.

He grabbed her by the throat when she got close enough, and he just pushed her away. The thought of grabbing one of the guns off the table and blowing her head off crossed his mind, but he decided against it. He just stepped over the money and walked out of the kitchen. His heart was crushed more than anything, and Niya knew it. She knew she had fucked up, and there was nothing she could do about it.

Master lay on his side, going in and out of consciousness when Detective Rose and Detective Butler walked into his room. Despite the couple of family members sitting in the room, they did what they did best and started asking questions.

"Mr. Miller, do you know who shot you?" Butler asked repeatedly every time Master's eyes would open.

The bullet had caused some damage when it entered his back. It was still stuck inside of him, and the doctors weren't too optimistic about removing it, because it was resting against his spine. One wrong move and the bullet could paralyze him. Gwen wasn't even aware that she had hit him. She saw him crash but didn't stick around to find out why.

"Can you leave him alone?" one of the women sitting in the room asked the detectives.

"Ma'am, we need to find out who did this," Detective Rose responded while Butler continued to question Master.

Both detectives knew that they had a short window to work with in finding the shooter, and now would be the best time to question the victim. Morphine mixed with pain added up to the strong possibility of a confession. The chances of Master telling them who shot him were better now than if he were fully conscious. The detectives just hoped that he would slip up and give them a name.

Chapter 7

"Yo, hurry up in there. We're gonna be late fuckin' around wit' you," Mayo yelled out to Prada, who was still in the bathroom.

Prada had managed to get some Kevin Hart tickets at the last minute, and she persuaded Mayo to take her to the comedy show. It was grown and sexy night, so Mayo had on a brown-and-blue cardigan with a Polo button-up underneath, a pair of dark blue Diesel slacks, and Gucci loafers. On his wrist was a Rolex. He tried to keep it basic for the night, considering after the show there was the after party.

"I'm coming, I'm coming," Prada grumbled, coming out of the bathroom.

"Damn!" Mayo said out loud, looking over at her.

Prada had on all white and a pair of gold Louis Vuitton heels. She was stunning. This was the reason why she had made it this far with Mayo.

"You better be on ya best behavior tonight or you'll miss out on dessert," she teased in a seductive manner. "I know it's gonna be a lot of bitches there, so let me give you something to think about before we leave this house," Prada said, walking over to Mayo, who was sitting on the bed.

She dropped to her knees, right between his legs, unfastened his pants, and pulled them down to his ankles. Mayo sat back on his elbows and watched as Prada took him into her mouth. She slowly swallowed every bit of nine inches of meat, causing Mayo's toes to curl in his loafers. The warm, wet spit could be felt running down his balls as Prada continued to suck. Her head bobbed up and down, going faster and faster the more she got into it. She periodically took it out of her mouth so that she could French kiss the top of it. She looked up at him so she could see the look on his face while she performed.

Mayo was at the point where he could feel himself about to cum. He tried to grab her by the back of her hair and pull her off of him, but Prada just kept sucking and sucking. He even tried to get up, but she pushed him back on the bed. He was about to cum and she could feel it.

"Shit!" he yelled out, now resting both of his hands on her head. He started pushing her head up and down on his dick until he couldn't hold it anymore. He exploded inside of her mouth with force.

"Aahhhh," he yelled as he could feel his warm cum on her tongue.

Prada didn't waste a drop. She swallowed everything. She continued to suck on it for another minute or two, just to make sure it was gone.

"They're just now leaving the house," Niya said, getting back into the car with Alexus.

Niya and Alexus had been parked around the corner from Mayo's house for the past two hours, waiting for Prada to get him out. Tonight was the night for them to move on Mayo's safe. The only thing that really bothered Niya was the fact that she had to bring Alexus along for the move. Diamond was nowhere to be found, and Tiffany was at the hospital with her mom, so the only person left to accompany Niya was Alexus.

"Now, no matter what, don't get out of this car," Niya told Alexus while putting on latex gloves.

Prada had provided Niya with everything. The house key, the alarm code, and the safe's six-digit code were all she needed. It was as if she lived there, the way she calmly let herself into the house and disarmed the security system.

Mayo's house was huge. It was like a mini mansion, and for a second, Niya stopped to admire his house design: large comfortable sofas, beautiful paintings on the wall, a piano, and a large bearskin rug resting in front of a stone fireplace. All this, and Niya wasn't even out of the living room.

"You know, the only thing better than love is loyalty. That's what a good friend of mine told me," Mayo said, breaking the silence in the car. "Do you know anything about loyalty?" he asked Prada, cutting his eyes at her for a brief second before looking back at the road ahead of him.

The question came from out of nowhere, and it confused Prada for a second. She didn't know how to respond to that, or even if he really wanted her to. She had to sit and think about the answer she was about to give, but right before she could say anything, Mayo's BlackBerry started to chirp. He grabbed it out of the center console and looked at the text message that was just sent to him.

"What? You forget that you was supposed to take ya other girlfriend out today?" Prada joked, pushing the top of his shoulder.

He just looked at her and smiled. They were halfway downtown when Mayo announced that he needed to make a quick stop before the show. "Business," he told her as he pulled off the highway.

"Now, come on, boo. We're gonna be late," Prada pleaded, hoping to keep him on course.

"I can't miss out on this one, babe, but I promise you we'll make it to the show on time," Mayo assured her.

Prada didn't care about the show. She really just wanted to make sure Mayo didn't intend to go back to the house. If he did, he would be walking right in on Niya. That was something Prada knew neither Niya nor she could afford. Not only would he kill her, but he would most likely put two and two together and figure out that Prada had something to do with it, and then he'd kill her too. All Prada could do was sit back and hope that wasn't the case.

Niya looked up the long row of stairs, skeptical about going up. It was dark as hell, and to be honest, she was a little scared. She pulled the compact black-on-black .45 off her waist, thinking to herself that she had come too far to turn around now. She proceeded up the stairs with caution, cupping the gun in both hands and praying that there was no one in the house. Ironically, she was more scared that a ghost would jump out from somewhere instead of a human. It got so bad that she started to turn on every light switch she passed. Once she got to the room where the safe was, she became a little more relaxed, tucking her gun into her back pocket and pulling out the small piece of paper with the safe's code on it. She immediately started punching numbers into the small box on the outside of the door, but the safe wasn't opening.

"Two, five, one, one . . ." she mumbled to herself as she kept trying to punch the code in. "Damn, Prada," she mumbled, becoming frustrated.

She remembered Prada saying that she couldn't get the last number, but thought that it was the number one. With that, Niya began punching in the code, but changing the last digit every time one wouldn't work. "Yessssss!"

she yelled after she pushed 251167 into the keypad and the door unlocked.

When she opened the door, her eyes opened wide as fifty-cent pieces. She had never seen so much money, guns, and drugs in her life. Prada wasn't lying when she said Mayo had a safe. She looked at the small duffle bag she brought with her, and she knew for sure that she was going to need something bigger to carry this stuff out. Niya thought that she might have to make two trips to haul everything out.

When she turned around to see if she could find a trash bag in the house, a blow connected to her face, which felt like it had been hit with a sledgehammer. The impact of JR's fist to the right side of her face caused Niya to fall back into the safe, knocking stuff off the shelves on her way to the ground. JR grabbed her by the ankle and dragged her out of the safe. Niya was knocked out cold, but JR woke her up with several body shots.

"You dumb bitch. You really thought you was gonna pull this off?" JR said, standing over her. He then pulled a large .357 revolver out of his waist and pointed it at Niya's head.

She was still dazed and couldn't see very well, but she could hear the hammer cocking back very clearly. Chad and the twins were the only thing that crossed her mind. She knew that it was her time to die, and before she did, she began to pray.

Mayo pulled over into a rest stop right off the highway. Prada didn't have any problem with that, as long as he wasn't going back home. She was hoping that Niya and Alexus were handling their business, because she was so ready for this situation to be over. Not wanting to show her stress, she just looked out the window at the large eighteen-wheelers coming and leaving the rest stop.

"You know something that's crazy . . ." Mayo began. "I really like you, Prada. You got a lot goin' for yourself, and I can see the great potential in you. I just hope everything works out," he said, looking down at his phone as though he was waiting for a call or text.

"I like you too, May, but why are you talking like this?" Prada asked with a confused look on her face. *Has he picked up on my vibe?* she wondered.

Mayo continued, "All my life, I've learned that it's the people closest to you who will hurt you the most. I'm just hoping you're not one of them," he said, looking her in her eyes with a stern look.

Now he was making Prada nervous. He was starting to talk crazy, and Prada also noticed the change in his body language ever since he got the text earlier. Nervousness quickly turned into fear, and before she knew it, Prada was looking for an exit strategy. Looking outside of her window, she noticed that she really didn't have anywhere to go. Her best chance was a gas station that looked like it was about a quarter of a mile away. Mayo's phone ringing snapped her out of her thoughts.

"Yo, what's good, homie?" Mayo answered, looking over at Prada, who was looking back out the window.

"Yeah, you were right, bro. Shawty here right now wit' her hand in the cookie jar," JR said, looking down at a groggy Niya.

"Oh, yeah?"

"Yeah, and she got a *MHB* tattoo on her wrist," JR told him. "So what you wanna do?"

"You already know, homie. Take care of dat and get rid of the body," Mayo instructed and then hung up the phone. "Can you believe somebody broke into my house and tried to rob me?" Mayo said, turning his attention to Prada. "A bitch at that." He chuckled.

Prada's heart started racing uncontrollably, and the only thing she wanted to do at that moment was get out of the car, which she knew Mayo wouldn't allow. A vision of Niya being executed like Dro flashed through her mind. Just the thought of losing her best friend brought tears to her eyes.

"Don't cry, sweetie. Yeah, I know it hurt, shawty. She's as good as dead," Mayo taunted, having put two and two together in a matter of seconds.

"I'm sorry, May," Prada cried, knowing she'd been caught.

Tears fell down her face, but Mayo didn't pay the tears any mind. Prada reached for her bag as if she was looking for some tissue to clean her face. While she reached for her bag, Mayo was reaching for his gun that was located in the side panel of the driver's side door. Inside of her bag, Prada felt around, but it wasn't for tissue. Her hand locked on to the baby .380 auto that lived there. This was her only chance. It was do or die. As she began to pull her hand out of her bag, Mayo was pulling the gun from the side of his door.

It all came down to who was the quickest on the draw, and for Mayo, he saw Prada's stunt a mile away. She never got the chance to pull it out, as a single shot from his gun flashed before her eyes. The bullet entered the center of her forehead and never exited, killing her instantly. Mayo was glad he had invested in the hollow-tip bullets; that way, he didn't have to worry about the splatter of blood and tissue from the bullet wound.

He got out of the car and walked around to the passenger's side. He looked around a few times to make sure nobody saw what had happened, before pulling her body out of the car and tossing it to the ground like Prada was a piece of trash. He looked at her once more and shook his head in disappointment at her betrayal. The love he was starting to develop for her all but disappeared with the confirmation call he had received from JR. To Mayo, Prada was just like any other trick or nigga who had ever crossed him.

JR tucked his cell phone in his pocket and then looked down at Niya. He leaned over and pointed the .357 at her head. Finally getting her bearings, Niya looked up at the man who was about to take her life. "See you in the next life, shawty," JR said.

He put his finger on the trigger and was about to squeeze when out of nowhere, he heard a gun cocking back. He turned around to see Alexus standing there with a gun in her hand, pointing it right at him. He attempted to fire, but Alexus didn't hesitate. She began firing round after round in JR's direction. What she lacked in accuracy she made up for with numbers. JR managed to get off two shots in the midst of Alexus raining bullets on him, but neither one hit her.

It was the last two bullets that Alexus fired that made contact with JR—one hit his leg, and the other one tore through his gut. He dropped to one knee, but he still had his gun in his hand. Seeing that Alexus was out of bullets and JR was still moving, Niya reached for the .45 in her back pocket, popped the safety off, and began firing at JR before he could raise his gun again at Alexus.

Pow! Pow! Pow! One bullet hit him in the side of his face, and another hit his neck, splitting open his jugular. Blood shot out of his neck like a faucet, and he was dead before he fell the rest of the way to the ground. Niya got to her feet, gun in hand and still pointed at JR. She made sure he was dead then unarmed him before running over to the bed and pulling the sheet off of it.

"Lex, get over here," Niya yelled out. "Help me get dis shit out of here," she said, laying the sheet on the floor in front of the safe.

She definitely didn't have time to be making two trips, especially knowing that Mayo and Prada were more than likely on their way back to the house. As fast as they could move, Alexus and Niya loaded everything of value into the sheet, wrapped it up as tightly as they could, then left the house.

Mayo pulled into his driveway and saw that the front door was wide open. A lot of lights were on in the house as well, which made him proceed with extreme caution. He pulled the 9 mm from his waist then entered the home. It was quiet, and he still wasn't sure if it was safe.

"Yo, homie," Mayo yelled out, seeing if JR was gonna respond.

There was no answer. Mayo continued up the stairs until he reached the room where the safe was located. He could now see why he wasn't getting an answer from JR. His friend was lying dead in a pool of blood, with his eyes open. Frustrated, hurt, and mad as hell, Mayo walked over and looked into his safe. It was pretty much empty except for the jewelry Niya had left behind.

He walked back over to JR's body and kneeled down next to it. Mayo placed his hand over his dead partner's eyes and wiped them closed. He shook his head in disbelief at the outcome of his plan. This bitch Niya had not only robbed him again, but now she had taken the life of someone he really cared about. He took a huge gasp before speaking out loud to his deceased childhood friend.

"Damn, homie, I'ma hold you down, family. That's my word. All these bitches gonna pay, my nigga. I put that on everythang," Mayo said, resting the gun on the side of his head.

Book 2

Chapter 1

Security was a little tight in the emergency room, due to the rash of violence in Charlotte over the past night. Cops were everywhere, but that didn't stop Gwen from entering the hospital with one thing on her mind, and that was to find out why Master had tried to kidnap her. She had gotten word through some street connections that he was now housed up in the ICU at Carolina Medical Center. The thought of that nigga still breathing wasn't sitting right with her, and despite JR promising he was going to take care of it, she wasn't in the mood for waiting.

A large pair of Gucci frames covered a nice portion of Gwen's face. That, along with a full-length blond wig, made the perfect disguise for her in the event Master forced her to do more than question him at that time. Instead of bringing her gun into the hospital, Gwen brought her trusty butterfly knife, so that if she did decide to kill him, it would be quiet.

After getting Master's room number from the nurse at the front desk, Gwen proceeded to the fourth floor where he was. Walking down the hall, Gwen played back in her mind that day when they came after her. It made her more and more furious just thinking about it. She looked up at every room number she passed by until she finally came upon the number the nurse had given her.

"Four twenty-two," she mumbled to herself, looking into the room to see Master lying in the bed with all kinds of needles and tubes sticking out of him.

"Who are you?" a young female asked, startling Gwen.

It was Master's sister, sitting in the chair off to the side. Gwen hadn't noticed her upon entering the room. She was pissed that Master wasn't alone, but she still managed to fake a smile and answer the curious young woman's question.

"Hi, I'm a friend of Master's," Gwen lied, thinking fast. "I just stopped by to see how he was doing."

Master's sister wasn't too alarmed. She just figured that Gwen was another one of Master's girlfriends who was checking in on him. "Well, he's doin' a lot better. The doctor said that he should make a full recovery. He just needs to get his rest," she informed Gwen.

Gwen looked over at Master, mad as hell after hearing he was going to be all right. Master's sister didn't think anything of it when Gwen walked over and stood by his bedside. She looked down on him, placed her hand on his side a few inches away from his bullet wound, and squeezed. There wasn't enough morphine in his system to stop him from feeling that. His eyes shot wide open, the heart monitor started beeping fast, and the bullet wound in his back started to bleed.

"He must be happy to see me," Gwen looked over and told his sister to try to take her attention off the suddenly rapid beeping noise from the monitor. Master's sister simply dug her face back into the hair magazine she was reading.

Gwen turned her attention back to Master, who was still somewhat in shock. She leaned in as though she was kissing the side of his face, in order to talk without being heard by his sister.

"Why?" she whispered in his ear as she held a firm grip to his side.

The pain mixed with a dry throat made it hard for him to speak. He was trying to say something, but Gwen couldn't really hear him through the oxygen mask. She pulled the mask down from his face, but the moment she did, the heart monitor started going crazy. It was too loud for Master's sister to ignore. Not only his sister, but also a nurse came rushing to his bedside. Gwen just backed up and let the two women attend to him.

"What happened?" both women asked her simultaneously.

"I don't know. I just gave him a kiss on the cheek and he woke up. I think he pulled his mask off to say something to me."

While the nurse and Master's sister focused back on Master, Gwen quickly disappeared from the room.

Detective Rose and Detective Butler pushed through the early morning traffic to arrive at the Pilot rest stop off Highway I-85. When they pulled up, they were greeted by the patrol officer who was first on the scene. He walked them over to where Prada's blood-soaked body was, right next to an eighteen-wheeler. Off the top, Butler could see the cause of death was a bullet wound to the head.

"She's too well put together to be a hooker," Detective Rose said as she analyzed the body.

"Whoa, we got a gun," Butler said, looking into Prada's Louis bag that was off to the side.

Butler looked deeper into her bag and found her ID, along with some cash. From that, he quickly ruled out the possibility of a robbery.

"We got a witness, too," the patrol officer announced, grabbing both Rose's and Butler's attention.

You could see the excitement in their eyes. Homicides without the proper evidence were the toughest cases to prove in the criminal justice system. Anyone who had ever viewed an episode of *The First 48* understood that.

But when there was a witness, an eyewitness to the crime, it was like a blessing from God for homicide detectives.

The patrol officer walked the two detectives around to the other side of the eighteen-wheeler, where John, the truck driver, sat. John retold them the story of how he was asleep in his truck when he was awakened by a pop. He didn't think much of it, considering where he was, but curiosity made him take a peek out his window. That's when he saw a man pulling the body of a female out of his car.

He said that he didn't get a real good look at the man; however, he was sure he was African American. He also was certain that the car was a Mercedes-Benz S550, all black. Because the car turned around so quickly, he didn't get a chance to see the rear license plate, but he had seen the front vanity plate clearly. He remembered trying to figure out why someone would put the name of some mayonnaise on the front of such a beautiful and expensive car.

"The tag read *Mayo*," he repeated to both detectives.

Rose asked if he would be able to identify the man who was driving the car if he were to see him again. John said that he was not sure, but he would try. Even though it was a small lead, it was a break in the investigation, and it had happened in less than thirty minutes of the detectives being on the case. Now came the hard part: having to make the trip to the victim's family's home to give them the sad news of their loss. Both officers dreaded this part of the job the most.

Gwen had wisely left the hospital after drawing all the attention to Master's room. She was just gonna have to wait until he was a little better before confronting the situation again. She headed back home with a somewhat bitter taste in her mouth.

When she finally did make it home, it was the line of older cars with twenty-four-inch rims sitting out front of her apartment building that caught her attention first. This wasn't the kind of complex where the occupants drove those types of vehicles. Gwen became more concerned when she could hear the sounds of men laughing and joking coming from the inside of her front door.

Pressing her ear to the door, she could hear the faint voices of men inside of her apartment. She looked up and down the hall, not sure what she should do, because she had no idea what was on the other side of the entry. Before she had a chance to react, the apartment door swung open and a short, stocky black man stood before her with the grimiest look on his face. The look alone scared the shit out of her.

"Yo, come on in, shawty," the man said, stepping to the side so that she could enter.

Gwen looked at him like he was crazy. Before he got a chance to say another word, Gwen took a step back, dropped her pocketbook, and pulled the 9 mm from out of her back waist. It happened so fast that the guy at the door didn't have time to do anything but put his hands in the air.

"Who da fuck are you, and what you doin' in my apartment?" Gwen shouted, hoping to get her next door neighbor's attention.

"Whoa, whoa, whoa," Mayo yelled as he ran to the door. "Gwen, it's me," he said, hoping it would calm her down.

Gwen began to slightly lower the gun after seeing a familiar face, but she was still cautiously hugging the trigger of the firearm. "And who da fuck is you, acting like I supposed to know your ass?" she asked, still pointing the gun at the first guy.

"I'm Roni, a friend of JR's. Remember I met you at his mom's house when she had the Thanksgiving dinner last year?" he explained.

Gwen was still on edge with the whole kidnapping situation, so she eased up a little bit, but was still watchful. "Why are y'all in my apartment?" she asked, lowering the gun all the way now but still keeping it in her hand. "And where the fuck is JR?"

Mayo lowered his head, preparing to give Gwen the sad news. He still had the memory of seeing JR's dead body in his house.

When he did that, Gwen knew that it wasn't good news. She poked her head farther into the apartment and saw a couple more guys sitting on her couch with sad looks on their faces.

"JR was murdered last night, shawty," Mayo said in a low tone with a quiver in his voice.

It was like somebody had taken a knife and stabbed her directly in the heart when she heard those words. She backed up until her back hit the living room wall. She slid down until she was sitting on the floor. She couldn't even stand up anymore, and the more the news registered in her head, the more she cried. JR had always been there for her, and even though she never could love him as much as he had loved her, there was a special bond between them.

Niya woke up to see Jasmine playing with one of her toys in the living room. Niya was still in the doghouse with Chad, so the couch had become her new best friend. At this point, it wasn't clear where her and Chad's relationship stood, but the one thing she knew was that she didn't want to lose him. In her heart, she felt guilty because she knew the sacrifices he made by getting out of the game, and she knew that those sacrifices were the best thing for their family.

"Jazzy Pooh," Niya said, calling Jasmine by her nickname. "Where's ya bro-bro?" she asked, looking around the room for Jahmil.

"Heee up dere," baby Jasmine said, pointing up.

Niya's ringing cell phone interrupted the short mother-daughter time they were having. She ran to get it, hoping it was Prada finally returning her many calls. She was waiting to hear how Mayo was taking the loss of the contents of his safe. Niya didn't even look at the screen; she just hit accept and began talking.

"Damn, bitch, it took you long enough to return my calls. That nigga must have been crying all night on your shoulders," Niya spoke with a little chuckle.

"Ni, it's D," Diamond uttered in a low tone.

"Oh, what up, D? I thought you were Prada," Niya answered, sitting back on the couch.

The phone went silent for a second, and then all Niya could hear was Diamond crying on the other end.

"D, what's wrong?" Niya asked. "Talk to me, Diamond. What's going on?" Niya pleaded through Diamond's sobs.

"Sheee's gone, Ni," Diamond cried out. "He . . . killed her," she managed to get out.

"Who, Diamond? Who got killed?" Niya asked frantically.

There was a moment of silence on the phone. In that moment, a million and one thoughts ran through Niya's mind. She knew who Diamond was talking about, but nothing inside of her wanted to believe it. She began shaking her head from left to right as her eyes filled up with tears. "No, I don't believe you. You lying, Diamond!"

"Prada is dead, Ni!"

"Diamond, you take that shit back. Don't you play like that!"

"They killed her, Ni," Diamond cried out, this time even louder.

Niya dropped the phone and fell to the floor. It was as if hearing the words collapsed her heart. There wasn't a single term in the dictionary that could describe how she felt, not only to have lost a friend who was like a blood sister, but to know that she was the cause. She knew she should have gotten Prada out of harm's way earlier. Her stomach began to knot up, and the tears poured out of Niya's eyes. Baby Jasmine began crying, matching her mother's screams.

All the noise brought Chad running down the steps to see what was going on. When he arrived and saw the two most important females in his life on the floor wailing their eyes out, he went over and picked up Jasmine in one arm, and pulled Niya close to him with the other.

"Ni, what's the matter?" he asked, trying to calm her down so he could understand her words.

"Prada is dead. They killed my best friend. I killed my best friend!" Niya shouted out.

Chad didn't ask any more questions. He had lost enough friends in the street to know now wasn't the time. He just pulled Niya closer to him and held his two girls in his arms like he never wanted to let go.

Detective Rose sat at her desk searching the police database for the alias name of "Mayo." She wasn't having much luck; that was until another officer suggested she try the domestic violence crime record.

"You know the ladies are always down here taking out restraining orders on these guys, and they always seem to list every alias or nickname they know," the young beat cop spoke.

She logged out of one search engine and into the domestic crimes search. Rose typed in the name Mayo, and a huge smile came across her face when she saw the name Marquis Harper pop up on the screen with a photo beside it. She then immediately cross-referenced his name with the DMV records, and her smile got even larger. She instantly picked up the phone and called her partner, Detective Butler.

"Hey, guess who I just found? And guess what kind of car he has registered in his name? Yep, a black S550 Mercedes-Benz," she spat out before Butler was able to answer one of the questions.

"That's great! Text me his address and I will meet you over there," Butler added.

Thirty minutes later, Rose pulled up to Mayo's house. Butler had already arrived and was across the street at one of Mayo's neighbor's homes. He came walking back over as Rose got out of the car.

"Well, we may have something. The owner of that house, a Mr. Carey, said he heard shots being fired from inside Mr. Harper's house last night. He also said that he saw Mr. Harper and his girlfriend leave last night, not too long before he heard the shots," Butler explained.

Rose was about to go up to Mayo's door and knock to see if he was home, but Butler stopped her. "I'm not done. Lastly, Mr. Carey said Mr. Harper returned in the wee hours of the morning and the girlfriend was not with him. The neighbor also said he left back out about two hours ago."

"Damn, so the neighbor saw all of this?" Rose asked Butler with a curious look on her face.

"Yep!"

"Thank God for nosey neighbors," Rose said with a laugh.

"Yeah, thank God," Butler added while nodding in the direction of the house across the street with an old white man sitting on his porch.

Chapter 2

The number of people who showed up to the church was in the hundreds, all to see off a good friend and great person, Kiara Monique Thompson, also known as Prada. Prada's grandmother was so surprised; she didn't even know that her granddaughter knew so many people. Prada had touched a lot of people during her time on earth, and it was a known fact that the people who loved her outweighed the few enemies she had made. It showed, because not only was everyone from Charlotte there, but there wasn't a set of dry eyes in the building. All that could be heard echoing in the church were expressions of grief.

The small church, which usually held 500 to 600 members and guests on Sundays, was bursting at the seams. The older, light-complected pastor stood up and requested for everyone to turn in the Bible to John 14:10. His voice was so low that the ushers had to ask the people whispering to quiet down. That didn't last long, because it seemed that the more he spoke, the louder his voice became. Pastor Culbertson was no longer speaking the words, but rather singing them. He began to talk about everyone having to get prepared for their day.

"Don't you cry for Sister Thompson. She's in a better place! You better be worried about yourself, because every one of us is going to have to follow Kiara," he continuously taught.

"Her grandmother told me just a couple of weeks ago that Kiara told her that she was coming back to church. She knew she had to get her life together with God again, and I know she made it right with Jesus before He called her home." All the church ushers and elders who had seen Prada grow up bore witness to the pastor's statement.

Even Niya felt some comfort from the words of the minister. She and the girls were actually holding their emotions together quite well; that was until Pastor Culbertson turned and requested the choir to sing a song.

The elderly choir director stood up first then motioned for the rest of the choir to stand. They did as they were instructed and then began to slowly and soulfully sing:

Never would have made it, never could have made it without you. I would have lost it all, but now I see how you were there for me . . .

The old man's voice was deep but very well toned. The pain of his years of living and the firsthand knowledge of the words he was singing poured out through his voice.

Diamond was the first to break. She let out a yell so loud it forced all the ushers to come running to her aid. It was good that more than one responded, because Tiffany was the next to go, and it was taking three women and one man to hold Diamond.

Niya's legs were shaking, and Chad could see that she was about to lose it, so he grabbed Jahmil out of her arms and handed him to a lady sitting behind them. He did it just in the nick of time, because Niya totally lost it. She ran up to the casket just as the funeral director was attempting to close it.

"Prada!" she yelled. "Prada, please, I love you, sis. I love you. Get up, Prada. Please . . . Please. God, please."

Prada's grandmother and Chad came up to get her. They were having a difficult time, because Niya was fighting them off, but finally her body went limp. Chad was trying to hold her up, and Mrs. Thompson wasn't being much help.

Chad could feel the presence of somebody walking up and standing right next to them. He looked over and couldn't believe that it was Gwen standing there with a T-shirt on that had a picture of Prada on the front with the letters *RIP* over her image. On the back it had the letters *MHB-4-LIFE*. She also had on some black jeans and a pair of white AirMax. She looked so hood, but so good in the way she was representing a fallen comrade.

She went over and motioned for Mrs. Thompson to let her help. She grabbed the other side of Niya. The whole time she stood there helping to hold Niya, she didn't say a word. The pastor continued by asking the pallbearers to come forward. The men grabbed the casket and escorted it out to the awaiting car.

After the body had been carried out, Prada's grandmother thought that it was best for the girls not to go to the gravesite. No one argued, and Niya found herself in the church's bathroom with her face in the sink. She picked her head up from the sink after splashing water on her face, just in time to see Gwen walking through the door.

"What the hell happened to Prada? This shit got ya name written all over it," Gwen said, leaning against the stall.

Niya's sorrow quickly turned into anger, and the tension in the room became thick in a matter of seconds. "Now is not the time for the dumb shit, Gwen," Niya replied with an attitude, drying her face.

Gwen thought that there wasn't a better time than that day. She had some shit she had wanted to get off her chest for quite some time now. The deaths of JR and Prada, and the fact that she knew Niya had something to do with them, was pretty much the breaking point.

"I'ma ask you one time, and I swear it's only going to be one time," Gwen said, turning around and locking the bathroom door. "Did you have something to do with this?" she asked with a dead serious look on her face.

"I think ya best bet is to move from in front of that door and mind ya fuckin' business," Niya said as she attempted to walk toward the door.

The confrontation went from zero to sixty in the snap of a finger, when Niya reached over Gwen to unlock the door. Gwen just took off, punching Niya in her mouth. Niya's reaction time was on point as she returned the blows. It was an all-out fight. Gwen grabbed a handful of Niya's hair with her left hand and was punching her in the gut with the right. Gwen was landing punch after punch. She had an advantage because of the way she was dressed in sneakers and jeans. She had come ready to fight.

Right when it looked like Gwen was getting the best of Niya, the tables turned. Once Niya got out of her heels, instead of fighting against Gwen and pulling her hair, she stepped into it. She jammed her thumbs into Gwen's eyes.

"Ahhh, bitch!" Gwen yelled out, letting Niya's hair go.

Right, left, right, left, right, left. Niya was whaling on Gwen, who could barely see. Gwen kept on punching too. They stood toe to toe, going blow for blow for a good sixty seconds.

"Let me go check on Niya," Tiffany mumbled to Diamond.

When she got downstairs in the basement where the bathroom was, she could hear the thumping and yelling. When she turned the corner, Tiki was standing outside the bathroom door eating sunflower seeds. She had seen when both Niya and Gwen left from upstairs, and she was going to take the opportunity to talk to both of them together, but when she got downstairs, they were already fighting.

"Just let it happen," Tiki told Tiffany when she walked up. "It's better if they get it out of their system now rather than later."

Tiffany couldn't do anything but respect the veteran call. They both just stood by the door and waited for the fight to end.

For females, Niya and Gwen had a lot of wind. They had been fighting and wrestling for over ten minutes straight. Now the fatigue started to settle in, and the punches became slower, until the point where neither of them could throw another blow. They finally broke, falling to the floor on opposite sides of the bathroom.

Niya was the first to get to her feet, stumbling to the door and unlocking it. She was shocked and somewhat embarrassed when she opened the door and saw Tiki and Tiffany standing there. Tiki just shook her head.

"Y'all done with that bullshit?" she asked. "Well, clean up and get back upstairs," she instructed the two women before turning around, grabbing Tiffany's hand, and heading back upstairs herself.

Butler, Rose, and D.A. Joseph Harrison sat in Joe's office trying to figure out the best way to proceed with their main suspect, Marquis "Mayo" Harper.

"Do we have enough for a warrant yet?" Detective Butler asked Detective Rose, who was finishing up the paperwork to present to the judge.

"We got enough to get a warrant for questioning," she said, passing him the affidavit for the warrant.

"I think we have enough information to bring him in for questioning, but I think that's all we got," Butler explained. He wanted to make sure the case was a slam dunk before he made the arrest.

"Look, detectives, I been doin' this for a very long time," the D.A. began. "I got a neighbor who saw him leave the house with Ms. Thompson that evening. I got a truck driver who can, at the very least, identify the kind of car he watched a man toss her dead body out of. That car happens to be the same kind of car that's registered to Mr. Harper," D.A. Harrison broke down. "If that's not enough for me to get a guilty verdict, then I shouldn't be a D.A."

After hearing it come out of his mouth, the case sounded a little more solid than before. Both Butler and Rose agreed. "So what do you wanna do?" Butler asked.

"Bring him in," Harrison said then walked out of his office.

"I understand what the D.A. is saying; however, I'm not gonna lie, Monica. I think we're gonna need more," Butler said, calling Detective Rose by her first name. "Once we get him in here, I'm not tryin' to let him go, and looking at his criminal history, I'm sure he's gonna lawyer up before giving a statement."

Butler was 100 percent right about Mayo. He'd been through the wringer when it came to the justice system. Butler knew from experience that guys like Mayo were hard to prosecute. Before he made the mistake of messing up this case, Butler was going to be sure that all his ducks were in line.

Chapter 3

Niya pulled up to the apartment building where she had rented a two-bedroom for Alexus to stay. This was also Niya's new stash spot, considering what took place with Chad finding the last one. Everything Niya took from Mayo was here, and this was actually the first time she'd had a chance to do inventory.

Alexus was in the kitchen making something to eat when Niya walked in. Even though Alexus was still in her nightwear, Niya could see what drew Dro and men like him to the young girl. Alexus had a small, long, shapely frame. She couldn't have weighed more than 130 pounds, but she had an ass like a woman twice her size. Her perky young breasts sat high up on her chest, while her nipples protruded through the thin T-shirt she was wearing. Alexus had her long, curly orange-brownish hair pinned up in a ponytail. She reminded Niya of Draya from *Basketball Wives*.

"I see you're getting used to doin' for yourself," Niya joked, entering the kitchen.

"Oh, I'm sorry, Ni. I got hungry and saw the chicken in the freezer and—" Alexus spoke before being cut off by Niya.

"Girl, I was just joking with you. You better not be waiting around for me to come cook. Shit, you will starve to death." Niya chuckled. She looked over at Alexus, who had her head dropped to the floor. "Lex, you do know this is your home also. You can eat what you want, baby girl," Niya added, now seeing that Alexus had taken her comment seriously.

"Thank you, Ni. It's just that most of my life I've lived with different people and family members, and I know how they can be about eating their food."

Niya could see the hurt in her eyes. She knew that although Alexus was young, she had been through a lot. She walked over to her and raised her head up until they made eye contact.

"Lex, babe, we are family now, and I love you just like a sister. If there is anything you want or need, don't you hesitate to ask me, and if it's some food in this house or any of our houses, you are more than welcome to it. You hear me?"

Alexus nodded her head. Niya wiped away the tears that were forming in Alexus's eyes and then kissed her on her forehead.

Ever since the day Alexus had saved Niya's life, they had gotten closer. Niya took her under her wing and also looked out for her on the strength of Prada. There was something about Alexus that drew Prada to her, and the more Niya hung around her, the more she could see why.

"Come on, I need ya help," Niya said, pulling Alexus away from the stove.

They got to Niya's room, where Niya pulled the large sheet containing the contents from Mayo's house out from under the bed. Everything was separated first. The money was in one pile, the guns in another, and the drugs in another. Niya didn't know much about the drug game, but she figured the brick-like packages were cocaine. The smell coming from the packages was so strong that Niya was becoming nauseated.

"That's heroin," Alexus said, pulling her shirt up to her nose.

"Heroin. How do you know that?" Niya asked with a curious look on her face.

"That's the same stuff Dro used to bag up before he took it around to the trap houses," Alexus answered.

"What da hell am I supposed to do with heroin?" she said, counting the packages. "So what is this supposed to be?" Niya asked, holding up a different colored package that was wrapped the same way.

Alexus took the package and examined it. There was a little white residue coming out of the side of it. She took some of it and placed it on her tongue. Her face looked like she had eaten a Sour Patch when she tasted it.

"This is cocaine," Alexus said. "Dro used to sniff this stuff twenty times a day. He got me to try it, but I didn't like how it made me feel," she said.

Altogether, there were three keys of heroin and two bricks of cocaine. The guns included an MP5 submachine gun, an AR-15 assault rifle, an AK-47, two .45s, two 9 mm and a Glock .40. Mayo kept enough firepower in his house to take on a small army. Amazed by the size of the guns, Alexus stood in front of the mirror and posed with each gun, causing Niya to laugh a little, something she hadn't done in a while.

It took every bit of two hours for the girls to count up the money. It was broken down in every kind of bill. At the end, there was a little more than $1.2 million there, more money than either Niya or Alexus had seen at one time. They sat in the middle of the floor just looking at the money for a while, before Alexus spoke.

"I think you should give Prada's grandmother some of this money," Alexus said, breaking the silence. Alexus felt kind of out of place by making that kind of suggestion. "I'm sorry."

"No, don't be sorry," Niya said, cutting her off. "I think you're right. Part of all of this is Prada's anyway. I'ma give her a hundred thousand," she said as she began separating the money.

"Oh, I can't forget about you," Niya said, tossing Alexus a stack of money.

It was 50K. Alexus looked at her curiously. "What's this for?"

Niya just smiled. "That's so you can buy something to eat. Oh, yeah, and for saving my life." Both girls laughed at the comment.

Gwen sat in the apartment staring at a picture of JR all day. His funeral wasn't until the next day, but Gwen felt like it was happening right now, the way she was crying. The last time she'd been in love with a man was when she and Chad were together.

A light knock at the door snapped her out of her daze. Even though she was mourning, she was still on high alert. People trying to kidnap her, folks breaking into her apartment, and a boyfriend who was just shot to death all kept her on her toes. She had just dropped Zion off to Chad, so there was no reason for anybody to be knocking at her door, lightly at that. Gwen reached between the cushions of her couch and pulled the chrome .45 out, then tiptoed to the door.

"Who is it?" she yelled, pointing the barrel through the peephole.

"Ay, it's Mayo, Gwen. I need to talk to you," he announced in a nonthreatening manner.

"Give me a second, Mayo," Gwen said, running to her room to put on some pants.

When she opened the door, she could see the stress written all over his face. Gwen figured it was because of the funeral the next day, but it wasn't. It was something a little more serious. He didn't even know where to begin, or even if it was safe to talk to Gwen, but at this point he felt like he really didn't have anywhere else to go—at least nowhere else he would feel safe.

Mayo could see the comfort that Gwen brought, just like JR had told him about. JR would always brag that he had the best of both worlds, because even though Gwen's body was country thick with measurements of 36-24-42, she had the ability to show the demeanor of a caring young woman one minute, then fight and go hard like a gangsta who was seven feet tall, 300 pounds the next.

"What's goin on, Mayo?" Gwen asked, taking a seat on the arm of the couch.

"Everything's bad. I pretty much lost everything. I don't have a muthafuckin' dime to my name. On top of that, my lawyer told me that I got a warrant out for my arrest, for murder," he explained. "They probably think I had something to do with JR's death."

This was the perfect opportunity for Gwen to get some understanding about what exactly had happened with her boyfriend. The first time he and the crew came by to tell her about JR's death, Mayo really didn't want to talk about it, and he barely answered her questions, but now, Gwen could see that he was vulnerable, so she began quizzing him.

"Mayo, I know you're goin' through some shit right now, but can you tell me what happened to my man?" Gwen asked in a low, sad, and sincere way. "I think I got the right to know," she said, now taking a seat on the couch right next to him.

He became quiet for a moment. He had recapped the whole night a thousand times in his head. "It was some chicks," Mayo began. "First they robbed one of my trap houses. I can't believe I fell for this bitch," he said, thinking about Prada.

"Do you know where these females are from?" Gwen cut in, looking for something to work with.

"Nah, but one of them had the letters *MHB* on her wrist. She's the one who killed JR in my house."

"Hold up, did you say *MHB*?" Gwen asked.

"Yeah, why? Do you know someone like that?" Mayo said, turning to face Gwen.

"Nah, I'm just wondering what those letters meant," she lied. "And that's who killed JR?"

Mayo told Gwen about the last phone call JR made to him, telling him how he had the girl at gunpoint in his house. He couldn't understand how the female got an opportunity to kill JR. The more Mayo talked, the more Gwen just sat there and listened. He told her about Mike the Realtor, and how he was involved with a girl who had *MHB* tattooed on her neck. It was through Mike that Mayo knew Prada was with that crew. Mayo even told Gwen that he killed Prada, not knowing that Prada was like her sister.

Gwen wasn't tryin' to hear anything else that came out of Mayo's mouth. Thoughts of blowing his head off right then and there crossed her mind, but Gwen had other plans. She was going to use Mayo to the best of her ability, and when the time was right, she would make him pay for Prada's death.

It took Chad over an hour to finally get the twins to take a nap. Even on his day off, he was still at work. It really wasn't a problem, though. He loved being a father. He loved having the opportunity to raise his kids. Every day he woke up and was afforded that joy, it reminded him that getting out of the game was well worth it.

Falling asleep himself, Chad felt Niya climb into the bed and wrap her arms around him. Her naked body pressed against his back, and warmth covered his shoulder. It had been a little while since they had been intimate, and it was more than obvious that they both needed it.

Chad rolled over to face her. Words needed not to be spoken for him to know where this was about to go. Niya climbed on top of him, leaned in, and kissed him ever so gently. Chad couldn't resist even if he wanted to. Her soft, warm body on top of him made his dick rock hard within seconds. She was so beautiful. It was as if his hands had a mind of their own as they fondled her bare 38DD breasts.

"I love you," Niya said, looking into his eyes as she kissed down past the center of his chest.

Once at his manhood, Niya took it into her mouth, making the nine-inch member disappear. Chad moaned from the warm, wet sensation of her throat, and the more she sucked on it, the wetter her mouth got. He could feel the spit from Niya's mouth drip down his balls and onto the bed. She looked up at him in order to see how good it felt to him. His eyes were shut, and his hands gripped the sheets.

When she finally came up for bit of air, it sounded like she was taking a Popsicle out of her mouth. She didn't skip a beat when she climbed back on top of Chad. Her juice box was soaking so much she didn't have to guide him inside of her. It just slipped in on its own when she sat on it. Her pussy felt wetter than her mouth, and as she swayed her hips back and forth, Chad palmed her ass cheek with one hand and reached up and grabbed her throat with the other. He pushed his dick deeper and deeper inside of her until she could barely take any more.

"I'm cumming, daddy. Dis ya pussy," Niya yelled out as she sped up the pace.

Now palming both of her ass cheeks and watching how her titties bounced up and down, Chad could feel himself about to bust. Niya's walls tightened up, and her body began to shiver. "Aaahhhrrr!" she yelled, releasing her fluids onto his dick.

Chad also exploded, sending about an ounce of his thick cum inside her. He could feel both his and her cum running down his balls. It was exactly what he needed. It was exactly what they both needed. Niya flopped down onto the bed. Both of them fell asleep, hot and sticky, in each other's arms.

Chapter 4

JR's funeral was packed. He didn't have as many people there as Prada had at hers, but all in all, it was a full house. One thing his family didn't have to worry about was security. There were more thugs at his funeral than a Biggie Smalls concert. Just about every one of them was strapped. These were all of his friends. These were the people who loved him. The hood loved him, and this was the first time Gwen witnessed how much.

"Yo, ma, sorry for ya loss," one man said to Gwen after he viewed JR's body.

It seemed like everybody who was there apologized to Gwen for her loss. She was shocked that people even knew who she was, especially since she didn't know almost anybody there. It was normal for it to be that way. In the hood, the homies might not ever really see her that much, but they definitely know who the wifey is. Gwen had to admit, she felt like a mob wife, and being honest with herself, she kinda liked it.

A knock at the door briefly took Mrs. Thompson's attention away from the hundreds of pictures she had of Prada laying out on the dining room table. She was surprised but happy to see Niya, Diamond, Tiffany, Alexus, and Tiki standing on her porch. She felt comfortable around the girls, especially Diamond and Niya, whom she'd known the longest. After hugging and kissing everybody, Mrs. Thompson led them to the dining room table, where everybody sat. Alexus set the large duffle bag of money at Mrs. Thompson's feet. Mrs. Thompson looked at the bag and then looked up at the girls.

"It's just a little something we all put together for you," Niya said. "And please don't be stubborn, Mrs. T. I know how you can get," Niya teased.

In Niya's heart, $100,000 wasn't enough. She wished she could have given her life for Prada's right now. That's just the kind of bond MHB had with each other. There wasn't a person sitting at that table who wasn't hurt, not even Alexus.

"You must be Alexus," Mrs. Thompson said, looking over at her. "My granddaughter told me all about you," she said with a smile. "Ya family now, so if there is anything you need, my door is always open to you."

Everybody turned to look at Alexus as if she were the golden child. Those words coming from Prada's grandmother meant a lot. Alexus wasn't even aware of what just happened, but in time, she would understand.

"Mama T, I want you to know that I'ma . . . we are gonna do everything in our power to make the person who did this pay," Niya said, looking down at the picture of her and Prada when they graduated high school.

"Oh, baby, I'm not worried about retribution. The good Lord is gonna deal with whoever done this," she said, raising one hand to the sky. "He's goin' to jail, baby."

"Mama T," Niya said, getting Prada's grandmother's eye contact. "I swear by the God that you hold ya hand up to that if I find him before the cops do, he's not gonna make it to jail," Niya admitted.

Mrs. Thompson sat there for a second. Her eyes began to water. She smiled at the sincerity and conviction Niya had. She looked Niya in her eyes and without blinking, said, "Well, you make sure his ass never get a chance to kill again," Mrs. Thompson said.

***

After the funeral, Gwen met up with Mayo so that he could help her get rid of the cocaine she still had. She wasn't too sure about dealing with any of her people after the attempted hit by Master, so she reached out to Mayo for help. He was on the run, but he still had all of his clientele and a couple of goons on standby. Moving the product was the least of Mayo's worries. He really just wanted to get his money up and then get out of town before he went to jail. Gwen was all for taking advantage of his situation.

She saw it as an opportunity, especially when Mayo offered Gwen his connect after he got his bread up and right before he skipped town. That was potentially big for her; it would mean no more middleman jacking up the prices. No more being one of the people caught up in the drought. No more having to worry about owing anybody. Gwen was gonna be free, and well enough in a position to take over the city. She loved the idea of not only being her own boss, but everybody else's boss as well.

"Now, this little spot belongs to a nigga named Dollaz," Mayo said, pulling up to the corner of Cummings Avenue. "He's good for nine ounces a week, sometimes more," he told Gwen.

Just as he said that, Dollaz came out of one of the trap houses to investigate the unknown car on his block. Gwen took his appearance in with one quick look. He was a Lil Wayne lookalike with dreads falling all the way down his back. He had on an orange T-shirt with the words TRUCK FIT written in black. He wore the shirt with some khaki pants and orange-and-black LeBrons. Every part of his body that wasn't covered by the clothing was etched with tattoos. The one that stood out to Gwen was the THUG LIFE that sat on the left side of his neck.

Boldly, he walked right up to Gwen's car and looked in the window. He didn't care who it was; they was in his hood and on his block, so he knew if anyone should have had fear, it was the occupants of the car, not him.

"Gotdam, baby boy, what it look like?" Mayo said, rolling down the window and also easing the mood.

"Aww, man, I see you ridin' in somethin' new," Dollaz shot back, looking around to see who all was in the car.

"Yeah, this my peeps' ride. I got her chauffeuring a nigga today," Mayo responded while pointing at Gwen. "You going to be seeing her more often, so I wanted to introduce y'all myself, you dig?"

"Brah, you know I don't care who bring it as long as it gets brought," Dollaz uttered back.

The small talk was over in a matter of seconds, and before Gwen knew it, she was serving Dollaz nine ounces of powder cocaine. This was the first of many more transactions to come. The only thing Gwen didn't like was when Mayo introduced her as his girl. She was about to correct him, but she realized that was something so small compared to the big picture.

After leaving Prada's grandmother's house, Tiffany, Diamond, Alexus, and Niya went back to Alexus's apartment. The girls sat at the kitchen table in silence, waiting for Niya to come out of her room. Niya had to think long and hard about what she was about to get herself into. She had to weigh the options herself before she could ask anybody else to join her.

It took half an hour for her to emerge from her room with a book bag over her shoulder. She tossed the bag on the table and took a seat at the head. Still, everyone was unaware of where she was going.

"I want y'all to understand that this is a very difficult task that I'm about to ask you to do," Niya began. "I love each and every one of y'all like you were my own flesh and blood—"

"Ni, what's goin' on?" Diamond interrupted, feeling like something was wrong.

"Let me finish, let me finish," Niya said, holding a finger up. "Look, I'm tired of struggling. I'm tired of wasting my time runnin' around this city tryin' to set niggas up. I'm tired of wishing and dreaming to own my own club, and every day I wake up, I get pushed further and further away from my goal."

Diamond could tell that Niya was serious. She had never heard her speak with so much passion before. Tiffany felt the same way. This was the first time she saw Niya in this form.

Niya stood up from her chair and grabbed the bag. She emptied the contents of it onto the table. It was the three keys of heroin and the two bricks of cocaine. Diamond looked at the packages, and then back at Niya. Tiffany grabbed one of the bricks of cocaine and started to examine it.

"I'm tryin' to get into the game," Niya announced, looking around the room.

"The drug game?" Tiffany asked, staring at the brick.

"Yeah, the drug game," Niya shot back. "I'm not just tryin' to get in the drug game; I'm tryin' to take over," she declared. Niya had come to the conclusion that it was going to be all or nothing. There was no point being in the streets if you wasn't gonna go hard.

"What about dese niggas out here? You know they not gonna just let us sell drugs in their hood," Diamond said, picking up one of the bricks.

Niya nodded to Alexus. She got right up from the table, went into Niya's room, and came back out with the AK-47 in her hands and two of the handguns sticking out of her pockets.

Diamond looked over at Niya. "You serious, Ni?" she asked.

"As I ever been," Niya replied with a stern look on her face. "So what y'all wanna do?"

The whole apartment became silent. Diamond and Tiffany looked off into space for a moment. It didn't take Diamond long to come up with her answer. It was a proven fact that there was nothing she wouldn't do for MHB. Not only that, but she liked the idea of competing with the same niggas in the hood she used to run around chasing.

"Fuck it, I'm wit' you," Diamond said, pulling one of the handguns from Alexus's pocket.

"Y'all bitches ain't gonna leave me out of the picture!" Tiffany said, grabbing the other handgun from Alexus's pocket.

Niya looked around the room, and she was satisfied with who she had on her team. This was a new beginning for MHB, and if Charlotte was sleeping on the abilities of the women, MHB was about to wake up the town.

"Search warrant!" Detective Butler yelled before kicking Mayo's front door off the hinges.

He led the tactical unit inside of the house, clearing each room. Detective Butler had a feeling Mayo wasn't going to be there, but he decided to be sure of it. Once Mayo got the heads-up from his lawyer that a warrant was being issued for his arrest, he never even thought about going back home.

"He's still in the city. I can feel it," Butler told Detective Rose as they stood in the center of Mayo's front lawn.

"Yeah, well, we got plenty of doors to kick in today, and I'm sure he's gonna be in one of them," Rose said, walking back to the car.

It was an all-day affair, kicking in door after door, looking for Mayo. They went any- and everywhere he'd lived before he had become a target for the detectives. They even got the green light from the district attorney to raid several of his known trap houses, information courtesy of an informant. It was pretty much an all-out manhunt, and if Mayo was still in the city, it wouldn't be much longer until he ran into the people who were looking for him.

There was some unfinished business Gwen had to deal with before she could hit the streets full-fledged, and Niya was at the top of her list. She knew for sure now that Niya had killed JR, and a need for revenge was running through her brain. At the same time, she struggled with her heart. She wasn't sure if she could actually commit the act of killing Niya. So much had happened over the years, and the wedge between them had gotten uglier, but the fact still remained that she held some love for Niya. More importantly, they had both made the oath never to put anything before MHB, not even a nigga. Gwen honestly didn't know what she was going to do, but one thing was for sure, and that was Niya had to answer in some kind of way for killing JR.

The traffic light turned from green to yellow, but Mayo wasn't stupid enough to go through it, considering his delicate situation. He'd never been this cautious in his life, and before long, his caution turned into paranoia. Every cop car he saw made his heart just about jump out of his chest. The only reason he was doing his own driving now was because Gwen had to pick up her son. Mayo had some important errands to run. There was still a lot of money on the streets that belonged to him, and he needed every bit of it.

While sitting at the light, Mayo glanced in the rearview mirror and noticed a cop car pulling up a few cars back. His paranoia kicked into overdrive. The cop wasn't even thinking about him, nor did his rental car draw any attention. If the cops had been looking for him to be in any car, it would have been the Benz.

"Shit," he mumbled to himself, turning on his signal to make a right turn when the light changed. He was trying so hard to avoid the cop car that he didn't even notice that the cop had his turn signal on to make the right at the light. All Mayo had to do was keep going straight ahead, but as soon as the light turned green, he made a right.

Moments later, the cop car made the same right turn. Mayo almost defecated on himself when he saw the cop car behind him. He looked to turn into a little shopping center, and he actually made the gesture of turning, but turned his wheel back and decided to keep going straight. That motion, along with the fact that he was black, made the officer turn his lights on for Mayo to pull over.

When Mayo pulled to the side of the road, he reached under his seat and grabbed the 9 mm. He looked in the rearview again to see if the cop was alone, or if he had a partner. Mayo wasn't tryin' to go to jail, but if he didn't do something now, he wasn't going to have much of a choice. His chances of getting away were getting slimmer by the second. They grew even slimmer when two police officers got out of the car.

Everything was happening so fast. He knew it would be suicide if he got out of the car and started shooting now. He waited for the officers to get as close as his back doors, then he threw the car in drive and stepped on the gas. The officers got back in their car and began the pursuit. Mayo punched it, but his efforts were put to a halt when a car shot out of the mall's parking lot.

Mayo slammed on the brakes, but it was too late. He crashed into the back end of the car and spun out of control. His car hit the pavement and turned over. His body was slung around like a ragdoll. The only thing he could hear before he passed out was the sound of the two cops yelling, "Do not move!"

Detective Butler got the call that Marquis Harper was in custody and had been taken to a nearby hospital after the car crash. Butler and Rose were at the hospital within minutes of the call. They had expected for his apprehension to be a little different than this, which would have included multiple shots being fired and somebody, if not him, being killed.

"How long has he been out?" Detective Butler asked the officer outside of his door when he walked up.

"Ever since the accident. The doctor said that he should be fine, though," the officer answered.

Butler relieved the officer, grabbed a chair, and set it right next to Mayo's bed. He was going to make sure that he was the first person Mayo saw when he woke up, and it would be then that the real party would start.

Chapter 5

Niya didn't know the first thing about heroin, or where to begin, for that matter. The heroin game was a whole lot different from the cocaine game. There were a lot of problems that came along with it, mainly the amount of time one could get for selling it. The risk was greater, but the money was crazy. A key of heroin cost about 80K, while a brick of cocaine went for 20K.

"So you sure you know what you're doin'?" Niya asked Mandy, watching her crack open one of the keys of heroin.

Mandy was an old friend from back in the day when Niya used to live in the projects. Mandy had moved to Betty Ford Road after high school, and she had been there ever since. She knew so much about heroin because that's all her neighborhood was known for. Betty Ford Road was the most violent street in Charlotte, because of the heroin trade. Heroin junkies were worse than crackheads. A crackhead could go cold turkey and quit, but a heroin addict would need years of treatment and methadone shots to kick the habit.

"Look, I'ma put you on to my cousin. He got this neighborhood on lockdown," Mandy spoke through the mask as she blended in the cut to the heroin. "If you sell it right, you can come up around here, girl," she joked.

"Who's ya cousin?" Niya asked, not really up for dealing with people she didn't know.

"His name is Master. He just got out of the hospital. I'ma walk you over there when I get done."

It had taken her a while, but Mandy had cut up a whole key of heroin for Niya. She even broke it down into ounces so that it would be easier for Niya to manage if she chose to just sell weight. The prices were the only thing left to discuss, which, again, Niya had no knowledge of. However, with her messing around with Mandy, she was definitely about to get a crash course in the dope game.

Gwen checked to make sure she had a bullet in the chamber before getting out of the car. Master must've been crazy to think that the beef was over between him and her. She had made her mind up a long time ago that Master had to go for pulling that stunt. Gwen just wouldn't be able to sleep right knowing that he was out there healing from his wounds and would be up and rolling again in a short time.

Her phone started ringing the moment she got out of the car, and her first thought was not to answer it. Then she remembered that she was waiting on a specific call.

"Yeah," Gwen answered, tucking the .45 into her back pocket.

It was exactly who she thought it might have been. She quickly accepted the call from the county jail, knowing that it could only be one person.

"Yo, shawty, what's good wit' you?" Mayo said.

"Nothin' much. I'm just about to go and take care of something," Gwen said, looking down the street.

"Well, look, I'm not gonna do too much talkin' over the phone. My visiting day is on Saturday from eleven to one p.m.—"

"Say no more. I'll be up there," she said, cutting him off. "Other than that, are you good in there?"

"Yeah, I'm good. I'll see what they're talking about when I go to court next week. But look, I was just checkin' up on you. We'll talk when I see you," Mayo said before hanging up the phone.

Gwen hung up too, but this time decided to leave the phone in the car as opposed to keeping it on her. She proceeded to Betty Ford Road with one thing on her mind. She didn't know what house Master lived in or even if he stayed on that street, but Gwen remembered that every time JR would bring him stuff, he'd be sitting on one of the porches. That's all Gwen was banking on.

"What up, cuz?" Mandy said, walking up to him with Niya in tow. "Yo, dis my girl, Niya," she introduced.

"What up, shawty?" he said, looking up at Niya.

Niya looked down at the short, dark, muscular man. He had a bald head and sweat ran down it, even though it wasn't that hot outside.

Master's words were limited because he was still in pain. The weed smoke helped somewhat, but it was still hard for him to do things such as talk, walk, laugh, or sleep comfortably.

"Yo, cuz, my girl got some work she's tryin' to get rid of, and I told her that you could help her out."

"Oh, yeah? What kind of work?" Master asked with a curious look on his face.

Niya stepped in and passed him one of the ounces she had brought outside with her. He looked at the plastic bag then put it to his nose. The smell was so strong he caught a little contact. He didn't have to ask what it was. He knew that it was heroin.

"Where you get dis from, shawty?" Master asked, looking at Niya.

"Does it matter? I got it for sale," Niya snapped back. "Do you wanna buy it or what?"

Master looked at the bag and then at Mandy. He never pegged Mandy to be a setup artist, but Master was still cautious because he knew the police had been lurking in the hood lately. Betty Ford Road was always a target for the local vice cops. Master waved for one of his dopefiends to come over so that he could taste the product for him. Niya approved it, wanting to know herself exactly what she was working with.

The fiend took one sniff of it then wiped some around his gums. After a few seconds, he was bent over with his head between his legs. His mouth was drooling with spit, and he didn't respond when Mandy smacked him on the back of his head.

"How much you want for it?" Master asked in a hurry. He knew that this kind of dope was hard to come by nowadays.

"How much is it worth to you?" Niya said, looking to get some understanding as to what the prices were.

Master could tell from that simple question that Niya didn't know what she had or how much to sell it for. He figured that she just stole it from her boyfriend and was trying to make a few dollars. Either way, he was going to play the game with her.

"I'm sayin'. Somethin' like this go for about fifteen hundred," Master lied. The average ounce of heroin would run anywhere from $2,000 to $2,300 an ounce. Master knew that, but Niya didn't. She thought $1,500 was more than enough per ounce, especially since Mandy just cut it up and brought back fifty ounces off the key. She did the math within seconds and saw that she could make seventy-five grand off a brick if she sold it that way.

"You got a deal. Give Mandy that fifteen hundred, take my cell number, and call me when you need some more," Niya said, flipping out her cell.

"How much of dis shit you got, shawty?" Master asked with his mind already on the angles.

"Enough. Just hit me up when you're ready," she replied then walked back to Mandy's house.

Gwen looked up and down the street a few times before she came out of the cut. Seeing Niya talking to Master only made Gwen furious. She came from the corner pulling the .45 out of her back pocket. The gun was almost as big as her, but she was well aware of how to work it.

Master was looking down at the dope when he saw a pair of AirMax coming up the steps. By the time he looked up, he was staring down the barrel of a gun, and on the other end of it was a woman he prayed he would never run into again.

"Hey, Master," Gwen said with a devilish smile on her face.

"Come on, shawty, it wasn't like dat," Master pleaded. "You don't gotta do dis."

"Oh, yeah, I got to. You think I'm going to let a nigga who tried to kill me live to get a second chance at it?"

Gwen looked into his eyes before she squeezed the trigger. *Boom! Boom!* Gwen let the .45 cannon blow. All three shots pierced his forehead, knocking him backward in his wheelchair. She then turned the gun on the dopefiend and was about to pull the trigger when she saw that he was already dead off the dope. She turned around, tucked the gun into her pocket, and walked off as if nothing had happened.

"Oh, shit, girl, get down," Mandy shouted, grabbing Niya's arm and pulling her to the ground away from the window.

It was typical for shootings to occur around Betty Ford Road, but this one shocked Mandy because they had just left from outside. Not hearing any follow-up shots, Mandy deemed it safe to go outside to see what happened.

Niya wasn't too crazy about the idea, but she pulled the 9 mm from her waist and followed Mandy out the door. Other residents were coming out as well to see what was going on. Mandy took a couple more steps up the street and could see that a crowd was gathering around Master's trap spot.

"Master!" she screamed, running onto the porch.

Niya followed closely behind her. When they arrived at the spot they were just standing at less than thirty minutes before, both ladies looked up to see half of Master's head peeled back.

Damn, Niya thought, *I'm back at square one.*

Chapter 6

Diamond and Tiffany weren't taking any prisoners. In a matter of days, they already had a trap house set up over on Milton Road, and they were pushing up on a few corners that weren't really established. Diamond took the lead role in moving the cocaine. She got with one of her old boyfriends, a young nigga name Dollaz, to help her cook up. In return, she gave him coke for cheap. There was a method to her madness. Her eyes were set on Washington Street, because she knew the potential it had after seeing the old crews make millions out there when she was young.

"How do you know so much about cocaine?" Tiffany asked Diamond, who was sitting at the table watching a couple of crackheads bag up the product.

"My dad used to sell this shit, my mom used to smoke it, and my uncles used to cook it in front of me when I was yea high." She motioned with her hand.

"Damn, bitch, you were made for dis shit," Tiffany joked.

A loud bang at the door grabbed everyone's attention. All activities ceased, and the first person to get up to go check the door was Tiffany. Although Tiffany was cute, petite, and reminded everyone of Rihanna, she had an instinct to kill without remorse. She was the quiet type who nobody would expect to do anything.

Tiffany pulled the blinds back on the window slightly. It was a young cat with Chief Keef braids. He was by himself, but she could tell he carried an attitude with him by the way he was standing.

Tiffany walked back to the table, grabbed the 10 mm, then proceeded to the door. Diamond motioned for the workers to finish doing what they were doing, knowing that whoever was at the door, Tiffany was going to take care of it. Tiffany took the several locks off the door and removed the large two-by-four from in front of it.

Ignorant to what was on the other side of the door, the guy pushed his way in. Tiffany just backed up and pointed the gun at his face.

"Whoa! Whoa!" Diamond yelled, getting up from the table.

The guy didn't even have a gun in his hand, and if it weren't for Diamond, he would have been dead. He took a good look around the house at all the people who were there. He was acting as if he didn't care that Tiffany had him at gunpoint.

"Who y'all bitches?" he asked with a confused look on his face. "Y'all bitches trappin' in here?" he said jealously.

"Us bitches? Who da fuck is you?" Tiffany shot back, not liking his tone of voice.

GoGo was a local hustler who had just come home from jail and opened up shop in the same house a few weeks before. He had only a little bit of work that was given to him by one of his connects, who felt like it was only right to bless him with the drugs since GoGo hadn't snitched on him.

GoGo considered this spot to be his trap house, even though he hadn't been around for the last two weeks. He had been out trying to come up on a new connect since he had spent the money from the dope his connect gave him. While on the streets, he heard through the grapevine that there was some action going on in the house. He came to find that it wasn't just action; Diamond had picked up the pace dramatically. Dealers in the surrounding trap houses were starting to feel the effect.

"GoGo, you don't run my house. I can have whoever I want in here," Ms. Daisy said from the table.

Diamond walked over and lowered Tiffany's arm that had the gun still pointed at GoGo. Diamond had known GoGo since he was a little boy, and she knew that he really wasn't a threat. She also knew that he was broke and trying to come up; but most importantly, Diamond knew that he was still young and could be easily manipulated by the right person with the right things.

Diamond walked all the way up to him, looked GoGo in his eyes with the most innocent face she could put on, and asked, "GoGo, you wanna make some real money or what?"

The visiting room was packed. It took Mayo forty-five minutes to get downstairs to the visiting area. The process irritated Gwen, but she knew that this visit had to take place to insure a better future for herself. Today's objective was to get his drug connect's information, so that she could start making her own moves. Since Mayo was booked for murder, Gwen wasn't even sure if he was going to do what he said he would do, but she felt like she had to take the chance. Besides, Mayo had to know that he was looking at a long stretch of time and would surely need someone on the outside looking out for him. If he hadn't thought about it, Gwen would definitely bring it to his attention.

"What up, shawty?" Mayo said, walking up and standing there like he was expecting a hug.

She really didn't want to, but she did it anyway. Mayo wasn't her man, nor did she care anything about him. For all she knew, Mayo was the one who was responsible for

JR's death. If it were up to her, his ass could rot in jail for-ever; but right now she kind of needed him. It was hard as hell trying to find a supplier who did business straight up in Charlotte. Local drug dealers always wanted to boost the prices up for drugs they had stepped on a few times.

"I'm sorry I can't stay that long. I got to pick my son up," Gwen said as her excuse not to have to sit there too long.

"Naw, that's cool, because I need you to get right on top of this anyway," he said.

Mayo broke down the whole situation as far as with his case and what evidence the D.A. had against him. He expressed his concern about getting a paid lawyer, because all he had now was a public defender. Gwen sat there and listened to him, but she really did not pay attention to what he was saying about his case. She didn't care. It wasn't until he started talking about his connect that Gwen focused on what he was saying. She had to remember the name and phone number he had given her.

"Now look, I know that there is nothing I can do to bring my boy JR back, and I hope that you don't think that I don't hurt over his death, because I do. Me and that nigga grew up together, got money together, and did time together. On the real, that was my right-hand man, and for that, I'ma make sure you and ya son is straight. I'm giving you my house so that you don't have to worry about having a place to stay."

"Mayo, you don't have to do that," Gwen responded with a surprised look on her face.

"I know, but I want to. You can do whatever you want with it. Just to make sure I get a lawyer at the end of the day," Mayo said with sincerity and sorrow in his eyes.

Gwen wasn't prepared for this other side Mayo was displaying. For a moment, she could actually see the hurt in his eyes when he talked about JR. That's when Gwen knew that it was time to end the visit. She didn't want to generate any type of feelings for Mayo, not even on the strength of JR.

Before the end of that day, Diamond had GoGo in the trap house moving work. He was soft for a cute face. That and the fact that he was about to be making good money was enough to get him on the team. This was all part of Diamond's takeover plan. She knew that no one could beat them on price, considering their dope had come free to them. Well, not free, since it had cost Prada her life, and nearly Niya's too, but they didn't have money tied up in the drugs, so they were able to sell it at a cheaper price than everyone else. They were also able to pay a higher commission to the workers. MHB was on the move, and Diamond was the main face on the streets. For the next couple of weeks, all she planned to do was push up on corners and run down on potential trap houses. Her motto was, "Either get down with the movement or get found not moving."

On her way out of the trap house, Diamond's phone started ringing. She waited until she got out on the porch to answer it, because she didn't want anyone hearing her conversation. It was Mike calling.

"Hey, stranger," Diamond said, looking up and down the block. Ever since Diamond had started moving the cocaine, she really didn't have time for Mike. It was during this short period of time that they both found out that some feelings were starting to get involved.

"Hey, beautiful. I was wondering if I could see you later tonight," Mike said, looking out of his office window.

Diamond had to think about it. Her mind was really on money right now, and that night she was supposed to get with Dollaz about some business. She wanted to take this opportunity to try to get Washington Street, or at least set up a trap house a couple blocks over.

"You still there?" Mike said, breaking the silence on the phone.

"Yeah, yeah, I'm still here. Naw, that's fine. We can hook up later on," she said as she calculated a time that would be good for her. "How does eleven sound?"

"Like a booty call," Mike chuckled, "but I'll take what I can get."

They both laughed. This was one of the things she enjoyed most about him. He was so easy to get along with and always understanding. At the same time, she couldn't ignore the feeling she had in her gut that things between them weren't going to last. She had been down this road before, and she knew that most perfect relationships were too good to be true; however, this one was someone different. Mike was white, so maybe, just maybe, this could work.

Gwen left the county jail and got right on the phone. She had already hit up the realty guy Mayo had told her to call about selling his house. Mike had told her she could easily borrow $80,000 to $90,000 against it. She didn't know how far ninety grand was going to take her with the new connect, but she sure as hell set up the meeting to discuss it. She had a couple of days before the meeting, so until then, Mayo gave her the okay to collect the rest of the money he had left out on the streets, so that she could add to the pot. Gwen's mind was made up, and she came to the conclusion that she was going to tackle the drug game full time, with conviction. This would be her year to get paid and put herself in the position she had been hoping for all her life.

***

Mandy and Niya stood at the table in Mandy's kitchen, breaking down another key of dope. It had taken almost thirty minutes to move all the half-empty cereal boxes and the dirty dishes Mandy had all over the table. Niya was trying to hold her tongue. Any other time, she would have told Mandy that even though you live in the hood, the inside of your house don't have to look like it. One thing Niya could say for her mother was even though they were in the projects, her mother always made sure their house was clean. Niya figured this wasn't the time to discuss good housekeeping skills with Mandy. She needed her to show her how to cut and package this work. This time, it was for street-level sales instead of weight, so the money would be even greater than what she could have made with Master.

Master had been dead for a couple of days, but Niya wasn't going to let that death derail her from cornering the market with her product. Diamond and Tiffany were handling the coke, and she and Alexus were taking care of the heroin. Niya had taken one of the most dangerous and violent places to start. This hood was crawling with hustlers and thieves who didn't mind killing for what they wanted, but Niya knew that this was also the best place for the quickest and most lucrative come-up.

"Niya, it's a lot of shit you don't know about the H game," Mandy said, passing her a mask to cover her face. "It's a lot of shit that comes along with it, and if you wanna survive, you got to be willing to act and think like a nigga," Mandy explained.

Mandy wasn't lying. She knew how the dope game was and the drama it brought, not only with the dealers and the dopefiends, but also with the law. On the flip side of it, you could become a millionaire overnight.

"Now, you sure you wanna go through with it?" Mandy asked before even starting the process of cutting again.

Niya shot her a "bitch, please" look. "Mandy, if I wasn't sure about this, I wouldn't be here. Now, if you having second thoughts about getting this money, then let me know," Niya answered.

Mandy looked at Niya and could see that she was dead serious. She cut the key open and spread it across the plastic-covered table, while Niya grinded up the Bonita, also known as cut. Masks and gloves were obligatory if you didn't want to get high off inhaling and touching the dope. Many people got strung out on heroin just because of the contact during the cutting process. It was the fastest way to lose everything before you had a chance to gain anything.

After about an hour and a half of chopping and bagging, Mandy handed Niya the shoebox of work. "Now look, I got enough dime bags in here to last you a couple of days. After that, I'ma take you to the store where they sell boxes of them," Mandy said as she continued to blend the cut into the heroin that was still left on the table. "The dope you got right here is an excellent grade. I might be able to turn this one key into two keys, or at least one and a half keys, depending on how much cut it can take without losing its potency. Oh, and I got to put you up on the prices so you can make the max on ya profit."

Niya looked at Mandy, amazed at how much she knew about dope. She was like a mad scientist in the lab, carefully doing everything with precision. Niya knew for sure that she had to have Mandy on her team, no matter what her house looked like or the cost she would charge for mixing the product.

Chad sat in the house, playing with Jahmil. He had been with the kids day and night for the past three days. Gwen had to attend JR's funeral, so Zion was also there.

He didn't mind spending all this time with his kids, but even Super Dad needed a break, and Niya wasn't a lick of help lately. She was rarely home, and by the time she did come in late at night, Chad was too tired to even argue. He had to be honest with himself. He was starting to feel like the bitch of the relationship. He was doing all the cooking and cleaning like he was a housewife. It was getting old real fast, and Niya was so far gone in her own little world that she didn't have the slightest idea what was about to hit her.

He had reached his breaking point, and asking Niya to step up and be the mother and wife he and the twins needed was getting old. Chad was really feeling like the best thing he could do for all involved was take a break and give the marriage some separation to see if they both still wanted to be there. He wasn't sure how he was going to break it to Niya, or even if she'd care. What he did know was that something outside had a hold on her greater than him.

Chapter 7

"Harper, you got a visit," the guard said, tapping on Mayo's cell door.

Mayo looked around with a confused look on his face. He wasn't expecting anyone, so he wasn't sure who would be coming to see him.

He took his time getting to the visiting room, but once he got there he almost turned around on his heels when he saw Detective Butler and his partner, Rose, sitting in the legal booth. He looked around the room to see who else was around, and coming from the vending machine was his lawyer.

"What's all this about?" Mayo asked his lawyer with a concerned look on his face. He didn't know what the detectives were there for, seeing as how he had already been charged with Prada's murder.

"Look, these guys wanna talk to you. They might be willing to make you a deal if you can help them out," Mayo's lawyer said, passing him one of the sodas he'd gotten out of the machine.

Reluctantly, Mayo went into the room with the detectives, only intending to see what they were talking about. He stood there with his back against the wall, while the detectives and his lawyer sat down.

"What y'all want?" Mayo said with an obvious attitude.

"Mr. Harper, a man was murdered in your house, and we know that you weren't home at the time it was done," Butler began. "But I am willing to bet just about anything that you know who did it."

Mayo didn't know if he was talking about Dro or JR. "Well, just like you said, I wasn't home at the—"

"You're right, because you were out killing Ms. Thompson," Rose cut in. "Look, Mr. Harper, if you wanna go to prison for the rest of your life, then that's okay with me, but if you ever want to see the light of day again, I suggest you put ya pride in ya back pocket and take advantage of this opportunity," she said, pointing at him with her pen.

Mayo didn't think about it as an opportunity. He knew that they wanted him to be a rat, something he never considered until now. Life in prison had been his only thought since the day he was arrested, and it was a sure thing that life was what he would get for Prada's death. This was his seventh offense and third felony.

"Yeah, so what you wanna know?" he asked, walking over and taking a seat in the chair.

"We wanna know who killed ya friend JR in ya house that night," Rose said.

Mayo opened up the soda and sat there trying to convince himself that what he was doing was self-preservation, not snitching. This was by no means easy for him to do. He had his pride and street credit on the line, but sometimes, even for a so-called real nigga, there is a breaking point, and he had reached his.

"So what's in it for me?" Mayo asked, putting all that pride to the side.

Detective Rose smiled and motioned for his attorney to fill him in on the deal they had already discussed.

Gwen hadn't slept a wink all night; she was constantly tossing and turning, and the same dream, or rather nightmare, was continuously playing back in her mind. It was nights like these that she wished for JR or any man to be there to hold her so she could fall asleep. Looking over at the clock, she read the bright red lights announcing 9:00 a.m. She had been up all night, with no sleep, and to make matters worse, she had a busy day planned and she need to get it started soon. Realizing that it didn't look like she was going to be getting any sleep anytime soon, she figured she would grab a good hot shower.

Once she was in the bathroom, Gwen turned on the water to let it run until it was at the right temperature. The room was filling up with steam quickly, and before the mirror fogged all the way up, Gwen took in the beauty of her naked body and smiled. She knew she had everything a man wanted when it came to a woman, and once she got the money and power to go along with it, she would indeed be that bitch!

Gwen felt so relaxed standing under the hot water in the shower stall. It was too bad she couldn't enjoy it a little longer. A knock at the front door brought her right out of her comfort zone, but she was well aware who it was. Chad was dropping Zion off for the weekend. She still couldn't believe that he'd had him all week. Chad was really trying to stick by his word of spending more time with his son, and Gwen really appreciated it. She threw a towel around her wet, naked frame and rushed to the door.

"Hi, Mom," Zion said in a low tone when she opened the door. He leaned in, gave her a hug, and then went straight to his room.

Gwen curiously watched him walk away, then looked back at Chad. "What you do to him?" Gwen joked.

"We been up all night playing Xbox and watching movies," Chad said with a proud smile.

"Oh, ain't that cute. I know he beat the wheels off your ass," Gwen said jokingly.

"Yeah, he did." Chad laughed.

"You wanna come in for minute?" she offered, stepping to the side.

Chad peeked inside and looked around suspiciously. He had never been inside of her apartment before.

"Ain't nobody in here." Gwen laughed, grabbing him by the arm and pulling him inside.

Chad sat down on the sofa and looked up at Gwen. "I wanted to tell you, on some real-nigga shit, I am sorry to hear about ya boy," he said sincerely.

Gwen had damn near forgotten about JR until he said something. She had a depressed look on her face, but Chad knew this wasn't from JR's death. He had seen this look too many times during the course of their relationship.

"Was it one of those nights?" he asked, this time with an even greater look of concern on his face.

Gwen understood that Chad knew her too well for her to lie to him. "Yes. I haven't been able to sleep all night, and my bed was soaking wet from all of the sweating."

Her eyes began to water up, and so did Chad's. He remembered all the nights of Gwen tossing, turning, and waking up screaming with her body covered in sweat. It took nearly two years before Gwen finally confessed that she had been suffering from nightmares. Chad thought back to that night and the horrific story that Gwen recalled.

She was seven years old and had been sent to live with her grandmother and grandfather for the summer. She always loved going to Norfolk, Virginia, even though the town was small. Her grandparents would take her shopping and to the nearby beach. The days were beautiful and sunny, and she would always play with her cousins who lived there.

One night, tired from a full day of swimming, her grandparents took her to McDonald's before going back home. Gwen ate the Happy Meal and played with the toy on the short ride to the house. Her grandfather gave her strict instructions to go upstairs and take a bath. He gave her some scented liquid soap and the scented lotion to put on afterward. Gwen loved the smell; it was the same scent her Aunt May wore, and it made her feel like a big girl.

Once she had finished her bath and put on the lotion, she got dressed in her nightshirt and went to bed. She was so tired that she fell asleep immediately. She remembered dreaming about all of the stories she would tell to her friends and classmates once the summer was over.

Gwen's beautiful dream was interrupted when she felt a body pressed up against her from behind. Gwen awoke groggily, unable to see anything in the pitch-black room. The body behind her tightened the grip around her small frame. Gwen was about to yell, thinking that the boogieman was real, but before she could utter a sound, a larger hand covered her mouth. She could feel something sharp up against her butt.

At the young age of seven, Gwen realized quickly that this wasn't a boogieman who haunted kids' dreams. She recognized the familiar smell of Old Spice cologne as her grandfather's scent, but she couldn't figure out what he was doing in her bed.

Her grandfather released his grip around her body, only to pull her pink polka dot panties down until they were around her knees. Then suddenly, Gwen felt the worst pain she had ever experienced in her life in an area her mother had always told her to never let anyone touch. She could not believe that this was happening to her. Her young mind could not understand why the same man who'd been so kind and caring to her was inflicting so much pain.

Her heart raced as pain and fear encompassed her entire being. Her instinct to fight back kicked in, and she squirmed and wiggled to prevent the inevitable from happening. She figured that if she made it inconvenient enough, he'd lose his patience and it'd be over. When that didn't work, she cried and pled with him to stop, but he wouldn't. Instead, he persisted at trying to force his way into her seven-year-old womb.

After nearly twenty minutes of fighting, her body and will to protect herself had been exhausted. It was clear that her grandfather wasn't going to give up until he got exactly what he wanted. He was finished in less than five minutes. Once he was done, he got up and told her to go wash herself up.

"You better not tell anyone, or you won't be able to come up here anymore. You hear me?" he asked. Gwen didn't respond. She just went into the bathroom.

Her grandfather would repeat the same shameful action every summer until Gwen was twelve. Whenever summer was close, her nightmares would start. Even though Gwen had often pleaded with her mother not to send her to her grandparents, her mother enjoyed the summers when Gwen was away. It made her feel like she was single again, with no responsibilities.

Finally, when Gwen was twelve, her grandfather passed away. She would then overhear a conversation between her mother and her Aunt May. Her aunt shared that her father had molested her for years, and it was the reason she had run away from home at such a young age.

Over the years, Gwen had taken the anger and hurt and put it to use for what she felt was her benefit. She would use the face of her grandfather whenever she had to kill. It had served as a surefire way for her to murder with no remorse. She promised herself that she would never be a victim again.

Chad had always kept the hurt and anger in his heart also. He wished that cancer hadn't delivered the painful death he so want to give to Gwen's grandfather. Chad took her in his arms. "If you want, I could hold you and let you get some sleep."

Gwen had to admit that Chad was looking good sitting in front of her with a well-fitted V-neck T-shirt, a pair of Robin jeans, and some black leather high-top Jimmy Choo sneakers. The smell of his Polo Black cologne traveled through the air, lighting up the whole room.

"Let me go change real quick," Gwen said, remembering that she didn't have anything on underneath the bathrobe.

Gwen went into her bedroom and put on a pair of boy shorts and a white tank top, no bra, no panties. On her way back into the living room, she walked by Zion's room. Gwen quietly opened the door just enough to see that Zion had fallen asleep on his bed with all of his clothes on. She shook her head and smiled, going into the room where Chad was waiting.

"What you do to my . . . our son?" she joked.

When Gwen arrived back into the room, Chad couldn't take his eyes off her. She looked so good. Her body was crazy. Even without a bra on, her breasts sat up like she had implants, and when she got into the light, he could see her nipples poking through the cotton tank top. The boy shorts she had on were so snug, her vagina print stuck out like a baby camel toe. Chad had to adjust himself on the couch, because he was beginning to get hard despite the attempts his brain made to block out her beauty.

She came over and placed herself in his arms. "Gwen, you crazy." Chad smiled.

"What?" she asked, looking down at what she had on. "It ain't like you haven't seen me like this before. Shit, you done seen me naked. What's the problem? Do I make you nervous?"

She was joking, but Chad was dead serious. His mind started wandering off, thinking about all the stuff he used to do and now wanted to do with Gwen. It seemed like everything was playing back in his mind, and the main thing was how good and wet she always was. On top of that, Gwen had mastered the Kegel exercises, so she stayed tight. Chad and Gwen had a chemistry like neither had experienced before or since.

Chad could feel pre-cum oozing from his dick when he thought about Gwen's full, juicy lips wrapped around him. "Yo, I got to go," he said, jumping up from the couch.

Gwen jumped up, too, but stood in front of him so he couldn't leave. Somewhat ashamed for having sexual thoughts about him, she put her head down, but when she looked down, she could see the bulge in his pants. She knew he was hard, and that only made her even wetter. Her breathing intensified.

"Chad, I'ma keep it real wit' you," Gwen said in a low, soft and sexy voice. "I'm horny as shit right now, and my pussy been wet since I opened that door and you were standing there."

"Come on, Gwen—"

"No, let me finish," she said, getting closer to him. "It's not a day that goes by in my life that I don't think about you. I miss daddy's dick," she said, reaching down and grabbing a handful of his member through his pants.

It had been a couple of years since they had sex, but every time Chad saw Gwen, he also had sexual thoughts about her. Today, there was more than just those thoughts. There was something different about Gwen that Chad was attracted to—something that was better than just having sex. Chad looked into Gwen's eyes and could see that she was still in love with him.

Chad grabbed Gwen by her throat, pulling her closer. The strength of his large hands made her body heat up. She closed her eyes and waited for impact. His soft lips pressed against hers as he pulled her body into his. The kiss alone was electrifying, causing both of them to examine the inside of each other's mouth with their tongues.

"Zion," Chad said, thinking about his son.

"He is asleep," Gwen shot back as she began lifting his shirt up.

Chad reached down and scooped Gwen up, wrapping her legs around his waist. Passionately kissing her, Chad walked her over and slammed her back against the wall. With one arm holding her against the wall, he used his free hand to pull off her shorts. His jeans hit the floor at the same time her shorts did, and before she knew it, his manhood had invaded her nectar box. She wrapped her legs around his waist as he stuffed every bit of himself into her. Deeper and deeper, he pushed his rock-hard penis into her. Gwen wanted to scream at the top of her lungs, but she couldn't. She didn't want to wake Zion, so she just bit down on Chad's shoulder and clawed her nails into his back.

"It's still yours," Gwen whispered into his ear.

This only made Chad crazier. He kept digging deeper and harder, until he felt Gwen's walls tighten from her orgasm. Chad could feel the wetness of Gwen's nectar thicken. He grabbed one of her breasts while he prepared to cum as well. His strokes became longer and faster, until finally, he came, shooting his load into her waiting treasure box. After a few finishing strokes, Chad let her legs down, but Gwen was far from being done. She grabbed him by the hand and led him back to her room.

"You ready for part two?" she asked.

Chad didn't respond. His face said it all: he wasn't going nowhere anytime soon.

***

"Ohhh, my God!" Alexus said as she held her hair high above her head and closed her eyes.

She jumped at the stinging sensation of the needle buzzing on the back of her neck. It was initiation day for her. Niya, Tiffany, Diamond, and Tiki were all at the apartment for the event. Alexus was officially becoming a member of MHB, a move that would change her life forever.

"I don't know why you chose the back of your neck for your first tattoo, girl, but you got balls," Tiki joked as she put the finishing touches on her work.

"She MHB now. She better be able to take it," Tiffany said, laughing.

It was a celebration. Everyone toasted to the new member of the crew. She had definitely earned her spot when she saved Niya's life inside of Mayo's house, but it was Prada's grandmother who sealed the deal, opening up her heart to Alexus. This marked the start of a new life for Alexus. From this day forward, she was no longer considered a child. This was womanhood, and Alexus didn't see it happening any other way. She felt blessed to be part of a family who would die for her, a family who would kill for her, and, if need be, a family who would do time in prison for her. This was the unbreakable bond.

Niya was the first to start the chant. "Am I my sister's keeper?"

"Yes, I am!" the others responded.

"Am I my sister's keeper?" Niya asked again, even louder.

"Yes, I am!" the ladies responded loud enough to match Niya's voice.

"Then what true sisterhood has put together, let no man take under!"

***

"You look tired. You should go home and get some rest," Detective Rose leaned over and told Butler, who was falling asleep at his computer.

"I done looked up just about every logo, and I still didn't come across anybody with *MHB* tatted on them. I mean, I got *MOB*, *MMG*, and *MBM*, but when it comes to *MHB*, it's like looking for a ghost," Butler said, rubbing his eyes. He was starting to think that the information Mayo had given him was false.

Mayo couldn't give him Niya's name, because he didn't know it. He only knew Prada's, and the information Mike told him about MHB. In a city of a million people, finding MHB was like looking for a needle in a haystack. The only thing about Detective Butler was that once he had his eyes set on something, he was gonna chase it until he got it.

Niya jumped out of the shower and tried to creep into the bed with Chad as if she didn't just come in the house at two in the morning. She was under the false impression that she was going to give Chad a shot of pussy to make up for the bullshit she'd been doing lately. She slid under the covers completely naked and grabbed his shoulder to try to roll him over.

Chad pressed his body in the other direction. Niya kept pulling, until he gave in. Chad finally turned over and looked at her. He didn't have any sign in his eyes of being asleep.

Niya leaned in to kiss him anyway, but Chad didn't move his lips. He just looked Niya in her eyes, regretting having to say what he had to tell her. "This not working anymore, Ni. I think we both need a break," he said, wiping her lip gloss off his lips.

"What? Boy, you better stop playin'," she said, leaning in for another kiss.

This time, Chad moved his whole face out of the way. Niya leaned back with a curious look on her face. She still wasn't sure if he was joking. "Are you serious?" she asked, seeing that Chad wasn't smiling.

"Look, Ni, we going in two different directions. I love you, I really do, but I'm not going to play second fiddle to another man, woman, or the streets. I'm tired of coming in here having to cook and clean like I'm some bitch-ass nigga who don't work. I'm tired of having to take care of the kids like they don't have a mother. Whatever it is that got a hold on you in them streets has a tighter one than me, and I'm through fighting it for your time and attention. We had a good run. We got beautiful twins out of the deal—"

"Wait, wait, Chad," Niya pleaded, now realizing that this wasn't a game.

Chad was at the end of his rope with Niya. He felt that he'd already been there before with Gwen, when he decided to get out of the game. Niya was doing the same stuff Gwen was doing, by staying out late, coming home with money he knew he didn't give her, and having something Chad identified as guilt sex. That was the kind of sex Niya was sitting there trying to have right now.

"You can have the house."

"Please don't do this, babe," Niya pleaded.

"You can keep the car," Chad said, yelling over her. "And I'll come see the twins—"

"Chad. Chad, please," Niya cried. "I'm sorry."

"Niya, trust me, we both need this time and space. If not, we could lose each other forever," he said then rolled back over. Chad didn't want to see the hurt on her face. He had thought about this long and hard, and as much as it was hurting him to do it, he really felt like it was for the best, before he started to have a real hatred for Niya based on how she was treating him and the twins.

Niya wiped the tears from her eyes and then climbed out of the bed. She was crushed, and she knew that their relationship was at a breaking point. When Chad said something, he meant it, and the cold look he had in his eyes said a thousand words by itself.

Niya got up and hesitantly put some clothes on. She went inside the twins' bedroom and hugged and kissed Jahmil. She then gently pulled the covers off Jasmine's sleeping body. Niya crawled in beside her and held her as tight as she could without waking her, and then she cried herself to sleep.

Chapter 8

Curious as to why the crackhead traffic had slowed down, Tiffany stepped outside of the trap house to see what was going on. She looked up and down the street, which was like a ghost town. That was odd, because yesterday Tiffany and Diamond couldn't bag up the crack fast enough. The trap house had made a 360-degree turnaround from doing a hundred dollars a day to now moving over $4,500 in a shift, and that was all in a little over a week.

Tiffany was a little relieved when she saw a crackhead on the next street over, walking toward the trap house. That quickly changed when the crackhead made a beeline at the corner. It was as if somebody was calling for him. Tiffany went back into the house and grabbed the .40-cal off the table and stuffed it in her waist before heading back out the door.

When she got to the corner of the block, she was shocked to see about ten crackheads lined up against the wall and a young cat going down the line, serving each of them with a little bag of crack. As they copped their crack and left, more heads walked up, doing the same thing. Tiff went straight into gangsta mode on him.

"Yo, my man, ya gotta take dat shit somewhere else," Tiffany said, walking up on the young dealer.

"Shawty, you got me fucked up. I do my thing wherever the fuck I want," the guy said as he continued to make sales.

"Dis ain't the stuff from your house?" one of the crackheads asked, looking over at Tiffany.

"Naw, that ain't from our spot," Tiffany replied. "If y'all want that real shit we known for, then go up the street," Tiffany yelled out to the crackheads who were waiting in line.

Just about all of them came off the wall and headed up the street, despite the younger dealer trying to push them back. The commotion on the corner caught the attention of a couple of guys standing on their porches.

"Shawty, what the fuck is your problem? Yo, you got me fucked up," the guy said, stepping closer to Tiffany like he was about to do something.

For Tiffany, the talking was over at that point. She pulled the .40-cal from her hip without hesitation and squeezed off a round into his leg. The young dealer grabbed his thigh, but at the same time tried to reach out to grab Tiffany. She let off another round into his gut, backing him off her. When he dropped to the ground, Tiffany stood over him and was about to finish him off. She looked around and could see a couple of people standing on their porches. It didn't matter. That was just what she wanted. She had to make an example out of somebody in order to establish dominance in this area.

"Don't kill me. Don't kill me," the young cat screamed out, looking down the barrel of her gun.

Diamond turned the corner in the nick of time, running up and grabbing Tiffany right at the moment she squeezed the trigger. The bullet just missed his head, hitting the sidewalk instead.

"No. No," Diamond said, pushing Tiffany back up the street.

The young dealer got up and jumped into his car, hoping Tiffany didn't follow. The dudes who were standing on the porch looked on, impressed with Tiffany's work. If they really wanted to, they could have killed her before she even pulled her gun out, but they really didn't like the young cat she had shot anyway. Tiffany had gained the respect needed to operate in that neighborhood.

Gwen pulled into the parking lot of South Park Mall where she was supposed to meet up with the new connect Mayo had promised. She was accompanied by Rell and Browny, two of Mayo's boys who he'd put at Gwen's disposal for the time being. These were two men who stayed strapped and wouldn't hesitate to kill anything moving. Mayo knew this was exactly what Gwen needed.

She leaned against her car with Browny and Rell within a few feet of her, just in case they had to get her out of there in the event something went wrong. It wasn't that they didn't trust the connect; it was more of being on point.

"I hate when people are late," Gwen said, looking down at her watch.

As soon as she said that, two SUVs pulled into the parking lot; both were Yukons and both were all-black with tinted windows. They stopped right in front of Gwen's BMW, making her and her two bodyguards look small. The driver of the second SUV got out of the truck, went to the back door, and opened it. He motioned for Gwen to get in the back seat without even saying a word. Browny and Rell stood between Gwen and the truck like they weren't about to let her get in. Both men had their guns visible.

"I don't have all day," a voice yelled from the back seat.

Shockingly, the voice sounded like that of a woman, catching Gwen's attention. She squeezed from between her two guard dogs, motioning to them that it was cool.

When Gwen got into the truck, she was greeted by a young, light-complexioned, long-haired woman. She was very attractive, and she was dressed in business attire. Gwen couldn't believe the boss was actually a chick, and for a second she felt inspired.

"You must be Gwen. I heard some good things about you," the woman said.

"Yeah, likewise," Gwen shot back.

"By the way, my name is Brianna," the lady in the truck said, extending her hand for a shake.

Standing outside of the truck, Browny and Rell stood attentive, as well as Brianna's men, who had gotten out of the first SUV. It was like a staring match between them, and everybody seemed to have their chests poking out to show dominance toward the other.

"Men." Brianna chuckled, looking out the window at them all. "That's what's wrong with the game now. It's got too much testosterone and not enough finesse."

Gwen looked out the window and smiled at the sight of all the mean faces everybody had on.

"So what can I do for you, Gwen?" Brianna said, getting back to business.

"Look, Ms. Brianna, I'ma be real wit' you. I know about drugs, but I never been on this level of play before," Gwen began. "All this is new to me, and I pretty much inherited this," she said.

Brianna smiled, thinking about how she, too, had inherited this life. She looked Gwen in her eyes with a look of concern and asked, "So is this something you really wanna do?"

"Yeah, I want this. I just wanna make it worth my while," she said, looking at Brianna. "I got 100K right now, so whatever you can do for me, I'ma make it happen as long as you look out for me."

Brianna admired Gwen's honesty. She saw a lot of herself in her. Gwen came humble and respectful, and that was a plus with Brianna.

"I normally charge anywhere between 25K to 30K for a key of cocaine," she said. "I don't even know you, Gwen, but I like you. You got the same look in ya eyes that I had five years ago when I was on my come-up." She chuckled.

The inside of the SUV got quiet for a moment as Brianna looked out of the window. Gwen didn't know what to think. "Gwen, I'ma give you five keys for that 100K. What you do after that will determine whether you really wanna be in the game," Brianna said, breaking the silence.

Gwen didn't know how good she had it by paying 20K per key. Cocaine prices were at an all-time high. Brianna could have easily charged 30K a key to anybody else on the streets. Mayo was even paying 30K a key. It had to be a female thing.

"Sounds good to me," Gwen responded, pulling the money out of the knapsack she held. Brianna motioned for her to stop.

"Look, Gwen, I like you, but this will be the only conversation you will have directly with me about this business for a while. From now on, you will either meet with Kasey or my lady in charge, Selena. Once we get some time and trust under our skirts, we will sit down again and discuss new terms if need be. Understood?"

Gwen shook her head to let Brianna know she comprehended her words. Everything in her being was telling her that this was the moment she had been waiting on. The life she so desired was about to be reality, and Brianna was going to be the woman to put her on.

Ralphy looked around a couple of times before jumping into the back seat of the unmarked car. He was a drug dealer turned informant and had been for a couple of years now. The information he gave normally led to an arrest and a conviction, which in turn gave him a free pass to sell drugs in Charlotte.

"Give me some good news, Ralphy," Detective Butler said, looking at him through his rearview mirror.

"Yeah, I got something good for you, but I need a favor from you."

"Yeah, yeah, we'll deal with the favors later, Ralphy. Just tell me what you got," Butler said.

"MHB stands for Money Hungry Bitches. It's a group of chicks who hustle in the neighborhood," Ralph informed them.

"What do you mean *hustle*?" Rose cut in, trying to get some clarity.

"Well, I know one of the chicks just opened up shop, selling H on Betty Ford Road. She might be small time, but business looks like it's picking up," Ralphy said.

The detectives looked at each other. They couldn't believe that they had just heard that a female was moving heroin, and on Betty Ford Road at that. If there was any truth to it, they knew from experience that she wasn't gonna last in that area very long.

"I need a name. Give me a name," Butler demanded.

"Niyesha . . . Nairobi . . . Niya . . . It's something like that," Ralphy said, unable to remember exactly what he had overheard somebody else call her. "I'll give you a call later with an exact on her name, but in the meantime, how about that favor that I need?" he asked with a smile.

"Yeah, what is it?" Butler questioned with a pissed look on his face.

"Man, really it ain't even a real favor. Shit, I'm looking out for y'all and being a good citizen with this one."

"Just spit it out!" Rose chimed in.

"Okay, okay. Well, it's this nigga named TJ who be hustling over on the east side. I got his address right here and his tag number," Ralphy continued while passing Butler the paper. "He keeps dope and guns on him always, and I know the nigga's a felon."

The detectives' eyes widened. "And what did this poor bastard do to you to make you such a concerned citizen that you would point us in his direction?" Rose asked.

Ralphy just smiled again, this time even wider. "The muthafucka been fucking with my baby mama, and I told the nigga I had something for his ass. The time he going to get when you niggas see him is just what that bitch-ass nigga need."

The loud sound of laughter caught both Mandy and Niya's attention as they headed out the front door of Mandy's apartment. Niya looked down the street. She could see a crowd of her new workers huddled in a circle, cheering on whatever was going on in the middle. Niya, curious and wanting to get some control and order over her block, went to go break up the fun. To her, this was not playtime, this was money time, and she needed these people to understand that.

When she got over to the crowd, she couldn't believe what she was looking at. She had to do a double take just to make sure that it was real. On all fours in a doggie-style position, a dopefiend named Chelsey was allowing Max, a red-nosed pit bull, to hit her from the back. Max was humping away like he'd been there before. What was even crazier was the look on Chelsey's face. It actually looked like she was enjoying it. As much as Niya tried to hold her composure, she couldn't.

Niya screamed out, "Get that fucking dog off her. Are you niggas crazy?"

She and Mandy started trying to break up the situation. Everybody was laughing, but Niya didn't see anything funny. She was still cussing and directing the men to break that shit up. Two of her workers began trying to pry Max off Chelsey's back, but he was putting up a strong fight. Niya and Mandy pulled Chelsey off the ground, while the guys were finally able to free her from Max's grip. Niya couldn't help but to wonder what would make a woman allow herself to do such a thing.

Then she noticed the dime bag of smack Chelsey tightly held in her right hand. Niya was almost ashamed, now realizing that it was the dope she was selling that had this black woman, a mother and elder, doing what she was doing. While everyone else continued to laugh and joke after Chelsey got up and left, Niya was coming to understand that if a woman would stoop this low, then what would a man or woman do for the goods she now held? It was at this point she knew she needed to step up security on herself and her girls. The streets had already cost her one friend, and she was determined not to lose another.

In just three days, the block was moving over eight grand a day. "Yo, we're gonna have to find another stash house," Niya suggested as she and Mandy got into the car.

"Yeah, I agree. And we're gonna have to start having shifts for our workers, so we can put a hold on the excess people around doing nothin' but making us miss money," Mandy said, nodding to a dopefiend standing up against the wall, waiting to cop his drugs.

It was understood that Niya needed to put the clamps on just a little tighter. Her presence was there, but it needed to be felt. At any given time, somebody on the block might think about tryin' his hand at robbing Mandy and Niya. It wasn't just the workers on the block; it was also the dopefiends who Niya had to worry about. She'd just witnessed with her own eyes that they would do just about anything for a hit. Killing her wasn't something that was too far off.

***

Gwen was paranoid as hell, driving back home with five keys in her truck and a .45 automatic under her seat. She made sure that she was careful when approaching traffic lights and using her turn signals properly. Rell and Browny drove behind her the whole time, just in case they had to become a decoy for the cops. Gwen picked up her phone and called Browny to let him know she had something else to take care of. He was cool with it and just stayed behind her. Gwen really couldn't afford to make any stops right now, but this would be quick, plus it was en route to her spot.

She was about to be doing a lot of cooking and bagging, so she needed to go to Premiums, a store that sold just about everything that a drug dealer needed. As she drove down the street, Gwen happened to look over and see a familiar car parked right in front of the store. She knew that it was Niya's Range Rover by the Carolina Panthers sticker attached to the back window. Gwen drove by and glanced at the license plate to be sure, and saw that she was right.

"Dis bitch," Gwen mumbled to herself as she looked for a good spot to park.

There hadn't been a day that went by lately that Gwen didn't think about the attempted kidnapping on her, Niya murdering her boyfriend, and then catching Niya talking to Master. She was all but sure Niya was the one who was behind the kidnapping. The only reason Gwen hadn't run up to Niya's house and blown her head off was on the strength of Chad and the twins being in the house, but Gwen vowed to herself that if she ever caught Niya out on the streets, they would finish what they had started in the basement of the church. This time, she was going to deal with her in accordance with the laws of the streets.

Gwen parked at the corner of the road, making sure nothing was blocking her in. Browny and Rell pulled up behind her. Neither had any idea what Gwen was up to. Gwen grabbed her .45 from under her seat, checked and made sure there was a bullet in the chamber, and then exited her vehicle. She didn't have any plans to shoot Niya, but she felt like she needed to be prepared just in case Niya was ready to take it there.

Rell could see the change in her behavior, plus the .45 she had tucked in her pants.

"Yo, shawty, you good?" Browny asked, also seeing the look Gwen had in her eyes.

"Just come on," she said, heading for the store.

She could see Niya and another female coming out of the store together. Gwen started jogging to close the distance between them. Browny and Rell were right behind her. Pedestrians on the sidewalk started moving out of their way, noticing that it looked like something was about to go down.

Then it happened. Gwen and Niya made eye contact as Niya walked around to the driver's side of her car. Mandy had also seen Gwen and her two goons approaching, and she quickly went for her gun. Niya tried to tell her to hold up. Although she knew Gwen wanted to start some shit, she also knew that she wasn't about to take it to gunplay. Besides the fact that they had Chad and the children in common, they were both still MHB to their deaths. This was like a family who could fight each other every day but would never think of killing one another, and would kill someone else who did think of harming either.

Niya's cry was too late, because Mandy was already pulling the trigger. Gwen had caught a glimpse of the shine of Mandy's chrome .38 semiautomatic pistol, and had pulled her own Glock .40, returning fire. Everything went into slow motion.

"Oh, shit. Mandy, get down," Niya yelled, slipping behind the car.

Boom! Boom! Boom! Pop! Boom! Boom! Boom!

Gwen was letting her pistol scream in Mandy's direction. Browny and Rell were also letting it fly.

Niya got low behind her truck, while Mandy took cover behind another parked car. Niya reached down, pulled her pistol, and began firing as well. All she could do was reach the gun over the truck and keep pulling the trigger. She and Mandy were sitting ducks, because they were caught off-guard. The sounds of bullets knocking holes in the truck flooded the street, that along with people running and screaming trying to get out of the way. In a bold attempt, Niya reached up and grabbed the driver's side door handle, trying to get it open. A bullet crashing through the window forced her to yank her hand back.

Seeing what Niya had tried to do, Mandy crawled to her feet and shot out from behind the parked car and made her way over to where Niya was. Mandy reached up and grabbed the back side door handle, opened it, reached in under the seat, and grabbed a shotgun. She jumped up and started returning fire, covering Niya so that she could get her bearings and possibly get the truck started so they could get the hell outta there.

By the time Niya got the truck started, Gwen was already retreating to her car. She screamed for Rell and Browny to follow. Mad as hell, Niya placed the truck in drive. She yelled for Mandy to jump in. As soon as she was sure Mandy was securely in the truck, she took off out of the parking lot.

"Who da fuck was that?" Mandy yelled, climbing out of the back seat into the passenger's side of the Range.

Niya couldn't believe what had just happened. Never in a million years did she think that it would come to this, but now there was only one person that could save Gwen, and that was God. "That was a fuckin' ghost," Niya said, speeding the truck down the narrow road. "That was a muthafuckin' ghost," she repeated.

Mandy looked down and saw a red spot on Niya's shirt. With her adrenaline still pumping, Niya didn't realize that she had been shot. It wasn't until Mandy said something that the burning sensation began. She reached down and lifted up her shirt to see a hole the size of a dime in her stomach.

Detective Rose and Detective Butler took a ride down on Betty Ford Road out of curiosity. They parked a couple of blocks away so they wouldn't draw any attention to themselves. Right off the bat, they noticed the heavy traffic of dopefiends going to and coming from an off street. It was almost impossible without getting close to see who they were getting their stuff from.

"I think our boy Ralphy was right about this one," Butler said.

Betty Ford was a little more active than it usually was. Ever since Master was murdered, the violence had gone down, and it had created a spike in the financial department.

The dispatcher screaming over the radio caught the detectives' attention. "Shots fired! Shots fired! All available units to Cedar Street," the dispatcher announced.

Rose looked over at Butler with a smile on her face. She knew he couldn't resist responding to the call, even though he tried to play it cool.

"What?" he said, looking at her like he wasn't that interested in the call.

Rose put her head up and back-counted from five. She didn't get to three before Butler started up the car and pulled off. His hunger for action wouldn't let him sit there any longer.

Chapter 9

Mayo sat in the dayroom staring up at the TV as Judge Mathis was giving some poor sucker a rundown on being a man. It was hard for him to keep his mind occupied, because he hadn't heard anything back from his lawyer since he had given the info on Niya and MHB. Also, Gwen hadn't been back to see him, he still didn't have a paid lawyer, Gwen's phone was turned off, Browny and Rell weren't answering their phones, the detectives had been giving him the runaround, and on top of all that, he was dead broke. He couldn't even buy a ramen noodle soup, and it seemed like his problems were only getting worse.

"Homeboy, let me holla at you for a second," a voice said from behind, followed by a tap on Mayo's shoulder.

Mayo turned around to see a skinny, five foot seven inch, 150-pound kid standing behind him. The young man was brown-skinned and had the image of a crown tatted under his right eye. He didn't pose a threat at all, and at first Mayo sort of brushed him off, not really feeling like being bothered.

"Damn, homeboy, you ain't hear me?" the young thug said, this time in a little more aggressive way.

Mayo jumped up, irritated and ready to set this young'un straight. He stood in front of him with a look that said, "Is this what you wanted?" The young kid started walking down the hall toward Mayo's cell. Mayo followed, and so did all the other eyes in the unit. Everybody on the pad knew that li'l Terry was wild. He was small, but he put in big work.

"Fuck you want, homie?" Mayo snapped once he got into the cell.

As soon as he spoke, Terry started swinging. Mayo outweighed him by more than seventy pounds, so he proceeded to toss Terry halfway across the cell, then slammed him to the ground with ease. However, what Terry lacked in weight he made up for when he pulled an eight-inch flat knife from his boot. At first Mayo didn't realize he was getting stabbed. It felt more like someone was pinching him, but then he saw the knife in Terry's hand with blood all over it. He began to feel his heart rate increase, and his breath was shortening.

Mayo kept trying to throw punches, but his vision was becoming blurry. The fight continued, or rather the stabbing continued, because Terry just kept poking and poking Mayo every time Mayo threw a punch.

The loss of blood was starting to take its toll on Mayo. He knew that if he didn't get out of that cell, Terry was going to kill him. He took a couple more punctures from Terry, but he made it to the door, pushing his way out of it and onto the pad. There was blood everywhere.

The guard on the unit saw Mayo's orange county jail jumpsuit covered with blood and quickly pressed the emergency response button. Within seconds, ten officers strapped with vests and beanbag guns rushed the unit.

The doctor entered the room with Niya's chart in his hand. The bullet went in and out, missing all of her organs but damaging a lot of tissue and nerves. "You're gonna make a full recovery, Niya. Just try to get some rest," the doctor said before leaving the room.

Niya lay in the hospital bed and explained everything about Gwen and the shooting. Diamond, Tiffany, and

Alexus couldn't believe it. They didn't understand why Gwen would go this far. Niya couldn't understand it either. In her eyes, the last beef they had was about Prada's death, but the fight in the bathroom was the end result of that. It wasn't cause for Niya taking a bullet in the gut.

"So now what?" Diamond asked.

"You already know what gotta happen," Tiffany cut in.

"Naw, naw. Whatever the beef is, it's between me and Gwen. I'm not getting the crew in the middle."

"Shit, if something was done to you, we in the middle," Alexus added.

Niya could appreciate her loyalty, but all the same she knew Alexus wasn't aware of the love she and Gwen once had for each other, or the family connection they shared. "Thanks for your concern, baby girl, but I'ma take care of that. Y'all just keep doin' what y'all been doin'," Niya instructed. Unfortunately, Niya didn't have the slightest idea that Gwen was holding her accountable for JR's death and the attempted kidnapping.

"I know that now isn't really a good time, but I wanted to let you know where we are at with the work," Diamond said, pulling up a chair next to Niya's bed.

"Nah, it's cool," Niya said, a bit curious about the progress anyway.

"Girl, this shit is movin' fast," Diamond said excitedly. "By Sunday, we will be done sold a whole key, and the traffic is only picking up."

"Yeah, soon we are gonna have to find a plug, Ni," Tiffany cut in. "I know a couple niggas, but I really don't trust them like that," she continued.

Up until now, Niya hadn't thought about what she was going to do once all of the work was gone. At the pace Betty Ford was moving, she too was going to have to find a heroin connect. Niya didn't know one person who sold heroin in weight, besides the people they had robbed, and there was no way she could go to any of them. The more Niya thought about it, there was only one person who came to mind who may be able to help her.

"Don't worry about it. I think I know somebody who can help us," Niya said. "I just got to get out of this damn hospital before I go crazy," she joked.

Butler and Rose raced through the hospital.

It was hospital policy that medical staff had to inform law enforcement when someone was being treated for a gunshot wound. Niya had come in late in the day, and it was busy around that time, so staff didn't get around to reporting it until the following day.

"Yeah, two people came in with gunshot wounds yesterday," the nurse told Butler. "One was a Mr. Alexander, who has already been released."

"Damn it," Butler yelled in frustration, looking up and down the hall. He knew that generally when there was a shooting victim there was a major crime involved.

"Well, can you give us his address or something?" Rose asked.

"He didn't have any medical insurance, and per hospital policy, once he was stabilized, he was discharged. However, the other shooting victim is still here; in fact, she is located on this floor."

Butler and Rose made their way down the hall and around the corner to room 208. When they got to the room, Niya's bed was surrounded by Alexus, Diamond, and Tiffany. Mandy was sitting in the chair off to the side. Butler started to enter the room but stopped midstride when he noticed something that froze him. He saw the letters *MHB* clear as day on the back of Alexus's neck. The tattoo still looked fresh, so it stuck out.

"Can I help you with something?" Mandy said, looking at Butler and Rose standing in the doorway.

Rose hadn't seen the tattoo yet, so Butler had to back her up out of the room before they drew any more attention to themselves. The girls looked over but didn't say anything.

"Sorry, we got the wrong room," Butler said, backing out.

"Tom, what's goin' on? Hey, Tom, what's goin' on?" Rose asked as she trailed behind Detective Butler.

Butler didn't even answer her at first. His brain was racing a million miles per second, and everything had properly registered before he could say something. He walked back up to the nurses' station and asked for the doctor who saw Niya. Rose was still lost. She didn't know what was going on, but she could see the excitement in Butler's eyes.

"Tom," she said, grabbing hold of him and making him face her. "What the hell is goin' on?" she asked.

"I just saw *MHB* tattooed on one of those girls in there," Butler told Rose. "It was on the back of her neck, clear as day."

"Well, let's see what she knows," Rose said, turning around in an attempt to go back to the room.

"No, no, no, no, no," Butler said, grabbing and pulling Rose back. "This is our chance to get to the bottom of MHB. I don't wanna jump the gun on this one. Now that we got 'em, let's do our homework," Butler advised.

Rose caught on fast. This was about to turn into a full-fledged investigation, and given the circumstances of the latest string of crimes concerning MHB, this case had the potential of becoming something big. Rose and Butler both needed this kind of boost in their careers. For now, all the detectives had to do was sit back and see how it all unfolded.

***

Mayo lay on the hospital bed, handcuffed to the rail. Three guards secured his room while doctors worked on him. The stabbing was vicious. Terry managed to collapse one of his lungs in the brutal assault. Altogether, Mayo had about eighteen holes in him, ten of which required stitches. He'd come to find out Terry was part of the 704 Kings, a gang that was well aware of the $50,000 Niya and MHB had placed on Mayo's head. They had intended to cash in, and if Mayo hadn't made his way out of that cell, they would have certainly done so. Terry's whole intent was to kill Mayo, and he was about two centimeters away from doing it.

Chapter 10

"Where da hell are you goin'?" Chad joked, watching Gwen getting dressed in the mirror. She looked sexy as hell, he admitted to himself, seeing how crazy her body looked in the black-and-white Dolce & Gabbana strapless dress. The gold metallic nappa sandals made her already fat ass poke out even more. Chad had almost forgotten that she wasn't his girl, and he was about to make her go and change.

"Boy, I'm grown. I'm takin' my ass to the club tonight," she said, smacking her right butt cheek.

Chad looked at her and smiled. It had been a while since he had been out to a club, and he was damn near tempted to go too, but the reality of babysitting duties set in. He wasn't going nowhere with Zion asleep in the other room. That was part of the price that he had to pay for choosing Gwen's place to camp out while he and Niya took their break from each other.

Chad had been there for over two weeks, trying to get his mind right. He hadn't even called Niya the whole time. He knew the twins were fine, because Niya would have called him if something had happened. Gwen hadn't volunteered to tell Chad about her run-in with Niya, and since she was unaware that Niya had been hit, neither knew about her gunshot wound.

"You been cooped up in this house all week, so tomorrow I'ma take my boys out," Gwen said, walking over to the bed and climbing on top of Chad.

Chad was loving the attention that he was getting from Gwen. Niya hadn't made him feel this important in a long time, and that's probably why he hadn't left yet. For a minute, it felt like old times, minus Chad being in the game. It was crazy how in a few days of constantly being around each other, Gwen and Chad just clicked back in to their old selves. It was less than a month ago that JR was alive, and not even his recent death could affect the bond that had been built over the past ten years. Gwen had loved JR, and at times she missed him dearly, but there wasn't a man alive or dead she loved more than Chad. Chad also still had a significant amount of love for Gwen in his heart. She was the first love of his life, and had given birth to his first child. For that, she would always have a reserved spot in his heart.

"Make sure you bring ya ass home at a reasonable hour," Chad said, smacking Gwen's ass as she straddled him.

"Yes, daddy." She chuckled, leaning in and giving him a nice, soft, slow, passionate kiss.

She could feel his dick getting hard through his sweatpants. She knew that if she sat there any longer, she wasn't going anywhere that night. Gwen leaned in and gave him one more kiss, then jumped up and ran out the door before Chad could grab her and change her mind.

Butler stood in front of the chalkboard with little sticky pads, writing down and pinning evidence. The main topic and probably the only topic was MHB. Within a couple of days, he had managed to take photos of everyone who was in Niya's hospital room, including Niya herself. The doctor who was treating Niya at that time confirmed for Detective Butler that she had an *MHB* tattoo on her wrist. So far, out of all the women, Butler had only found her with

MHB on her wrist. That matched up with what Mayo had told them about JR's murderer as having an *MHB* tat on her wrist, and Niya was placed at the top of the pyramid.

Hospital records provided her first and last name, and almost everything else personal about her life. It was already understood that this whole case was going to be built around Niya, and anybody else who was under MHB was going to be feeling the heat.

Club Onyx was blazing, but it was as if everything stopped when Gwen walked through the door. This was her stomping ground, and all eyes were on her. Tagging along right behind her were Browny and Rell, doing what they did best, which was protection. A lot of people thought that she was there to party, and in a sense she was, but at the same time she was there on business. Every drug dealer from Durham to Fayetteville was there, and this was her time to try to lock people in. Brianna was a hell of a connect, and in two weeks of hustling nonstop, Gwen was ready to cop again, this time even more than what she'd purchased before. She pretty much had taken Mayo's clientele and branched out a little further, with the small clients she already had.

"Damn, shawty, I been tryin' to holla at you for a minute now," Boss Hog yelled over the music. He had Durham on lockdown, but the prices he was paying were too high. He was paying 26K per key, and he was buying anywhere from five to ten keys every couple of weeks. If Gwen charged him 23K per key and he bought five in one week, that was a 15K come-up a week for Gwen, because she was only paying 20K a key. If she could do that with five to ten dealers on a daily basis, Gwen wouldn't have to worry about selling nickles and dimes. She could just sell weight.

After a brief discussion, numbers were exchanged, and just like that, Gwen booked another customer. This was her real purpose for being there that night; that and a little bit of dancing wouldn't hurt. She did that until her feet started hurting, then straight to the VIP booth she went.

"Yo, you got a couple niggas who wanna holla at you over at the bar," Browny said, coming into the VIP booth with Gwen.

"Tell them I'll be over there in a few minutes," Gwen said, pouring herself a shot of Patrón.

Gwen sat in the VIP area, taking in the atmosphere. Everything was going good in her life. She was getting money, she had Chad at the house, and she was on the verge of putting the whole of North Carolina on her back. There was only one thing missing in her life that she wished she had, and that was friends. That was one thing she missed about MHB and the sisterhood behind it. She missed having people who were there for her. She missed that ride or die bond with bitches who was willing to kill for you or take a bullet for you. She really was in need of some true friends she could share her good fortunes with.

Niya limped up the steps to the second floor of Gwen's apartment building. She was still sore from the bullet wound, so she had to take her time moving around, or the wound could possibly reopen. She had barely been out of the hospital a day, and she had decided that she was going to pay Gwen a visit and finish what Gwen had started.

Niya had tossed and turned on what to do with Gwen since she left the hospital. Although there was no doubt that they were no longer friends, she still had a tremendous love for Gwen. It just sat so far deep in her heart.

Niya would try with all her being to forget about it. Even with everything that had gone down with the Chad situation between the two ladies of MHB, Niya had to admit that she never thought it would come to this. She never in a million years believed it would come to one of them taking the other's life. They had fought together, cried together, and loved together.

Gwen was the only person with whom Niya was able to share the pain of growing up in a house where she was constantly being sexually abused by the boyfriend of her mother. Niya's mother had to have the relationship in secret, because Niya's father, Nate, along with his twin brother, Norman, were known killers. There wasn't anyone crazy enough to mess with one of their ladies. Not only would it be certain death for the man, but also Niya's mother. So, Fitzgerald, aka Fitz, would come through late at night and see her mother. He would always spend the night and go to work from their house.

Niya's mother would leave to catch the bus at 4:40 a.m. Once she was out the door, Fitz would make his way into Niya's room. The first time it happened, Niya wanted to tell someone, but Fitz had told her that her father would kill her mother for cheating on him. Niya was stuck. She didn't want her mother to die, and Fitz only took about five minutes, so she endured the abuse for nearly a year.

Then Fitz started to get violent, and one morning he choked Niya until she almost passed out because she wouldn't skip school and spend the day with him. Gwen was the first person to see the marks on Niya's neck. She questioned her best friend until Niya broke down and shared the agony of her situation. Gwen seemed like she was the one who was being abused; she was crying, and Niya could feel the anger steaming off of her. Gwen devised a plan where she would spend the night with Niya, and when Fitz came in that morning, they would make sure together that he never came in again.

The plan worked to perfection, because that was a morning that Fitz would never forget. The scars on his face and back wouldn't let him. When he climbed on top of Niya, she reached under the pillow and grabbed a small pocketknife Gwen had given her. She tried to stab Fitz in the neck, but he moved and the blade pierced his right cheek. The small, sharp blade nearly tore his face apart.

When he tried to retreat, Gwen was standing behind him with a knife of her own. They both commenced creating puncture wounds over his entire body. Fitz ran out of the house butt-ass naked, covered in blood. He never came back around, and when Niya saw him again a couple of years later, he quickly turned and ran.

Niya chuckled at the memory. Gwen was her girl then; but all that was now behind them, because Gwen had attempted to take her life. Niya was now at the point of kill or be killed, and she wasn't ready to leave this world. She pulled the Glock .40 from her Tory Burch bag, placed the bag by the stairway door, and proceeded toward the apartment. Niya had a key to Gwen's apartment ever since Gwen thought she lost them at Zion's birthday party a few months earlier. Niya had found them but didn't return them, in case she had to use them one day. This was gonna be that day.

Niya cocked a bullet into the chamber, walking down the hall, looking up at the apartment numbers. She got to Gwen's apartment and prayed that she hadn't changed the locks within the last eight months. It was like magic when she stuck the key in and unlocked the top lock, and then did the same to the bottom door handle.

She locked the door behind her once she was inside. The light from the kitchen provided just enough light for Niya to maneuver. She didn't give a fuck who was in there; all she wanted was Gwen. She knew that Zion wouldn't be there since it was the weekend. Even though she hadn't heard from Chad in nearly three weeks, she knew that he always picked up Zion on the weekends, and she was sure he was still doing the same.

As she walked down the hall, the first door she came to had a Spider-Man poster. She knew it had to be Zion's room, because that boy loved him some Peter Parker. She walked a little farther and passed by the bathroom. There was only one door left in the place. Niya pointed the Glock in front of her, turned the knob quietly, then eased the door open. She couldn't believe her eyes. It was as if her heart was being snatched out of her chest. She looked down into Gwen's bed, and there was Chad, sound asleep in nothing but a pair of Champion sweatpants.

Niya just stood there, almost dropping to her knees in front of the bed. She leaned against the wall for support. *He left me for her? He left me for this bitch? This is where his heart is at? This is the family he wanted?* Niya thought, looking down at him. No wonder Gwen had decided to raise the stakes and take it to gunplay. She wanted her out of the way, and from the looks of it, Chad did too. Niya was crushed. Her tears wouldn't stop flowing, and for a second, her weeping almost woke Chad up.

Her heartbreak quickly turned to anger, and then hatred. She wiped the tears from her eyes and walked closer to the bed, until she stood directly over of him. She pointed the gun at his head and then closed her eyes. She didn't want to see it, but she felt like it had to be done.

Visions of the twins popped into her mind, then visions of Chad playing with Zion. She had just witnessed Prada's funeral, and she wasn't sure if she could make it through Chad's; but then came the visions of Chad making love to Gwen in the very bed he was sleeping in. She had thoughts of him and Gwen laughing at her lying in the hospital bed. Fuck it; she wanted to see it. She wanted to see the bullet crash though his skull. He deserved it. He deserved everything that he was about to get.

Niya opened her eyes to see Chad one more time, only to find him looking back up at her. She mustered up everything she had in her to pull the trigger, but she couldn't. It killed her not to, but she didn't. The tears started flowing down her face once again. Chad didn't say a word. He couldn't, and the guilt was evident on his face. Niya didn't speak a sound either, and started slowly backing away from him, until she backed all the way out the door.

Chad didn't even attempt to get out of the bed. He had absolutely nothing he could think of to say that would set the situation right. He was also just relieved that Niya hadn't ended his life. For a moment, he truly believed he was a dead man. However, Chad did know that he was now dead in one place, and that was in Niya's heart.

"So what exactly are you asking me for?" the police chief, Rodney Monroe, asked, sitting at his desk.

"I'm pretty much asking you for everything," Butler said, taking a seat. "I need resources, money, manpower, every kind of surveillance equipment we got. Most importantly, I need to be the point man over this case," Butler pleaded.

Butler was asking for everything but the kitchen sink to put into this case. After seeing everything that MHB was involved in, he knew that this was going to be something big. He wanted to be the one to bring Niya and her crew down before the feds got a whiff of what was going on. The feds were like vultures when it came to indictments. They would sit back, wait for local or state authorities to gather the hard evidence, and then swoop down and take the whole case from them. Butler was trying his best to avoid that.

Chief Monroe gave in with a little more convincing, and at the end of the day, Butler got the green light to head the investigation. He was given everything that he requested and more. The police chief figured that one of two things were going to happen: either Butler was going to bring them down the biggest cases since BMF, or he was going to lose his job and probably his pension trying. The chief was fine with either.

Chapter 11

Gwen changed into the bathrobe provided by the day spa staff, then headed to the steam room where Selena was. She walked in and was blown away by Selena's body. With only a bikini bottom on, Selena stood in the corner of the room dripping with sweat. Her stomach was flat as a board and her breasts were perky and rounded perfectly. Her long black hair became a dark brownish color because it was wet, and she allowed for it to hang down over her shoulders. This was Gwen's second time meeting up with Selena since Brianna had handed her off to her right-hand chick.

"I'm not gay or anything, Selena, but damn you got a body on you, girl," Gwen said, taking her robe off and hanging it on the hook.

"Likewise," Selena replied when Gwen took off her bra. Gwen's body was crazy too; so much so that Selena had to ask Gwen if her breasts were real.

"So did you really want to come to the spa today, or was this ya way to see if I had on a wire?" Gwen joked.

"Trust me, Gwen, if you were a cop, I would know. We got more friends in the Charlotte Police Department than you can imagine." Selena smiled. "I honestly felt like being pampered today. In this business, it's hard to find some time, you know. Like now, even though I am trying to relax, I am still doin' business." She chuckled.

Gwen sat there and listened to Selena talk. People lied when they said that most pretty girls were dumb, because everything Selena was saying made sense. It got to the point where Gwen started taking mental notes of their conversation. In a way, Gwen was being schooled. That was big, considering that Selena and Brianna rarely took the time to talk to any of their clients; but Brianna had told Selena that there was something about Gwen she really liked, and Selena was feeling the same.

"So how much are you spending this time?" Selena said, getting back to business.

"Two hundred K," Gwen said, proud of her accomplishments over the past few weeks.

"Damn, girl, you on your shit for real, right," Selena responded.

First it was 100K, then 125K, then 150K, and now Gwen was spending 200K. She was definitely heading in the right direction, Selena thought. She didn't know that Gwen had this kind of hustle in her. It reminded Selena of how she used to be, and as long as she was moving the cocaine at this rate, Brianna was gonna keep feeding her.

Tiffany stood on the porch, watching the traffic going up and down the block. She wanted to make sure that there wasn't another hustler sitting in the wings, taking customers. The steady flow of traffic showed that the shooting in broad daylight had served its purpose.

"Damn, shawty, you run a tight ship around here," Toast said, walking up to the steps.

Instinctively, Tiffany reached for her back pocket, where Anna, her gun, rested. She wasn't sure if Toast was coming as friend or foe, and she wasn't about to take any chances.

"Slow down, baby girl. I ain't come here for dat," he joked, throwing his hands up.

His demeanor was calm, cool, and collected, and his tone of voice was smooth. Tiffany could also see the gun on his waist bulging through his shirt.

"So what you here fo'?" Tiffany asked, resting her hand on the butt of her gun.

Toast couldn't help but to think about how sexy she looked standing there. She had on a pink lace bra under a fresh wife beater, a pair of 7 For All Mankind jeans that showed off her curves, and a pair of Jordans. Her hair was pulled back into a ponytail, which brought out the few freckles she had on her light brown–skinned face. She was pretty, sassy, and a cold gunner: a combination Toast admired in a woman.

"Nah, shawty. I just wanted to let you know that I'm feelin' the whole takeover thing you got goin' on," Toast said, looking at one of the crackheads pass by him and go into the house.

"Yeah, well, I don't see too many niggas around here getting money. Why not jump at the opportunity?" Tiffany said.

Tiffany didn't have the slightest idea who she was talking to. Toast was a vet in the neighborhood. He was the reason it was safe to sell drugs on East Falls. He'd put more work in than anybody in the history of that block. The only reason he was letting Tiffany and Diamond do their thing was because it was what the hood needed. Not only were they bringing in more money through the block, they were also willing to bust their guns for the cause. Diamond and Tiffany were reppin' East Falls better than the men who were under Toast. The benefits were great if the girls stuck around.

Today was play day for both Niya's and Van's twins. The park was always the kids' favorite place to go, and believe it or not, it was also chill time for the moms as well.

"What's wrong wit' you, Ni?" Van asked, seeing the blank look she had on her face.

Van and Niya were cousins on their fathers' side. Neither had grown up with the two brothers in their life, but their grandmother, Mrs. Maggie, had always made sure that her grandchildren knew each other. She knew her two twin boys were womanizers, just like their father, and had stayed in and out of jail most of their lives. She always felt it was up to her to keep the family together. Niya and Van would always visit each other when they were young, and when the family reunion came around yearly, they were inseparable.

Once the issues of a new connect for the dope came up, Niya remembered the big trial her cousin Van's husband had gone through a couple of years ago. It was all on the news for like three weeks, and Van had spent the night with her a couple of times when she came to visit. Niya figured that even if her husband, Q, was no longer in the game, he could surely point her in the right direction, so she had reached out to big cuz and put the meeting together.

Van asked again, "Ni, what's wrong with you, baby girl?"

"I'm good," Niya said, picking her head up to see Van's son Khadir playing with Jahmil on the slide.

Niya had so much on her mind that she didn't know what to do or where to even begin. She felt like Chad had betrayed her and crossed the line of no return by being with Gwen. She couldn't help but think about what would have happened if she had pulled the trigger and killed him, and at that moment, she wished she had.

"I need a connect," Niya said, turning to look at Van.

"A connect on what?" Van asked.

"I need boy and girl," Niya said, speaking the street names for cocaine and heroin.

"You need it, or your husband needs it? I thought he was out of that life."

"He is, and he ain't my husband. The work is for me and my crew. I need it bad, cuzzo, or I'm about to lose my blocks quick."

Van was a hustler's wife, so she knew how important it was to keep a steady flow of dope coming in. There was always competition just waiting for a chance to take over your clientele. Niya was family, so there wasn't an option of saying no, but she still had to ask, "Since when did you get into that?"

"Since I'm out here by myself with those two mouths to feed," she spoke, pointing at her twins. She knew how to push her cousin's buttons. Niya knew that Van was as loyal as they came and there was nothing she wouldn't do for her kids or family—and she and her twins were that by blood.

Van smiled. She knew Niya had added that to seal the deal. "I see you still know how to work a bitch's heart," Van said, laughing. She and Niya high-fived each other and both broke out with loud sounds of amusement. "Exactly how much work are you looking for?" Van asked, already having someone in mind who could supply it.

Niya explained how she needed at least twenty to thirty kilos of both cocaine and heroin. Betty Ford Road was starting to go off the charts with numbers with heroin. Word traveled far and fast if some good dope was on the block. Dopefiends were coming from everywhere. Niya was moving every bit of 25K a shift, working three shifts a day, and that number was still growing on a day-to-day basis. Diamond and Tiffany had the trap house on East Falls doing around 20K a day, and that number was also growing.

"Well, when I get home, I'ma make a few phone calls for you. Just keep ya line open," Van told her. "Now on another note, what the hell is goin' on with you and hubby?" Van pried.

"Nothing I can't handle," Niya replied. "Nothing I can't overcome."

Van knew that was the response of someone who didn't want to talk about it, so she left that conversation alone and they started talking about the kids.

Mike looked across the table at Diamond, who was eating the dinner that he had cooked. He had spent half the day preparing the steak and baking the baked potatoes and apple pie. He went to three different stores to find the right apples for the pie, and went to the farmer's market to get the veggies for the salad. He got so much enjoyment watching Diamond devour the meal. He wasn't that hungry, and this wasn't really the reason he had asked Diamond over. He had something on his chest that needed to come off, something he had wanted to tell her for a while now. The feelings he had developed for her sort of blocked out his judgment, but this was something he felt she needed to know if their relationship was to go forward.

"I need to talk to you about something," Mike said, dropping his fork onto his plate.

Diamond looked up and could see the seriousness on his face. She thought for a second that he was about to ask her to marry him or something. The thought of him doing something like that made Diamond smile. Even though she would have to shoot him down, just hearing him ask would have been cute. Diamond stopped eating, crossed her hands, and rested her chin on them, giving Mike her undivided attention.

"I been tryin' to figure out how to tell you this for a while now," Mike began. "It's a guy named Mayo who wants you and ya friends dead," he said flat-out.

Diamond's chin almost hit the table when he said that. This was the last thing she'd expected him to say. "What did you just say?" Diamond asked, only wanting to make sure she heard him correctly.

"I said this guy I know named Mayo wants y'all dead," Mike repeated.

"Wait, wait. How da fuck do you know Mayo?" Diamond shot back with a confused look on her face.

Mike dropped his head and began explaining everything that had gone down from the start. He told her about the robbery plot, and how he knew that Mayo killed Prada. He told her about how Mayo knew about MHB. He even went so far as to tell Diamond that he was the one who told Mayo that she was MHB and that he saw Prada with them that night at the club.

Diamond just sat there at a loss for words. She really didn't know what to say. She had really started to like Mike; however, now he was sitting there telling her that he was part of the reason why Prada was dead.

"So you mean to tell me . . ." Diamond started to say but stopped. Tears began flowing down her cheeks.

"I'm sorry, Diamond," Mike pleaded. "I never—"

Diamond got up from the table and walked into the kitchen. Mike didn't even want to get up and go after her, knowing that he had really messed up. He just sat there with his head down. Diamond, on the other hand, was hot. She started thinking about Prada and how much she loved and missed her. Knowing that Mike had something to do with her death ripped through her heart. Then guilt started to set in as she thought that it was her fault. If she hadn't been so into Mike, he would have never been coming to pick her up, and he would have never seen Prada.

She looked up to the sky and pleaded with Prada for forgiveness. When her head dropped, she knew that there was only one way to make it right with her girl. Diamond took a deep breath, grabbed a larger knife out of the knife holder, and walked back into the dining room.

Mike sat at the table with his head in his hands. He was so far gone into his thoughts that he didn't even feel Diamond standing behind him. She grabbed a handful of his hair, pulled his head back, kissed him on his forehead, looked him square in the eyes, and sliced his neck from ear to ear. She had cut so deep into his throat that his Adam's apple was dangling. Blood squirted out across the table and pretty much all over the dining room.

Mike reached for his throat but stumbled out of his chair and onto the floor. He died in less than a minute from all the blood he had lost.

She grabbed a cloth napkin, wrapped up the knife, and placed it in her purse. Diamond stepped over his body, grabbed the rest of her things, and walked out the door. Tears were still flowing down her face. She had started developing real feelings for Mike, but those feelings could never be like the ones she had for Prada. Mike had to die, and she had to be the one to do it.

Chapter 12

Gwen pulled up to Washington Street and beeped the horn twice, like she always did when she was serving Dollaz. On cue, he came out of his trap house and got into the car. The fact that Gwen was now serving major weight and getting real money, it was making her a little peeved with coming to get these crumbs from Dollaz's small-time ass. She knew this was most likely going to be the last time, so she had a little arrogant demeanor when Dollaz got in the car.

"What you need, Dollaz?" Gwen asked as she looked out the window.

Dollaz noticed her new attitude but didn't pay it any mind. He just grinned to himself, digging in his pocket and pulling out a large stack of bills. Gwen still wasn't looking over at him. She was feeling herself a little too much.

"You can give me the usual, shawty," Dollaz said, reaching into his other pocket.

This time it wasn't money that he pulled out; it was his gun. Gwen still didn't know what was going on, until Dollaz stuffed the 9 mm into her gut. Gwen jumped, looking down to see the slide of an automatic weapon. She then looked up at Dollaz like he had lost his mind.

"Beep the horn," Dollaz commanded, nodding at the steering wheel.

"You must got a death wish," Gwen said, looking in the rearview mirror at Browny and Rell sitting behind her in their truck.

"Nah, I don't got a death wish, but if I gotta ask you one more time to beep the horn, I'ma make sure you'll never be able to have any more kids," he said, shoving the gun deeper into her side.

Gwen was mad as hell, but she did exactly what she was told to do. Once she tapped the horn, Tiffany came out of the trap house with an AK-15, running right up to the driver's side of the truck that Browny and Rell were in. Browny and Rell were tempted to bail out of the passenger's side, but had second thoughts about it when Alexus came out of the garage across the street with a chopper in her hands.

"Dollaz, you better kill me right now," Gwen said, looking at him with hatred in her eyes.

A tap at the driver's side window caused Gwen to turn around. Diamond stood there motioning for her to roll down the window. Gwen rolled her eyes and did so, having much to say.

"Dis how y'all ridin', D?" Gwen said, looking at Diamond with the same look she had for Dollaz.

"It ain't my call, baby girl. You'll get ya chance to holla at her," Diamond said, speaking of Niya. She then gave Dollaz a nod, signaling that he could exit the vehicle.

Gwen turned to look at Dollaz, but the last thing she saw was his fist. He almost took Gwen's head off with one punch, knocking her smack out cold. After stripping Browny and Rell of their guns, Diamond gave them ten seconds to get as far away as they could before Tiffany and Alexus opened fire on them. All you heard was the engine in their truck screaming down the street.

"Niya Walker, Alyah Shaw aka Alexus, Daneill Smith aka Diamond, and Tiffany Grey aka Tiff," Detective Butler announced, standing in front of a small classroom of plainclothes officers. "These are our subjects, and please don't let the innocent, pretty faces fool you," he warned. "You are not here to make any arrests right now. Our goals and objectives are to build an airtight case against each and every one of these women and anybody who is associated with them. You will all be broken up into teams and assigned to one of these women. If Ms. Walker decides to take a shit, you better be recording what kind of toilet paper that she used to wipe her ass. And if Daneill decides to have sex in the middle of the night, I wanna know the name she screamed out and what kind of sausages they had for breakfast the next morning," Butler yelled.

Once Butler was given the green light on this case, he turned into a drill sergeant. He wasn't about to screw this up for nothing or nobody. Dealing with people like Niya, Butler knew that he had to be at his best. He broke down everything from what kind of money they had to work with during the investigation all the way down to the names and phone numbers of all five informants he had working for them.

Butler was smart. He was starting this investigation right at the start of MHB's reign. This way he would be able to grow with them and watch their rise to the top before bringing them down. Butler knew one thing beyond a shadow of a doubt: it was a guaranteed fact that he and the rest of the officers in that room were in for a hell of a ride.

Jamaica was a vacation destination, and was one of the most beautiful places in the world, unless you left the tourist part of the island and went into the slums. If one of the tourists traveled too far away from the hotels and found their way into the hood, there was a slim chance he would make it back out of there alive.

Niya and Van rode on scooters down a longer dirt road through the outskirts of Kingston. Niya noticed the way the locals stared at them, and she prayed that the scooters wouldn't run out of gas before they made it to their destination. The dirt road led them into a small village. Van pulled over and parked right in front of an old, beat-down shack. Niya looked up at the shack and wondered how in the hell she was going to find a new connect here.

"Ingaaaa," Van yelled, getting off the scooter.

"Girl, me gon' kill ya callin' me name like dat." Inga laughed, coming out of the shack with open arms.

Niya just sat on the bike. She didn't know what to do, until Inga walked over to her and grabbed her by the arm.

"You must be Niya," Inga said, walking her into the shack.

The inside of the shack looked nothing like the outside. It was nicer and more Americanized than anything. Inga even had tea ready to serve. Niya took a look around and noticed that Van didn't come into the shack with them.

"Don't worry about Van; she out back wit' da dogs," Inga said, seeing the concern on Niya's face. "So, before we talk about anything, let's talk about business," Inga said, sipping her tea. "Why are you here?" she asked.

"Well, Inga, I'm looking for a connect. Not just any kind of connect. I need somebody who can consistently supply me with grade A cocaine for the best possible price," Niya explained. "I also need for this connect to supply me with heroin. Not just any heroin. I'm talking uncut, fresh-out-the-opium-plant type of work, and I need good prices on that as well," Niya said, sipping her tea.

"Damn, mon, Van was not playin' when she said you come direct." Inga chuckled. "Look, me gon' take real good care of you. Van my sista, and she say you family."

Inga got quiet for a minute. She sat back in her chair and put her finger on her chin. There was a lot to calculate, considering she was more than likely gonna have to get the cocaine and the heroin over to the States. "I can go as low as eighteen point five a key for the cocaine, minimum of ten key per purchase a trip," Inga said, sitting up in her chair.

"And what about the heroin?" Niya asked.

"Heroin come wit' a lot of problems. I gonna have to charge you a little more, but I give you de best, so you make ya money back. One hundred K a key is the best I can do right now," Inga said. "My people risk a lot bringing it to the States. You keep buying, we can talk about the price next time," Inga said in her Jamaican accent.

The numbers didn't sound that crazy at all to Niya. She had made close to 300K from one key of heroin, and Diamond brought back 50K off one key of cocaine. In her eyes, the math was cool and the prices were gonna get cheaper the more they bought.

"Yaw good in here?" Van said, coming back to the shack with two pit bull puppies in her hand.

Niya nodded her head with a satisfied smile on her face. "Yeah, we good. We are definitely good," Niya said, sipping on her tea.

Detective Butler got straight to business and had his team watching East Falls, Betty Ford Road, Niya's house, Diamond's spot, and Tiffany's apartment. The only place they didn't have surveillance on was Alexus's apartment. The surveillance team assigned to her never could seem to follow her around as much, because she used public transportation when she wasn't with the other girls.

Butler and Rose staked out Betty Ford Road personally. Butler had become infatuated with Niya and the way that she moved. He put her at the head of MHB, and he was determined to see to it that when it was all said and done, Niya would fall the hardest.

***

As soon as Niya and Van got off of the airplane, Niya's phone began to ring. It was a reminder that it was back to business, even though the two-day trip to Jamaica was business in itself. The first shipment was gonna be delivered in three days, and Niya couldn't wait.

"What's good?" Niya answered, seeing that it was Diamond calling.

"Yeah, everything taken care of," Diamond said then hung up the phone.

A big smile came over Niya's face. She had to quickly check it, though, because Van started asking questions. Niya knew that Van had met all the girls of MHB before, and she had a real liking for the realness of Gwen in particular. She also loved the sisterly bond the women had with each other, so Niya felt that Van would never understand why she was about to kill Gwen. For that reason, Van needed not to know anything that was going on.

Chad woke up from his sleep to the smell of smoke. It was so thick in the apartment he could hardly see. He jumped up from the bed and ran straight into the kitchen to see a frying pan on the stove engulfed in flames. He grabbed the pan and threw it into the sink then turned off the stove.

"Fuck is goin' on?" he mumbled to himself, looking around for the smoke detectors. The first thing that came to his mind was that Zion had tried to make something to eat and went back to bed while the food was cooking. Mad as hell, Chad steamed down the hall then busted into Zion's room, ready to whoop his ass. When he got there, the boy wasn't there.

"Zion," Chad yelled out in the house.

He called out his name a few more times, but still there wasn't any answer. He looked around the room and almost didn't notice the piece of yellow paper sitting on his pillow until he was about to leave the room. He picked up the paper and began reading. The contents of the letter were so severe it made him take a seat on Zion's bed. His knees became so weak he couldn't muster the strength to stand up.

Chapter 13

Gwen barely opened her swollen eyes, looking around trying to figure out where she was and how long she'd been there. She could taste the blood in her mouth as it seeped down her throat, and her hands became numb from the wire that bound her hands behind her back. As she looked around the room, she could tell that she was in a cellar or some type of basement of a house.

The sounds of footsteps crept through the cracks of the floor above her, and before she could yell to her abductors, the cellar door opened. It was no surprise when Niya made her way down the steps and walked over to the mattress Gwen was lying on. Niya had a large chrome .40-caliber in her hand, but at the same time, she seemed relaxed. She was calm and showed no signs of anger. In fact, she had a creepy little smirk on her face, as if to say, "Bitch, I got you!"

"Ch . . . Chad is gonna k . . . kill you, Niya," Gwen managed to utter out of her bloody mouth.

Niya just chuckled at Gwen's words, shaking her head as she walked up and squatted right next to Gwen's body. "Do you really think for one second that he's gonna miss you? You foul, Gwen, disloyal and ungrateful," Niya said, waving the gun in Gwen's face. "Not to mention the fact that you tried to kill me. You lucky it's not him down here ready to blow ya fuckin' head off."

"I didn't try to kill you, Niya. If I wanted you dead, I could have done it a long time ago," Gwen shot back in her final attempt to preserve her life.

Deep down inside, Gwen knew that this was her last ride. Too much had transpired over the past couple of weeks, and there was no other way this story could end. In an instant, Gwen could see her whole life pass her by, and the thought of Zion actually brought tears to her eyes. Even then, she didn't let 'em fall, determined not to let Niya see her in her weakest state.

"Fuck you, Niya," Gwen screamed through her bloody mouth. "No matter how hard you try, he will never love you the way that he loves me," Gwen said then spit a mouthful of blood in Niya's direction.

If it weren't for Niya's quick reaction, it would have hit her in the face. *The nerve of her,* she thought as she rose up over Gwen. "See, that's why it can only be one," Niya said, raising the gun to Gwen's head.

This was the end of the road for Gwen, and not even Jesus Himself could walk down the steps and stop Niya from pulling the trigger. Niya took the safety off, looked Gwen in her eyes, and took a deep breath.

"Good night, baby girl," Niya said.

The sound of the basement door swinging open temporarily grabbed Niya's attention. She looked up to see someone unexpected walking down the steps. It was like the whole world was caving in, but before she would let Chad change her mind about killing Gwen, she quickly focused her attention back on her. Now, anger showed all over her face. Her palms were sweaty, heart was racing, and her finger was on the trigger.

"Ni, don't shoot her," Chad yelled out. "Please, babe, I'm begging you."

Niya stopped and turned to face him. He had never begged her to do anything, and the tone in his voice sounded like he was scared of something or someone. Niya took her attention off Gwen for a moment to see what was going on with Chad. He only had one chance to speak before Niya put a bullet in Gwen's head.

"He got my son," Chad said, damn near breaking down. "Da nigga Mayo took my son, and she's the only one who can get him back."

"Noooo," Gwen yelled, hearing Chad. "My son. Oh, God, my Zion," Gwen cried, trying to wiggle out of the restraints.

"You kill her, you kill my son. You kill my son, then you might as well kill me," Chad said with a dead serious look in his eyes.

Niya didn't believe him at first, but then beyond his anger, Niya could see the hurt in his eyes. This changed everything. There was no way in hell that she was going to be able to pull the trigger. It would be killing three people with one bullet, a heavy price to pay for such a selfish act. She lowered her gun, tucked it into her back pocket, and headed for the steps. She stopped at Chad.

"For what it's worth, I hope you find ya son. Ya family needs you," Niya said, looking back at Gwen; then she turned around and went up the steps.

Those words coming from Niya's mouth were like a bullet. Niya and the twins were his family in his eyes, and they always had been. As bad as he wanted to run after Niya, he couldn't right now. He just had to worry about getting Zion back.

"Detective, we've got Niya and Tiffany leaving Niya's house, and it appears that Tiffany has a large-caliber rifle in her possession. Possibly an AK-47," the surveillance officer told Detective Butler over the radio.

"Do not engage. I repeat, do not engage," Butler yelled over the radio.

With the right lawyer, Tiffany wasn't gonna be facing that much time for the rifle. Butler thought that it was best that they just let her go for now, instead of risking the possibility of being exposed. It would be hard to investigate someone who knew that they were being watched by the police. It was still early in the investigation. Time was the only thing Butler was counting on having, and the more time MHB had, the deeper they were gonna dig their own graves.

The silence in the small two-bedroom apartment was so heavy that it was difficult to focus. Resting her head in her left palm, Gwen clicked the hammer of the empty .38 Special and focused on the sound to pass the time. The thump of the revolver clicking seemed to echo throughout the kitchen. Chad, meanwhile, sat in the living room on the couch with his head in his hands. He would look up every few minutes to check the display on the cell phone, which rested on the table. Both he and Gwen were silently praying that the phone would ring at any moment. The house held an odor that emanated from both of them. Hygiene had been the furthest thought from their minds. Zion had been gone for nearly two days, and they had not moved since being advised of his abduction.

Gwen pulled the trigger of the gun several times. The sound of the chamber clicking was replaced with Zion's voice crying out to her. Images of him tied up in a basement, alone, scared, hurt, or possibly worse crowded her headspace. He was her only child, the center of her life, and the reason for her existence. Her chest became tight, the room seemed to shrink in size, and the air became thinner. The only thing that Gwen could clearly focus on was the handgun and the bullets that were lined up on the glass top of the table.

Zion's voice echoed in her head. She placed a bullet into the cylinder and positioned the barrel against her chest. She closed her eyes and touched the trigger, longing for the heat of a bullet to end the ache that now existed in her heart. Her baby was gone, due to her own greed, ego, and selfishness. Without him, there was no need to keep breathing. She moved the barrel of the gun until it rested against her temple. She took a deep breath.

"What the hell you doin'?" Chad said softly as he walked into the kitchen. He looked at Gwen with the firearm raised to her head and sat down slowly next to her. He knew one wrong word or move could result in her brains being sent all over the kitchen. "Look, I don't know what's running through ya mind right now, but our son needs you," Chad said in a low tone. "I need you," he said in a louder, sincere voice. "We gotta be smarter than this, Gwen, in order to get him back. This shit right here, this ain't gon' get him back. We gotta get our heads straight. Come on, baby, fight it. We gon' get our boy back, but it's gonna take both of us."

The tears began to pour down Gwen's face. She heard his words, but they didn't stop the pain that was in her heart. She didn't know what to do; she had never felt this helpless before. She wanted her baby back. Having him in her arms or dying would be the only way to stop the pain. She applied pressure to the trigger.

"Gwen, please don't do this and leave me here alone," Chad pleaded softly.

Chad searched for Gwen in her eyes, but they were blank. Her soul was missing. He inched closer to her. Her mind had shut down, and he knew it was only a matter of seconds before her finger squeezed the trigger. Time stopped as he reached for the gun.

Before he could take the gun, the sound of the metal clicking echoed in the room. He yelled as he snatched the gun from her hand, and she fell back onto the floor. "Fuck, Gwen, fuck! No!"

He sobbed as he lay on top of her. He was afraid to turn and look at her. He had blown plenty of brains out of niggas without blinking, but he knew he couldn't handle seeing Gwen like that.

The impact had broken the chair. Tears ran down his face as he looked at the gun in his hand. Shit, he had lost his son and his love; the pain was too much. He felt arms around his shoulder and breath on his neck. He turned his head. Gwen was sobbing against his shoulder. He opened the cylinder to see the bullet still resting in the chamber.

"Fuck, Gwen!" Relieved and angry, he picked her up and held her.

The sound of the cell phone ringing in the next room brought them both back to reality. Chad didn't realize that he was running with her in his arms to the living room.

Gwen jumped out of his grasp, grabbed the phone off the table, and hit the accept button on the screen.

"Hello!"

Book 3

Chapter 1

Niya sat back in the chair. She wore a white linen wide-leg jumper and orange Tom Ford pumps. The neckline dipped down to her navel, displaying the long silver waterfall necklace with matching earrings. Her hair was pulled back in a neat ponytail, and she had applied little makeup other than the cocoa shade of lip gloss that made her full lips sparkle.

Sauce was mesmerized by the beauty who sat across the table from him. He looked over at Dirty, who was leaning against the outside bar on the deck of the Italian bistro. The Mob-like scene seemed cliché, but an appropriate place for the two underworld bosses to meet. Diamond and Tiffany sat at the table behind Niya, each wearing designer shades. Sauce laughed to himself at the three of them.

He adjusted his body in the chair and got a quick glance of Niya's partially exposed breasts. Niya ran her manicured French tip across the top of the wineglass. As Sauce continued to adjust himself, he remembered Dirty's warning that she was a viper. He cleared his mind and told his other head to settle down.

Sauce sat back and took a swig of his Henny and Coke, and then he leaned forward to inhale the sweet scent that came from her. He cleared his throat. "So, let's get to business, shawty," he said, breaking the silence. "What you lookin' to buy? An ounce or two, or maybe some weed?" he asked as he placed a piece of bread in his mouth.

Sauce had no clue what this meeting was about. Dirty had advised him to meet with these chicks because they were from his hometown. He had told Sauce that they probably were looking to buy some weight, and that they were on the come-up back in Charlotte. Dirty was his right-hand man, but looking at these broads, he wondered if Dirty was thinking with the right head. Niya looked like a chick who would be in a corporate office, not a drug kingpin. He checked his watch and sipped some more of his drink.

Niya didn't smile. She sat back, giving him a better view of her breasts.

Shit, this bitch is fucking ridiculous! he thought.

"Honey, I'm not here to buy nothin' from you," Niya began. "I'm here to make you an offer that can be lucrative for both of us." She took a small sip of the white wine and leaned forward.

"Boo, what could you possibly have to offer me that could make me more money than I already make? I mean, you fine and all, but I ain't into pimping." Sauce laughed as he raised his drink in Niya's direction and winked at Diamond and Tiffany. "My boy Turbo, that is who you need to talk to. He into that pimping shit, not me."

Niya took a deep breath. This nigga had no idea who the fuck he was talking to. He might have had Durham on lock, but the lock was loose. He had everyone thinking that the money flowed to him, but it was only a trickle compared to what he could have with her. This nigga was thinking this little trickle made him a boss. The prostitute comment he made had her trigger finger itching, but she needed this dude for the moment, so she settled her temper.

"Sauce, I don't sell ass, and I don't appreciate the disrespect. Now, if your junior high schoolboy tactics are over, I am here to talk business. I am not talking about business where you are making low six figures, but the kind that will gross nine figures on a constant." She studied him for a moment and then checked her reflection in a spoon. She could tell his mind was starting to spark and his interest was piqued. She was intentionally silent for a few more moments.

He had shifted his position in his seat again. He no longer was relaxed and casual. He locked his fingers, rested his elbows on the table, and leaned forward.

"Durham has a lot of potential, but you are not supplying the right fertilizer to produce a quality crop. You think ya eatin' well right now?" Niya sipped the Chardonnay then swirled it around in the glass. She leaned forward and smiled. "So how much is a key costing you these days? Forty, forty-five?" Niya had connections in the area who had informed her of the rising cost and risks involved with the powder in the region. At this time, Sauce was the only one who seemed to be able to pull it together enough to supply the street, but it was weak quality.

Sauce sat back. Yeah, he was paying about 35K per key, and that was because his connect was giving him a break, due to him bringing in business. Shit, nobody in Durham was even trying to compete with him right now. Hell, he even had the mayor and police force in his back pocket. He wasn't no business major, but he knew he could always stand to make more money.

"So, shawty, what you offering me?"

"I am offering you a chance to work for me. Working for me, you can get it 30K a key, with higher quality. It is better than that talcum powder you're selling now." Niya sipped her wine again and took out her phone to check the time. She needed to set the tone now that if he worked for her, it would be on her terms and her time. Even with Inga's price per key going up slightly, she still would make a profit of about eight grand on each key by selling them for 30K. Sauce might not have had the quantity or quality to work with, but he had Durham's streets on lock. His name had power, fear, and respect behind it. She needed him to make Durham a new acquisition for the MHB empire. He had the reputation, and she needed him as a part of her "corporation." The streets bowed to him, and the transition would be smoother if she had him on her side.

Shit, Sauce thought, *why this broad got me over here thinking shit over like it is a difficult decision?* He would be saving five grand a kilo if what she was offering was true. "How fast can you bring me a key? I'ma buy one off you, and if it is what you say it is, we can do business," Sauce said, leaning back in his chair.

"I would not make you an offer and show up unprepared to give you what ya need. You got what I need on ya right now?" Niya stared into Sauce's eyes.

Sauce licked his lips and then laughed. He looked over at Dirty, who was already digging in his pockets and pulling out two large wads of money. Sauce grabbed the rubber-banded bills, took Niya's hand, kissed it while placing the money in it, and leaned back.

"Yo, we eatin' ova here, shawty." Sauce chuckled. "Now show a nigga what you working with."

Chad and Gwen pulled into the KFC parking lot and parked in the space where the kidnappers had instructed them to park. They had advised Gwen to come alone, but Chad wasn't trying to entertain that. They both sat quietly; no words or looks were exchanged between them. Gwen scanned the surroundings and tucked an extra clip for her .40 Glock into her boot.

Chad checked the chamber of his chrome Desert Eagle. Besides the beating of Gwen's heart and the occasional sound of a passing car, the inside of the '68 Chevy was dead silent. Chad tapped her shoulder as a maroon Ford Explorer approached and slowly entered the parking lot. Gwen grabbed the latch to the door; Chad had to pull her back.

"The chances of Zion being in that truck are slim to none. They wouldn't risk bringing him down here," Chad said, holding her arm. "You need to be calm. We need to think smart, baby. Come on." They exited the car.

The doors of the Explorer opened and two men stepped out. The one on the left made sure that they could see the gun in his waistband. Chad recognized one of them as they continued walking toward each other.

Spice nodded to Chad and threw a phone to Gwen.

"Hello." Gwen spoke as she placed the phone to her ear.

"Mommy?" Zion's little voice was quivering.

"Hey, baby, Mommy's right here. Are you okay?"

"Mommy, I wanna come home. Please come and get me."

The line went dead.

Gwen wanted to scream and pop the two niggas who were in front of her. She looked at the screen and saw the name 4Pound. She memorized the number before tossing the phone back to Spice. She looked at Chad; his eyes were telling her to be calm.

"Check it out. Killing kids ain't my thing, but when it comes to my family, I wouldn't give a fuck who it is," Spice threatened.

"What the fuck you want? If y'all mistreating my son, I will—"

"Bitch, shut the fuck up and listen. Do what I say and you can have your kid back; then y'all can go back to being a hood happy family." Spice laughed and pounded his partner. "Like I said, we don't kill babies." He lit a Black & Mild that he took from behind his ear. "My cousin Mayo is sitting in jail, facing life. Ain't no way he'll do that kind of time as long as he gots his family. The state got two witnesses who's gonna testify against him. I was gonna pop them myself, but for some reason, Mayo wants you to do it. Says it's business between the two of you, and you need to close a deal or some shit. Mayo go to trial next week, and he needs dem two snitch-ass bitches taken care of. Yo' ass got 'til Monday to get this shit handled." Spice blew smoke rings out his mouth and leaned back on the hood of the SUV.

Gwen gritted her teeth. Mayo was behind this?

Chad ran his hand over his face. He heard the words, but it took a moment for him to process what Spice had said. Gwen was ready to light the niggas up. She would shoot Spice in the stomach; she wanted him to suffer. She needed him alive, just long enough to tell her where they were keeping Zion, and then she would send him to hell. Her head was spinning. She needed to sit down for a moment. She leaned against a white Honda that was near the SUV.

"Oh, yeah, and Mayo said he want a quarter million along with the witnesses being dead by the end of the week. You know, the bread is for his and my pain and suffering. Ya feel me?" He laughed. "And before you start the bullshit with you ain't got that type of paper, cuzzo already let me know you got the bread, 'cause he knows who ya connect is. You make it happen, and your son will be home in time for y'all to go to church on Sunday. If not, then ya son is dead. Don't worry about living without him, 'cause I'ma kill your black ass next. And you." Spice nodded at Chad.

Gwen's hand was trembling. Her mind envisioned this dude coughing up blood on the ground as a bullet ripped through his gut.

Chad nodded his head and threw a Spider-Man backpack to him. "Hey, make sure Zion gets this and takes this medicine. He has asthma."

Spice opened the bag and inspected the contents. After inspecting it, he threw it in the truck. "Y'all need to get this shit done quickly. Shit, we ain't running no fucking daycare or medical place."

Chad spit on the ground near Spice's white Nikes. Spice glared at him and motioned for his boy to get in the truck. His boy, Made, walked backward toward the door. "Come on, man, they know better than to try some shit."

Gwen held her Glock. She flexed her hand over the handle and watched them drive out of the parking lot. She and Chad walked back to the Chevy. She closed the door and placed the gun under the seat. Gwen placed her head on the steering wheel and let out an anguished scream.

Niya's mind was on the exchange at the bistro. Lining things up would give MHB what they needed to lock down North Carolina. This meeting was the first step. Once she pulled Durham under her belt, she would take on Guilford County. Shit, she may even hit Virginia. She smiled as she thought of how she could have runners doing shit like this for her soon. She could even establish a legitimate business and give the perception of a normal life.

Breaking her out of her thoughts, Diamond cleared her throat and placed her phone in the cup holder. "Did you hear anything about Gwen getting Zion back?" Diamond asked, looking over at Niya.

Niya gripped the steering wheel tighter. She hadn't thought about the Gwen situation. Today was a good day for her, and just mentioning the trick's name put her in a foul mood. "Naw, I hadn't heard nothing," Niya replied as she switched lanes. "And to be honest wit' you, that's not my issue," Niya said, taking out a piece of gum and placing it in her mouth.

Although they had met at the bistro, she and the girls didn't eat. It was business, not a social call. Now her stomach reminded her of the fact that she hadn't eaten anything all day. She cursed Diamond under her breath for bringing up Gwen and Chad's situation. The two of them had burned her so badly that she needed a skin graft on her heart. Chad was her husband and Gwen was MHB; both had betrayed her. Gwen tried to kill her, and to put the icing on the cake, Chad was sleeping with her! She mashed the accelerator.

"Damn, you a cold bitch." Tiffany chuckled from the back seat.

Niya swerved over into another lane. "Cold? Let me tell you what's cold. Dat bitch tried to kill me, and then I catch my husband lyin' up in her bed half naked. That's some cold shit. No, that's some arctic shit!" Niya said.

"A'ight, Niya, slow down! We can't afford to get pulled over," Tiffany said as she fastened her seat belt and looked back.

Niya loosened her grip on the steering wheel and eased off the accelerator. She took a deep breath and put the SUV on cruise control. "I feel sorry for li'l man, and y'all know I got mad love for him, but Gwen and Chad got to deal with that. My kids are safe and sound," she said, looking straight ahead.

She pressed the volume control on the steering wheel. Maybe music would change the mood. The radio was tuned to Magic 103.7, a hip-hop and R&B station. Lauren Hill's "To Zion" pumped through the speakers:

> *Unsure of what the balance held, I touched my belly overwhelmed by what I had been chosen to perform; but then an angel came one day . . .*

Niya was glad she had her sunglasses on. Her eyes began to water as she thought back to her and Gwen in her room, singing this song at the top of their lungs. Lauryn was one of their favorite female rappers, and this song was what made Gwen give Zion his name. Gwen felt that the lyrics spoke directly to her, especially when everyone around her was telling her to get an abortion.

She and Niya had cried together when she took the pregnancy test and those two lines appeared on the plastic stick. Niya promised her that she would be there for her and Zion. Every time things got hard, Niya made sure she was there to hold Gwen up. Hell, Zion was like her first born. She had spoken those words about the situation out of real fear of what had happened to him.

She sniffed as the next song blared. She was glad it was loud. She didn't want the girls to see her being emotional about Zion's situation. She had to keep her head straight and grow her empire. Shit, Gwen was a bad bitch, and Niya was sure she could get this handled.

Diamond studied Niya. She knew that the words Niya spoke were not from her heart; they were from hurt. No one had ever hurt or threatened one of their kids before. They put everything on hold when it came to the little ones. Diamond leaned back against the door of the SUV. She knew that the next thing she said would make the tension rise and pierce their hearts.

"Shit, she's still MHB," Diamond said. "And that baby ain't got nothing to do with grown folks' problems. He is innocent, and this is some bullshit that he had no power over! MHB, remember that shit?" Diamond repeated then put her earpiece in and turned on her iPod.

She had been trying to stop smoking. She reached in her pocket and took out the blue electronic cigarette. She pulled the nicotine into her mouth and allowed the vapor to circle her head. Although it was not tobacco, it had a slight odor, and she secretly hoped it fucked with Niya's sinuses.

About twenty miles outside of Charlotte, Niya decided to pull off at the next exit and grab something to eat. Her stomach had begun to punch her spine. She exited the expressway. A sign showed that a Waffle House, Burger King, and a Cracker Barrel were to the left. She stopped at the light and looked over at Diamond, who had her eyes closed. Her last statement still resounded in Niya's mind: *She's still MHB; he is innocent.* Zion's little face entered her mind, and her eyes began to sting again. She was lost in his big brown eyes.

"Ni, what you waiting for? The damn light is green. Shit, pull into the Waffle House and let's get some breakfast food. You know I love me some chicken melt and eggs smothered and covered," Tiffany yelled from the rear of the truck.

"Damn, Tiff, give a bitch a chance to hit the gas, with your greedy ass." Niya laughed.

Diamond was still reclined in the passenger's seat. She had her eyes closed, her breathing was normal, and no snoring was coming from her.

Niya pinched her arm. "Diamond, get yo' ass up. We know you not 'sleep, because yo' ass would be snoring so loud we would not be able to breathe in this bitch from you sucking out all the air."

"Really, you going there, Ni? Really, how 'bout this? Trick, you paying for my damn food," Diamond responded while stretching and yawning.

Niya pulled into a parking space that was under a light. They exited the truck and Niya clicked the alarm and checked her reflection in the glass.

"Come on. Who you primping for, Ni?" Tiffany asked, already nearly inside.

Diamond stood by the door, waiting for Niya to walk across the parking lot. Pointing inside, she spoke. "Look at Tiff's greedy ass."

Tiffany was waving to them as she sat at a table by the window. Niya and Diamond took a seat. Niya was glad that she could see the truck from their table. She had her stash in the truck. This little hick town might seem sleepy, but she didn't want to take any chances.

The waitress took their drink orders, and then the whole table was quiet. Either they all were hungry, or tense from the conversation that had taken place in the SUV.

The silence was broken when the waitress returned with their drinks and they gave her their food orders.

Tiffany sighed and stretched. "I am going to go ham on this food. My stomach is speaking in tongues!" She sipped her tea and scanned the faces at the table. The day had started well, but the mention of Gwen, Chad, and Zion had taken the buzz out of the group. "So, tricks, tell me about some good spinal and hamstring stretching," Tiffany said, hoping to change the mood. She looked at Niya then Diamond while she sipped the sweet tea.

"Don't look at me," Niya responded. "I told you earlier, my nigga been acting like his dick is community property."

"All right, well, it sounds like you need to start lining up some new bucks, bitch. I know you ain't gon' be abstinent. Let that shit go, girl. Ain't nothin' like a long, thick, luscious rod hitting bottom to make the memory of another one disappear. What about you, Diamond? Now I know you ain't even being celibate!"

"Damn, with all that's been going on, shit, I don't even remember." Diamond shook her head. "I mean, it has been a minute. Well, whoever the next dude is, he better drink ginseng and do some pushups. Hell, he might even need to bring backup!"

"Damn, you nasty. A threesome? You know you a freak! But on the real, if you do that shit, call me. I am going to watch!" Tiffany laughed while high-fiving Niya.

The girls laughed and joked while they ate their food. They each named some dudes who could be potential playmates, and joked about their skill level. With all the stress they had been under lately, it felt good to joke and laugh. They were going to have more money and more days like this soon, Niya promised herself. Her personal life may not have been where she wanted it at the moment, but it would pass.

After finishing their meal, the girls piled back up in the truck and headed for home.

Chapter 2

*Ohhhh oh ohhh, all I see is signs; All I see is dollar
signs; Ohhhh oh ohhh, money on my mind; Money,
money on my mind . . .*

Niya turned the radio down as she noticed the Crown
Victoria mimicking her turns. She placed the .45 automatic in her lap and checked the rearview. She did not
recognize the car, but after making a turn down three
different streets and seeing the Crown Vic do the same,
she was sure it was not her imagination that she was
being followed.

"Who da fuck is this?" she said to herself while trying to
get a better look at the car in her rearview. Niya chewed
her lip. Good thing she noticed the car early enough to
take them on a little detour from her home. Since Chad
had moved, and after Gwen's attempt on her life, she had
relocated. She was careful not to let anyone know where
her new spot was.

Niya stopped at an intersection. A car had gotten
between hers and the Crown Vic. She waited for the light
to change and did a quick U-turn. The Crown Vic quickly
went around the blue Toyota.

"Shit! Damn fucking cops!" The lights flashed and
Niya moved over to the shoulder. She slowly eased the
automatic into the console. She had two bricks in the
trunk and a .45 in the console. She knew they were not
stopping for just a traffic violation, and a search of her car
would give her some serious time in a six-by-eight.

She checked her side mirror. Butler was approaching the passenger's side of her car. She opened her visor to take down her ID, registration, and insurance card. She always kept it in the visor. Cops get real nervous when they see blacks reaching for shit at a traffic stop. She wished he was on the driver's side, so maybe he could accidentally be hit by a car that didn't see him.

He tapped on the passenger's side window.

She rolled it down and faked a smile. "Yes, Officer?"

Butler snickered and hit the button to unlock the door. Niya felt her pulse quicken as he sat down in the seat.

"Niya, Niya, how are you doing?"

Niya regretted putting her gun in the console. She never had a pig get in her car before. "I am fine, Officer."

"You know, Niya, most detectives would tell you to get your black ass out of town, or lock you up. But me, I enjoy having you around. You are the kind of woman who inspires me to get up every morning and come to work," he said, looking straight ahead. "Yeah, Niya, you are inspiration and motivation for me."

"I am glad you enjoy your job. Is there a reason why you stopped me?"

"Niya, this is a nice SUV, and well, you are always put together so well. You like nice things, and looking good like you do. You know everybody who works has to pay taxes, and well, call me Uncle Sam. Think of today as April fifteenth."

Niya sighed. This was a shakedown. It had never happened to her, but she was expecting it. She knew that as she began to move up, the damn sharks with dirty badges would start circling for flesh. "How much do you want?" she asked, looking out the window. She had to count to ten to stop herself from reaching in the console and blowing this fool's head off.

"We'll discuss that another time. Right now, I just wanted you to know who I am," Butler said as he began to exit the car. "Oh, and for the record, if you're gonna go to jail for something, make sure what you going for is worth it, not a damn traffic violation for making an illegal turn. I'll see ya around, Niya," he said then slammed her door.

Niya sat there for a moment and rested her head on the steering wheel. Her heart was pounding. What the hell had just happened? What did he want? Maybe he knew she didn't have enough cash on her to amount to anything. The bricks would have been hard for him to move, but the cash would have paid her "taxes."

She took a deep breath, checked her side mirror, and pulled back onto the road. She needed to get the hell out of there before another fucking pig showed up who wasn't crooked like the one who just left her car. She did not want to think about being in a six-by-eight for twenty-plus years, and if paying a pig taxes guaranteed that, then so be it.

"What was that all about?" Detective Rose asked Butler when he got back into the car. Rose studied him for a moment. Butler had alerted Niya to the fact that she was under police surveillance, and she was aware of what he looked like. Why would he show his hand like that? This woman wasn't stupid, and now it would be even more difficult to get what they needed on her.

"I just wanted to ruffle a few feathers." He chuckled. "Now that she knows she's being watched, she's bound to do something stupid. Nine times out of ten, she's going to fall back and let somebody else do the heavy lifting," he said. "We need to be able to pull all this shit down, and the more they think they are outsmarting us, the more mistakes they will make. This ain't no damn television series where the drug dealers are these groups of cunning, smart people. They are all the same. They all end up making the same mistakes; they just take different roads to their demise." Butler pointed to the road to let Rose know it was time to go.

He laughed to himself. He had been doing this shit since heroin was big in Charlotte back in the day. Hell, he had spent so much time undercover he could predict what the next move would be for these motherfuckers. Yeah, that time in Miami had taught him a lot—and made him a lot.

"I don't get it," Rose said as she turned onto the street.

"Rookie, that is because you are still on the bench." Butler smiled. "I'm about to put ya in and on to the game."

Zion stacked the chicken nuggets on the table. He was not really hungry, but he did play with the Avengers toy a little.

"Come on, li'l man. You gotta eat somethin'," 4Pound said to Zion as he sat at the kitchen table. "You gotta eat, so you won't get sick; then we can go out back and throw the Frisbee with Hermes."

"I wanna go home," Zion whined, taking the toy and pretending to make it climb the nugget mountain. "You said my mommy was gonna come get me."

4Pound smirked at Zion. Little dude was not slow. He had begun asking him more questions about how he knew his mother and why he didn't take him to the store with him. Little dude told him his mother told him never to talk to strangers, and he kept asking why he took him out the house when he was sleeping, and why his mother hadn't told him he would be staying with a friend.

Zion took a bite of a nugget, looked at 4Pound, and pouted. If his mommy or daddy didn't come get him soon, he was going to go find them himself.

Gwen put on the black latex gloves and took the .45 out of the grocery bag, along with the clip. She cocked the bullet into the chamber and checked the street. The large red bush gave her the perfect shield from any prying eyes. After all, she didn't want to make the same mistake as fucking Mayo. She felt sick to her stomach. Her conscience was yelling at her not to go through with taking this man's life. She shook her head. It was his life for the life of her baby. She had to send this man to the afterlife so her son could have a life.

She conjured up the image of Mayo in court smirking at her, and her blood boiled. Taking a rachet nigga's life was easy for her. There was never any thought behind her separating their fucking brains from their skulls. This was different; this was a decent man who had done nothing wrong to anyone. She knew that taking his life would leave a mark on her soul.

She heard Zion's voice on the phone, begging her to come and get him. She opened the door and began walking toward Mr. Walker's house. The road seemed to stretch on forever, and her legs felt like she had forty-pound ankle weights on them. She stopped and inhaled.

"Gwen, buck the fuck up. You are doing this for Zion. You will make it quick and painless." The words *quick and painless* echoed in her head as she made the trek to his home. It was only a block, but she felt like it was ten miles. Damn. If Chad was the dude she knew years ago, he would do this shit without thinking about it. Now he had a conscience, and she could not afford to leave Zion's life in the hands of someone who would pause to do what needed to be done. After all, she was the mama bear, and bears do whatever it takes to protect their cubs.

She stopped and pretended to tie her shoe as she looked up and down the street in front of the old man's house. She checked the numbers on the mailbox and checked the street again for any nosey-ass neighbors. The cropped wig she wore had long bangs that partially hid her eyes. She checked her watch; it was 9:00 p.m. The old man was probably settling in for the night. She walked on the porch and rang the doorbell. The light damn near blinded her. Duke Energy had mailed people those energy-efficient bulbs, and they were bright as hell.

Mr. Walker opened the large mahogany door and looked out. Gwen could hear the news playing in the background. He stood behind the thick glass door and squinted. "Can I help you?"

Gwen forced a smile. He was small and frail. His voice had the treble of age, and his genuine smile made Gwen's heart ache. She pulled Zion's face to her mind. She had to get this over with so she could get him home. Mr. Walker had probably had a good life, and she would make his end swift.

"Yes, how are you? I was jogging by, and I saw that your garage door was open."

"I tell you, that thing. I could have sworn it went down this time."

"Yeah, mine does that too. You might need to clean your sensor."

The old man mumbled as he turned and walked toward the kitchen. Gwen looked around and opened the glass door. Typical man—they never locked the outside door. She made her way into the home, into the kitchen, and through the door. Mr. Walker was looking at the sensor, cursing under his breath.

When he turned, Gwen raised the .45. She paused for a moment. Her heart ached, and she felt like she needed to tell him why he had to die.

"Young lady, whatever you need, just take it. Just take it."

Gwen swallowed, took two steps. "I'm sorry." She closed her eyes and pulled the trigger.

The bullet went into the center of his forehead. She stood over him and fired a second round into his temple. She removed the silencer and threw the gun under the car. She grabbed the gold watch from his wrist, went back into the kitchen, and turned the television and the outside light off. She looked around the room for a moment. There were pictures of two women about her age, and small children.

She shook her head and closed the door. Mr. Walker's azalea bushes were tall. She stood behind them for a moment to check the street. Jumping off the porch and jogging toward her vehicle, she felt something heavy over her heart, something she had never experienced after killing someone: guilt.

"So you mean to tell me that you had two bricks in the trunk and a gun under ya lap, and the cracker let you go?" Tiffany asked, shocked by what Niya had told her and Diamond about the encounter she'd just had with Detective Butler.

"Yeah, the peckerwood had me red-handed and he didn't lock me up."

"What you think that was all about?" Diamond asked, walking into the kitchen and taking a seat at the table with Niya and Tiffany. She placed the two ice-cold daiquiris she had just made in front of them.

"I don't know, but he did say that he would be in touch. And I ain't even gonna lie; the motherfucker got a bitch a little shook," Niya said, thinking about possibly having to go to jail and having to be away from her children. Shit, any- and everything Niya did, the thought of the twins' welfare was always on her mind. They meant everything to her, and she didn't make a move without thinking about their well-being first.

"So what now?" Diamond asked Niya.

"I don't know. I guess we'll play it by ear. Just be on point and try to avoid ridin' dirty until I find out what this cop is up to," Niya instructed.

"We need us some intel on this cracker," Diamond said, getting her laptop. "If he dirty, we have to be careful who we ask in the street, but the Internet, that is a cool bitch." They all laughed and pulled their chairs closer to her.

Gwen sat in her car for a moment. She reached in her pocket and took out the silencer. She opened the grocery bag that contained a box of Baggies. With her gloves still on, she opened a Baggie and placed the silencer inside, then zipped it. She opened a second Baggie and placed Mr. Walker's watch inside. She placed them both back into the grocery bag and drove out of the development.

She drove down Cottage Grove Court. They were building new houses, and she knew the development would be empty at night. She drove to the end of the cul-de-sac, reached under her seat for the small planting shovel, and looked around. She knew the developer had not paid for security to be there yet, due to it only being marked for lots. She dug into the red clay they had outlined for the foundation to be poured. She wanted to make sure the hole would be deep enough so that the contents would not be discovered before they poured the foundation.

She took the silencer and watch out of the grocery bag, dropped them into the hole, and covered it. The street didn't have any streetlights, which meant no cameras, but just to be safe, she had her hoodie pulled up and the SUV parked at an angle that made it hard to see the license plate. Even if they did see the plates, it didn't matter, because she had stolen them anyway.

She got back in her vehicle and drove down the street. Reaching in the console for her cell phone, she waited until she was about eight blocks away and turned it back on. She took off the black latex gloves and placed them in her pocket. The screen showed she had three missed calls, all from Chad. She had not spoken to him since this morning when she left to go to Mayo's hearing. They had discussed and agreed that Chad would take care of the witnesses. She was supposed to go to court, gather information, and give it to him to handle. She knew that there was going to be a blowup when she told him she had taken care of Mr. Walker. She swiped the screen. The phone didn't even seem to ring once before he answered.

"Yo, where you at?" Chad answered with an attitude as he sat waiting in the apartment.

"I'm on my way home now. I had to take care of something," Gwen said, looking off onto the highway.

Chad knew Gwen, and to anyone else she may have sounded calm, but he could tell that something had her upset and shook. Thinking back to her recent attempt to take her own life, he decided not to press her too much. "A'ight, babe. You coming home now, right?" Chad said as he checked the bullets in his clip.

"Yeah." The phone clicked.

Chapter 3

Butler kneeled next to Mr. Walker's dead body. The old man still had his eyes open, which meant that he saw what came at him. Butler cursed himself for being so sloppy. His focus on MHB had caused him to be careless and not take care of his homicide witnesses. He knew Mayo had this done; it reeked of him. Smooth, clean kill. He might be locked up, but he still had his goons to do his dirty work. Although he had given Butler valuable information on MHB, he was still a ruthless kingpin. He only provided information to save his own skin.

"You think Mayo had something to do with this?" Detective Rose asked.

"What do you think, rookie? This old man didn't have any enemies. Who else would gain anything from his death? I mean, we still need to investigate this like any homicide, but I am pretty sure that bastard ordered this!" Butler said, passing Rose a clear Ziploc bag with the gun in it.

Butler couldn't even think about Mr. Walker. His mind was on MHB. He shook his head and closed Mr. Walker's eyes.

"I think we need to put the other witness into protective custody before they get to him next," Rose suggested.

"Yeah, get that done." Butler almost stepped over the body, but he stopped and walked around. Damn, he was off his game.

He walked into the kitchen where the neighbor was being questioned. She had come over to check on Mr. Walker when she didn't see him taking his morning stroll, and found his body in the garage.

Mayo had given him information on MHB, but Butler did not want him on the streets. He had murdered two people he knew of, and an animal like that needed to be in a cage. He remembered the saying his father would always quote: "Sometimes you may have to dance with the devil, but you need to leave him in hell."

Selena touched Gwen's arm. She had been sitting at the table, looking off into space for the last five minutes. Her bottom lip was cracked from her chewing on it, and her skin didn't have its usual glow to it. Her hair was pulled back off her face, and the bags under her eyes were so large that she almost appeared to have two black eyes.

"Gwen, you look troubled, ma. What's going on?"

Gwen finally looked at Selena for a moment, then looked back at the wall behind her. She licked her lips and rubbed her eyes. "I really don't wanna get you involved with my problems," Gwen answered without looking her in the eyes.

Selena studied her for a moment. She had lost weight and seemed to be on edge. She looked into her eyes and didn't see a light. Something dark had taken hold of her. Selena didn't like it at all. She had grown fond of Gwen. Being a woman in a nigga's game wasn't easy. She squeezed her hand and gently turned Gwen toward her.

"Gwen, you gotta know by now you can trust me, boo. You got problems, I'll do whatever I can do to help you," Selena said as she looked into Gwen's tired eyes.

Gwen sat there for a minute. Her eyes began to well with tears as she thought about her Zion and how much she wanted to hold him in her arms.

Selena looked around the nail shop. They needed to be away from potential eavesdroppers. She grabbed Gwen by the hand and pulled her into the waxing room. Selena nodded to Ming to keep herself and others away.

"Now, you're really not leaving until you tell me what's going on," Selena said as she sat Gwen down on the table and pulled up a stool.

Gwen started breaking down. She told Selena the whole situation with Mayo, her deceased boyfriend, JR, and about her son being kidnapped. Gwen cried the whole time. As she spoke, she felt something lift inside of her, just having someone else besides Chad. He had lost his heart when he decided to go straight. The street prince she fell in love with was not there anymore. She was pissed when he said they should go to the feds about Zion. She looked at Selena, and she could see wheels turning in her head.

Selena listened to every word she said, while trying to wrap her mind around the words and thinking of how she could help her.

"Mayo has made me a monster, just like him. I took the life of an innocent old man, Selena," Gwen cried out. "I just want my son back," she cried.

"Shhhhh, we're gonna get ya son back," Selena assured her, pulling Gwen into her arms. "Whatever you need from me, I got you. We got resources everywhere. We got this. Don't worry. Zion will be back with you."

Gwen wanted to believe what Selena was saying, but she had not told her everything. She was on a ticking time line. All she had was the other witness's name and no idea where he was. If the cops had found Mr. Walker, they had surely put the other witness in protective custody, which meant it would be even more difficult to get to him. She knew the longer she took, the less time Zion had to stay alive.

***

Niya quietly opened the door to the twins' room. There was a soft glow from the nightlight, and sounds of soft snoring coming from both of them. She pulled the door closed with a sigh, then stretched and grabbed her laptop. She checked some of her social networking messages and laughed at a few pictures some fools had posted. She had "liked" the page of Mr. Marcus, one of her favorite porn stars. Looking at his pictures made her squeeze her legs together. She laughed as she thought back to the conversation that she and the girls had earlier about riding a black stallion. She logged on to Mr. Marcus's Web site and searched through the on-demand movies. She had a paid membership and could watch all his movies any time. It was worth the twenty bucks a month. Dude had some backbone and pelvic skills.

She stood and pulled her pink Bob Marley T-shirt over her head, took off the matching boy shorts, and placed them on the chair beside the door. She opened her nightstand drawer and cursed, remembering that she could not find her toys after moving. What she needed more than anything after today was a moment of release. She slid between the sheets, put her earbuds in, and plugged them into her laptop. She closed her eyes and listened to the moans of the light-skinned chick as Marcus enjoyed her clitapop. His long tongue slid up and down her clit.

Niya pulled on her nipples and bit her lip. She bent her legs so that her pussy was wide open. She imagined that she looked down between them and saw the top of Marcus's hat. The sounds of him licking and sucking old girl's pearl made her own button throb. She didn't touch it, although it begged for her fingers to massage it. She began grinding her hips while she sucked one of her nipples into her mouth. In her mind, she was grinding against his tongue. She opened her eyes. He had the female on her knees, bent over on the couch.

Niya got on her knees and faced the monitor of her laptop. Keeping her right hand on her right nipple, she slid her left middle finger over her swollen lower lips.

"Ahh, yeah." The girl moaned as Marcus slid his hooked cock inside her.

Niya moaned with her as her finger moved up and down her own moist, erect clit. Marcus grabbed her ass and slid slowly in and out the chick's pussy. Niya moved her finger faster up and down her clit. She watched as Marcus did his signature move: turning that baseball cap around. Niya placed a pillow under her stomach. She let go of her nipple and used her left middle finger to move in and out of her creaming box while pinching her clit with her right hand. Marcus began pounding old girl. Niya could hear her fingers going in and out of her over the moaning. She moved her fingers faster, grinding against the pillow until she felt the river flow down her hands.

"Oh, shit!" The sound of Marcus banging against the chick's hips caused her to erupt again. She fell on her stomach, out of breath, and somewhat satisfied. "Damn, Marcus!" She giggled and closed the laptop.

It had been weeks since she'd had any release. She lay back on the bed and exhaled, enjoying the silence. Her cell phone rang and she grabbed it from the nightstand. Mandy was calling. She hit accept as she walked over to the chair to put on her T-shirt.

"Yeah," Niya said as she slid the shirt over her head and pulled up her boy shorts.

"We got a problem. I need you to come through as soon as you can," Mandy whispered.

Niya could hear police sirens in the background along with some yelling. She cursed. It had to be a fucking raid. "What am I walking into?" Niya asked, looking around the room for a pair of jeans to slip on.

"A nigga got killed on the block. It's crawling with cops, so don't come dirty," Mandy advised.

The sweet release she had only moments ago had lost its calming effect. She placed the phone on the bed as she pulled up her jeans, and it began to buzz again. The face on the screen made her stomach tighten. The last time she had spoken to him was when the two of them were in the basement with Gwen. She wanted to answer the phone, but her heart told her to let it go to voicemail. Shit, for as hard as she had to be in this life, she was still soft when it came to affairs of the heart. Chad had crushed that part of her. She still loved him, but forgiving him was something she knew she would never be able to do. *Let him talk to the voicemail,* she thought while opening her bedroom door and going to knock on her nanny's door.

"Ms. Emma, I need you to watch the twins. I gotta go out," she yelled.

She then walked down the stairs, grabbed her keys, and walked out the door.

"I really think I can do it," Detective Rose told Detective Butler.

"What makes you think Niya would trust you enough to let you get close to her?" Butler shot back.

"I can do this. I know I can," Detective Rose said as she sat on the edge of the desk. She and Butler had been going back and forth about her going undercover in MHB. She wanted to do this, partly because she needed the intel on the organization, and partly because in a twisted way, she admired a group of females taking on a male-dominated business, even if it was illegal. She was a female detective, and she had to take it from men like Butler every day, thinking she was green and too weak to be an effective part of the team.

She snatched her file off his desk. From what she had observed of the MHB, she would fit right in with them. She was Dominican and black, five foot seven, athletic build, and, hell, she was street smart. She had grown up around chicks like MHB; hell, she could have been one decision away from actually being MHB. When she put on the right outfit, she looked more like a video vixen than a cop.

"I don't know about this, Monica. I gotta think about it," Butler said.

Detective Rose sat in her chair and stewed. If she were a male rookie, the bastard would not think twice about putting her in undercover. Like every other person on the force who didn't have a penis, she would have to work twice as hard at proving herself.

Niya parked a couple of blocks away, got out, and walked to Betty Ford. As she walked down the street, the coroner and his staff were placing the body in the medical van. She blended into the crowd that stood behind the yellow tape. Detectives were attempting to speak to people in the crowd, but they were getting no answers. Mandy grabbed her hand and pulled her to the side.

"You're not gonna believe this shit," Mandy said as she took a drag off her Black & Mild.

"What da fuck is going on?" Niya asked, looking over at the bloodstained street where the body had been.

"Eagle unloaded his clip in HB over a sale. Fed that nigga the entire clip to the head." Mandy shook her head and blew smoke out her nose.

Niya listened to Mandy describing how the altercation had taken place. Damn, she knew that Eagle had a short fuse and that his temper would be an issue. His street name was Eagle because that was his weapon of choice, and due to his keen eye. He could spot bullshit product and niggas a mile away. What the hell possessed HB to cross this fool?

"So where da fuck is Eagle at right now?" Niya asked, trying to process everything Mandy had told her.

Mandy looked over at the crowd of people. Eagle was standing in the crowd as if he were a bystander. Niya's heart stopped when a detective actually began questioning him. She knew this fool probably still had the murder weapon on him. He wasn't the type of dude to think ahead; he was a reactive nigga—good to have when something popped off, but a problem when it came to looking down the road.

Her cell phone buzzed again, and Chad's picture appeared on the screen. She hit ignore and whispered to Mandy, "Tell Eagle I need to holla at him," as she put her phone in her back pocket.

Niya leaned against her Toyota, and Eagle walked up to her with his usual grimace. She glared at him and got in the car. Eagle opened the passenger's side door and sat down. Niya looked at him for a few minutes. Eagle looked straight ahead. She could see the vein protruding from his temple.

"You know you costing me a lot of money, Eagle. What the—"

"Wait, don't be talking to me like I am one of these pussy-ass niggas around here," Eagle said without making eye contact. His jaw became tight, and he flexed his right hand.

Niya was silent for a moment out of shock. Most of the niggas around her didn't say shit back to her or Mandy as long as they were getting their part of the cake. They were quiet and bowed down to them, but Eagle was from a different mold. Answering to anyone or bowing down to anyone was not the way he was raised. She knew he had an issue with the fact that she was a woman who sometimes had to get her hands dirty. He was raised by men of honor, men who felt that women were supposed to hold their men down and be protected from the dirt and grime of the street. He had a different set of morals and honor.

"That nigga," he said, tossing a pack of dope in her lap, "was cutting your shit on the side. One of the fiends came to me after he complained to HB, who busted a few teeth out his mouth for questioning him. I had to shut that shit down, ma. He flexed at me, so I flexed back."

Niya looked at the pack. It had a different color from her product. Eagle may have handled it with a little too much aggression, but HB could have ruined Betty Ford with this inferior shit. She had no idea how long HB had been cutting her shit and making money on the side. Blocks that had poor-quality dope didn't last too long. Niggas would move on to blocks that had shit that gave them that dragon they wanted with that fire. Although Eagle had a hot head, this incident made him come up in the ranks in her eyes.

"Damn, this nigga was fucking me without even kissing me first. Thanks, Eagle."

Eagle's jaw loosened for a moment. He stared straight ahead. "I don't wanna hear that shit. Take me to get something to eat."

Niya sat back against the door and looked at him. They both busted out laughing, something that Eagle rarely did.

Niya noticed Mandy approaching the car and rolled down the window. "I'll be back."

Eagle looked shocked as she started the engine. Niya smiled to herself. If this dude wanted a meal, hell, he was going to have a meal, if for nothing else but looking out for her and saving her block.

***

Detective Rose sat at her desk, looking at all the information that she had on MHB. She was focused on the head of the crew, Niya. She studied the surveillance video, photos, and wiretaps they had managed to get in some of the cars, with the help of informants.

Butler walked over to her desk and stood there until she looked up.

"Remember the Realtor who was murdered?" Butler asked as he sipped his soda.

"Yeah," she answered as she continued reviewing photos on the monitor.

"Daneill Smith's fingerprints were all over the bedroom and bathroom of his house. Chang is on that case and just brought it to my attention when they came back." He dropped the case file on Rose's desk.

Rose sat back and snatched the blue folder. She opened it. There was a mug shot of Smith, aka Diamond, her print sheet, and prints from the crime scene of the Realtor's murder. This was a waste of time. If there were no witnesses, they didn't have a case. She threw the folder back on her desk and went back to studying the photos

"So what do you wanna do, bring her in for questioning?" Rose asked.

Butler sat there in silence for a moment. He knew that what he was about to say could mean the beginning or the end to Rose's career. "Do you still wanna go undercover?" Butler said, sounding as if he regretted the words as they escaped his lips.

Rose began to smile like the Cheshire cat. She smacked the desk with her hand then composed herself. She cleared her throat and sat back in the chair, ignoring the worried look on Butler's face. This was going to be her chance to prove herself. She was finally being let out of the stable!

"Don't make me look like a fool, Monica," Butler said, heading back to his cubicle.

"I won't, sir," Rose responded, looking down at the picture of Diamond. *Yes,* she said to herself, *this is going to be my chance to shine.*

Chapter 4

Voicemail again. He had not spoken to or seen Niya since the day he stopped her from killing Gwen. He missed her and his twins. It had been almost a month since he had seen any of them. Niya was so angry at him that she moved, and he had no idea where she was living.

Chad stood and walked into the kitchen. He opened the refrigerator and grabbed a beer, but thought better of it. He needed to have a clear head. He grabbed one of Zion's orange juice drinks.

As he walked back into the living room, the apartment door opened. Chad quickly hung up just as Niya's voicemail began to play. He definitely did not need Gwen finding out he was trying to reach out to Niya, especially with her being so wound up. There was enough going on without adding wood to the fire. Right now, the slightest thing could cause Gwen's fragile state of mind to crack.

Gwen flopped down on the couch. Chad sat down and placed her legs on his lap. She was exhausted, running on nothing more than adrenaline.

"Did they call you?" Gwen asked as she placed one of the throw pillows under her head.

"Naw, they didn't call me yet. I gotta try and find the other witness," Chad said as he pulled out his phone, hoping he could get a signal strong enough for the Internet. He kept forgetting to ask Gwen for the code to her wireless, but he knew that right now her mind was so strained she probably couldn't even tell him.

Chad watched Gwen as she struggled to keep her eyes open. He sighed as he thought about how his presence in the street was no more of a threat than some knucklehead. All his boys were dead or locked up. He had no connects anymore. New blood was on the street, and they had no idea and didn't give a shit about who he used to be. He had become a square-ass nigga, just working and getting a W2 like the everyday law-abiding dude. He had become soft, and his instincts were dulled. Given time, he knew he could pull the beast out of him, but time was something that he didn't have. He needed to get the beast in shape and hit the streets hard to save their son.

"Yo, I'ma take care of the other witness, give these niggas the money, and get our son back. You just got to trust me. I know you might feel as though all of this is your fault and that you gotta do everything on ya own, but you don't. He's my son too," Chad said as he rubbed her legs.

Gwen was knocked out cold. He was glad she finally crashed. She needed to rest, but he couldn't fall asleep. He needed to figure out what his next move was going to be, and figure it out fast. He grabbed the remote and turned on the TV. *SportsCenter* was on ESPN, but his mind was on how he was going to get his firstborn home safely.

"You're making things harder on yourself, Mayo," Butler said when Mayo entered the room.

"I don't know what you're talking about," Mayo said smugly as he pulled out his chair.

Mayo's lawyer, Hinson, eyed him with a warning to shut up as he sat down.

Butler tapped the pen on the notepad and glared at Mayo. He knew that he'd had the witness killed and that there was no way for them to trace it back to him.

"Mayo, this has your stench all over it, and I am going to put you so far in the hole, sunlight will be a distant memory for you. I'm gonna check every phone call you made, every letter you got in ya cell, and every visitor who came to see you since you been here. And if I find out that you had something to do with the death of one of the witnesses against you, I'll make sure they put a needle in your arm." Butler had intentionally eaten an omelet with extra onions. He made sure his breath cascaded in Mayo's direction.

"I ain't kill no witness," Mayo said as he leaned back and placed his hand over his nose. "I ain't had nothing to do with that shit. I'm innocent, and the witnesses are wrong. Somebody obviously is trying to set me up."

Butler stopped tapping the pen and stared at Mayo for a moment. "Set you up? Why?"

"I'm guessing MHB is looking for a little retribution and don't feel that the government will do me justice. If I am found innocent, I will be back out on the streets, and they probably feel like dey need to handle me their way. They think I killed one of their crew."

"Who? Prada?" Butler asked.

"Yeah, Prada. And if they get me out of jail, they would be able to kill me themselves. I know that's what I would want to do," Mayo said, shrugging.

Butler chewed on the pen. Mayo had a point that MHB wanted his head on a stake. It had been proven that they were a ruthless bunch. The body count around them seemed to keep rising the more they took over the drug game in the QC. Niya was the type to exact retribution, and taking the lives of two witnesses to get to the one who she thought murdered one of her own would be just collateral damage. The MHB family was growing more affluent and dangerous as time passed. An organized crime family was what they were becoming, and he couldn't allow that to grow in his city.

"Like I said, Mayo, if I find out you had something to do with this, you better get right with God," Butler said as he walked out of the room.

Mayo patted his lawyer on the shoulder. Things had to line up for him. He would let the white man get Niya and MHB off his streets. Soon, Gwen would take care of the other witness, and when that was done, he would take her out, along with Chad.

The little boy, Zion, well, that little nigga gonna be my little prince. Shit, I can raise him better than those two motherfuckers. They let his ass get kidnapped. Maybe I won't kill Gwen. Maybe I'll sell her ass to them Russian dudes. Killing her would be too easy. Yeah, I could sell her ass to them and make sure she knows all the while that I am raising her boy. Shit, might sell Niya's ass too. Get a good little hit off dem two bitches. He snickered to himself. Niya and Gwen underestimated him. He'd had time to think while he recovered in the infirmary from being stabbed and slashed. Shit, he was a boss, and these bitches would feel the pain of crossing him.

Niya loved the sound of the bill counter. With each drop of a stack of bills, the number on the display increased. Diamond, Tiffany, and Alexus sipped their drinks and stacked the cash to be placed in the slot and counted. Alexus's apartment was the unofficial MHB headquarters, and her kitchen had become the MHB boardroom. Alexus had taken some precautions since Diamond had told her about Niya's run-in with Butler. Alexus's geeky-ass cousin had installed scramblers in the apartment. If the police or anyone had bugged the place or were outside trying to record MHB, the sound would be distorted. Alexus had zoned out as her cousin explained how it worked. She just told her to handle it and then paid her.

"I wanna run something by y'all, and I want you to think about it before you answer," Niya said, pushing the money to the side.

The girls stopped their conversations and looked at Niya. When Niya made that statement, they knew it was going to be something they needed to hear.

"I been thinking about taking MHB to the next level," Niya said.

"Oh, yeah?" Diamond asked, fanning herself with money.

"I was thinking that maybe it's time to expand MHB," Niya began. "It's a lot of young girls out there who's hungry right now, just like we used to be. I think we're in a position now to bring some new faces to our clique," Niya suggested.

"You wanna start recruiting?" Diamond asked, excited about the idea. "That's crazy, 'cause a few people been asking me if they could get down with us."

"Damn, we can have our own little gang," Tiffany added.

"Not a gang. MHB is a family," Niya corrected her.

After the incident with Eagle and HB, Niya had an epiphany. Women were proactive; they tried to see a problem and resolve it before it became an issue. Men, they were reactive, which usually resulted in impulse reactions like unloading a clip in a nigga's head. Being proactive in the Eagle and HB situation would have resulted in less bloodshed and less heat from the cops. Her block would not have to cool down business for a moment, and her money flow would still be the same.

"You know what this means, right?" Tiffany said. "It's gonna be a lot of angry niggas out there, 'cause once we expand, it's gonna be hard for a nigga to eat." She laughed.

"No, no, no. We're not saying a nigga can't eat. We just sayin' a nigga can't eat off of our plate or at our table,"

Niya said as she dropped another stack of bills in the bill counter.

MHB had taken over some major hoods north and east of Charlotte. She knew niggas were already hungry and angry. If they wanted to eat, they would have to move outside the state. Shit, for that matter, they'd better move to the lower part of South Carolina, because she had already started to lock down the upstate. Yeah, MHB was about to get everybody's attention. They needed to ramp up with sisters who were ready to ride.

"You know, since we're goin' down this road, we gotta pick a boss," Diamond said, tracing the top of her glass with her fingers.

"We don't need a boss," Niya shot back. "It's working perfectly fine just the way it is."

"Come on, Ni, we do need one," Tiffany butted in.

"Every family has a head to it," Alexus chimed in.

Niya smacked her lips and continued dropping cash in the bill counter. The room was quiet. Niya looked up to meet the stares from everyone in the room.

"Everybody who wants Niya to be the head of the MHB family, raise ya hand," Diamond said, raising her right hand high.

Everybody at the table raised their hands without hesitation. Niya sat back and looked each girl in the face. She saw the love they had for her in each of their eyes. She shook her head, smiled, and nodded. She knew the love she had for them was unconditional, and their love for her was the same.

"So, it's final. Niya is the head of MHB," Diamond said, standing. She walked over to Niya.

Niya stood, and Diamond wrapped her arms around her and kissed each of her cheeks. Tiffany and Alexus encircled Niya and blessed her the same way. Niya embraced them as she fought back tears. She was the official MHB boss.

***

Gwen opened her eyes and realized she was in her bed. She looked beside her, expecting to see Chad. He wasn't there. She looked at the clock and saw that she had been asleep for a few hours. Feeling energized, she called for Chad as she got up.

"Chad!" she yelled as she walked down the hall. She looked in the living room and walked in the kitchen.

"Where the hell are you?" she said to herself as she grabbed her phone off the counter. She checked the screen and saw she had no missed calls. She stood there for a moment, and panic hit her. Had he gotten a call from the kidnappers and left without telling her? Did they call him? Shit, was Zion okay? She dialed Chad's number; voicemail picked up. She tried again, and the same thing happened.

"Fuck!" She began pacing the floor. She looked down at her cell phone. Damn it, she was late to meet with Selena. She ran back to the bedroom and grabbed a T-shirt and her black leggings, slid her feet into her jeweled Donna Karan sling-back sandals, and headed out the door.

"Harper, get ready for a visit," the guard said, tapping on the door with his flashlight.

Mayo had been moved to a different pod after the stabbing incident. He was still healing from the attack, and the pigs didn't want him dead before he could give them what they needed in regard to MHB.

The ankle restraints were causing one of the stab wounds to burn as he walked in front of the corrections officer. He winced as he sat down in the seat across from the stranger. He studied his face. The man's glare could have melted the Plexiglas that was between them. They sat in silence for a few minutes.

Chad's rage was so intense that Mayo's face actually became blurry for a moment. He didn't blink. This dog had his seed kidnapped.

Mayo picked up the phone after a few minutes. "Who you, fam?" Mayo asked. He couldn't place the dude's face. Mayo paused again, thinking that maybe the guard had made a mistake with the name. As he stared at the stranger, he saw the hatred in his eyes, "Oh, you must be Gwen's baby's daddy. Chad, right?" Mayo laughed and reclined in the chair. He broke away from the man's glare for a moment. He had never seen the nigga before, but he knew his name because of the tattoo on Gwen's arm. Chad snatched the phone on his side and he inhaled before he spoke.

"Yeah, so, dude, you snatch kids? That is a bitch move, nigga, and low. You feel like you powerful and in control now 'cause you snatched a eight-year-old to get yo' shit resolved? I know I been out the game a minute, but street code is niggas don't touch babies."

Mayo sat back and looked at Chad. "Yo' baby mama should have stayed in a female's place, nigga, on her knees. When you dealing with bitches, you got to make sure they hear ya loud and clear. Whateva done happened to your son happened because of yo' baby motha and them MHB hoes."

Chad looked down for a moment. MHB? What the hell was that? And what did they have to do with Zion being taken? Chad was so far out of the game that he didn't know what Mayo's reason was for having Gwen handle this business. Chad didn't know anything about the women around him. He had no idea that the reason his son's life was in danger was due to the two women's ambition to take over.

"Look, man, I don't know what's goin' on between you and Gwen, but I do know it doesn't have nothing to do with me or my son, which is why I'm asking you, man to man, to let him go." Chad relaxed his posture and softened his glare.

Chad studied Mayo's eyes. He may have been out the game, but he knew niggas, and this nigga was one of those bastards who didn't give a fuck about anybody. There was no soul behind those eyes. The only thing that was there was self-preservation. Dudes like this had no sense of honor or respect for anybody but themselves.

"Look, dude," Mayo said as he stood up. "I don't know who has your son. I hope and would think he is safe. If baby mama comes through like she is supposed to, you can be throwing a baseball to him real soon. Your baby mama shouldn't have tried to play me. She got my connect then left me in here. All she had to do was pay my lawyer, and that is real." He hung up the phone and tapped on the door.

Chad sat there and watched Mayo disappear through the gate. He slowly hung up the phone and stared at the door for a few moments. He stood slowly, feeling the weight of the situation hit him hard. He was helpless, tired, and had no idea how he was going to pull off getting Zion home safely.

"Hey, girl. Whoo, you got a lot of loads to wash, huh?" Gwen said as she sat on top of the washing machine next to Selena.

Selena folded a shirt. She smiled at Gwen and placed her hand on Gwen's thigh.

Gwen put her hand on top of Selena's and forced a weak smile. Even when Selena tried to dress down and blend in, she was a stunner. She had her hair tied up in a golden silk scarf, white Capri leggings, and a white baby tee with black rubber-bottom flip-flops.

Gwen looked around the Laundromat; the front and back door were guarded by two large, armed men.

"Girl, how are you holding up?"

"I'm trying to hold together, but it's getting harder every day my baby is gone."

Selena's heart ached for Gwen. "My sources found out the last known address of the second witness, but they have him in protective custody now. I haven't got the location of the safe house." Selena handed her a piece of paper. "Sometimes, even Bri's money doesn't open lips, but I will keep trying. That is the best I can do for ya right now."

Gwen took the paper. She already had his name, and now the last address. Her mind was racing so fast that she didn't hear Selena until she shook her shoulder.

"So now what?" Selena asked, holding both of Gwen's shoulders.

"I gotta do what I gotta do," Gwen said, looking down at the small piece of paper. "Thank you," she told Selena as she hugged her and then shot out the door.

Selena watched her leave. She would continue to track down information, but at this point, time was not on Gwen's, Chad's, or Zion's side. She sighed and whispered to herself, "Do what you gotta do, Gwen."

Niya parked at the end of the street. It gave her the perfect view of the block. She watched the junkies trickle in to her crew for their fix. Business had slowed down as expected since Eagle executed HB, but she knew it wouldn't be slow for too long. These fools loved the platter she was serving them, and Eagle was back on the block conducting business as usual.

She scanned Eagle as he handled the transactions with the junkies. He was definitely attractive, standing there bare-chested, wearing khaki cargo shorts, mid red court Adidas, and a white towel slung over his gleaming brown skin. He wiped the sweat from his face with the towel. His tatted chest glistened with his perspiration.

Niya's hand rested between her legs as she looked at his full lips that were outlined with a trimmed beard. Like a typical young dude out the pen, his body was sculpted. Wide chest, slim waist, and abs that looked like she could stand on them.

Niya licked her lips and squeezed her hands between her thighs. "Damn," she said to herself as she stared at his hard body. She was so mesmerized by him that she didn't hear Mandy tapping on the window. She shook her head and unlocked the door.

"Damn, what you lookin' at so hard?" Mandy asked, getting into the car.

"Traffic," Niya lied. "I see it's starting to pick back up again."

"Somewhat. I think we might have a little problem with that though," Mandy uttered, looking out the window at a couple of dopefiends walking past.

Niya looked away from Eagle. The words *we might have a problem* definitely were enough to warrant her attention. "What kind of problem are you talking about?" she asked with a curious look on her face.

"When HB got killed, every fiend that day went to Ronheart Street to cop their dope, since we was shut down. The word is getting around that they got some good dope, maybe even better than ours," Mandy said.

Ronheart Street was owned by a nigga named Rell. Ronheart Street, along with Miller Road, were the only dope strips that were making as much money as Betty Ford. Miller Road belonged to a nigga named Ant, and Ant had a wild li'l crew. Issues like this were the reason why the family had to grow. She needed more members to help handle their competition. Although MHB was making money and had the streets handled, she needed more queens to help guard and expand the kingdom.

"Well, I guess it's time I pay Rell a little visit," Niya said, turning her attention back to Eagle.

Niya was going to play it smart and meet with Rell like a businesswoman; however, if this nigga wanted to take it there with her by exchanging gunfire instead of words, so be it.

Chapter 5

Gwen opened the door to her apartment, and she paused at the sight of money that covered her coffee table. Chad walked out of the bedroom carrying a duffle bag and began shoving the money inside. Gwen watched as he frantically checked the time on his cell phone and stuffed the money in the bag.

"What the hell is going on?" Gwen asked as she closed the door and sat down on the couch. Chad stopped for a moment, sat down beside her, and continued putting the money in the bag.

"The kidnappers called. They said that if we pay them the money now, they would take care of the other witness," Chad said, stuffing more money in the bag.

She looked at Chad. She wasn't sure when he had actually slept last. Maybe it was sleep deprivation or the fact Chad had been out of the game too long that was making him react without really thinking this through. She could smell that something wasn't right. She wanted to believe that what Chad was saying was true, but the hairs standing up on the back of her neck gave her reason to pause.

"Where the fuck is you supposed to be taking this money—I mean my money—and what exactly did they say?"

Chad zipped the bag and stood. "Look, I'm supposed to meet them on State Road, near the firehouse. They are supposed to bring Zion there in exchange for the money."

Gwen knew this didn't sound right, but what if there was a chance it was true? She could be holding her baby in her arms. There was nothing on State Road around the firehouse, and this reeked of a setup. She checked her .45 and placed it back down the waist of her pants.

"I'm coming with you," she told Chad.

Chad began to protest, but he knew that it would fall on deaf ears. Gwen felt adrenaline flowing through her veins. She had to get her baby boy back, and for the sake of the motherfuckers who had him, he better be in the same condition he was in when they took him.

The Beemer with the limousine tint and the new Cadillac DTX pulled into the parking lot. It was about 11:00 p.m. when the doors of the cars opened. Diamond, Tiffany, and Niya stepped out wearing black hoodies, jeans, and black sneakers. Even wearing street gear, the women exuded sex appeal. Diamond and Tiffany walked in front of Niya as they walked to the truck where Rell stood. He and one of his crew were leaning back against the hood. Diamond and Tiffany parted as Niya walked between them.

"Damn, I feel like I am meeting with a real boss or somethin'," Rell joked, tapping his man who was standing next to him.

"What's up, Rell?" Niya said, taking the hoodie off her head. "I hear you doin' big things nowadays."

"Hey, shawty, what's up? I got word you wanted to holla. So holla."

Diamond and Tiffany scanned the parking lot. They kept their hands in their hoodies, just in case these fools flexed the wrong way. They counted three of them. Rell and his boy were in front of the truck, and a dude was standing near the passenger's door.

"All right, I will get straight to it. I know you got Ronheart Street on lock. I'm just curious to know how much you payin' for a key of dope these days," Niya inquired.

"Who da fuck is you again, shawty?" Rell asked in an annoyed tone. He no longer leaned on the truck, but stood and looked Niya up and down. He had heard about a chick running Betty Ford, but he hadn't had any interest in that until today. His interest was piqued when he was told this bitch was bold enough to ask for a meet-up with him. Now this ho was asking him how much he was paying for his weight? His jaw tightened as he put his hands in his pockets and moved the toothpick in his mouth with his tongue.

"Again, who the fuck are you?" Rell said with more bass and menace in his voice.

"No need to get ya boxers in a bunch. I'm Niya." She smiled at him. "I only wanted to meet with ya 'cause I think I might be able to help your bottom line grow." Niya rubbed her hands together as she looked Rell up and down.

Rell leaned back on the hood and laughed. "How da fuck can you help me, shawty?" Rell shot back.

Diamond and Tiffany felt their pulses quicken, Rell's demeanor and tone made them squeeze their pieces in their hoodies. Niya looked back at them. She smoothed her hair as a sign for them to calm down. She turned back to Rell. "Look, I can get it to you for eighty a key, and my shit raw to the core," Niya said.

"Bitch, get the fuck out of here. I tell you what: *I* can get that shit to you for eighty a key, and if you twerk that shit the right way, I will take it down to 78K a key," Rell said as he squeezed his dick.

Niya smiled. The dick was the downfall of many a nigga. She felt the heat coming off Tiffany and Diamond. They both had taken the safety off their guns and were ready to light these niggas up; however, that was not the way she wanted it to go down.

Rell flicked the toothpick with his tongue. He said a few other perversions and then stood up straight. "Y'all bitches got me fucked up. Y'all really don't know who da fuck I am," he said as he lit his cigar.

Niya stood there and listened to him. He talked shit and threw a few more insults at her. When he finished, she flashed a smile at him again. She inhaled and looked him in the eye. "So, Rell, this will be the first and only time I ask you. You wanna do business or not?"

"Bitch, who is you talking to?" Rell snapped, grabbing his gun from his waist. He didn't point it at her, but left it down by his side. The two women behind Niya already had their guns drawn and on him and his partner before they had a chance to respond.

Out of nowhere, a red beam shone on Niya's chest. Niya looked down at the beam. It was coming from Rell's truck. Rell wasn't confident that Niya's crew wouldn't still pop anything that moved. Niya turned around and nodded to them, and they slowly lowered their guns. Rell lifted his right hand, and the beam disappeared from Niya's chest.

"That was probably the best move you made since pulling up here. Now, you and yo' hoes betta get the fuck out of here before somebody get picked up in something flashing," Rell said as he held the Glock.

Niya nodded and slowly backed up to her car. Diamond and Tiffany waited until she was behind them and began backing up to their car with their guns drawn. Niya got in her Beemer, looked in her rearview to make sure Diamond and Tiffany were in their vehicle, and sped out of the parking lot. Rell had given her his answer, and now she had to respond. She respected the game and his stance, but it was time for MHB to let the streets know what those three letters meant.

***

Gwen sat in the car beside Chad. Her stomach was doing flips. She knew something wasn't right about this meeting. Although she had been around Mayo for a short time after JR's death, she had gotten to know him and his ways. This was too easy, and he damn sure wasn't the type to do anything that didn't have a profitable gain for him. Not only that, but he was a nigga big on retribution, and she knew he was salty at her. She hated she wasn't there when the call came in. Her instincts were keener than Chad's. She could have judged what the fuck was really going down with this meeting. Chad was green, and he was etting his emotions rule his common sense. She sure would have found a better location than this dark-ass road. The only light on it was an almost burned-out streetlight that flickered. She felt a chill go up her back as they rode down the quiet black street.

"Pull over right here real quick," Gwen told Chad as soon as they got near the middle of the long road. "Pop the trunk."

Gwen got out and walked back to the trunk of the Chrysler 300. She moved a few things around, pulled a few latches here and there, and then up came a small section of the floor. Inside of the compartment was a vest, a 9 mm Taurus, and two extended clips. She strapped the vest to her chest, threw her hoodie back on top of it, and tucked the 9 mm in her back waist.

"You good?" Chad asked when she got back into the car. She tapped on the vest, letting him know that she had one on.

Gwen's mouth became dry as they drove farther down State Road. There were no streetlights at all, and the silence of the street was heavy.

Chad's phone whistled. He checked the text. "They want me to pull over," he told Gwen, placing the phone on the dash.

Gwen pointed to a parking lot in front of a pet store. They pulled in. Chad's phone whistled again. "What it say?"

Chad grabbed the bag. "They want one of us to get out with the money."

Gwen grabbed his arm. "Fuck, Chad, get your head clear and right. We gotta be smart. Tell them we need to see Zion first."

Chad looked at her for a moment then grabbed his phone and texted the number back. A few minutes later, a Chevrolet Traverse pulled in the parking lot. Gwen tried to swallow as the headlights of the Traverse went off.

"Stay right here. Let me see what's going on," Chad said, opening his door.

Gwen was dizzy with the anticipation of seeing Zion. She couldn't stay inside the car. She opened her door and got out, trying to look in the van for a sign of Zion, but the tint was too dark.

Spice got out of the driver's side and his partner, Made, jumped out of the passenger's side. Both of them had guns in their hands, and Made was carrying something that looked like an assault rifle.

"Where the fuck is my money?" Spice said, seeing that neither Gwen nor Chad had a bag in their hands.

"Where da fuck is my son?" Chad snapped back, gripping the butt of his gun a little tighter.

"Money first, nigga!" Spice demanded.

"Show me my son, fucker," Gwen shouted back.

Spice looked over at Made and gave him a nod. Made went to the side door of the minivan and pulled Zion out. Made held him by the back of his collar, with an assault rifle to the child's head.

Gwen's blood boiled, and without thinking, she began walking toward him. "Hey, baby," Gwen yelled with her arms outstretched.

Spice raised his gun to her. "Money!" he shouted then looked over at Made, who threw Zion back into the minivan and shut the door.

"Hold up, hold up." Chad opened the door before Gwen could stop him.

"Let my son go," he said, walking over and tossing the bag at Spice's feet. Gwen looked at Chad. This nigga had really lost it. Giving this fool the money gave them no control of the situation.

Kneeling down and still holding his gun on Gwen, Spice unzipped the bag. He grabbed a few stacks of money, inspected them, then zipped the bag. He tossed the bag in the door.

"Fuck yeah," he said while getting in the van. He held his gun on Gwen. "Now we gon' put your son out at the fire station. Give us about five minutes; then you can pick him up."

Gwen pulled her gun. "Nigga, let my son go now. We ain't doing this shit." There was no way she was going to let them drive off with her son.

Spice signaled for Made to get in. Made opened the door, and the dome light shone on Zion in the back. Gwen cocked her gun back. She had to think of how to stop them without hurting her baby. Spice knew they couldn't open fire on them with the boy in the car.

Gwen screamed at Chad, "Do something!"

Chad could see Zion's position, due to the interior light. He prayed and opened fire on Made as he tried to get in the van. Gwen's mind raced. She aimed for the tires, trying to take them out so the van couldn't move. Spice began firing at Gwen. Made began popping rounds in Chad's direction.

Rat, tat, tat, tat, tat, tat, tat! Boom! Boom! Boom! Boom! Pow! Boom!

Zion heard the bullets and jumped to the third row of the crossover. He got on the floor and covered his head. His chest became tight, and he couldn't breathe. He tried to claw at the tape over his mouth, but his chest began to burn. The sounds of the bullets flying around him caused his little hands to shake. He finally got the tape halfway off, but he couldn't catch his breath. He felt in his jeans for his inhaler, but it wasn't there. The sounds of the bullets became softer as darkness surrounded him.

Made continued forcing Chad back. Chad took cover behind the car. Gwen and Spice were exchanging fire in their own shootout. Spice got out to get a better shot at her. She was out in the open, and he was behind the door of the van.

Gwen was shooting at the tires. She didn't want to shoot in the van, for fear of hitting Zion. She jumped behind the pole of the pet store sign as Spice continued firing at her.

"Just let him go," Gwen screamed out, sending four quick shots in Spice's direction.

Made fired until he was out of ammo, then jumped in the van. Spice jumped back in, still firing in the direction of the pole. Gwen cursed as she dropped the empty clip and loaded a new one. As she came from around the pole, Spice fired again, hitting her in her solar plexus. The force of the shot knocked her to the ground. That was the time Spice needed to throw the car in reverse and tear out of the parking lot.

Chad fired the last two rounds he had left and ran over to Gwen. "Come on, babe, you gotta get up," Chad yelled, helping her up off the ground.

They got in the car. Chad nearly lost control as he drove on the road. They approached the firehouse. The van was sitting in front of it. Gwen jumped out of the car before Chad stopped. She fell to the ground then jumped up and ran to the van. She checked the back, the front, and under the seats. "Zion, Zion!" Gwen yelled as she looked inside.

She collapsed, realizing that he wasn't there. She started, beating the butt of her gun against the ground, holding her stomach as a wave of nausea hit her and she vomited. Her son and her money were gone!

Chad grabbed her by the waist and dragged her to the car. He threw her in the passenger's seat and took off, leaving the lights off. He could hear the police sirens wailing as he drove down the dark road.

Diamond leaned against Niya's car. Her pulse had finally slowed down from their encounter with Rell. She looked at Niya. "So now what?" Diamond asked.

Tiffany sat on the trunk. "I think we should leave them niggas alone before I end up having to kill one of their asses," Tiffany suggested while putting on some lip gloss.

Niya kicked a can that was near her foot. She knew that taking over Charlotte's drug flow wasn't going to be easy. There were more Rells in Charlotte than she cared to think about, but like anything, MHB would have to take things one step at a time. Rell's reaction had numbered the days—no, the hours—he had left above ground. Dicks thought they controlled the streets, but Niya was going to show them how big real-pussy control worked.

"Look, I told you this shit wasn't gonna be easy, but at the same time, I told y'all that we can make it happen. Now, the nigga Rell made his choice, so he gotta bear the weight of his actions," Niya said, looking from Tiffany to Diamond. Niya knew that MHB had the crew it needed to make MHB the royalty of the Queen City drug game.

"We gotta get on some otha shit right now," Niya said. "We gon' have to put some real work in to make these niggas feel our presence. We got to show these mother-fuckers we about this life!"

"Shit, we came this far, and I ain't turning back now," Diamond replied, hugging Niya.

They both looked over at Tiffany, who was lighting up a blunt. Tiffany was the wild card of the bunch, and they really didn't have to ask her if she was riding, because they knew she was with whatever.

"What y'all looking at me for? I'm MHB to the death of me," Tiffany said, taking a toke of the sour.

"Yeah, and what's that supposed to mean?" Niya asked jokingly, only wanting to hear some slick talk from her girl.

Tiffany exhaled the weed smoke, jumped down off the car, and faced both of them. "You either go hard or blow ya own fuckin' brains out," Tiffany said and then walked to her car.

Chapter 6

Shopping is the activity that bonds women—shoes, purses, dresses, all the things every girl needs to have and must have. Many girls' nights out started with a group of friends shopping and then deciding to show off their finds on the dance floor.

Niya and Diamond entered the food court of North Lake Mall. It had been a while since they actually had time to enjoy the money they had been making, and today they would dip into it and make a sizeable dent. Niya and Diamond walked through the food court, laughing and talking. They walked into their favorite store and were greeted by Misha, one of the salesgirls. Misha knew when she saw these girls that her commission was going to be lovely.

"Ladies! It has been too long." Misha hugged each of them and air-kissed each cheek.

"Hey, Misha, how are you?" said Diamond as she walked over to a purple cocktail dress.

"I am great. So are we looking for anything in particular today?" Misha asked.

Diamond held up a pair of Chanel satin Capri pants. "I like these. Do you have them in another color?"

Misha took the pants and walked to the back of the store.

"This will be cute on you," Diamond said as she held up the purple cocktail dress.

Niya felt the material and then held it in front of Diamond. "I think it will look better on you. I think I will go with pants or something."

"Yeah, how many people ya think will show up tomorrow?" Diamond said as she looked at her reflection in the glass.

Niya was silent for a moment. The next night was the recruiting meeting. She had extended several Purple Party invitations to some of Charlotte's most intelligent, sexy, and street-savvy broads. She and Diamond continued talking and grabbing things off shelves that caught their eye.

Diamond laughed. "You made sure this shit was exclusive and private. I ain't heard shit on the street about it."

"The invitation was clear. This event was by invitation only and was to be kept quiet. I made sure that invitations were hand-delivered to broads I been watching for a minute—the kind I know can keep their mouths shut, and the kind who want to be a part of something like MHB."

Diamond walked into the dressing room. Misha returned with pairs of white, purple, pink, and lavender Capris.

"This is our newest item. We have not had a chance to put all of them out yet. It actually has a matching halter. We also have some wide-leg cotton pants that are screaming your name and would be just sizzling with the halter."

Niya took the purple Capris from Misha. "It's kind of hot to be wearing wide-leg pants."

"No, this is really light and flowing cotton. Let me get them for you, and one of the halter tops."

Niya smiled at Misha as she fluttered off. Diamond opened the curtain and did a runway walk to the mirror.

"Yeah, bitch, that is you. You look good. That is a keeper," Niya said as she walked around Diamond. The dress stopped above her knees and displayed her thick legs. Material clung to her hips and her breasts. Diamond had a naturally flat stomach that Niya envied, due to the fact that the bitch never did a crunch in her life.

"That dress definitely says come get it."

Niya and Diamond turned around.

"Sorry, didn't mean to barge in on your conversation, but that dress is ridiculous on you. Shame I can't say the same about this one." The girl sighed as she looked at herself in the mirror.

Niya scanned her for a moment then looked at Diamond.

"Girl, that dress is fire on you. What are you talking about?" Diamond laughed.

"You think so? Is it hot enough to make a dude wanna use his hose on me?" The girls all laughed. "I just want something that is going to make his Latin blood boil and his American wallet open."

"I know that's right, girl, and I think that dress is going to have him hearing Alicia Keys in his head when you walk up," Niya said.

The woman had long, curly hair that flowed down to the center of her back. The dress wrapped around her small waist and high hips. She was making that dress sing sexy as she walked to the mirror. Niya noticed the Hermès bag on the stool in the dressing room stall. Niya scanned it and could tell it was not a knockoff. This chick was far from low budget; she was carrying a $20,000 handbag.

She began pulling the dress up and looking in the mirror. "Yeah, it will come far enough for him to hold me up against the wall and make me go up and down his pole."

Diamond and Niya looked at each other, then at the woman. The room was quiet for a second, and then all three erupted in laughter.

"Girl, you are crazy!" Diamond said, walking back into the dressing stall.

"Where you from, girl?" Niya said as she sat down.

"I just got here. I am originally from Brazil, but I been in Miami for a little minute. My name is Millie." She extended her hand.

Niya nodded and took her hand. "I'm Niya, Millie." She could tell the girl had class, but there was an edge to her also. "That is my girl Diamond in there."

"Well, nice to meet both of you."

Misha returned with an armful of clothes for Niya. Niya took the lavender cotton pants and the dark purple halter and held them up to herself in the mirror.

"Damn, Misha, you know me so well. This is orgasmic," Niya said. "Girl, when I come in here, I ain't even got to worry about looking around, 'cause you already know. I'ma take all that shit."

"Well, I have some accessories for you to look at too."

"Misha, girl, do your thang. I know you got me," Niya said, smoothing her hair.

"Hey, boo, I'm gon' take all these," Millie said as she handed Misha her credit card.

Niya noticed the diamond dolphin pendant that hung from her wrist. This broad had some loot. Niya got a good vibe off her. She was definitely worth inviting to the party.

Diamond walked out of the stall holding the dress and three other outfits. Niya and Diamond walked out of the dressing room. They bought their items and handed Misha an invitation.

"Give it to the lady who was in the dressing room," Niya said as she grabbed her bags. Misha placed the purple envelope on top of the clothes the girl was buying.

"Next time, don't stay away so long, ladies," Misha said as they left the store.

Detective Rose walked out of the store with her bags. She looked around a few times before walking across the parking lot and jumping into the unmarked Crown Victoria.

"So did you see them while you were in there?" Butler said, looking over at Rose going through her bags.

"Yup, I saw them," she answered, pulling out one of the dresses she purchased.

Butler stood there waiting for Rose to say something. "Well?" he said, tugging playfully at her bags.

"They invited me to a party," Rose said with a big smile on her face.

She had casually followed Niya and Diamond around the store, listening to as much of their conversation as she could. She seized the opportunity to listen to them when they went into the dressing room. The booth gave her the perfect shield. She got the chance to get a feel of the type of women they were, and how to best interject herself into their world. She knew that Niya had a keen eye for fashion. Renting that Hermès bag and wearing the bracelet her ex-boyfriend had bought her was just the type of thing she knew Niya would notice. It was pure luck that they were having a recruiting party, and luckily, she had played her role so well that they invited her.

"So, when is the party, Rose?" Butler asked with a grin.

"I'm not supposed to tell you. It's a secret." She chuckled. "Oh, and don't call me Rose anymore. I am Millie from Miami."

Gwen couldn't believe that she was so close to her baby. They had let them take him again. She had nothing left to barter with. She knew that Spice took Zion because he wanted more money. She was down 250K and had maybe $15,000 left. For a moment, she actually thought about contacting the police. She felt helpless and useless.

"Do you think we might have killed our son?" Gwen asked, sitting up in the bed. "Did we do that?" she said as she began to cry.

Chad couldn't comfort her. He was trying to deal with his own pain. He had no idea why they didn't let Zion go. Had he tipped his hand when he gave them the money? He thought back to how frail Zion looked, and his heart felt as if it were in pieces. Shit like this was why he got out of the drug game. Was this karma for his past deeds?

"Yo, one thing I am not gonna let you do is start blaming yourself," Chad said, sitting up behind her. "These niggas took our son, and I swear to God that—"

"That what, Chad?" Gwen snapped. "You shouldn't have let them take our son in the first place," she yelled, getting up from the bed and heading to the bathroom. "You was right in the other room when they came and took him."

Chad stared at the bathroom door. The conversation with Mayo sang in his head. He swung the bathroom door open. Gwen jumped back.

"So, you blaming me for this shit?" Chad yelled.

"You weak, Chad. You supposed to be a fuckin' man," she said, pointing her finger at him. "What kind of man lets somebody come take his child right from under his nose, huh? You tell me, Chad."

Chad took a deep breath. His head was spinning, and the room seemed to be moving. He looked at Gwen. He had to fight the urge to wrap his hands around her throat and squeeze until she turned purple. Her words stung him, but she was crazy to try to put this all on him. Due to her fragile state of mind, he had not really asked too many questions as to why these people would take their son. Fuck it; he felt for sure that Zion's life was more than likely gone. He didn't give a fuck how Gwen felt now.

"You know, I went to see your homeboy Mayo the other day," Chad sneered. Gwen's eyes widened at the mention of Mayo's name. "Yeah, he told me that he gave you his connect, and how you were supposed to look out for his legal fees. He also said you left him to fucking rot in jail. Played the grimy bitch role. Mayo took Zion because of you and your fucking greed, Gwen! You da reason our boy could be dead. You did this shit! You put our boy in the ground, and for what?" He shook his head and walked out of the bathroom.

Gwen began to shake. She could no longer think. She wanted to make Chad regret saying that to her. She ran out of the bathroom and laid a blow to the side of his face. Chad stumbled, but before he could regain his balance, she laid another blow to his nose.

Chad caught her fist as she came in for another hit. Before he realized it, he had knocked her across the room. She hit the wall and slid down to the floor. Her body hitting the wall caused Chad to immediately panic at his reaction. He ran to her and tried to help her up. Gwen kicked him and slid back up the wall.

"Gwen, I'm sorry," Chad said. Damn, he had punched her like she was Mayo.

She spit at him, wobbled to the bathroom, and shut the door. She fell to the floor and began sobbing. She knew that this was not Chad's fault; it was all hers. Zion's blood was on her hands. She had fought so hard to bring him into this world, only to lose him due to her stupidity. Hearing Chad say the words just made it all the more real that she had possibly killed their baby. She stood and looked at her eye in the mirror.

She heard Chad's footsteps and then a door slam. She fell back to the floor and curled up in a fetal position.

"Oh, God, what did I do? What did I do?" Gwen cried out, hoping her heart would just stop and the pain would go away.

Chapter 7

Niya licked her lips as she pulled up. *Damn, Eagle is standing there looking like he needs something other than a belt around his waist,* Niya thought as she gazed at him.

Eagle flashed his crooked smile at her and began walking toward her car. As he walked over, Niya felt the heat between her legs intensify. She had gone to the lingerie shop and bought a little toy that had an eagle as a button tickler. She had burned the batteries out using it and thinking of how the real Eagle would probably put it down on her.

"What up, Ni," he said, leaning against the car.

He smelled like he had just stepped out of the shower. Niya rested her hand between her legs and smiled at him. "What up, E. Where's Mandy?"

"I don't know. I think she went to get some Baggies," he answered. "Yo, why don't you step out of the car for a minute," he said, stepping back from the door.

"What I gotta step out of the car for?" Niya asked. She studied his face and scanned his body.

"I need you to step out of the car so you can make my day," he said, giving her a view of his white teeth.

"What? Boy, you better stop playin'." Niya chuckled.

"I'm serious. I wanna get a view of you. It will keep me motivated. You know it ain't gon' be long before you and me become an *us*. I just want to see what my future is working with. I will settle fo' seeing that sexy-ass body in dem clothes right now. Come on," he said, opening the door.

Niya felt her face heat up. Dude had some swagger, and it was natural. She found it sexy, and this was not the first time they had flirted. She rolled her eyes and got out of the car. She crossed her arms and leaned back against the door.

"Happy?" Niya teased.

"Nah, nah, now that I see you, I need to see how you feel," he said as he stepped closer.

Niya put her hand on his chest in a weak protest. "Boy, I know you done lost your mind," Niya jokingly responded.

Eagle continued to move closer. "Come on, girl, I just want a hug. We fam, right?" he said, flashing that damn smile again.

She kept her arms folded as he embraced her body. Damn he smelled good, and she could feel how hard his pecs and stomach were as he held her close to him.

He looked down into her eyes. "Yeah, damn. See, that ain't gon' be enough. You got a nigga hungry now. I need to know how ya feel without dem clothes on, and your arms around me instead of folded across that beautiful chest," Eagle said as he stood back and rubbed his hands together.

Niya tried to keep her face straight, but feeling him on her like that had caused things to tremble.

"Shit, man. Li'l man ain't looking so good. You know how to give him that shit?" Made asked Spice, nodding at Zion, who was lying on the couch. His color was an ash gray, and he was barely breathing.

"I don't know. I gotta think. Shit," Spice said as he walked over to Zion to feel his face. The child felt cold to his touch, but Spice thought he was still breathing. "Shit, dey gon' hafta give us some more bread. I mean, me and cuzzo cool and all, but we got to get ours too." Spice loved

Mayo like a brother, and Mayo had always done right by him, but he was tired of living on handouts. It was time for him to come up on his own. Kidnapping in North Carolina could get you some serious time. He had never snatched a kid, and it was just his luck to snatch one who was fucking sick.

"So, what about Mayo?" Made asked.

"Mayo is gonna be good. Da bitch is just gonna have to come up with another 250K to get her son back."

"Shit, dude, where is his backpack? We need to give him his medicine. Where the fuck is 4Pound?" Made said as he looked at Zion.

"I don't know. I'ma try him again. You right, li'l man ain't lookin' right." Spice stood away from Zion. If this kid was dead, it would put a kink in his plans.

Gwen let the Patrón linger on her tongue before swallowing. The effects of the shots were starting to numb her for the moment. The apartment seemed to close in around her as she thought about Chad's words before he left. She looked at the pictures of Zion on her cell phone. His smile touched her in a way that made her smile and caused a stabbing pain in her stomach. As she scrolled through the pictures, she downed another shot. She looked at Zion in his soccer uniform and touched the screen. She looked at the mustard stain that was on his number. She laughed as she remembered him saying the stain was worth it because he got to eat his corn dog.

As she stared at the number four, she put the shot glass down. Something sparked in her brain. *Shit, the name 4Pound.* That was the name on the caller ID when she talked to Zion. She had memorized the number and put it in her phone when she got back in the car after meeting Spice and Made the first time. She scrolled through her address book. Her hands were shaking. She stopped when she saw the number four listed as the name. She sat there for a moment. Damn, should she call him?

"Think, Gwen, think." She held the phone in her hand and stared at the number. Shit, she didn't know if it was a TracFone or what. She ran to her bedroom and grabbed her laptop. She keyed reverse lookup in Google. The yellow pages reverse lookup site popped up. She keyed in the number. Pam Jamison came up. The address wasn't listed; the site asked for a credit card. Gwen looked around for her purse. She took out the prepaid Visa and completed the form.

Pam Jamison, 28 Providence Road. Gwen grabbed her gun, her clips, and sprinted toward the door.

Tiffany could hardly stand. Her thighs burned and her stomach was cramping from the pound that Toast had just laid on her ass. Nigga had hit bottom. The way that thick, ten-inch dick punished her pussy made her dizzy! Toast had been schooling her about the game, which was why her spot in East Falls was moving 30K of dope like an assembly line. Toast grabbed her hair from behind, pulled her back on the bed, and kissed her. She giggled and lay beside him.

"Yo, you holla at Niya fo' me about what we discussed?" Toast said as he puffed on the electronic cigarette. He was on probation and had to stay clean. Cigarettes seemed to make him want weed more. One of the white boys he worked with told him to try these vapor things. They calmed his nerves and curbed his need to have something in his mouth.

"Not yet. I told you I would," she said, kissing his chest.

Toast had been trying to get Tiffany to holla at Niya about investing in the real estate game. He had pulled a bid in prison a couple of years ago, and while there, he studied up on the real estate game with plans of getting into it upon his release. But he had never made the type of money that was needed to get started. Toast knew that MHB was making serious money. The best way to keep the feds off ya ass was to show some legitimate streams of income. The real estate bubble had burst while he was locked up, but there was a lot of land and houses up for bid, due to the fallout. Real estate would be a way to get a stream of income in, and a legal way to stack some cash. In the Carolinas, property and land were the only things of value for black folks. He had seen so many niggas murdered or locked up because of the drug game, with nothing to show for their efforts. He wanted to make sure he could do what the white boys do: raise money and invest in something legit. All he needed was startup.

"Yo, you need to start thinking about ya future, Tiff. This way of life don't last forever. And I know you probably don't wanna hear this from me right now, but I am only telling you this because I care about you," he said, rubbing his fingers through her hair.

"You really care about me?" Tiffany asked, looking up at Toast.

"Yeah, I care about you. You wouldn't be here if I didn't," he answered, kissing her on the forehead. "Just get the loan from her, and I will help you do the rest."

Gwen looked up and down the street a few times before proceeding to the house. *Shit, this is Mayo's place. Why didn't I think to look here before?* She looked up and down the street again before pulling the hoodie over her head. It was noon. Although that southern sun was beaming down, there were a few people outside. She waited until the woman adjusted her sprinkler and went inside.

Gwen reached in her pocket and took out the key she had to the house. God was smiling on her right now. She was lucky she still had the key Mayo had given her.

Once inside the door, she held the knob as she closed it. She looked around and took out her Glock. Taking a deep breath, she stepped into the foyer. She could hear the television playing in the living room and voices coming from upstairs. She checked the living room and other rooms before going toward the kitchen with her finger on the trigger, ready to blow away any motherfucker who came at her.

"Babe, you want something to drink?" a female voice yelled out from the kitchen.

She had no idea how many people were in the house. She didn't know who the bitch was in the kitchen, but she decided she would deal with her ass first. She looked at the staircase when she heard the male voice yell down for a soda. Gwen heard the refrigerator door open and close.

The woman walked into the dining room. Gwen put the gun to the back of her head and covered her mouth. "Say a word and I will pull the trigger," Gwen whispered in her ear. The woman almost dropped the soda, but gripped it tightly. "Walk, bitch. Try to scream and I will fucking splatter your brains. You understand?" The woman nodded and headed toward the stairs.

"Yo, tell dat nigga to call me as soon as you hear from him," 4Pound said into the phone. He was talking to Made, trying to figure out where Spice was. 4Pound stood by the bedroom window, looking out at the landscape. He nodded to Pam as she entered the room.

He turned back to look out the window and then slowly turned back to Pam. She fell to the floor. 4Pound was staring down the barrel of a gun that a female was holding. He was caught. He couldn't even get to his shit, or maybe he could, but he wasn't sure how quickly this chick could fire one off in him or Pam.

"Is your name 4Pound?" Gwen asked, stepping a little closer to him.

4Pound looked at Pam as she lay on the floor, then back to the woman. He closed his eyes and nodded his head, hoping his answer didn't cost him his life.

"Where's my son?" she asked through clenched teeth, gripping the gun even tighter.

"Shawty, I don't know what you're talking about," he shot back with a straight face.

Gwen reached into her back pocket, grabbed her phone, and pressed the number on the screen. The room was quiet for a moment, and then the phone in 4Pound's hand began to sing Gucci Mane's "Trap God."

"You don't know anything? Your boy handed me his phone, and this number was on it when I spoke to my son after he was kidnapped. Now, for the last fucking time, where is my son?" Gwen gripped the gun with both hands.

4Pound swallowed. He knew this shit was going to go wrong as soon as he saw that little boy. "Shawty, I don't know where he at," 4Pound lied.

"Get on ya stomach and put ya hands on ya head," Gwen said, squeezing the gun tighter.

"Shawty, I am not getting on the ground. If you're gonna shoot me, then shoot," 4Pound shot back, hoping this chick didn't have the heart to take him out.

Gwen reached in her hoodie. She held the gun in front of her as she put the silencer on the end of the barrel.

4Pound felt his stomach drop. Shit, this bitch was serious.

"Last chance," Gwen told him, looking him in his eyes.

"Just get down, boo," Pam said from the floor.

He thought about it. He wondered if he could reach his shit. Gwen's eyes were focused on him. He fell to his knees and then lay on his stomach.

Gwen told Pam to get up. She directed her to yank out the cord to the satellite box and tie his hands behind his back. Once she tied his hands, she directed Pam to sit on the bed.

Pam sat down, never taking her eyes off Gwen. She wasn't a street chick at all. Gwen knew she didn't have to worry about her by the way her hands were shaking and how quickly she moved when Gwen told her to get the cord.

"Now, one way or the other, you're gonna tell me where my son is at," Gwen said, walking over and grabbing his phone off the floor. "And if you don't tell me, I'ma kill you and her," she threatened as she waved the gun from 4Pound to Pam.

Pam was terrified. She had no idea what was going on, but she could tell this woman would kill them both if 4Pound didn't give her what she wanted. Shit, she knew this nigga would be the end of her, but love made her stay with him. Now she may be with him forever.

Niya pulled up to Washington Avenue, where Diamond and Dollaz were sitting on the steps. Diamond sat a step below Dollaz, her head resting against his stomach. The girl was in love with dude. Niya smiled at them. They made a cute couple, and the fact that Dollaz was holding the block down for MHB was an added bonus.

"Awwwwww," Niya teased out the window.

"What you want?" Diamond joked, throwing up her middle finger.

"Dollaz, can I steal her for about two hours?" Niya yelled out.

Dollaz smiled. "Two hours is a long time," he shouted back, wrapping his arms around Diamond.

The two exchanged a few more kisses. Niya pretended to gag, and Diamond got up. Dollaz smacked her on the ass and she giggled.

"Dis better be good," Diamond said, getting into the car.

"Naw, this is gonna be great," Niya replied with a sinister grin on her face. "But before we do anything, we got to get Tiffany."

"What are you up to, Ni?" Diamond asked, looking at her.

"We got a party tomorrow, so I want us to do it big. That's all that I am going to say about that right now," Niya said, putting her shades on and pulling off.

Chad cautiously approached Mayo's house, not really sure what to expect. All he knew was that Gwen had called his phone several times. When he decided to pick up, she told him that she needed him to meet her. After receiving the address, he got in his car and headed out. He could tell by the sound of her voice that it had something to do with Zion. He put their earlier fight out of his head, hoping that their son was still alive.

The sun was going down and the house was dark. Chad gripped his gun as he approached the porch. He slowly turned the doorknob with his gun raised. A television was playing in the living room. He checked the rooms downstairs and made his way up the stairs. He took out his phone and texted Gwen:

I'm downstairs. Where you at?

"I'm up here," Gwen yelled.

Chad proceeded up the stairs slowly. He had his gun raised, ready to fire. When he reached the top, he could see a light in the first room to his right. He walked in. Gwen was sitting in a chair. A woman was on the bed, and a man on the floor.

"What's goin' on?" he asked, looking around the room.

"He knows where Zion is, but he is not saying anything."

"I told you I don't know where ya son is at," 4Pound yelled from the floor.

"Fucking liar!" Gwen yelled as she kicked him in his stomach. "I talked to my son from ya phone, you lying bitch."

Chad grabbed her before she kicked the dude again. He looked down at the man. He was missing a few teeth, and his right eye was swollen. He coughed, and blood sprayed from his mouth onto the tan carpet. Chad made sure Gwen was seated, walked over to 4Pound, and rolled him onto his back. 4Pound let out a painful moan. Chad put the barrel of the gun to his forehead.

"Check dis out, homeboy. I don't know who you are, and I really don't give a fuck either," Chad said, kneeling down next to 4Pound. "All I want is my son back."

"I told you, I don't—"

Chad pressed the barrel into his forehead. "You got kids, homie?" Chad asked, cutting him off.

4Pound looked over at Pam.

"Yeah, you got kids," Chad said, looking at the expression on Pam's face. "Listen, homie, and I'ma keep it one hundred wit' you right now, 'cause I don't got time for games. I don't care about you; I don't care about Mayo or the niggas who got my son. If you tell me where he is, I give you my word that I will let all of y'all niggas live. I'll take my son and move to the other side of the map. You will never see me again," Chad said. "But if you don't tell me where my son is at, I'ma find whatever kids you and shawty got," he said, nodding to Pam, "and then I'm gonna slay 'em. I'ma kill you, her, ya mother, ya father, ya brothers and sisters, and anybody else in ya family I can find. I'ma wipe out ya whole lineage. I swear on my son's life, I'ma kill everybody you love, my nigga, and they won't go fast, either," Chad threatened as he applied more pressure to 4Pound's forehead with his gun.

4Pound closed his eyes. He knew he should have walked away from this shit as soon as he saw little man. He really thought Made and Spice would give the little boy back to his parents. He looked into Chad's eyes. Ol' boy didn't look like the type to spray a nigga's brains everywhere, but he looked like a father on edge. He thought about his family. Mayo, Spice, and Made were on their own. He had to save his blood.

"A'ight, man, just give me my phone. I'm gon' help you get little man back," 4Pound said as he looked at Pam's terrified face.

Chad parked his car at the convenience store. He walked down the block of abandoned houses. He shivered to think that his boy was in one of these rat traps. Gwen was back at Mayo's house with 4Pound and his girl, in case the information he had given him was bogus or a setup. 4Pound had asked Made to meet him at one of the trap houses to deal with a problem. He told Chad that Spice would be the only one in the house.

He looked at the faded numbers on the mailbox. Forty-two, it read. He checked the chamber and listened at the door. He heard the TV and someone talking, so he listened to the conversation and determined that the male must have been talking to someone on the phone, due to Chad not hearing another voice respond to the man. He put the key that 4Pound had given him in the door and slowly opened it.

Spice was walking into the bathroom. He didn't notice that Chad was standing there, and he began peeing. "I don't give a fuck what 4Pound said. Get da fuck back over here and help me wit' dis shit, nigga," Spice yelled into the phone before hanging up.

He flushed the toilet and turned around to see Chad standing in the bathroom doorway. Spice dropped his phone in the toilet and his eyes widened. "Fuck!" Spice said as he attempted to lunge at Chad.

Chad moved and cracked the butt of the gun in the top of Spice's head. When Spice hit the floor, Chad fired a round into his stomach. He rolled him over and put his foot on the wound.

"Where da fuck is my son, nigga?" Chad said through clenched teeth as he stepped on the bullet wound.

Spice bit down in pain from the bullet wound. He tried to get up, but Chad wouldn't let him.

"Where da fuck is my son?" Chad yelled in fury, smacking Spice in the face with the butt of his gun.

"Fuck you, fuck you, nigga," Spice said, knowing that at any minute his life was about to end.

"Zion!" Chad yelled out to see if he would answer.

Chad looked around the room and called for Zion again. He noticed a large black duffle bag on the floor in the kitchen. His eyes scanned the room, but when he looked down at Spice, he noticed that his eyes were on the duffle bag. The terror in his eyes confirmed Chad's fear. He looked at the bag, and then at Spice.

"Look, he just stopped breathing, and I didn't know . . ." Chad fell back against the wall.

Spice took a chance and made a run for the door. One flash and he hit the floor.

"It was an accident," Spice pleaded, still trying to get out of Chad's grasp.

"God, please, please." Chad walked into the kitchen. He fell to the floor and unzipped the bag. He opened the bag, and Zion's pale face appeared. Chad yelled, "No, no, no, no, nooo!"

He reached in and grabbed his son's body out of the bag. His entire body ached, and his lungs were on fire. He cradled Zion in his arms, screaming to God to bring him back. He didn't even care about the police sirens approaching, and he made no attempt to get up. Chad held his firstborn in his arms and rocked him. Then he pulled out his phone. He had one more phone call to make before the police got there.

Gwen sat on top of the dresser, looking over at the TV. 4Pound was still lying on the floor, and Pam had started to nod off on the bed. The sound of Gwen's cell phone ringing made everyone jump. Gwen quickly reached over and grabbed the cell phone.

"Yeah!" Gwen answered, jumping down off the dresser. There was silence on the other end of the phone. "Hello," Gwen said as she listened to the police sirens in the background. "Chad, what is going on?" Gwen asked frantically as she paced back and forth across the room.

Chad tried to speak. His voice cracked, and Gwen could hardly understand him.

"Baby, please tell me what's wrong," Gwen pleaded.

There was silence, and then she heard a loud crash as the police announced themselves. She heard them yell for Chad to put down the gun.

"Zion's gone," Chad cried into the phone before dropping it to the floor. The words echoed through her soul.

"Chad! No, no, don't tell me that. Where is my son?" Gwen yelled at the phone. She fell back against the chair as the phone slid out of her hand.

Ten minutes later, she stood up and abruptly stopped screaming. She stared out the window then turned and headed out of the room.

Pam looked at 4Pound, surprised at Gwen's exit. 4Pound dropped his head. From the sounds of it, he and Pam only had a few moments left on this earth.

Terror struck Pam as she looked at 4Pound. She tried to free her hands from the duct tape. She looked at the door and she slid off the bed, still struggling with the tape.

"Come on, baby. She's gonna kill us," 4Pound pleaded. "Just get up and come untie me," he begged.

Pam placed a foot on the floor and froze. Gwen came back in the room. Her eyes were cold and lifeless. Pam looked in her hand and saw the lighter fluid. She jumped off the bed and ran toward the window. Gwen fired, hitting her in the back of the neck. She fell back beside 4Pound. Gwen looked down at him.

"Come on, shawty. Don't kill a nigga," 4Pound pleaded as she stood over him.

Gwen didn't hear his voice; she heard Zion calling for her. She just began spraying the fluid on top of him, mainly in his face. She sprayed some over Pam as well, and then sprinkled the rest of the bottle around the room. She went back to him and saturated him with the fluid. Gwen tossed the bottle to the ground, tucked her gun into her back pocket, and then pulled out a book of matches. She lit the whole book and tossed it onto 4Pound's face. He briefly screamed in agony before the flames shot down his throat when he tried to inhale.

Gwen just stood there for a moment, watching him wiggle around on the floor, trying to escape the pain. The fire quickly spread over to Pam and then across the room. She slowly exited the area, looking back one more time to see the flames eat away the flesh of Pam and 4Pound. She walked down the stairs and out the door to her car, looking back as the second floor erupted in flames.

***

The EMTs came running into the house as the police were attempting to pull Zion's pale body from Chad's arms.

"Sir, let go of the child," one officer screamed,while the other one was instructing Chad to raise his hands. Chad did neither; he just continued to hold and squeeze Zion.

The EMT realized that it was hopeless to try to remove the son from the man he assumed was the father, so he simply placed his hands on the young boy's neck. "We have a pulse. We need a defibrillator in here now!" he screamed. "Sir, let go if you want me to save your boy!"

Chad let go of Zion. As soon as he moved back, he was pushed to the floor by cops. He watched as the EMT performed CPR on Zion. "Come on, baby boy, come on," Chad said.

Two more EMTs entered the house with a machine. Chad didn't move from the floor; he kept his eyes on his son. An EMT took a pair of medical scissors, cut off Zion's shirt, and began placing white stickers to his small chest. The other one began connecting the wires that were coming out of the machine he held in his hands. Everything was a blur as the medics worked on Zion.

The police had to carry Chad out of the house. They placed him in the back of a patrol car. He sat in the back seat, looking out the window as they rolled Zion out of the house and placed him in the back of the ambulance.

Chapter 8

Club Cameo looked as if they were having a summer fling in the parking lot. It was full of women dressed in purple, waiting to get inside. The variation of women went from hood to corporate, from tall to skinny, lipstick lesbians to butch, fat to thin. The crowd was diverse, and no penises in sight.

Niya, Diamond, Tiffany, and Alexus pulled into the parking lot. The valet ran to each car and opened the doors. Heads turned as Niya stepped out of her two-door Bentley wearing a purple silk Chanel halter with lavender wide-leg pants. She wore matching purple Chanel open-toe sandals, with a silver-linked Chanel belt around her waist. Tiffany followed behind, stepping out of her Maserati Quattro wearing a purple miniskirt with matching cowboy boots and a sheer purple blouse. Diamond slid out of her silver Aston Martin Vanquish. She wore the curve-hugging Chanel cocktail dress, and Alexus slinked out of her black-on-black CL55 Mercedes. Niya had instructed each girl to make sure that they brought glamour, class, and their big-girl toys out tonight. She wanted to make sure that the potential recruits could see what could be obtained by being with MHB. The parking lot was filled with whispers.

Once the women stepped inside, Niya looked around at all the impressed faces in the crowd.

"Damn, I didn't know this many people was gonna come out," Tiffany said once they made it to the VIP section.

"I know. Shit, it gotta be over five hundred girls in here," Diamond said, looking out at the dance floor.

Club Cameo was packed with chicks from the security to the DJ. Niya looked at the crowd on the dance floor.She had so many broads to choose from. To be a part of MHB, a girl had to be smart and attractive; if she wasn't good-looking, she had to exude confidence that made people find her attractive. She watched the women dance and observed what they ordered at the bar. She made mental note of the ones who caught her eye, and went through her checklist of attributes she saw in each one. She smiled as she sat back. Later that night, there would be a way to separate the kittens from the female tigers.

"Is he talking yet?" Detective Gibson asked, walking into the interrogation room next to the room where Chad sat.

The detectives had been trying for the last forty-five minutes to convince Chad that Zion was not dead. They told him that Zion was in the hospital, but Chad still had not said a word to them. Chad thought they may have been just telling him that so he would talk. It had been a little less than twenty-four hours since they brought him into the station. At this point, without him saying anything, they had not charged him. The detectives had assumed that the boy was Chad's, and that something had happened to cause him to shoot the man in the house. The boy's body was halfway in a duffle bag, and Chad was distraught when the officers kicked in the door. They needed him to fill in the blanks for them, and he was not saying a word.

"No, he hasn't said a single word," Detective Rodgers replied, looking at Chad through tinted glass. "He didn't ask for nothing to eat, nothing to drink, not even a damn cigarette. Hell, he hasn't even asked to use the damn bathroom," Detective Rodgers said, shaking his head while watching Chad sit in the chair.

Chad stared at the gray walls of the interview room. His mind and body were exhausted. What kind of father was he that he couldn't protect his child? Why didn't he hear them when they came in the apartment? His boy was gone, and right now, the only thing he wanted was to hear Zion run up to him and call out, "Daddy." He wanted to feel those little arms around his neck and hear him laugh when they played the belching game.

Detective Rodgers opened the door due to the commotion he heard outside. He and McFadden stepped out to see a woman and a man talking to one of the officers. He heard the man say that his client had rights.

"What in the hell is going on out there?" McFadden said as he approached the man and woman.

"My client has rights, and I don't think you want to violate them," the man in the suit said.

McFadden cursed under his breath. With Chad having a lawyer, he knew that any chance of getting a statement from him was now gone. "I'm Detective McFadden. I'm the lead investigator."

"Well, is my client being charged with anything?" Donald Mac, Chad's lawyer, asked.

"Look, I'll be straight with you. We didn't file any charges against him yet because we're trying to figure out what's goin' on, but your client hasn't been very helpful. What we do know is we got a severely injured child and a dead body in a house. Your client was sitting right in the middle of them. Now, unless y'all got a good explanation for this, I'm gonna have to hold him until he tells us what happened."

"Hold up. Did you say an injured child?" Gwen asked, wanting to make sure she heard the detective correctly.

"Yes, and if he don't tell us what happened, we're gonna have to charge him with both cases," Detective McFadden tried to explain.

"So, are you telling me that my child is alive?" Gwen screamed. "Where is he? Please tell me where he is." Donald Mac had to hold Gwen.

McFadden could see that this woman had been through hell, but he needed answers. "Look, before I can go into the information on the young male victim, I will need you to tell me everything you know. I can tell you that he is alive, and I can have an officer take you to the hospital as soon as you give me a statement."

Mac looked over at Gwen and nodded that it was okay for her to tell the detective what had happened. Leaving out some specifics, she told the detectives that her son had been kidnapped and held for ransom. She and Chad were too afraid to come to the police, due to the kidnappers watching their every move. She had no idea why they targeted them. Two of the kidnappers had allowed her to speak to her son, and she memorized the number that was on the screen. From there she was able to track them down through a reverse lookup. This was after they had given them the money and they did not return her son. They became desperate. They knew they should call the police, but they just wanted their son back safe. After finding the address, Chad went to get their son back.

Detective McFadden looked at the woman, who could hardly speak for sobbing between words. She was so distraught that he patted her shoulder, trying to calm her down. He thought of his own children and was sympathetic toward the couple. It would be up to the D.A. to decide how he wanted to proceed. He still needed to hold Chad until he confirmed everything Gwen had said.

"Well, we're gonna check that story out, but until then, he's gonna be in our custody. Now, I will have an officer give you a ride to Carolina Medical Center, where your child is." He nodded to a uniformed officer. "Officer Starnes will take you there, ma'am." He walked out of interview room 12 into room 11, followed by the lawyer.

"Give me time with my client please."

McFadden closed the door. He only had twenty-four hours left to decide if he was going to charge Chad or let him go. He walked to his desk to call the D.A.

Boy, don't even try to touch this; Boy, this beat is crazy; This is how they made me; Houston, Texas, baby; This goes out to all my girls . . .

"Run the World (Girls)" by Beyoncé was blasting through the speakers. The girls were upstairs enjoying the party, and the heads of MHB were in the basement with twenty-five handpicked females. Niya, Diamond, Tiffany, and Alexus sat behind a table looking over each one of them.

Niya whispered to Diamond.

"Porsha, Tasha, Kea, and Millie, step up," Diamond said, smiling at each of the four. Niya had decided on these girls due to them passing the test.

During the 100K money drop, these four did not bend down to pick up one bill. Porsha actually stepped back and allowed the other women to grab the cash. Niya watched her watching the women, and then smiled as she walked to the bar to get a drink. Alexus had asked her why she wasn't grabbing the money, and she replied that she wasn't going to get a nail broken trying to pick up money she could make in about an hour. She was a college girl but had a weed contact who paid her tuition, rent, and other things. She had most of the campuses in Charlotte locked down.

Tasha and Kea told Tiffany that they didn't need any money. They got what they needed from their clients. They ran a high-end escort agency.

Millie told Niya that she should step up her game if she trying to test folks. Niya really liked her. She was smart, and smart went further than stupid. Each one of these chicks possessed a trait that Niya needed and liked.

"I hosted this party tonight for one reason, ladies." Niya stood and walked toward the four women. "I was looking for the elite women of Charlotte. I was looking for some new recruits to join Money Hungry Bitches, M . . . H . . . B." She looked each woman in the eye as she said the letters. "You four possess qualities that our family needs. We will take over Charlotte, then expand to both Carolinas.

"We are family above everything else, sisters with bonds that cannot be broken. We are not a gang of stupid thugs. We are a family, an organization that will have status like the top ten on the *Forbes* list. Ladies," Niya said as she leaned back on the table, "this is an invitation to join us. Being a part of MHB will change your life. So, if you want to find out more and become part of this young, growing empire, step forward."

There were whispers from the twenty-one other women in the room. The hoods knew MHB was a group of bad-ass bitches that was about making their money. Not a nigga among them, just broads about their business. Only a few in the room had no idea what MHB was or how much of a hood honor it was to even be considered. One by one, Porsha, Tasha, and Kea stepped forward. Millie took some time. She looked at each of the ladies at the table. After a couple of minutes, she stepped forward.

Diamond handed each of them a glass. Niya poured from a bottle of Ace of Spades into each of their glasses.

She raised the bottle. Tiffany, Alexus, and Diamond stood beside her and raised their glasses.

"And let me be the first person to welcome you to MHB," Niya announced and then took a swig from the bottle.

It was late at night when Detective Butler got the word that two bodies were found burned to a crisp in Mayo's house, but even still, he had to see it for himself. When he entered the morgue, a chill shot straight down his spine. No matter how many dead bodies he had seen in his career, going into a morgue always did something to him. The remains of 4Pound and Pam were horrific. Both of their bodies had been burned beyond recognition. An accidental fire was quickly ruled out by the fire department, determining that an accelerant had been used to start the blaze.

"The autopsy determined that the female was shot in the back of the neck," the medical examiner said while leading Butler to metal slabs.

"So, they were already dead when the fire started?" Butler asked with a curious look on his face.

"Actually, she wasn't. I found her lungs full of smoke, which means that she still was alive. This fella here got it bad," the examiner said, touching what was left of 4Pound's head. "It was like somebody had poured gasoline right on his face. We sent both sets of teeth to the lab, so hopefully we can identify them in a day or two," the examiner concluded.

Butler stared at the bodies. This killing was malicious and personal. This happened at Mayo's house. Mayo would be his first stop after leaving the morgue. His phone rang. Officer Starnes advised him of Chad's arrest and his son's kidnapping. Butler listened, but what Starnes said next made his antenna go up. It was the mother of the boy. Williams advised Butler that she had a tattoo of *MHB* on her ankle. Starnes worked the gang unit, and when he saw the tattoo, he recognized it from being undercover off Rozzell Ferry. He knew that Butler was investigating MHB, and felt he needed to know what was going on.

"What's the name of the female you got?" Butler asked out of curiosity.

"Gwyneth Wright," Starnes answered as he looked over at Gwen sitting in the lobby of the hospital, waiting to see Zion.

Until now, Butler didn't have Gwen on his radar for being MHB. He didn't know her, but he had a gut feeling. She was off the radar for a reason, and he wanted to know exactly what that reason was. "I'll be there in twenty minutes," Butler told Starnes before hanging up and leaving the morgue.

Detective Rose finally made it home after a long night, and the first thing she did was use the bathroom. She'd been holding her pee ever since the club. She really wasn't a big liquor drinker, so the four shots of Patrón had her feeling tipsy. She didn't want to drink, but she knew this party was more than just a gathering. She knew that the group was watching everyone closely, so she had to partake in the festivities.

"What did I do? Shit, this thing itches," Rose said, standing in front of the mirror, looking back at herself.

She slowly pulled her shirt off and tossed it into the hamper then looked down at her waistline. The MHB tattoo was clear as day, and it was starting to swell. This was the first tattoo Rose had ever gotten, and she couldn't believe it was a gang tat. It was a mixture of pressure and excitement that got her to let Niya brand her. It was like a rush that Rose couldn't describe, being around all of those women. For a second, she almost forgot that she was a cop, and she was actually enjoying herself.

Rose continued staring at the tattoo in the mirror, but she was interrupted by her cell phone ringing in the other room. When she reached the phone, she could see that it was Detective Butler calling. She thought about not answering it, but quickly remembered this was a prescheduled call.

"Rose," she answered, kicking her shoes off and walking into the kitchen.

"How did you make out?" Butler asked, pulling into the hospital parking lot.

"I did pretty good," Rose responded, opening the refrigerator and grabbing some leftover chicken. "I think that is safe to say that I am officially a member of MHB."

"You sure about that?" Butler questioned with some doubt. He had confidence that she would do well, but not in such a short time.

"Yeah, I think I'm pretty sure I am MHB," Rose said, looking down at her tattoo. "Look, I got my first meeting tomorrow, so I need to get some sleep. I'll meet up with you afterward, and we can go over the details," Rose said, trying to rush off the phone.

"All right. Make sure you call me the first thing in the morning. I want a full update," Butler said and then hung up the phone.

Gwen paced in the hospital waiting room. The nurse had informed her that they were still working on Zion. She had not given her any other details. She promised Gwen that she would send the doctor to her as soon as Zion was stable. Gwen bit her nails and sat down in the blue chair.

Officer Starnes stood close by for a moment, but then he disappeared down the hall with his phone to his ear. She rocked back and forward in the chair and stared at the steel doors. She needed to see her baby.

Detective Butler walked into the hospital waiting area. Starnes nodded to him as he walked toward him.

"Detective Butler," Starnes greeted him as he walked up to him. "Let's go over here for a moment and I will bring you up to speed," he told Butler as he walked away from Gwen's earshot.

Officer Starnes broke down everything he had on the case. When they walked back over toward Gwen, Butler got a good look at the *MHB* tattoo on her ankle, but that wasn't the only thing that he noticed as he sat beside her. He stared at her for a moment.

Gwen turned to him. He had his arm around the back of her chair, causing her to draw back. Why was this dude all up in her personal space? "Can I help you?" Gwen said.

Butler only smiled, took a deep breath through his nose, and leaned in closer.

"Again, can I help you?" Gwen repeated with a little more aggression.

"Why do you smell like gasoline?" Butler asked, not blinking or breaking his stare.

Gwen frowned at him. She wasn't sure how to respond to the question, and his closeness to her made her extremely uncomfortable. What the hell was wrong with this cracker? She was about to speak when the steel doors opened and a nurse pointed to her. A short Asian doctor began making his way toward her. She forgot about Butler and jumped up to meet him. He barely took four steps before she was in front of him.

"Hi, yes, how is Zion? You are his doctor?" she asked.

"Yes, my name is Doctor Gen, and your name is?" he said as he extended his hand and led her to a chair.

"Oh, I'm sorry, my name is Gwen. Gwen Wright, and my son's name is Zion," Gwen responded. "Please tell me he's alive and is going to be all right. Please," she continued.

Dr. Gen touched her hand. He had kind eyes. He took a deep breath. "Well, the good news is Zion is stabilized for the moment. It appears that his oxygen supply was cut off for some time, but through some miracle, he hung on just long enough for help to get to him. It appears he had an asthma attack. Do you know why he wasn't able to get his inhaler or breathing treatment?"

"He was kidnapped. So, can I see him?" Gwen asked, trying to fight the urge to push Dr. Gen out of the way and run down the hall screaming for Zion.

"Mrs. Wright, Zion is in a coma. There could be possible brain damage, and also damage to his heart. He is young and has a fifty-fifty chance of a recovery, but even with recovery, he will have a long road ahead of him."

"What?" Gwen asked, looking at the doctor as if he were speaking his native language instead of English. "Okay, okay, so can I see him please?" Gwen asked a second time.

"Yes, of course," Dr. Gen responded. "Nurse Patterson will take you to him."

Gwen looked at the nurse. The nurse smiled at her and pressed the button to open the large steel doors.

Detective Butler and Officer Williams walked over to Dr. Gen. They were not able to question Gwen right now, but they could get information on the boy's condition.

Eagle was sound asleep when his ringing phone awakened him. He quickly reached over to the nightstand where the noise was coming from and turned off the ringer. He did not want to be bothered by anyone. About a minute went by, and then the doorbell started to ring.

Now that was unusual, since only a few people knew where he rested his head when he wasn't on the block.

He got up, grabbed the Desert Eagle handgun that was lying next to him, and crept downstairs to the front door. He quietly moved the curtains to take a look outside. At first, he didn't see anyone on the porch, which made him become even more concerned.

It wasn't uncommon in Charlotte for stick-up boys to run up in someone's house when they thought there was money there, and if they thought Eagle was going to be their next victim, they had another think coming. He wasn't going for that, so he took the safety off the large-caliber handgun then took another peek out the window again.

This time, he saw the small frame of a woman walking back down the steps. Looking a little closer, he could see a white Bentley Continental coupe sitting curbside. He quickly opened the door to see who it was, but he still kept his hand wrapped around his gun.

"Yooo," he said, stepping out onto the porch.

Niya stopped and turned back around to see Eagle standing there shirtless. His body was ripped to the core, and as she looked at him from head to toe, Niya gasped at the sight of his dick print showing through his sweatpants.

"Damn, what's up, Ni?" Eagle said, noticing who it was.

"I'm sorry. Was you asleep?" Niya asked, walking back up the stairs. "You know what they say about sleepers."

"Yeah, the only thing that comes to them is a dream," he said, finishing her quote. "So, what's up? Something happened on the block or something?" Eagle asked, still not sure why Niya was there.

Niya looked at him and laughed. "Yeah, you must still be 'sleep," she said, walking past him into his house.

He took another look at the Bentley before following her back into his home. Niya was really feeling high tonight, not just because of the few drinks she had, but because of the success of her recruiting efforts. She was riding around in her $200,000 car, and she had made $100,000 rain down at her first official MHB party. Life was good for the female boss! She had everything she needed, and now she was here for something she wanted.

"So, E, you alone?" Niya asked, walking up to Eagle. "Or do you already have company?"

Eagle looked at Niya like she was crazy. "So, how many drinks did you have tonight?" he joked.

"Shut up." She laughed, punching him in his chest. "I'm serious. Are you alone? If yes, I want to see how that chest feels against me without clothes—or how did you say it? Oh, yeah. Arms between us," she said, sliding her hand down his stomach.

Niya's eyes pulled Eagle into her seductive gaze. Feeling her hand on his body made his stomach tremble. He looked at her full lips and the way the halter top dipped to her navel, exposing her soft breasts. He picked her up and carried her upstairs. Eagle had been attracted to Niya since the first time she pulled up in her Benz, wearing the hell out of some jeans. This was what he had been waiting for, the chance to feel those caramel thighs around his waist. He placed her on the bed and stood back to take in the view of her.

"You sure you wanna go down this road?" Eagle asked, hoping that she didn't have any second thoughts.

Niya untied her halter and unzipped it at the waist, then threw it to Eagle. He licked his lips as he looked at her hard nipples. She stood and allowed her pants to fall to the floor and then stepped out of them. Still wearing her stilettos, she walked around him, stood behind him, and slid her hands into his sweatpants.

"Damn, umm, is that for me?" Niya stroked him while pressing her body against his back.

Eagle closed his eyes and enjoyed her soft hand going up and down his shaft. He felt her tongue playing behind his left ear. He turned to her and kissed her then lifted her in his arms. She wrapped her legs around his waist and grinded against his erection.

"Damn, Ni." He dropped his sweatpants to the floor. His dick was against his stomach. He rubbed her hot, wet box up and down the shaft of it. She moaned and reached down to caress his balls. He needed to be inside her, but he also wanted to take his time. He lifted her up higher so that her breasts were near his lips, and he sucked one of them inside his mouth. As he tasted one of her nipples, Niya began playing with her clit while he held her in the air.

"No you don't. That's for me." He placed her on the bed and buried his face between her legs. He moved his head from side to side, tasting that sweet, wet pearl. *Yeah, I'm gonna have her thinking about a nigga after this.*

Niya looked down at him as she bucked against his tongue. "Ahh, ummm, E, shit!"

Eagle felt her pussy twitch. He turned her over and placed her on her knees. He took his wide dick and smacked her ass with it. Niya jumped with each hit. After spanking her, he flipped her back over and pushed his wide head between her moist folds.

Niya's mind was screaming, *Condom!* but her lower lips screamed for him to go deeper. She looked down, and although she had thought he was completely inside her, she noticed that half of it was still out. *Damn, this nigga a horse!* she thought.

"You ready to take this dick, huh?" he panted. "I'ma make this pussy mine!" Eagle slid his entire dick in.

Niya's eyes widened and she let out a scream. "Fuck, E! That is a big-ass dick! Ahhh, damn!" It was more than she could handle, but there was no way she was going to let this young nigga put her out. He held her ankles and slid in and out of her wet box slowly. She pulled her nipples and he picked up the pace.

"Yeah, baby. Damn, that pussy good." Each time he entered her, his strokes became more aggressive. Niya was biting her lip. He was hitting a painful spot. She tried to adjust her hips, and when she did, he went even deeper.

"Shit!" she yelled, holding her thighs. She didn't realize that the high-pitched scream was coming from her as she squirted all over his dick.

"Yeah, yeah, that's right. Rain on this dick, baby!"

Niya couldn't believe where she was right now. She never thought in a million years that she would be giving her goodies to a man other than Chad. Not only was she giving her goodies away, but she really was enjoying herself. Damn, Eagle fucked her, and she needed it. She needed it to forget Chad and to feel desired. The way this young boy was putting it down, it felt like he was really trying to mark her pussy.

They made love until dusk, and between the passionate lovemaking, the alcohol, and the long prior day, Niya was exhausted. Eagle had put her ass to sleep and then awakened her with his mouth on her ass.

"Damn, boy, mama didn't give you enough last night?" Niya said, laughing.

"No, I'm good for right now, but I will be needing seconds later on today, for sure," Eagle responded, rubbing her butt. "But right now, I need you to throw your clothes on and ride somewhere with me right quick," he said.

Niya studied him for a minute and then began putting on her clothes. She grabbed her car keys, followed him outside, and walked toward her car.

"Nah, we don't need to roll up in that where we going."

Niya looked at him. He had some good pelvic moves, but he needed to watch giving her orders. He smiled at her and touched her back. She followed him to his car and got in.

After about twenty minutes of driving, they pulled up to a small yellow house in the Cherry Community. Cherry was a black neighborhood that sat right beside Myers Park, one of the wealthiest communities in Charlotte. According to history, the Cherry Community was built for the servants of the Myers Park residents, so that their help wouldn't have far to travel every day to work, to clean and maintain their homes and children. Although at one time the community was considered middle class for the blacks who lived there, the crack cocaine days of the eighties and early nineties had left their ugly mark on the once prosperous area. The once beautiful ranch-style homes now looked dilapidated.

"Come on," Eagle instructed as he got out of the car and headed for the front door of a brick house. He turned and extended his hand to Niya as they walked up the sidewalk. Eagle was about to knock on the door when a soft voice came from the right side of the porch.

"Hey, baby. Grandma decided to come outside and enjoy this beautiful weather the Lord done blessed us with today," the elderly woman uttered from the large rocking chair that was sitting on the far left side of the porch. The large bushes that adorned the front of the home had shielded her from Eagle's and Niya's view when they were walking up.

Eagle went over and gave her a hug, and then introduced Niya to his grandmother.

"It's nice to meet you," Niya spoke while holding out her hand.

"And it's nice to meet you, with your pretty self, but mama don't do no handshakes. You come here and give me a hug," Grandma Maggie instructed.

Eagle and Niya took a seat on the porch. Grandma Maggie gave Eagle all the updates on what was going on in the neighborhood and in the family. She paused only to ask Niya if she wanted anything to drink. Before Niya could respond, she told Eagle to go inside and fix them all some glasses of tea.

"Eugene, go on in dere and get us ladies some tea. The lemon is already cut up and in a bowl with some foil over it."

"Yes, ma'am," Eagle responded.

Niya couldn't believe her ears or her eyes. Here was this killer and hell-raiser of the streets, acting like a well-mannered nine-year-old. She was amazed at the respect, love, and affection that Eagle was displaying to his grandmother. Niya made sure she got her chance to call Eagle by his government name.

"Thank you, Eugene," Niya responded jokingly when he handed her a glass of tea.

The three of them sat and talked for nearly three hours. Niya could tell that Grandma Maggie loved Eagle just as much as he loved her.

Chapter 9

The smell of eggs, bacon, and home fries wafted through Rell's condo. He got up and made his way to the kitchen where Kea was standing over the stove, wearing nothing but one of his white wife beaters. He slid up behind her and grabbed her small waist, pulling her fat ass up against his dick.

"What's the special occasion?" Rell asked, kissing Kea on the neck.

In Kea's mind, she was still celebrating the fact that she was MHB now. Even the backbreaking sex she'd had with Rell the night before couldn't compete with how getting her tattoo felt. She felt like she was a part of something, and not just another one of Rell's bitches. The relationship between the two was still fresh, but Kea felt Rell was too controlling. He said that she was the one, but after being together for nearly two months, she realized that he shared his bed and attention with more than just her.

Rell, for the moment, was a financial sponsor for Kea. The fact that his dick would hit spots that made her body shiver was an added bonus. She would see this through until something better came along. He treated her as an option, and that made him disposable.

"I gotta go take care of a few things in a couple of hours. I was hoping we could do a late lunch today," Kea said, turning around to face Rell.

When she went to wrap her arms around his neck, Rell got a glimpse of something on the top of Kea's right arm. He grabbed her arm. He did not notice the tattoo last night when he was pounding that ass, but now it was sticking out like a sore thumb. He looked at her as if she had just stolen something, and he jerked her around by the arm.

"What the fuck is that?" he asked, pulling her around to get a clear view. Rell's face changed, and his grip became painful.

She pulled her arm away and stood so that Rell could clearly see the letters *MHB*. "I got it last night. I am an official MHB member." She smiled as she slid her fingers across the raised skin.

"You MHB?" Rell asked, running his hand over his face. "You messin' around wit' dem bitches running around here thinking they taking over shit?" he snapped, stepping back and looking at Kea.

Kea looked at him. She had no idea about the confrontation Rell had with Niya a short time ago concerning his block. After that confrontation, Rell got the word that MHB was growing and had taken over a couple of strips. It burned him to think about a bunch of females playing like they were some bosses. Now they had gotten to his girl, bringing that shit in his house?

"Yeah, Rell, I am MHB. What's the problem?" Kea shot back. She could see the vein had popped on the side of his temple. She looked at the grease from the bacon and decided she should move away from the stove. "What's the big deal? Dang," she said, walking past him.

Rell's eye caught the *MHB* tattoo again. He grabbed Kea from behind and locked his hand around her neck. These bitches were trying to take his block and his woman. That shit wasn't going to happen. Shit, these hoes needed to learn their place, and he needed to start teaching the one in front of him.

"Go cover dat shit up on ya arm. You not MHB; you my bitch," Rell snapped, applying pressure to her throat.

Kea didn't understand what Rell's issue was and why he was acting like a psycho. She twisted away from his grip. She took an oath to MHB last night, an oath to her new family, and anyway, Rell was temporary. "I ain't covering up shit," Kea said. "Nigga, take me—"

Craaack! Rell smacked the shit out of Kea before she could finish her sentence. Kea grabbed her face and stared at Rell. Before she could react, he smacked her again, this time knocking her against the kitchen table.

"Bitch, who you talking to?" Rell shouted as he grabbed her by the hair.

Kea looked back at the bacon grease on the stove. She should have stayed by it to begin with, but she wasn't about to let this dude keep hitting her. As he held her by her hair, she managed to connect her fist to his chin. Rell grabbed his chin but didn't let go of her hair.

"Y'all bitches think y'all niggas? I'ma treat you like a nigga."

Rell punched her in the face and she fell back against the wall. Kea turned her face against the wall. She was seeing stars. This wasn't a fair match. She had to be smart, so she balled against the wall. Rell bent down. She could hear him breathing but was afraid to turn and look at him, for fear he would punch her again. The smoke alarm wailed as the smoke from the burning bacon poured from the pan.

"Bitch, I'm gon' say this once: Cover that shit up before I burn that shit off. You got me?" Rell said, poking Kea on the side of her head with his finger.

Kea was fuming inside, but right now, she needed to survive. She nodded her head. Rell stood, looked down at her, and placed his foot on her butt.

"Get this shit cleaned up, too," he said, pushing her with his foot and then walking into the bedroom.

"Harper, you got a visit," the corrections officer told Mayo as he finished his set of pushups.

Being in solitary confinement had it disadvantages, and one of them was Mayo not being able to have his ear to the streets like he needed. He wasn't aware of anything that took place with Zion's near-death experience, nor about 4Pound, Pam, and Spice. When he got down to the visiting booths, he smiled at the sight of Gwen sitting on the other side of the glass. The officer took off his cuffs and closed the door behind him.

Gwen stared at Mayo, concentrating on her breathing, and then picked up the phone. Mayo smiled at her and picked up the other receiver.

"What up, Gwen?" Mayo spoke into the phone. "How's the family?" he asked.

Gwen looked directly into his eyes while tapping her nails on her leg. She smiled at him, which caused Mayo to feel uneasy.

"I really just wanted to look into the eyes of the man who nearly killed my son," Gwen said, breaking her silence.

"What da fuck is you talking about?" Mayo shot back with a confused look on his face. Damn, he had not heard from anyone in his crew. He had told the fools that they were not to harm Zion. Mayo was a gangsta in every sense of the word, but killing kids was not something he would wear. What the fuck had happened? Where was Spice?

"You a weak, pathetic nigga. I wasn't sure what I should do at first. I was torn between going to the police and FBI to tell them what you did; or should I do something for you that you didn't do for my baby?" She sat back in the chair and allowed her words to settle in his mind. "You can die in prison or die in the streets. Either way, I don't care."

"I told you I didn't have—"

Gwen stood and began to hang up the phone. She looked at the guard, who began to open the door.

"The streets. The streets," Mayo yelled, banging on the glass.

Mayo was a hard-ass gangsta, but he didn't want to spend the rest of his life in a cement prison. He dropped his head. The guard tapped his shoulder and he stood. What the fuck happened? He needed to find out so he could come up with a plan.

Chapter 10

Detective Rose, who was known to MHB as Millie, was the first person to show up at the vacant lot. Niya had informed them that she wanted to meet there to discuss some MHB business. Rose checked her watch. Niya pulled in the parking lot, followed by Tasha and Porsha. Rose got out of her car and smiled at the women. She hugged each of them, and they chatted for a few minutes, until Alexus pulled up about ten minutes later

The area was desolate. The old grocery store that was once there had been demolished. There wasn't a building or a house for miles. They were damn near in the country. Alexus nodded to them as she popped her trunk. She took out a small duffle bag and slung it over her left shoulder. The women had parked their cars in a circle and stood in the middle of it. Niya looked at each girl.

"Like I told y'all bitches before, we taking over the city, so in—" Niya stopped and pulled her .45 from her waist. A car was slowly pulling into the lot. It was a black Jaguar with tinted windows.

Diamond, Tiffany, and Millie pulled their guns. The driver door opened. Kea stepped out with her hands raised. She wore large, black Donna Karan shades. As she approached, Niya noticed the bruises on her cheek and chin. The women stared at her but did not say anything. Niya decided she would discuss it with her later.

"You late, and you almost got yaself killed," Niya said, tucking her gun back into her back. "Like I was saying,"

Niya continued, "it's gonna get ugly out here, so you better be prepared to use one of these," she said, nodding to Alexus.

Alexus reached into the duffle bag and pulled out automatic handguns. She passed them out to each of the females. Instinctively, Detective Rose popped the clip out, looked to see if it was a full clip, slapped it back into the gun, and cocked a bullet into the chamber. Niya studied her for a moment and made a mental note.

"I want y'all to shoot at the target until ya hand starts to hurt," Niya instructed, pointing at the target paper posted up on the partial wall that had not been knocked down completely. "And when ya hand starts hurting, I want you to switch hands and do the same thing."

Tiffany and Alexus stood behind Kea and Millie with clips. The two began firing away at the targets.

"Whoever shoots the best is rolling with me," Niya leaned over and whispered to Diamond before heading back to her car to make a phone call.

When Gwen walked into the police station, she was met by her lawyer and Detective Butler. Butler had a gut feeling that Gwen had something to do with the two burned bodies found in Mayo's house, but he just couldn't prove it. The fire chief said that the house was deliberately set on fire, and the person who did it used gasoline or lighter fluid. Gwen smelled of one of those liquids in the waiting room, less than twenty-four hours after the house fire; however, his smelling that on her wasn't evidence enough to prove that she had anything to do with the charred bodies in Mayo's house.

"I have some good news," Mac said to Gwen as he pulled her to the side, away from Butler. "They dropped the murder charges against him, but they did charge him with the gun possession. They only did that because he was a convicted felon. If it weren't for that, they would have let him go," Mac explained.

The district attorney advised McFadden that they would not charge Chad with murder. McFadden had presented the facts to him. The D.A. advised him that this wasn't one they could win, and no charges would be filed against a parent trying to save his child.

"So, now what?" Gwen asked. She glanced over at Butler, who glared at the two of them. Gwen couldn't figure out why this cracker had so much hostility toward her.

"Well, his bail was set at thirty thousand dollars. Whenever you can pay it, he'll get out," Mac explained. "More than likely, the D.A. will cut him a deal on the gun charge, but as you know, that's gonna take some time," he said.

Gwen was glad he wasn't being charged with murder, but there was an issue with bail. She was broke. She had maybe $1,500, and that would not even cover a bail bondsman. The police had confiscated her money from the house as evidence. She thought about Selena and Brianna, but they were out of town. She had no one else to turn to for help.

Detective Rose's skills with the gun had earned her a seat next to Niya in the Bentley.

"So, you from Brazil originally?" Niya asked, breaking the silence in the car.

"Yeah, until I was like, sixteen. This is a nice car. I don't think I have been in the front seat of one before," Rose admitted as she looked around in amazement at the interior.

As they drove down the streets, Rose made up a story about her originally being from Brazil and her family moving to Miami. She lied about her age, family history, and where she had worked. She admitted to Niya that her father had taught her how to handle a gun.

"So, what about you, Niya?" Rose asked, looking out the passenger's side window.

Niya smiled. "That's a long story. Maybe I will tell you one day," Niya said, pulling the car over.

"So, what's up?" Rose asked, looking around the area.

Rose looked at the street. It had a few houses across from a wooded area. This was a perfect spot to kill and drop a body. Niya was so focused that she didn't notice Rose placing her hand on her gun.

"Remember when I told you that MHB ride out for each other?" Niya asked, reaching under her seat and grabbing a Glock .40-caliber.

"Yeah," Rose answered with a confused look on her face.

"Well, today you're gonna get a clear understanding about what that means," Niya said, cocking a bullet into the chamber.

At the end of the target practice, Niya had pulled Kea to the side. She asked her about her being late, and what had happened to her face. Kea explained what happened. Niya listened to her, and she swelled with pride. In less than twenty-four hours, Kea had taken a beating for MHB and stood her ground against a gangster-ass nigga for the family. This nigga had drawn the blood of one of her sisters, and now it was time for him the pay the price for his actions.

She looked over at Millie. "Just watch my back," Niya said and then exited the car.

They walked about three blocks, until they got up to Ronheart Street, where Rell watched his troops sell dope. They approached the street corner, and Niya could see Rell's truck parked on the pavement. Niya was on the right side of the street, while Rose was on the left. They walked toward the crowd of niggas.

"Millie, watch them," Niya told Rose, nodding at the two guys standing on the porch.

They were gunmen watching the block for stick-up kids. They noticed Millie and Niya, not as a threat, but rather as potential ass.

"Damn, shawty, let me holla at you," one of the men said, getting exactly what he asked for when Rose walked up on the porch.

Niya kept walking, counting five niggas total on the corner, and that included Rell, who was sitting in his truck with the door open.

"Hey, Rell," Niya said, pulling the Glock out of her back pocket. Before he could respond, Niya had jammed the barrel into his groin.

His crew was busy selling to the fiends. They didn't look back for a few minutes. When they turned around, they scanned Niya from behind, and it appeared she was standing between Rell's legs flirting. Rell always had bitches on his dick. They continued selling to the fiends.

"Bitch, what am I supposed to be, scared?" Rell said, looking Niya in her eyes.

"Naw, I don't want you to ever be scared. Mama say scared niggas will kill ya. I wantcha to be just dickless." She smiled and squeezed the trigger.

The two young niggas and the fiends hit the ground, hearing the gunshot. Niya pulled Rell out of the truck. He fell to the ground, groaning and grabbing his dick. Niya searched Rell and took his gun. She checked his sock and took the small .22 and then ordered the workers to throw their guns under the truck. The boys were young and shaking, so they obeyed without issue.

"Now get down and stay down," she ordered the two young boys.

"Arrrgggh, bitch, I'm going to kill you!" Rell yelled.

Niya stood over him. She took her foot and stood on his groin. Rell yelled in pain. Niya put all her weight on his crotch. The young boys stared at her. Rose had the two niggas on the porch lying on their stomachs. She had disarmed them. She looked toward Niya and knew she had to do something before things got worse. She could see Niya laying blows to Rell's face with the butt of her gun. Shit, she was going to kill him. Rose looked at the two goons and then back to Niya pummeling Rell.

One of the young dudes had taken a chance while Niya was beating Rell. He had run inside one of the houses.

Niya was exhausted from the blows she had delivered to Rell's face. She had beaten him so badly that his eyes were swollen shut and blood was coming out his mouth and nose as he exhaled. She stood and raised her gun to his bloodied face. Rell was wheezing. Niya felt her adrenaline kick in; she was happy seeing his ass struggling to breathe and knowing his life was about to end.

"Niya, it's too many witnesses out here. One of dem boys done ran in one of those houses. Come on, we got to go. Finish this shit another time," Rose said, walking up on her.

Time was of the essence, and she knew that they didn't have long before the boy would be back out the house, and armed.

"We gotta go," Rose yelled, pulling Niya away.

Niya yanked away from her. She wasn't done yet.

"Touch somebody else from MHB, and I'ma blow ya fuckin' face off!" Niya shouted through clenched teeth as she continued hitting him with the butt of her gun.

Bullets whizzed in their direction. Not only had the young boy brought fire, but the dudes on the porch had gotten up and gone inside. Just as Rose expected, one of the gunmen came rushing out of the house, this time with a large assault rifle.

He let off eight shots in one second, most of which hit Rell's truck. Rose grabbed Niya and pulled her around to the front of the truck. *Fuck!* Rose looked around for the best strategy to get out of there. Niya began returning fire toward the porch. Rose followed suit. She knew she could take each one of them down, but aimed for shoulders and legs. Rose hit the young boy in the thigh.

As the boy fell, Niya jumped into Rell's truck. Rose jumped in the passenger's side. Niya punched the gas, looked at Rell, and turned the truck then headed toward him.

Rose panicked. She had to do something, so she began firing back at the porch. Niya swerved, hitting Rell's legs instead of his head. They disappeared down the street.

Chapter 11

"Gwen, where are you going?" Ms. Wright asked, stopping her daughter at the door of Zion's hospital room.

Gwen was terrified. The thought of Zion not surviving this cardiac surgery, or the doctors finding no brain activity, was more than she could bear. "I really can't deal with all of this right now, Mom. I got some stuff I need to take care of, and the doctors don't need me to help them do their job," Gwen replied, grabbing the door handle.

As Gwen tried to open the door, Ms. Wright slammed it back then stood in front of it. Ms. Wright looked at her daughter. Gwen's face was sunken. She had lost weight, and she walked around like a zombie. She was pale and she was jumpy.

"Sit down. I wanna talk to you," Ms. Wright said, pointing at the chair.

"Mom, I don't have time."

"I'm not asking you, Gwyneth," her mom said, pointing to the chair.

Gwen knew not to test her mother when she took that tone. She sighed and took a seat in the green leather chair. Ms. Wright sat beside her. "You haven't shed one tear since you been coming over here to check on Zion. When you come, you only stay a little while, and then you leave. You look like hell, and I can tell you are not taking care of yourself. You gotta do better, baby, for Zion. Tell me what is going on." She took Gwen's face in her hand and looked into her eyes. "Come on, baby, tell me. You know I am here for you. Now, what's going on with you, Gwyneth?" she asked, already knowing the answer.

"Mama, I don't got time to cry. I gotta handle my business first."

"What business?" Ms. Wright asked.

Gwen was silent, thinking about her baby having a fifty-fifty chance of surviving or at least having a normal life. It caused her blood to boil. Mayo's face entered her mind. She needed to make sure there was a zero percent chance that he survived. She imagined pulling the trigger and letting the heat from her Glock enter his forehead.

"What business?" Ms. Wright asked, snapping her fingers and bringing Gwen back.

Gwen and her mother had a close relationship. There was nothing she could not tell her. Her mother was always there for her. Even when Gwen did wrong, her mother would scold her but stand right by her. There wasn't too much she hid from her.

She looked in her mother's eyes and kissed her cheek. "Mom, I gotta make sure the dude who did this to Zion pays for it with his life. I ain't gonna rest until I take him out, and anybody else who wants to get in my way. I can't sleep until he is six feet deep," Gwen answered.

Ms. Wright sighed and squeezed Gwen's hand. She knew there was nothing she could say to change her mind. The apple didn't fall far from the tree. "Listen to me, baby," Ms. Wright said, turning Gwen's face to her. "I can't imagine what you're going through right now, but please, baby, remember I am a mother too. I love you, and I can't take losing my only child," Ms. Wright said, kissing Gwen on the cheek. She touched her face and walked over to Zion's bedside.

Gwen walked over to kiss Zion. Her heart ached. Touching her baby's hand, she knew that he was no longer in that body. She didn't feel him there any longer. The machines were beeping and hissing, keeping his body alive, but his little spirit was gone. She knew what the brain scan test was going to show. She had already processed the loss of her only child in her mind, but she just couldn't get up the nerve to disconnect him from the life support system. She took her baby in her arms and held him tightly as the doctor and the reverend entered the room.

Detective Rose sat on the edge of her bed, staring down at her badge and gun on the floor. Her mind was still reeling from the shootout. She replayed the incident in her mind and shuddered as she thought about how close she came to losing her life. Niya was a crazy chick; she had responded to the situation out of sheer emotion for one of her MHB sisters. Rose grabbed the bottle of Moscato off the nightstand. She turned it up and sighed.

A loud bang at the front door caused her to jump. She grabbed her gun off the floor and walked up the hallway. She made sure the light was off behind her and placed her hand over the peephole first, then looked through it. Her heart stopped when she realized that Niya was standing outside the door. Her mind raced as she tried to figure out how she had found her home.

"I see ya shadow under the door," Niya said, letting her know that she knew she was there.

Rose unlocked the door and opened it slowly.

"What, you didn't think I'd find out where you lived?" Niya joked, walking past Rose.

"No, it's not that. I'm still on edge a little from the other day," Rose said, trying to play it off.

Actually, Rose was more than a little concerned. If Niya knew where she lived, how possible was it that she knew Rose was a cop? She had been to the station a couple of times since the shooting.

"Well, I just stopped by to see if you wanted to ride with me. I got some business to take care of, and since you handled yaself the other day, I thought I could show you the flip side of the MHB coin," Niya said, looking around the apartment.

"Yeah, yeah, that's cool," Rose said. "Come back here while I get dressed," she said, trying to get Niya away from the living room. "It's cleaner in my bedroom anyway."

She needed to guide her away from the living room. She didn't want to take a chance on Niya seeing the photo of her in her officer's uniform after she graduated from the academy. Rose still felt uneasy. Revealing where she laid her head was a big no-no in undercover work. She wanted to make sure she kept her gun accessible at all times. She wasn't taking any chances on what else Niya might have found out.

"You mean to tell me that you got one of ya balls shot off and you refuse to tell me who did it?" Detective Butler said, standing next to Rell's hospital bed.

Rell was a top player in the drug game in Charlotte. Detectives had files so thick on him that there was almost a whole filing cabinet in the station just for his files. Butler knew that trying to find out who shot him was useless. These people didn't come to the police for anything. He lost one ball to the bullet, and his face was jacked up too. He was missing teeth, and his eyes were swollen shut. His left leg was in a cast, and his right was elevated. He looked like something out of a horror movie or a sci-fi film.

"All right, look. I know you think courts of the streets will resolve this issue, but if a kid stubs his toe in Charlotte over the next month or so, I am going to be coming for your black ass."

Rell managed to lift his hand and shoot the bird at Butler. Butler shook his head and exited the room.

Rell didn't know if he was dizzy from his injuries or from the rage that was rising inside of him. As soon as he was released, Niya was going to wish she had never run up on him. His head began to ring with pain as he imagined Niya begging him for mercy. After a moment, the pain began to subside. Yeah, MHB would be nothing more than an urban legend when he got finished with them hoes. He was going to take all of them out.

Diamond and Tasha walked into the courthouse suited and booted, like they were about to begin a high-profile trial. The truth of the matter was that Diamond was only there for a hearing to get her criminal record expunged. She didn't have any convictions or felonies, but her arrest record made it hard for her to apply for a license to carry. Tasha just came along for the ride. Each senior MHB had taken on protégés: Diamond mentored Tasha, Niya mentored Millie, Porsha was with Tiffany, and Kea with Alexus.

"Walk me to the bathroom," Diamond told Tasha as they got off of the elevator.

"A'ight," Tasha replied.

When they got to the bathroom, Diamond stopped in midstride when she walked in and saw Gwen washing her hands at the sink. The last time Diamond saw her was when she put a gun in Gwen's face and kidnapped her for Niya to kill. Tasha felt the room vibrate with tension.

Diamond readied herself for a violent encounter with Gwen. Gwen took towels from the machine. She looked up and locked eyes with Diamond.

Diamond pushed Tasha behind her. Gwen thought back to how she had imagined the things she was going to do to Niya, Tiffany, and Diamond the next time she saw them, but there was nothing there right now for them. She was too exhausted to even try to fight this bitch. She had bigger things to handle right now.

Diamond stood ready to fight.

Gwen sighed. "I really don't have time for this. Are you gonna move from in front of the door so I can leave?" she said, throwing the towels in the trash can.

Diamond noticed how skinny Gwen was. She looked like hell, and she didn't feel the normal energy from Gwen. She unclenched her fists as she looked down at the *MHB* tattoo on her ankle. Through everything, Gwen was still family, and it looked like she needed family right now instead of an ass-whooping. Diamond moved to the side. Gwen began to walk by. Diamond took a chance and grabbed her.

"G, what's wrong?" She squeezed her hand. Damn, she wasn't accustomed to this Gwen. There was no light or fire in her eyes.

Gwen instinctively returned the squeeze to Diamond. She teared up for a second but fought back the tears. She had to stay focused and handle business. "It's nothing. I'm fine, Diamond," she replied.

"And how's your son?" Diamond asked.

Gwen wanted to fall onto her sister, but there was too much bad blood. She let go of her hand and opened the door. "My son is caught between here and heaven," Gwen said and then brushed past Diamond and right out of the door.

Diamond froze. Those words alone were like a blow to the heart. She'd really hoped that Gwen and Chad had gotten him back safely. It made Diamond feel guilty, because while Gwen was going through her situation, the rest of MHB stood by and did nothing to help her.

"Who was that?" Tasha asked, still a little confused about everything. "I see that she is MHB," she said, noticing Gwen's tattoo.

"That's our sister," Diamond said, walking out of the bathroom with her head down.

"Look, Millie, it's a lot of money in the drug business. You just gotta be ready to put in the work. Sometimes, as women, we gotta do just a little bit more for men to understand how serious we are," Niya explained as she drove down the highway.

This was the conversation Rose had been waiting for. It was the core of the whole investigation, and she knew that in order for the case to stick, she would have to get Niya to talk about how the business was run. It was going to take time and patience, and of course a whole lot of trust, which Rose was gaining fast.

"Do you know something about cocaine?" Niya asked, looking out into the highway.

"Yeah, I know a little something," she replied.

"What about heroin?"

"I can't really say that I do, except for what I heard about it in the streets," Rose lied, not really wanting Niya to know her full knowledge about drugs.

Niya pulled out her iPhone and tapped on the screen a few times. It rang once and a man picked up.

"You ready for me?" Niya asked, holding the phone away from her face.

"Yeah, come holla at me," the man said and then hung up the phone.

Niya placed the phone in her bra and reached under her seat for her gun. She steered the truck with her knees as she made sure she had a full clip.

Rose watched her and then turned to look out the window. She hoped they would not be dodging bullets again that day.

"Don't worry." Niya chuckled. "I don't think we're gonna have to use these." She smiled, placing the gun on her lap.

Niya made a few turns, until they arrived at a diner. Niya parked, popped the trunk, and jumped out. Rose sat there for few moments to look around before getting out and walking to the back of the car.

"Millie, look around the corner. You should see a big-ass dude with a blond beard. You can't miss his fat ass. He wants to buy two bricks." Niya pulled and pressed something behind the license plate. The left light popped out, and she grabbed a black backpack.

"A'ight, Mills, you need to start getting familiar with the business. I sell my bricks for 40K apiece to these niggas around here. You need to be able to know who these niggas are and how to handle their asses," Niya said, slamming the trunk and passing her the bag.

Rose's stomach tightened. Niya was serious about her business and making the new recruit ready to move. This seemed a little fast for her. She eyed Niya and wondered what was really around that corner. She pulled her gun from her waist and followed Niya down the quiet suburban street.

Gwen smiled a sinister smile as she walked away from the clerk of the court. She had gotten Mayo's next court date. As she walked to her car, she thought about Diamond. It actually made her feel good seeing her. She knew that Diamond's concern was genuine because Gwen was MHB for life. She noticed that the girl Diamond had with her had a new *MHB* tattoo on her left breast. So much had happened since the Niya incident that she wasn't sure if they still had beef or not. At this time, she didn't have time to play these high school games with MHB. She had adult shit to handle, and she needed to be focused on her business.

Chapter 12

"Yo, wake up, babe," Eagle said, tapping Niya on her ass.

Niya was exhausted and also annoyed that Eagle was waking her up. She looked at her cell phone. She had a couple hours until she needed to pick up the twins. She and Eagle had been kicking it for about a month and half now, and she had grown fond of him. He seemed like a good dude, but she needed a lot more time with him before he could be around her babies.

"Yo, Ni, get up," Eagle said, this time shaking her.

"Yeah, babe?" Niya rolled over to face him. He brushed the lock of hair from her eye and sat up. Niya sat up also, seeing that he was not smiling.

"Yo, I ain't gonna be able to work the block. You gotta find somebody else to do it, shawty," Eagle said.

Niya rolled her eyes. What the fuck did this nigga want from her? "Really, E, what's up? It ain't like you don't get paid. I mean, I feed your ass." Niya dropped the chick shit quickly and went into boss mode.

Eagle laughed, but it was without humor. He was trying not to snap on her for talking to him like he was some low-level street imp. "Shawty, dis shit ain't about no money," Eagle said. "I been getting money before you and always will be stacking it on my own."

"So, what's up?"

"You are the reason I can't do this no more. You—"

"Because of me?" Niya said, cutting him off.

"Ni, damn, would you just hold up and let a nigga finish what he trying to say?" Eagle snapped.

"E, you not making any sense. What does this—"

"Shut up. Damn, Ni," Eagle yelled over her. "Look, I been thinking about dis shit for a minute now. Niya, I love you," he said, lying back down and looking up at her. "I been feeling you for a minute, and I know right now you feel the same way about me. The more time I spend with you, the more my heart clings to you. Having said that, I can't be working for a chick who gots my heart."

Niya didn't know what to say to Eagle. He looked at her for a moment then pulled her to him.

"I got my own bread, so I can do my own thing in another hood. I don't need no handouts from you, and I know I can find my own connect. All I need you to do is be my girl, and if you don't love me the same way right now, that's fine. I just ask that you give me a chance to earn your heart."

Niya tried to fight the smile that stretched across her face. His words had touched the parts of her heart that Chad had trampled on. She wasn't sure if her feelings ran as deep as Eagle professed his did, but she did have feelings for him.

"Eugene loves Niya, Eugene loves Niya," Niya said, straddling him. "You better be careful of those words," she warned, leaning in to kiss him.

Eagle's and Niya's phones rang in unison. Niya looked at the screen on hers and answered. She slid off Eagle and sat on the side of the bed. Eagle sighed and grabbed his off the nightstand.

"What up, D," Niya answered.

Diamond wasted no time telling her about the run-in she'd had with Gwen and about Zion. Niya's heart ached. She thought about Chad. Zion meant the world to him, and for that matter, Zion meant a lot to her too. Even though she and Gwen had beef, she would not have wished this on her. The mood in the room quickly turned gloomy.

"I'm on my way to you right now," Niya told Diamond and hung up the phone.

As she stood to find some clothes, Eagle stopped on a news channel. She looked at the screen and fell on the bed. Flames were jumping from a house on Betty Ford Road. The news helicopter flew over the blazing homes. Smoke filled the area as flames leapt out of the house. The entire block looked like it was on fire.

"Ohhh, shit," Eagle said, putting on his pants.

"Is that the block?" Niya asked, placing both of her hands on her head.

Eagle didn't answer at first. He turned up the volume.

"This massive fire broke out about an hour ago on Betty Ford Road, claiming three lives so far. No one knows what sparked the blaze, but firemen are struggling to put the fires out," the news anchor reported.

Niya and Eagle looked at each other. Eagle put on a shirt and his shoes, and they ran out the door.

Bills don't stop coming because you have changes in your life. Rose had not checked her mailbox in the last few days. That didn't stop the mailman from filling it with bills. Being involved with this MHB thing had caused her to neglect some things. Utility bills, car note, and a car insurance bill greeted her as she looked through the envelopes. Damn, they were due in a few days. She was always on time with paying her bills, but she forgot to update her credit card information for her drafts. They probably made the attempt to draft, and it had been returned.

"Ms. Rose. Ms. Rose," Mr. Parker yelled, running up the steps behind her.

Hearing Mr. Parker reminded her that she was late on paying her rent too.

"I came to make sure you were okay. You are never late on paying your rent."

Rose smacked her head with the pile of mail. She almost began to tell Mr. Parker she would pay him next Friday when she got paid, but saw the $8,000 in her sling bag as she placed the mail inside. She pulled the money out and counted out the $1,500 for the rent.

She paused as she placed the drug money in Mr. Parker's hand. Mr. Parker's face lit up when she handed the additional sixty dollar late fee to him and headed up the stairs. She knew using the money was wrong, and the slope she was on was slippery.

Eagle couldn't get within two city blocks of Betty Ford Road, due to the thick smoke engulfing the block and the police and firefighters blocking off the area. He parked his car and proceeded on foot. He slipped under the yellow tape and headed down the block to check the extent of the damage.

"Eagle!" a voice yelled from a house on the side of the street that wasn't on fire. It was MeMe, standing in the door, motioning for him to come in. He walked inside. Most of the squad that worked for Niya was there, and they were shook.

"What da fuck is goin' on?" Eagle asked, looking around at everybody sitting down. The group was quiet for a moment. "Niggas, you gone mute? What the fuck happened?"

"It was dem niggas from around Ronheart Street," one of the workers blurted out.

"Ronheart Street? Who da fuck is on Ronheart Street, and why da fuck is they bringin' drama to the block?" Eagle asked, looking for an answer.

Nobody had one. Everything had happened so fast. Eagle looked in the kitchen and saw that a couple of females had gathered in a huddle. Some of them looked like they were crying.

"What's up wit' dem?" Eagle asked MeMe, nodding to the kitchen.

MeMe teared up instantly. "Mandy," she mumbled before covering her mouth. She began crying. "They killed . . ."

Eagle felt a sharp pain in his stomach. Mandy was like a sister to him. She had looked out for him when he was locked up, and she made sure he was straight when he got out. He looked in the kitchen at the females comforting each other.

"Dogg and Pete got hit up too," one of the street workers said.

Eagle heard him, but his head was ringing.

"Two niggas ran in Pete's house and shot him. Dogg and Mandy were bagging shit up when another nigga killed both of them. Me and Tone went for our shit when we heard the shots. When we got back, the houses were burning. Our shit was in the car. You know we can't hold it on us on the block," he explained.

"MeMe said niggas was pouring gasoline on the porches, and then they lit 'em up. I mean, I don't get it. They didn't take shit. They just smoked them."

Eagle stood and hugged MeMe. Dogg and Pete were cool, but Mandy, that was his nigga. He walked out the door without saying a word.

Niya traveled across town to Gwen's apartment. She had knocked on the door, looking for Gwen and Chad, but neither one of them was there. Niya sat in her car for a minute; then it hit her that Gwen was more than likely at her mother's house.

She pulled up to Ms. Wright's residence. It felt like home as she walked up to ring the doorbell. Ms. Wright opened the door and pulled Niya inside. She kissed her on the cheek. Ms. Wright's embrace was warm. Niya held on to her, wanting to take away the pain.

"Is she here?" she asked.

"Mom, is my phone down there?" Gwen yelled from upstairs in her old room.

Gwen turned around to walk out of her room and froze. Niya was standing in the doorway, holding her phone.

"You know, I remember that day," Niya said, pointing to a picture of the two of them hanging on the dresser mirror. "You were scared to death of Mr. Johnson's dog that day." Niya chuckled, passing Gwen her phone. "You could never run." Tears formed in Niya's eyes. This was her best friend since preschool, and some ill shit that didn't matter had happened between them. They were sisters beyond blood, and MHB.

"He gone, Niya. My baby gone." Gwen sobbed and fell to her knees.

Niya ran to her and held her. "You should've come to me."

"We just got finished trying to kill each other, Niya. How was I gonna come to you?" she said, sobbing. "I thought I could save him, Ni. I thought I could save him, but I lost him. I lost my Zion."

Niya held Gwen tightly. They lay on the floor and sobbed together.

"Damn, G, I'm sorry," Niya apologized, holding on to her friend. "I'm sorry. I should have been there for you."

"My baby, my baby," Gwen cried out.

They cried for Zion and for their friendship that had been broken. Zion had brought back together the two women, who had been his cheerleaders from the womb. It was a shame it took this to make them remember how much they meant to each other.

***

"Where the hell have you been?" Detective Butler asked Rose before she sat down in the car. He hadn't seen or heard from her in a few days.

"I've been undercover. That means sometimes I am not gonna be able to get away from the girls and call you. You acting like a rookie now," Rose said.

"So, what do you have for me?" Butler asked, trying not to pay her little attitude any attention.

"Nothing, really. Niya's a hard-ass. She got us doing a lot of training shit right now. By next week, I should have more for you," Rose replied. "I gotta get back to work." She opened the door and stepped out.

What the hell was that? Butler said to himself. He knew that going undercover meant that you had to keep your mind on your character at all times. He hoped Rose was just playing the role and not being drawn into the life. If she was, he would snatch her ass back and have her put in a cubicle working cold cases.

The two women let the recent hiccup in their friendship go. They needed each other right now, and Niya wasn't going to make the mistake of not being there when Gwen needed her, ever again.

"So, how do you wanna handle this?" Niya asked, getting right to the business. "I know you got a plan. All you gotta do is tell me where I fit in at," she said, looking down at Gwen as she rested her head in her lap.

"I have to get rid of a witness who could possibly keep Mayo in prison," Gwen said, sitting up on the bed and wiping the last of her tears from her face. "Dis nigga took my little boy away from me, Ni. I'ma kill dis nigga myself," Gwen said, grabbing a tissue from her nightstand.

Spending the rest of his life in prison was too easy, especially for somebody like Mayo, who was used to doing time. He still had the ability to make moves from behind bars. She knew he would order hits on Gwen and Chad as soon as he got the chance. No, she needed him out on the streets where she could handle him.

"Do you know where this witness is at?" Niya asked.

"See, that's the problem. My connections don't go that far into the police department, and I can't afford to wait until the next time he goes to court. He goes to trial in two weeks," Gwen said, handing Niya a Kleenex.

Niya stood up and looked out Gwen's window. She couldn't imagine what Gwen was going through, but she knew she was going to help her do what needed to be done.

"I think I might be able to help you out with that," Niya said, walking over to Gwen.

Gwen turned around with a shocked look on her face. "How?" she asked with a sense of relief.

"Just trust me on this," Niya assured her.

Butler walked into police chief Rodney Monroe's office to see three white men with suits standing there. At first he thought that they were Internal Affairs coming to question him about some foul shit he had done before in one of his cases; but after they introduced themselves as DEA agents, Butler knew exactly what they were there for. Just like vultures, the feds waited in the background and let the local police do all of the dirty work, until they felt like taking over the case. This time, however, it was a little different. The feds were already investigating MHB well before Butler was.

Butler looked at Chief Monroe. From the look on Monroe's face, he knew the vultures were there to take over.

MHB had managed to get the attention of the big-boy agencies due to the amount of drugs and money they had flowing through Charlotte. As they were moving weight, snitches jumped at the chance to have their time reduced, so they told or made up anything to sing to the feds and DEA.

The house where Chad found Zion was still covered in yellow tape, but there wasn't a cop in sight. Gwen didn't really know if she was ready for what she was about to do, but something inside of her wanted to see the last place her son had been.

Instead of going in through the front door, Gwen went around back. Even though the house had been secured by the police, and more than likely nobody was there, Gwen still pulled a .45 automatic from her back pocket before she ripped the yellow tape down and entered through the back door. The afternoon provided her light.

She walked into the living room and looked down at the bloodstained carpet. She heard a noise coming from upstairs. It sounded like some furniture was being moved around, and then the noise stopped. Gwen gripped her gun and listened. She walked into the kitchen as she heard footsteps coming down the stairs. She slipped by the refrigerator and listened to the person talking.

"Yo, I don't know what dis nigga done wit' the money," the person coming down the stairs said into his phone.

Gwen took the safety off her gun and then slowly peeked around the refrigerator to see who it was. She couldn't make out his face because the sunlight was shining on the back of the house, causing the living room to be dark. The man looked around, opened the front door, and walked out. Gwen went to the window to see where he was going and to get a better look at his face.

She ran out the back door and then darted through the alleyway, until she came out at the end of the block. Gwen began jogging, getting closer to the guy, who was still talking on his phone. As she got closer, she recognized him. She kept her gun down by her side as she jogged closer.

"Muthafucka," she mumbled to herself when she recognized Made from the first meeting and the shootout.

As Made reached for the door of the car, he caught Gwen running up on him out of the corner of his eye. He turned in time to see her raise her gun. He froze for a moment and then looked in the car at the glove compartment. He would never make it in time. As he began to run, Gwen fired. Bullets hit the driver's side window of his car in quick succession.

Bullets hit the windshield and his grill as Made ran away. He was glad she was so far away, because any closer and he knew she would have hit him. A bullet zinged his coat. He dropped it, disappeared between the houses, and jumped a fence.

Gwen continued running and shooting. She lost sight of him when he hit the corner of one of the houses. "Shit!" She ran back, grabbed his jacket, and ran to her car.

Chapter 13

"You made bail," the detective said, walking into the small cellblock where Chad was being held.

He was glad that he was getting out. He was numb as he waited for them to finish the paperwork and return his property. As he walked to the lobby, he stopped. Niya was sitting in the waiting area. He looked around and approached her.

"Hey, you," Niya said, standing up and giving him a hug. "I'm so sorry about Zion," she whispered.

"Damn, you the last person I'd expect to be here," Chad said, fixing his belt.

"I wasn't gonna let you sit here. I know things ended on a fucked-up note, but the fact remains that I still got love for you."

This was the first time he'd seen Niya since the apartment, and he missed her. More than that, he missed the twins. He just needed to hold them close to him. He and Niya had things to talk about, but this wasn't the day for that. Today he needed to try to begin to put back the life that had become so undone that he had actually thought about not living anymore.

Detective Rose pulled up and parked in front of Goldy's Bar. She was supposed to meet a dude named RJ. Niya was busy dealing with the death of Mandy and making the funeral arrangements. She had given Rose the authority to handle business. Rose was doing so well at the game that she almost forgot she was a cop, especially when the money was coming to her so easy and quick. This lifestyle had the same risk as being a detective, but with much higher pay.

"Damn, shawty, you right on time," RJ said, hopping into the passenger's side.

"Always on time. What you got for me?" she asked.

RJ reached into his pocket, pulled out a stack of money, and handed it over to Rose. "I need a whole loaf this time," he said with a smile on his face.

"You know they forty a pop," Rose said, looking at the money.

"Yeah, I know, shawty. It's all there," he replied, nodding at the money.

Rose reached into the back seat and grabbed a small grocery store bag and set it on her lap. The other good thing about being MHB was that niggas respected the movement. They knew that MHB wasn't falling short and that every female who repped it had no problems at all putting in work.

"Damn, MHB. Good working with ya, shawty." He grabbed his brick and headed out of sight.

Niya, Chad, and Ms. Wright sat downstairs, waiting for Gwen to finish getting dressed so they could visit Zion at the hospital. Zion had been in and out of surgery for the last couple of days, and his condition had not improved. He was still in a coma and unresponsive. The doctors had asked her to consider removing him from life support, and this was the day for her to render her final decision. Gwen had requested the alone time. She needed to try to get her mind together, and everyone understood this was going to be a hard day for her.

"I'ma get us something to drink," Ms. Wright said, getting up from the couch and heading into the kitchen. She couldn't take the quietness of the house, and she needed to move around. She left Chad and Niya alone. They were silent for a moment.

Chad looked at Niya. "I was wondering if you could let me see the twins. I really do miss them," Chad said with his voice breaking.

The pain in his voice brought tears to her eyes. Above everything else, Chad was a damn good father, and she knew that now of all times, he needed the twins close to him. She had moved to give herself some space from the situation, not to keep him from the twins. "I swear that right after the visit, I will take you to them, and you can spend as much time as you want with them," Niya assured him.

Before he could even respond, Gwen came walking down the steps. Her hair was pulled back in a ponytail.

"You ready?" Chad asked, getting up to meet her at the bottom of the stairs.

She took his hand. Gwen stopped when she noticed that people were standing outside her mother's house. She looked at Chad and Niya, who looked as confused as she did.

"Who's that?" she asked, pointing to the window.

They walked outside to see over thirty women standing there. Diamond and Tiffany stood at the bottom of the stairs, looking on.

"Diamond, what's going on?" Niya asked.

"I don't know. They all just showed up," she answered.

She looked into the crowd, and some familiar faces emerged. Tasha, Porsha, and Kea walked toward the front porch.

"Diamond told me about Zion," Tasha began, "so the girls wanted to come out and show their support. You said that MHB is a family, so we here to help family and support you during this time. You cry, we will all cry with you. Whatever you need, sis," Tasha said, looking up at Gwen.

Everyone had T-shirts with a picture of Zion on the front. The official members of MHB had on the MHB hoodies with Zion's picture on the back and MHB on the front. Gwen could feel the love and support coming from the crowd. They were all strangers to her, but today they were sisters, aunts, mothers, in prayer for her little angel.

Niya scanned the crowd. She smiled at Gwen and took her hand to lead her to the car that waited for them. The crowd parted as Gwen leaned on her.

"Are all these girls MHB?" Gwen asked Niya while wiping the tears from her face.

Niya looked back at the crowd as Gwen got in the car. She scanned the faces again and inhaled. Every woman there had passed the most important test to become a member of MHB: loyalty and support for a sister in pain.

"Every last one of them are MHB," Niya told her. "Every single one of them."

"We burned Betty Ford down. Now what do you want us to do?" Redd asked Rell, who was still laid up in his hospital bed. Due to his injuries, his stay in the hospital was longer than he had expected. They were concerned about a clot they found in his leg and advised that he needed to stay for further testing.

"Did you kill that bitch Niya yet?" he asked, wincing as he adjusted himself.

"Naw," Redd answered, looking him in the eye.

Rell had niggas that followed any orders given to them. He knew if they had access to Niya, she would be sporting a nice hole in her head. His crew would take her out, and anyone else who was around at the time. When she popped that hot lead in his dick, she should have put one in her head, if she wasn't going to finish him. These hoes playing with real niggas, and now they was gonna wish they kept to being on their knees and fucking keeping a nigga's belly full, instead of trying to jump in this game.

"Get my troops together, Red," Rell said as he turned to watch TV. "Let them know we got some bitches to put in their places. They fired the first shot, and now it's war."

Chapter 14

Niya pulled up and parked at the breakfast spot where she was supposed to meet up with Rose. After her two workers' and Mandy's deaths, Niya made a decision to cut back on her dealings in the hood for a few days. She needed to figure out how she was going to deal with the impending war that she knew was brewing between her and that nigga Rell.

Rose had taken the lead on situations that Niya was unable to handle, and Niya made sure she was being paid for every brick she sold and a bonus for picking up and dropping off to her hoods. Rose was making money hand over fist. This was making her more cash than a promotion to chief of police would produce.

Rose felt a twinge of guilt. Being with these women gave her a sense of sisterhood, love, and loyalty. Although what they were doing was illegal, it was still women fighting to get what was theirs in a world of men. These girls really cared about each other, unlike the intolerance she felt from her male counterparts at the department.

"It's about a hundred fifty thousand in the bag, and I still got two keys left," Rose informed Niya when she got into the car.

"Damn, bitch, you making a killing," Niya joked, tossing the duffle bag into the back seat.

"Yeah, girl, I'm trying to get out of that apartment," Rose shot back, looking out the window at people going into the breakfast house.

"I ain't mad at you, girl. Get ya money." Niya smiled. "Oh, it was something I needed to talk to you about."

"Yeah, sure, what's going on?" Rose said, turning to face her.

"Look, I know we've just met, and like every friendship, it takes time to build trust," Niya said, looking at the new *MHB* diamond pendant on her bracelet.

Rose sat there, nodding her head in agreement. She held her breath for a moment. The mood had changed within a few seconds.

"I just want you to know that you can trust me. When you became MHB, you not only became my friend, but you became my sister. That means I would put my life on the line for you, and I wouldn't hesitate to put a bullet in somebody's head for you," Niya said.

Rose looked at Niya. She could hear the sincerity in her voice. She bit her lip. The guilt that came over her felt like a thousand-pound weight on her heart. People who go undercover have to learn how to disassociate themselves from the criminals. She had seen, so many times, good people falling into the trap of money and loyalty from the people they were trying to put away. Part of her wanted to tell Niya she was only befriending her to shut down her entire organization, but she knew that she had taken an oath to serve and protect. That oath superseded her oath to MHB, even if she felt in her heart that MHB was truly more her family than the pricks at the department.

"I got you, Niya. Is there something I need to do for you?" Rose said.

Niya smiled and patted her thigh. "Naw, baby girl. I just wanna make sure that you would do the same thing for me. Just letting you know how deep you are in the fam, is all."

Rose smiled. She wondered how Niya would feel when she slapped the handcuffs on her.

***

Chad was having a great time with the twins. He hadn't seen them in about two months. They seemed to have grown since the last time he saw them, and they were squealing with joy as he played with them. He was glad Niya dropped them off. He really needed to have them near him.

Gwen watched Jahmil wobble around. He looked so much like Zion at that age. The air in the room seemed to become heavy. She needed to get some air. She picked Jahmil up and kissed his little chubby face. He laughed and pinched her cheek. She placed him back on the floor and walked into the other room. As she sat down, she noticed Jahmil crawling behind her. He touched her leg and pulled himself up. She looked into his eyes and saw Zion. She wondered if she would ever see Zion up and moving around like a normal kid again. She picked Jahmil up and held him close to her, inhaling his baby scent.

Chad stood in the door for a moment, watching them. "You all right, shawty?" Chad said as he sat down beside her.

"Yeah, I just got a lot on my mind right now," Gwen answered, kissing the baby and handing him to Chad. She lay across the bed and turned on the television. Gwen had so many thoughts running through her head. She wasn't sure if she was being selfish, keeping Zion on life support. What she did know was that she was going to make sure the men who were responsible would pay for their actions.

Those weren't the only things troubling her. About a week ago, she realized that she had missed her cycle. At first she thought it was because of all the stress she had been under. She knew this was not the time for her to be pregnant. The wound from Zion would take a long time to heal. As she lay there, a pregnancy test commercial was on the TV. She laughed at the irony. She sat up and slipped on her shoes. She was feeling a little woozy, but she tried to block it out and get her eyes refocused.

"I have to run to the store," Gwen said as she grabbed her keys.

Chad grabbed her arm. "What's wrong?" he asked as he held Jahmil.

"Nothing. I just need to get some air," she replied, smoothing Jahmil's hair.

Gwen began to take what she thought was a step, but when her leg moved, she found herself on the floor. Chad placed Jahmil on the floor and ran to Gwen. He checked her pulse and looked for his phone. He grabbed Jahmil and ran into the other bedroom. When he returned, Gwen was trying to sit up.

"Nah, babe, relax." He picked her up and laid her on the bed.

"What happened?" Gwen asked as she tried to sit up again.

"No, sit back. I am going to get you some water." He ran down the stairs and grabbed a bottle of water from the refrigerator. He almost leapt from the bottom stair to the top. Gwen had lain back on the pillow.

Chad opened the bottle and told her to sip it. "Babe, have you eaten anything today?"

Gwen closed her eyes, hoping the room would stop spinning.

Jasmine began to cry as Chad handed Gwen the bottle of water. "I need to call the ambulance."

Gwen shook her head. "No, no, I just got dizzy is all. I probably just need to eat. Go get the baby. I'm fine."

Chad touched her forehead. He knew there was something wrong, but he knew if Gwen didn't want to talk, it would be pointless to press her. After what she had been through, her body was finally reacting to the stress. Jasmine cried out again, and he left the room.

Nose walked into Rell's hospital room. Nose was Rell's right-hand man. He had been handling the business of the streets while his boy recovered. Redd was the enforcer and had blazed up Betty Ford Road.

"Yo, big bro, I got some good news," Nose said, pulling up a chair and setting it next to Rell's bed.

"Is da bitch dead?" Rell asked.

"Naw, big homie, not yet. I'm definitely working on that, too. But Ronheart Street is doing some crazy numbers right now off the dope. Ever since we burned down Betty Ford, the traffic on the block has doubled," Nose explained.

Since Ronheart was so close to Betty Ford, he already knew that the fiends would be coming to his block. He had quality shit, and them fiends loved it. Now that the block was shut down, he had taken MHB clientele. Why the hell wouldn't he just shut down all that shit? *Yeah.* Rell smiled to himself. They would shut down all MHB shit and then open up shop to get that money.

"Listen, I want you to shut down every block MHB has, and every crack house MHB owns. We're gonna kill this movement financially first," Rell instructed. "And if any one of those bitches get in ya way, make like a Mack truck and run dem hoes ova, ya dig?"

Nose nodded his head in agreement. "Yo, homie, just fall back and get ya rest. I'ma take care of it," Nose assured him as he stood. He pounded Rell and headed out to rain fire.

Diamond, Tiffany, Alexus, Tasha, Porsha, Kea, and Millie sat around the TV in Tiffany's living room with their eyes glued to the screen. They were watching a special report on CNN about the spike in drug activity in Charlotte. The murder rate was up 10 percent from last year, bringing the body count to 300, and it was only the end of August.

"State, local, and federal officials are working together to try to regain some order in this city," the police commissioner announced to the news reporters.

Tiffany looked over at Diamond. She was worried about the attention that the QC drug business was getting. Tiffany knew firsthand that when the feds got involved, it could mean some serious time, or someone could be put into a box. Her brother was serving twenty years for conspiracy to distribute. He wasn't a high-level dealer, just a street boy. The murder rate had gone up, along with the drug trafficking, which made the government twitch. They knew there was a lot of money, property, and drugs to confiscate in the name of the law. This would be prime time to get some bricks out there to people. Seeing this report, she knew that they would be grabbing what they could, due to the impending lockdown.

"We need to be careful who we fucking with," Tiffany whispered to Diamond.

"What you mean?" Diamond asked, leaning over to hear Tiffany but also keeping her eyes on the TV.

"The feds, you know they send snakes in the hen house. We need to be careful," she answered.

Niya and Gwen walked into the living room. Niya grabbed the remote and turned off the television. "We got some problems. There are some niggas who don't appreciate some chicks eating so well. They view MHB as the reason dey wallets on a diet right now. When a nigga hungry, you know they start looking for food and will do whatever it takes to eat."

Niya threw the remote on the table. This shit was about to blow up, and right now she needed to ramp up her members. She needed the best bitches in Charlotte to be with MHB. These niggas was going to come at them hard.

"So, what you wanna do?" Tiffany said, checking her Glock.

"We gotta be smarter than these niggas," Niya answered, taking the gun from Tiffany. "We are women, ladies. We think things through. It ain't always about bullets and shit."

"Fuck dese niggas out here. If they don't like what we're doin', I'll smoke any of dem niggas," Porsha blurted out.

The comment from Porsha ignited a spark in the room. Everyone pulled their guns.

"Stop, stop, stop," Niya yelled. "Listen to me. Like I said, we are smart. We don't want to get into gun battles with these fools. There are ways for us to handle this shit and make more money."

"So, what, are we gonna fuck our way to a peace treaty?" Tiffany laughed.

"Naw, the first thing that we gotta do is get our numbers up. It's time we take this shit to higher levels," Niya said. "I want every chick in the hood from ages eighteen to twenty-five to be a part of MHB. I want y'all to take the next week to find bitches who's just like you. If they understand what MHB is about and are willing to stand on our principle, then bring them in. We about to go to fucking war," Niya said, handing Tiffany back her gun.

"War?" Diamond asked. "War with who?"

Gwen went and stood right next to Niya. The whole room became quiet, and everybody was looking at her. "With these niggas who think we just some weak-ass bitches in a nigga's game," Gwen announced.

Chapter 15

The knock at the door startled Detective Rose. She closed her laptop. Since the last visit from Niya, she had locked away all evidence of her being on the force. She looked through the peephole and saw Niya and Gwen standing in the hallway. She looked back again to make sure she had not left any evidence out.

"Hey, y'all," Rose said, opening the door.

"You ain't got a man in here, do you?" Niya joked, entering the apartment. "Don't want to interrupt no headboard breaking." They laughed.

"Can I use ya bathroom?" Gwen asked, setting her shoulder bag on the couch.

"Sure. It's down the hall and the first door on ya left," Rose said, pointing down the hall.

"So, Millie, I need to talk to you about something," Niya said as she placed her automatic on the table. "I need your help. I need to find somebody who might be in the witness protection program."

"What? Um, how would I know how to find that kind of information out?" Rose said as the hair stood up on the back of her neck and arms.

Niya smiled at her. Rose felt something being pressed against the back of her head. Gwen pressed the barrel into the base of her skull.

"What's going on, Niya?" Rose asked.

Niya walked over to the wall where the picture of Rose in her uniform had once hung. "You didn't think that I

was that dumb, did you, Detective Monica Maria Rose?"
Niya said, turning to face her.

Rose exhaled and slowly sat down on the couch. Her
sixth sense had told her that when Niya dropped by the
apartment, her cover was blown. Her ego and the money
had clouded her common sense.

"The day we had target practice, I noticed how you
were intentionally not hitting the target every time, and
when you did, you hit it dead on. You even held your gun
like someone who had either military training or police
training. So, one day, I followed you home, and when we
walked through, I saw the picture of you in your uniform
hangin' up here," Niya said, patting the wall.

"So, why—"

"'Cause I wanted to see how far you was willing to go,"
Niya said, cutting her off.

As Rose listened to Niya with her narcissistic rant, she
slowly eased her hand between the cushion of the couch.
She felt the butt of her gun and wrapped her hand around
it. Niya walked over and sat on the coffee table, facing
her.

Rose took a chance and pressed the barrel into Niya's
chest. Niya looked back at her gun on the end of the table,
then back to Rose.

Rose had moved so quickly that Gwen didn't have time
to react. If she put a bullet in Rose's head, Rose might get
a shot off in Niya's chest before going down.

"Drop it," Gwen yelled out, pressing the gun up against
Rose's head.

Rose didn't move. She looked into Niya's eyes. She
knew these women had no issues with murdering people.
Her chance of survival was very slim at this point.

"Bitch, I'm not gonna ask you twice," Gwen yelled out,
gripping the gun tighter.

"You shoot me, I shoot her," Rose responded, not
losing eye contact with Niya.

Niya met Rose's stare. She smiled and leaned into the barrel.

"Now what?" Rose asked, breaking the silence.

"Well, that's gonna be up to you, *Monica*. I told you before, I came here because I need you to help me find somebody. We didn't come here for nothing else. Pulling that trigger is going to give all of us something we don't want. Believe me, Gwen don't have a problem popping your ass. We been through a lot, and today is just as good as any day to die; but I don't think anyone is going to die in here today. I know you gon' choose the right family and do what you know is right," Niya said.

"Why da fuck should I help you?" Rose snapped.

Niya motioned for Gwen to lower the gun. Rose kept her gun on Niya.

"I'ma give you one good reason, and if you don't feel like this reason is good enough, you could either pull the trigger or take me to jail," Niya said.

"What's that?" Rose asked, keeping her finger on the trigger.

Niya turned over her wrist. Rose saw the *MHB* tattoo, and she looked at her own tattoo. She was a damn cop, and yet the oath she took with this gang of women had her doubting the oath she had taken for the department. She looked at the letters and lowered the gun. She looked at Gwen, who walked around the couch and sat beside Niya.

A couple months ago, she swore her allegiance to CMPD, and now MHB's oath meant a little more to her. She looked at Niya and then Gwen. Niya smiled and placed her hand on her knee. She knew that MHB wasn't only tattooed on Rose's body, but it was on her heart too.

Special Agent Mark Atkins was heading the MHB indictment. They had cloned the MHB's cell phones and tracked their vehicles. They had been on MHB for months, and it had paid off. Now it was time for their work to pay all the way off, and to get these women off the streets before a war ensued.

Chapter 16

Rose sat at her cubicle, looking for the paper where she had written the address to the safe house. She could have sworn she wrote it down in her notebook, but the page was nowhere to be found.

"Surprised to see you here," Butler said, walking past Rose and taking a seat at his cubicle. "I didn't think you worked here anymore."

"Right," Rose responded, peeking into his cubicle. "I got some good news for you."

"Well, I got some bad news for you," Butler said.

Rose had been so caught up with the streets that she didn't even realize what was going on in the police department. She had no idea that the feds were in the building.

"You're off the MHB case," Butler informed her. "The feds officially took over the investigation. Come to find out they've been investigating them for some time now. If you were around or answered ya phone, you would know that," Butler said, taking a sip of his coffee.

"I can't be off the case. I'm this close to making a major deal and finally learning where Niya is getting her drugs from," Rose said as she opened her desk drawer. Rose couldn't afford to be off the MHB case right now. If she was officially off the case, she couldn't give the girls what they needed. She would be out of the loop, especially if the feds had taken over.

"Do the feds know that I was undercover in this case?" Rose asked, now having her own bit of an attitude.

"Of course they do, but you have been assigned to another case now. MHB is their problem now. There are other crimes going on," Butler said as he clicked his mouse through e-mails.

Rose found the paper with the address. She sighed and grabbed her keys. Butler was saying something, but she ignored him and walked toward the elevator. Butler caught up to her as the doors opened.

"Leave MHB alone," Butler warned Rose.

She stepped onto the elevator. Butler watched her as the doors closed. His gut was telling him that she was up to something. He just hoped it wasn't something stupid that could ruin her life and career.

Niya parked in the driveway of the house she and Chad had once shared. He had called and said he had to take care of some things and needed her to pick up the twins. He would get them back after he finished his business. Niya needed to spend some time with her babies before shit in the street exploded. She had made the decision to introduce Eagle to the twins. He had won her heart, and she felt today was a good day for him to meet them.

Chad may have been rusty in the streets, but not so much that he didn't notice a dude in the passenger's seat of Niya's car. He looked at Niya and then back to the car. Although the windows were tinted, he could still see the outline of a person. "Who da fuck is dat?" Chad asked as he stepped out.

"Really, Chad? Really? Boy, don't start today," Niya said as she picked up Jasmine and covered her little face with kisses. Jahmil babbled, and she picked him up to give him the same affection. Both of them squealed and giggled as she played with them. "Mommy missed you two."

"So, you just gonna ignore me? I know I asked a damn question."

Niya tried to keep her temper under control. Chad had lost all his rights to question anything in her life, except the babies. Although Eagle had touched her heart, it still was wounded by Chad.

Chad had enough heartache of his own right now, but Niya forgot that when she opened her mouth. "That," she said as she placed the twins down, "is my man."

Chad closed the door and walked over to her. "Ya man?"

"Yes, nigga, my man. My boyfriend. My dude, my boo, my significant other," Niya said as she poked his chest with her finger.

As Niya said those words, Chad clenched his fists then relaxed his hands. He walked over to the steps and stared at the car. He figured after everything calmed down he would get his family back. He had no idea that Niya had moved on; it had only been a couple of months.

"So, it's like dat?" Chad asked, looking Niya in her eyes.

"Look, Chad, you really hurt me. I loved you from the depths of all I am, but I just don't see us ever getting back to that. I do and always will love you because you're the father of my children. You and me? Too much has happened for that to exist anymore," Niya said. She opened the door and placed the twins inside. She closed the door and looked at Chad.

"Do you love him?" Chad asked, looking at the ground before raising his eyes to hers.

Niya thought about it for a second and then she smiled. She hadn't even told Eagle that she loved him, but she realized at that moment that she did. "Yes. Yes, I do love him, Chad," Niya said as she smiled at the car.

Chad's jaw tightened, his teeth clenched, and he balled his fists. He felt like Niya had just reached in his chest, grabbed his heart, and stomped on it. Niya stepped back against the door. Chad stepped toward her. His heart was aching; he wanted to knock her head around until she came to her senses.

"I wouldn't do that if I was you," she warned, putting her head down to break the eye contact. Niya knew that if Chad raised his hand, Eagle would not hesitate to raise his gun and blow him away.

"It's no need for all that, Chad. Let's just be parents to our beautiful kids," Niya said, going inside to grab the babies' bags.

Chad watched her and realized that he no longer had Niya. He had fucked up any chances of getting back his life with her. Someone had already stepped into his place.

"You want something to drink?" Diamond asked Dollaz as she stepped out on the porch.

Diamond did not find sitting inside a trap house all day to be romantic, but it was required if she wanted to spend some time with him. She was determined to make this relationship work. She had history with him, and they both had matured. Pouring the lemonade, she smiled to herself, replaying their lovemaking from earlier.

Her dreamtime was interrupted by the sound of glass breaking and bullets hitting the house. Glass and bullets were flying everywhere. Diamond dropped to the floor and crawled behind the couch, grabbing the 12-gauge pump they kept under it for protection.

Boom! Boom! Boom! Pop! Pop! Pop! Boom! Pop!

As quickly as it had started, the gunfire stopped. Diamond slowly rose from behind the couch with the shotgun drawn. She stood by the wall and looked out the window. She could see Dollaz at the bottom of the steps.

"Arrrghhhhhhhhhh!" Dollaz moaned.

A couple of workers who were out on the block started coming out from behind the parked cars. A few came out of the house across the street with guns in their hands. Whoever the gunmen were, they were nowhere in sight.

Diamond ran down the stairs. She took off her shirt and applied it to the two holes that she could see. "Hold on, baby," Diamond said, pressing down. She could see the bullet hole in his stomach and one in his shoulder. Blood was beginning to pool under him also.

"Call the fuckin' ambulance," she yelled out. "Hurry da fuck up," she told one of the workers.

She kept the shirt pressed against the bullet wound in his stomach. Hearing someone shriek, she looked in the direction of the bloodcurdling scream. All she could see were white Nikes on the ground behind a car.

"Come on, Dollaz. Hold on, baby," Diamond yelled out, trying to keep him awake. "Just hold on, boo. The ambulance is coming," she pleaded with him as she tried to stop the bleeding.

Tiffany pulled up to East Falls to see cops everywhere. Yellow tape blocked off her crack house, and the coroner was bringing out a body.

"What da fuck is goin' on?" she mumbled to herself, watching the cops bring bags of evidence out of the house.

The cops had GoGo, her main worker, sitting in the back of the squad car with the door open, asking him question after question. He sat there quietly as they continued trying to question him. They finally gave up, and he walked toward Tiffany. He knew the rules and respected the game too much to be talking to the cops. Where he was from, he was taught to have court on the streets only.

"Shit, Go, what is going on? What the fuck happened?" Tiffany asked as she looked at the house.

"I don't know. Some niggas just ran up in the house and started shooting. By the time I got downstairs, da niggas was gone," he explained.

"Who dat?" Tiffany asked, nodding toward the coroner's van.

"That's Ms. Daisy. She took a bullet to the chest. They said she was killed instantly," GoGo said, looking down.

Tiffany couldn't believe this shit. She patted GoGo on the shoulder and walked off. She heard Niya's words in her head about things getting ugly. Shit, they were down three already, and she hoped whatever Niya's plan was that she would kick it into gear before they had someone else in a black bag.

Eagle watched Niya play with the twins. For now, he was a stranger to them, and they showed no interest in him being there. Seeing this side of Niya made him love her and want to protect her even more. He knew she considered herself a boss, but at the end of the day, she was in a nigga's game.

"Do you smell that?" Niya asked Eagle, sniffing the air.

Eagle didn't smell it at first, and then the nanny, Ms. Emma, came running down the stairs. "Ya car, ya car!" the nanny yelled, pointing to the window.

Niya jumped up from the floor and ran to the window. Eagle was behind her. Niya's white Bentley was engulfed in flames. She looked at Ms. Emma, who grabbed the twins and ran upstairs. As she reached the top step, bullets cut through the walls and the windows. Eagle snatched her back and jumped on top of her.

"Get down," Eagle yelled, pulling out his Desert Eagle.

Bullets knocked chunks of wood out of the banisters going up the stairs. They hit mirrors and knocked pictures off the mantle, along with putting holes in the sixty-inch flat screen on the wall. Eagle lay on top of Niya, shielding her. The shooting stopped, but a thick, black cloud of smoke began coming through the window. Niya panicked. She needed to get to her babies. Eagle snatched her up and pushed her toward the stairs.

The smoke that was pouring through the house was coming from the BMW and the Bentley. Both cars were orange with flames. Tires screeched in front of the house as the shooters left.

Niya sprinted up the stairs. Emma and the twins were in a back room, unharmed.

Eagle stayed downstairs by the door. He looked up and down the street, making sure the gunmen were not returning. He could hear the sirens approaching. Niya stood at the top of the stairs.

"You ain't got nothing up in here, do you?"

"No. You know I am not stupid. I would never bring that shit around my kids or where I lay my head."

"A'ight, you know what this means, right?" Eagle asked Niya as he stood.

She nodded her head, still a little shook up by everything. She knew exactly what time it was, and there wasn't no turning back now. There would be no retreat. She needed to get her troops ready for battle, and she did not intend to lose.

Chapter 17

"Now look, this is no longer a high-profile case, so he's not gonna have round-the-clock security," Rose explained to Gwen as they drove down the highway.

"What about his family? Are they gonna be there?" Gwen asked, reaching into her bag.

"From what I know, he really didn't have much family. I think it's just him," Rose answered.

The ride to the safe house took about an hour and a half. They pulled up and parked a couple of streets away. Gwen slapped a clip into her .40-caliber, cocked a bullet into the chamber, and then tossed her bag into the back seat. She had that same funny feeling in her stomach when she killed Mr. Walker, the first witness. It was different this time. The first time she was killing an innocent, trying to save her son. This time, she was taking an innocent life to get the chance to take out the fool who took Zion from her. Even still, she had guilt, but her desire to make Mayo pay outweighed her guilt.

"Thank you," Gwen looked over and told Rose. "It really means a lot," she said before getting out of the car.

Gwen tucked her gun in her front right pocket and then threw her hoodie over her hair. The street was in a quiet rural area. The houses had acres of land between them and large trees to shield her from anyone. As long as a woman or child didn't answer the door, she planned to plant a bullet in the head of the person who did.

She took a deep breath and walked up to the door. Before ringing the doorbell, she tried the doorknob. It turned. She stopped for a moment then stepped inside. She looked around and didn't see or hear anyone.

"Mr. Johnson?" Gwen called out, hoping he would answer.

Gwen approached the living room; however, the voice that answered her caused her to freeze.

"Drop the gun and put ya hands in the air," a voice yelled out from the dining room.

Gwen could see someone standing by the china cabinet with a gun pointed at her. She didn't have hers raised. It was still by her side, and she didn't know how quick the other person was, but she doubted she could get a shot off before him.

"Put the gun down and let me see ya hands," Butler yelled out again.

Gwen hesitated for a moment. She slowly placed the gun on the table in the hall. Butler walked over to her and kicked her in the back of her knees, making her fall to the floor. He pulled her arm back and placed the handcuffs on her wrist. Butler had to give it to Mayo; he had proven to be useful. He thought for sure Mayo was lying, but here she was, trying to murder a witness.

"You goin' to jail for a long time, Gwen," Butler said, holstering his gun and doing a quick pat search of Gwen to make sure that she didn't have any more weapons on her.

"I can't let you do that," a voice said.

Butler looked up to see Detective Rose standing behind him with a gun pointed at his back. He didn't pay her any attention as he continued to put the handcuffs on Gwen. The sound of Rose cocking back the hammer to the revolver in her hand quickly caught Butler's attention.

"Are you serious?" Butler asked with a curious look on his face. "Do you know what you're doin'? Are you really willing to spend the rest of your life in prison for these crazy bitches?" Butler snapped, standing up to face her.

"Where's the witness?" Rose asked, looking around the house.

"Listen to me, kid. Just put the gun down and let's get MHB off the street," Butler yelled, pointing down at Gwen, who was still lying on the floor.

"Where's the fucking witness?" she snapped back.

"I can't tell you that, but what I will tell you is that if you don't put that gun down and assist me with this arrest, you'll be going to jail right along with her," Butler said, wiping the sweat from his forehead.

Rose could hear her heartbeat in her ears. She looked at Butler being honorable and loyal to his oath to serve and protect. She looked down at Gwen and the *MHB* tattoo on her ankle.

"Sorry I couldn't be what you wanted me to be," Rose said before squeezing the trigger.

Niya pulled into Chad's driveway. She almost forgot to put the car in park as she jumped out and ran to the front door.

Chad opened the door and the smell of smoke hit him. Eagle was unloading the kids from the car. Seeing another dude touching his kids caused his temper to flare. Seeing the look on Niya's face caused him to cool it quickly. He could tell that Niya was on edge as Eagle handed her the kids.

"What's going on?" Chad asked as he took Jahmil. Both the babies reeked of smoke.

"I know I just got them back, but I need you to watch the kids for me. I can't tell you when I will be back for them, but it shouldn't be but a couple of days," Niya explained, walking into the house with the bags and Jasmine.

Seeing her on edge made Chad want to close the door and not let her leave until she told him what the hell had happened. He looked at Eagle leaning against the car and decided it was no longer his place to question her.

Niya kissed the kids and instantly kissed Chad on the cheek. Their eyes locked for a moment before she ran out the door.

Gwen and Rose rode back to Charlotte without saying a word to each other. Gwen knew that not only was this Rose's first kill, but the kill of an innocent. She looked over at Rose as she stared out the passenger's side window.

Rose's mind played back the moment when she pulled the trigger and the bullet landed between Butler's eyes. She tried to find some type of emotion for taking the man down, but there was nothing there. She felt nothing. She had no guilt or remorse. Even though she said she was sorry, the words were empty.

"You know it ain't no turning back now," Gwen said, looking over at Rose.

Rose looked at Gwen. She was sure she had covered their tracks. They made sure the evidence that was left behind would point toward Mayo's boy, Made. They were covered. She took her phone out when she saw the city limits and turned it back on.

Gwen smiled. She knew that when Rose pulled that trigger, a piece of her flew out with the bullet. She would never get that piece back. The chick who was a detective had been buried in that house, and she left it as an official MHB sister—one who took someone down to save her family.

Chapter 18

Niya sat on the edge of Eagle's bed and dug deep in her mind for a game plan to regain her hoods and to take Rell's ass out. Even though they had recruited more than 150 chicks for MHB over the last week, she didn't know how many of them were ready to go into real battle for MHB against these niggas.

"You ready to go?" Eagle said as he grabbed his keys.

"Yeah," she answered, taking in a deep breath and getting off the bed.

She wrapped her arms around Eagle and kissed him, holding her lips against his for a moment. She still had not actually told him that she loved him, and she didn't know how tonight was going to play out.

"I love you, Eugene Malik Cole," Niya confessed, looking him in his eyes.

"I love you too." Eagle smiled and kissed her. "We're gonna be good. Stop acting like this is gonna be our last time being together. I will kill every last nigga in this cit before I let something happen to you. You hear me?" said, lifting her chin.

She felt safe with Eagle, and his words gave fidence that she could take over the city's dr they walked out the front door, a black SV the street toward them, and anothe opposite direction. Eagle and Niya bo ready to light up the trucks, but the of the doors were not there for war.

"DEA!" one of the men yelled. "Put da fuckin' gun down, now!"

Niya and Eagle looked at each other. They slowly lowered their weapons.

"Hello, Niya. Wassup, Eagle," Special Agent Mark Atkins greeted them, walking up on the porch.

Two other officers walked on the porch, secured the weapons, and handcuffed both of them. Niya's face showed the shock she felt as they put the handcuffs on her and Eagle.

"Don't look so surprised, Niya. You should have known we were coming," Agent Atkins said.

"I want my lawyer," Niya said to Atkins before he could say another word.

"Yeah, we'll talk about all that when we get down to the federal building," he laughed as he walked her to the SUV.

Diamond sat in the emergency room waiting area covered in Dollaz's blood. She had been sitting there ever since they brought him in. He had been shot five times in the chest, stomach, shoulder, and right leg. Massive blood loss, and the internal damage the bullets had done to him, made his chances for survival low. He had lost his spleen, one bullet was too close to his spine to be removed, and his right lung had collapsed. Dollaz had flat-lined twice, but he was still fighting.

Diamond rose and walked toward the chapel. She needed God to hear her prayer for Dollaz and spare him.

The thirty-minute ride to the downtown federal build-gave Niya time to process what was happening. Agent ns had tried to chat with her, but she kept quiet.

Although she wasn't familiar with the way the feds did things, she knew enough to keep her mouth shut. She wasn't saying shit, and this cracker better back up. Niya knew her rights, and she had asked for her lawyer, which meant he needed to sit his ass down.

Niya rubbed her wrist as she walked into the interview room. She sighed when she saw her lawyer, Sanders, sitting at the table.

"Hey, Niya," Sanders uttered.

"So, what's up, Tom? What are they talking about?" Niya asked.

"Niya, I haven't dealt with a lot of federal cases before. This is new territory for me," Sanders said. "They got some deep shit on you. Informants, surveillance, they are executing warrants of your homes and your associates' homes as we speak. Right now, they seem to have enough to put you away for life."

Sanders's words echoed as he spoke. These fools had everything from shootings she was involved in to how much she spent on her luxury vehicles that she bought with cash. They were not looking at Mayo or Gwen until Zion was kidnapped. They had been watching over MHB like a pack of vultures circling over a wounded zebra, just waiting for the right time to swoop down and feast.

"So, now what?" Niya asked, already picturing the judge slamming the gavel down, screaming the word, "Life!"

"Now, there's a flip side to every coin, Niya, and I am not telling you this as a lawyer. I am telling you this as a friend. These people outside that door wanna talk to you about a few things. I think you should hear what they got to say," Tom advised.

Niya really didn't have anything to talk about. She'd rather spend the rest of her life in prison before she gave up anybody from MHB. She stood on that loyalty, and she was not going to bend, break, or fold for anything. That was the oath she took that day the needle and ink pierced her skin, and that was the oath she was going to the grave with.

Three days later

The word about Niya and Eagle being locked up by the feds had spread quickly through the streets. Tiffany, Alexus, Tasha, Kea, and Porsha sat in the hotel room, armed. They were hiding from the niggas Rell had unleashed to put bullets in each of their heads. Tiffany knew that if they had gone after Niya, they would be hunting down the rest of the crew too.

"We can't stay here forever," Kea said, looking out the window at the cars going by. "We're like sitting ducks."

"I know, y'all. We should just get out of town for a while until shit dies down a little bit," Porsha said, pacing the floor.

"I say fuck dese niggas out here. We should strap up and go to war wit' dese muthafuckas," Tasha added, gripping the butt of the .45 resting on her waist.

"Everybody just chill out. We are gonna sit here until I figure this shit out," Tiffany said as she sat on the bed.

Everyone's eyes fell on Tiffany. With Niya locked up and Diamond not answering her phone, Tiffany had been shaken to her core. The silence of the room was cut by the sound of her phone ringing. Tiffany blinked as she looked at the screen showing Niya's number.

"Yo," Tiffany answered.

"Tiffany, where is Diamond?" Niya asked. "Her phone keeps going to voicemail."

"Niya?" Tiffany asked, still in disbelief. "They said the feds—"

"I know, I know, I know. I will explain," Niya said, cutting her off. "Take down this address and meet me there in two hours," Niya instructed.

Tiffany snapped her fingers at Alexus for her to pass her something to write with. "So, what are you about to do?" Tiffany asked after writing down the address.

"I'ma find Diamond," Niya said and then hung up the phone.

Chapter 19

Dollaz had gone through several surgeries before doctors finally got the bleeding under control. His condition was still critical, but he was stable for the time being. Diamond sat by his hospital bed, holding his hand, saying short prayers in hopes that God would answer them.

"Dollaz, if you can hear me, I want you to know that I love you," Diamond said, stroking his hand. "Please don't leave me. We still got so much to do," she cried, wishing that he would wake up.

Dollaz lay there with tubes and cables coming out of him. He was pale and lifeless. Diamond kissed his hand and laid her head on the bed.

Knock! Knock!

Diamond lifted her head up to see Niya walking into the room. She tried to walk to her but fell to her knees, sobbing. Niya took her in her arms and held her.

"How did you know?" Diamond managed to ask through her tears.

Niya had stopped at Washington Avenue to look for Diamond and saw the yellow tape and blood in the street. One of the workers told her everything that had happened. When he told her that Dollaz had been hit, she knew Diamond was at the hospital.

"Diamond, I need you to hear me, okay? All of our shit, every corner, dope house, street we owned, is being shut down. These dudes are playing for keeps. They are waging war on us."

Niggas in the city were exchanging gunfire so rapidly that the morgue was filling up. Niya explained everything to Diamond. She advised her of what the feds had on MHB, and how it looked like everyone would be serving some time in jail. She finally told Diamond that she had agreed to cooperate with the feds.

Diamond stood, shocked by the last statement.

"What do you mean you're cooperating with the feds?" Diamond asked with a disgusted look on her face.

"Let me ask you something, D. Do you love me?" Niya asked, looking Diamond in the eyes.

"You know I love you, but—"

"Do you trust me?" Niya asked, cutting her off.

Diamond looked at her for a moment. She didn't know where Niya was going with it. "Of course I trust you," Diamond said.

"Then I need you to come with me. I can't do dis shit without you by my side," Niya said with tears starting to flow from her eyes.

Diamond looked over at Dollaz and then back at Niya. She really didn't want to leave Dollaz, but she had to. Niya needed her, and it didn't matter what she had gotten herself into. Diamond was gonna be there for her. She loved Dollaz, but Niya needed her by her side, and that was where she was going to be.

The sounds of guns being cocked flooded Alexus's apartment. Tiffany, Alexus, Tasha, Porsha, and Kea were checking clips and strapping on vests.

"Did anybody call Gwen and Millie?" Tasha said, cocking a bullet into the chamber of her gun.

"Yeah. They're gonna meet us at the location. Make sure we got enough fire for everybody," Tiffany said, taking a pull of the weed she had lit.

Once everybody was locked and loaded, it was time to ride. Before they left the apartment, Alexus led them in a thug's prayer, asking God to protect them. They draped their hoods over their heads. MHB was going to the streets, and they were prepared to be the last ones standing after the smoke cleared.

When they exited the hospital, Niya made a sudden U-turn on a one-way street. Diamond gave her a strange look as if asking, "What the hell are you doing?" But the quick left turn she made onto Monroe Road gave away Niya's thoughts. There was only one place Niya would be going to on Monroe Road at this time of night. Less than twenty minutes later when they pulled up to Sharon Memorial Gardens, it was confirmed for Diamond. Sharon Memorial was an upscale burial site, the final resting place for Prada's physical body.

Both girls got out of the car at the same time. The emotion began to build up as Niya used her cell phone to illuminate the headstones lining the beautiful southern green grass. When she located Prada's grave, she bent down on one knee. The tears began to flow down her face as the hurt was building up in her chest. She tried to release the words from her mouth, but they seemed to weigh too much. Instead, Niya decided to speak to Prada with her heart, knowing that she could now hear her thoughts.

Hey, Pra, I know it's been a minute, but you know how hard it is for me to visit this place. Girl, I miss you so much. Damn, how I wish you was here with me right now.

Just to give you some updates, you know you was right about Alexus. She really stood up and has proven to be MHB born and bred.

You know Diamond is still rocking with your bitch hard. You see I had to bring her with me, and I know she better not be talking over me right now. You know she got to tell her story first all the damn time.

That comment made Niya smile outwardly, and as she peeked out the corner of her eye, she could see Diamond was indeed trying to talk over her to Prada, even in silence.

Tiffany is still holding all of us down. Also, you know me and Gwen are crazy. The bitch almost took my ass out, and you know I had to come back harder at her. I know you was probably the one who stopped us both from sending one of us to be with you early.

Okay, so now to the business at hand and the reason for this visit. Niya took a deep breath before she continued. *You know as usual, your girl done got herself in some shit, and I need you to be my voice of reason.*

She continued to ask Prada question after question, until Niya finally had the answer that she was sure Prada wanted to send her. She felt like a thousand-pound brick had been lifted off her shoulders, and she now knew precisely what she had to do.

Niya opened her eyes and Diamond smiled at her. They stood, hugged, and blew kisses to Prada.

For MHB, Downtown Charlotte was usually the place the girls went to have drinks and eat. They met in front of the yellow-and-blue building on Trade Street.

"Where the hell is she?" Porsha asked, looking up and down the street.

A car approached. Gwen and Rose got out, looking around, confused by the location of the meeting. Something was off. They stood there waiting for Niya.

A few minutes later, another car came down the block. Tiffany and Gwen recognized Eagle's car.

"Here she go," Tiffany said, watching the car pull up and then disappear into the building's parking garage. A few minutes later, as Diamond got closer, the girls noticed the bloodstained clothes she was wearing.

"D, what happened?" Alexus asked when they walked up.

"Come on, y'all. Let's just get inside," Niya said, directing everyone to the front door, where she punched a few digits on the keypad.

Niya stopped Kea at the door while everyone else entered the lobby. Diamond and everybody else watched as Niya talked to her outside. Nobody could make out what she was saying. Niya entered as Kea walked off.

As they entered the lobby, the sounds of their voices echoed. The girls walked forward to see the indoor pool and a gym. Niya motioned for them to get on the elevator. As it rose, they could see the city from the glass. Niya punched another code, and the elevator continued to a floor that did not show on the panel. When it stopped, the doors opened and the girls gasped at the penthouse. They had to be at least forty stories up. There were high-end electronics, furniture, and beautiful paintings on the wall. The panoramic view was breathtaking in the living room.

The penthouse caused the girls to forget about the reason they were meeting. Niya hit a button, and the surveillance cameras covered every angle of the building outside.

Diamond sat down at the bar. She wasn't fazed by its view or anything else. They needed to get down to business and plan their next move. She didn't fully understand why Niya was cooperating with the feds, and until she did, she would just sit back for a moment.

Tiffany touched her shoulder and took a seat beside her. It was time to get this shit on and poppin'.

***

"All right, guys. Niya said that they will be heavily armed and they are not afraid to use their weapons," Special Agent Atkins informed his team of agents and marshals as they geared up. "Expect resistance, and don't hesitate to put a bullet in anybody's head if they fire upon us. We will break up into about eight teams. Whatever you do, listen to your tactical leader. I put him in that position for a reason," Atkins said. "Remember, nobody moves until we get the call from Niya. Are we clear?" Atkins asked.

Federal, state, and local authorities teamed up for the sting operation. There wasn't a cop out on the streets right now. They wanted to make sure the arrests went as smoothly as possible, so the more manpower present, the better. They were definitely going to need it.

Chapter 20

"I know y'all thought that we would be going to war tonight, but that is not gonna be the case," Niya said, sitting in the middle of the living room with everybody standing around her. "I need to tell y'all something, and I hope you can understand the position that I am in," she said, looking around the room at the girls she hoped would still be her family after she finished saying what she had to say and doing what she had to do.

This was the most difficult situation Niya had ever been in, and she struggled with making the decision she had made. Tiffany, Diamond, Alexus, and even Gwen all looked up to her as a big sister.

"Sometimes in life, we might be called upon to make difficult choices and decisions, but in reality, it's the consequences from our decisions that we have to deal with," Niya continued. "I made a choice tonight that I am gonna have to live with for the rest of my life," she said, getting up and slowly walking over to the window to look out at the city.

No one noticed Kea walking in the hospital, wearing a pair of square-framed sunglasses and her hoodie pulled partially over her head. She stood in the elevator and watched the blue numbers change. The doors opened to the seventh floor. She stepped out of the elevator and walked down the hall, keeping her hands inside the pockets of the hooded T-shirt as she looked at the room numbers.

"Seven eighteen," she mumbled to herself, stopping in front of a halfway open door.

She looked up and down the hallway. It was quiet, as it should have been at 2:00 a.m. She walked into the room to see Rell watching TV. One of his boys was sound asleep in the vacant bed beside Rell's.

"Damn, shawty, visiting hours are over," he said as she entered the room.

"But, boo, it's your bitch. Ain't that what you told me?" Kea said as she took off the hoodie and raised the automatic weapon toward him.

She replayed the vicious beating Rell had given her when he saw her *MHB* tattoo, and then she fired at him. Two shots whistled silently to his chest for the slaps, one in the temple for the black eye, and one in the center of the forehead for being a dick.

The silencer had muffled the shots. His boy was still snoring in the bed next to him. She placed the gun in Rell's lap and disappeared out of the room.

Niya pulled out her cell phone from her back pocket.

Diamond and Tiffany walked over to the window and stood next to her. Gwen, Rose, and Alexus followed. Niya looked to her left to see Diamond, and then to her right to see Gwen. She smiled, looked down, and pushed the button to make a call.

"It's a go," Niya said into the phone and then hung up.

"What's goin' on?" Tiffany asked, not sure what to make out of what Niya did.

Niya didn't respond. She just looked out of the window and nodded her head. Everybody looked to see what she was looking at. At first, it was nothing there, but then, after about thirty seconds, a single cop car shot up Main Street with its lights flashing. Soon after, another one did the same thing. Then another one and another, until the city center was full of cop cars and flashing red-and-blue lights, all of which were heading toward the hood.

"Search warrant!" the U.S. Marshals yelled, knocking the hinges off the door of the dope house on Ronheart Street. The tactical team raided the house, locking up each and every person who was in the house. All kinds of evidence was discovered pertaining to the drug enterprise Rell was running. Everything from heroin to guns was recovered.

Ronheart Street wasn't the only street that was getting hit that night. FBI, ATF, DEA, and local police took part in the largest roundup in the history of Charlotte. Almost every drug house, drug corner, and known drug dealer was being searched and shut down. Everybody who was in the drug game was being shut down. The only ones not going down tonight were those who had MHB ink on them.

"After tomorrow, the city of Charlotte will belong to you. You won't have to worry about looking over ya shoulders, nor will you have to worry about going to prison," Niya said as she continued to look out of the window at all the flashing lights going toward the hood.

"Niya, you talking like you not gonna be here with us," Gwen said. "What did you do, Niya?" Gwen asked, grabbing her by the shoulders and turning Niya to face her.

A hard knock at the door grabbed everyone's attention. Gwen looked at the door, then back at Niya, who now had tears in her eyes.

"I did what I had to do," Niya said, walking away to answer the door.

Everyone was silent as they watched Niya walk to the door. She hadn't provided details as to what her deal with the feds was.

When Niya opened the door, Agent Atkins and another agent entered the penthouse. Atkins looked around the room and then pulled out one set of handcuffs. Rose saw the handcuffs, pulled up her hood, and looked out the window.

Niya could see Diamond's and Gwen's hands reach for their guns. She shook her head as the cuffs clicked.

"Niya?" Alexus yelled.

Nobody in the room knew why she was going to jail. They were blind to the fact that Niya had sacrificed her honor, her morals, her dignity, and just about everything that she stood for, for the sake of her team.

Originally, the feds wanted Niya to give up everybody in MHB, including her drug connect. With that information alone, she would be able to walk free. They threw everything at her, even a life sentence, but she didn't budge. She couldn't betray her family. In fact, she did the very opposite when she decided to save them from having to go to war and from having to go to prison.

In return for the immunity of everybody in MHB, Niya made a deal with the feds to help them bring down four major drug dealers in Charlotte, Raleigh, Greensboro, and Winston-Salem. She knew pretty much everything about their drug operations and how much money they were getting. That was because she was their supplier. She had no loyalty to them. They were just customers, not family.

The major drug dealer she gave up in Charlotte was Rell, so everybody else he had rallied up to go to war with MHB was a part of his organization, or at least that's what Niya made it look like to the feds. It was like killing two birds with one stone. She stopped the war and saved MHB from being indicted. Some might call her a snitch or a rat for what she did, but in her eyes, she was acting as a chief, saving her village from being destroyed, even if that meant sacrificing herself in the process.

Before Agent Atkins escorted her out of the condo, Niya looked around at the faces of the women in the world who meant the most to her. She realized that what she had done was worth it.

"I'll see y'all in a couple of years." Niya smiled, and the agents escorted her out the door.

Chapter 21

Six Months Later

"All rise," the bailiff announced when the Honorable Judge Linda Walsh entered the courtroom.

MHB filled the courtroom. Judge Walsh could not remember ever having her courtroom filled to capacity. "Are all of these people here for the defendant?" the judge asked, looking over the top of her glasses.

"Well, yes, Your Honor," Niya's lawyer answered. "These are her friends and family."

The judge took one look around and continued with the proceedings. Niya's lawyer had managed to get her a "conditional plea" of five years, so that was exactly what the judge would sentence her to. The government, along with her lawyer, also asked that Niya undergo the drug program while she was in prison. If completed successfully, her sentence would be reduced to four years.

"Do you have anything to say before I sentence you today, Ms. Walker?" the judge asked.

Niya looked at the judge and then turned to look at her family sitting in the back of the courtroom. There was nothing Niya could think about that she wanted to tell the judge. She hoped that the judge didn't want her to apologize for her actions and conduct in society, because that wasn't going to happen. There were a few things that Niya was sorry for in her lifetime, but this wasn't one of them.

"No. No, Your Honor," Niya said without an ounce of regret in her eyes.

After Niya's sentencing, Gwen made her way quickly out of the courtroom. Mayo's murder trial had been going on for the past two weeks, and Gwen didn't miss a day of it. Yesterday, the state had rested their case, so the jury was in deliberations. Gwen was torn. She wanted him to be found guilty and live the rest of his days in a cage, but she also wanted to make him stop breathing herself.

When Gwen finally made it to the courtroom, she knew that she had missed the verdict. She walked in just in time to see the bailiff escorting Mayo out of the courtroom. He looked over and smiled at Gwen before they took him through the door. She felt a chill go down her spine.

"What happened?" Gwen asked, grabbing the arm of one of the people exiting the courtroom.

"Hung jury," the man informed Gwen before leaving.

Gwen knew what a hung jury was, but she didn't know what was going to happen now. She played it cool, walking up to Mayo's lawyer as he was packing his things into his briefcase.

"Excuse me. My name is Michelle Harper. Mayo is my cousin, and I just got here," Gwen said as innocently as she could.

"Well, your cousin got a hung jury. All the jurors didn't believe the witness, I guess," Mayo's lawyer said.

"So what happens now?" Gwen asked.

"Now . . . Well, now, more than likely he is going to go back to trial. In the meantime, I am gonna get him a bail hearing to see if he can be put on house arrest until the trial," his lawyer said before grabbing his briefcase and walking off.

Gwen's mind processed what the lawyer said. Killing him wasn't going to be hard once he got out. She knew it wouldn't take long for him to come pay Gwen a visit once his foot hit the pavement.

"One last question, Detective. Did you or did you not know that the federal government picked up the MHB case?" the Internal Affairs agent asked.

All morning, Detective Rose had been grilled about her involvement with MHB and the death of Butler. They were trying their best to link her to crimes she committed with MHB after she was taken off the case. Their only problem was trying to figure out when she was made aware that she was officially off the case. Without Butler, they had nothing else to rely on except Rose's word.

"Like I said before, the day before my partner was murdered was when he told me that the federal government took over the case. I was reassigned to another case, and that's when my involvement with the group MHB stopped. I cooperated with the feds to the best of my ability in this matter, and I have no further information to provide at this time," Rose responded.

The board really didn't have anything else to do but reinstate her back to field duties, even though they didn't want to. One thing was for sure, and that was a guaranteed fact that the investigation was far from over. Internal Affairs was only going to give Rose enough rope to hang herself, and the FBI was at the head of the whole operation. They knew that Rose would do exactly what they wanted her to do, and that was to dig a hole and bury herself. If given a second opportunity, the feds were going to bring down the rest of MHB. This time, there wasn't anything anyone could use to bargain for their freedom. That was a one-time deal for Niya; they had no more cards left to play. MHB had a target over those letters, and the feds were aiming for them.

***

Niya took a deep breath as the corrections officer secured the cuffs around her ankles and wrists. After checking each inmate, the petite, full-figured guard yelled at them to move. Niya shuffled along with the other women toward the bus.

"Take a seat in the first empty seat you come to," the bus driver instructed as the females were herded in like livestock.

Niya did as she was told and took a seat at the front of the bus, looking around at the other women. She knew that most of them were probably on that damn bus due to some stupid decision they made involving some fucking dude. *Not me.* MHB was her family and her legacy. She had taken an oath to do whatever it took to protect her sisters from any- and everything, and that's just what she had done.

The bus began to pull out of the parking lot of the jail, and within what seemed like a matter of seconds it was on the interstate heading north. She looked out the window at the Charlotte skyline until it disappeared from her view. Niya thought about the years she had ahead of her. If the feds thought that by locking her up they could reform her, that was the biggest mistake they could make. Actually, they were putting her in a place with a bunch of other females. Shit, she already had some of the baddest bitches in Charlotte and surrounding areas riding with her. What the fuck did they think was going to happen in a place that had young, hungry females just waiting to be led by someone like herself? Not to mention all the other female bosses who would be around to school her.

She relaxed in the hard-cushioned seat and dropped her head back. A big smile came on her face at the idea that she would be assigned a number by the penal system, but in her heart she knew she would only be loyal to three letters: *MHB.*